She glanced at him. He wore khakis and a forest green V-necked sweater. It would bring out the green in his eyes, but she didn't look for it. What was wrong with her? The tips of her ears felt warm, and her throat was closing up. She had thought about him through the short night, first thing in the morning, and all day until practice at one this afternoon, when at last the matter at hand took precedence over that other, whatever *that* was. *Adrenaline…a crush…a moment in the snow…Christmas magic…*

He reached across the distance between them and squeezed her shoulder. "Miss O, you look like a deer caught in headlights."

She'd heard that one before!

"If it helps any," he said, "my deer's wearing a mask."

She turned toward him at last. He was smiling his rare smile; the one that diminished the ever-present military aura, the one that tricked her body into believing it was on a roller coaster, on the whooshing down side of the steepest climb. "I was trying to chalk it up to Christmas magic."

"Me, too."

The roller coaster careened around a curve.

JUST TO SEE YOU SMILE

SALLY JOHN

HARVEST HOUSE PUBLISHERS

· EUGENE, OREGON ·

Cover by Garborg Design Works, Minneapolis, Minnesota

Published in association with the literary agency of Alive Communications, Inc., 7680 Goddard Street, Suite 200, Colorado Springs, CO 80920.

JUST TO SEE YOU SMILE
Copyright © 2003 by Sally John
Published by Harvest House Publishers
Eugene, Oregon 97402
www.harvesthousepublishers.com

ISBN-13: 978-0-7369-2093-3
ISBN-10: 0-7369-2093-5

Library of Congress Cataloging-in-Publication Data
    John, Sally D., 1951-
        Just to see you smile / Sally John.
            p. cm.
        ISBN-13: 978-0-7369-0883-2 (pbk.)
        ISBN-10: 0-7369-0883-8 (pbk.)
    1. Christian fiction, American.   2. Love stories, American.   I. Title.
    PS3610.O28J64 2003
    813'.54—dc21   2002009617

Printed in the United States of America

08 09 10 11 12 13 14 15 / LB-KB / 11 10 9 8 7 6 5 4 3 2 1

To
Cindi, Tom, Jeff,
and our mother,
Mary Carlson

Acknowledgments

When a project like this is finished, the heart overflows with gratitude for those who had a hand in its creation. My thanks go to:

Friend Rhonda Cox, for her teacher's heart, for answering all my basketball questions without laughing, and for her devotion to coaching. Any mistakes are mine. Keep in mind the book is fiction.

Kelly Farmer, U.S. Marine wife, for graciously devoting time to answer a myriad of questions and thereby giving substance to "Joel." Technical mistakes are mine. I hope he lives up to the Corps' honorable traditions. If not, keep in mind he is fiction.

Daughter Elizabeth John, for clueing me in on athletic details and life.

Stephanie Begley and Anna Rehder, for the team stories.

Donna Begley and Judy Rehder, for the winter night bleacher memories.

Editor Kim Moore, for her unfailing sense of direction.

Tim, for believing in the possibility.

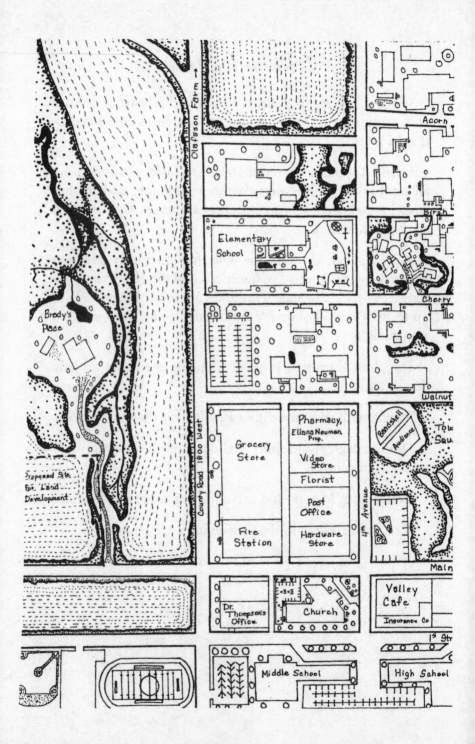

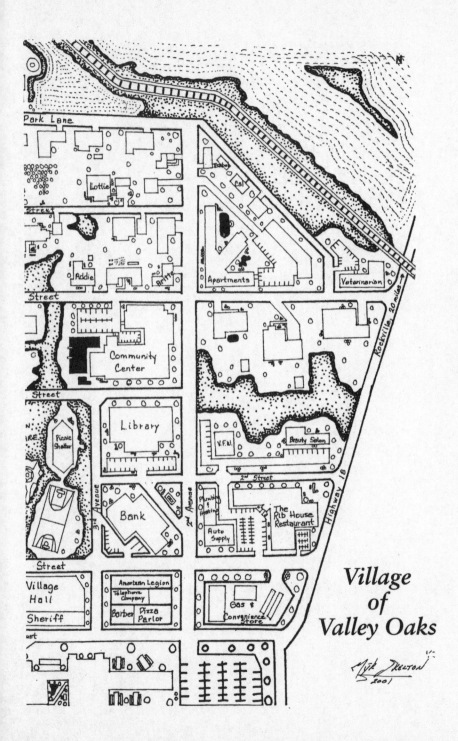

Village
of
Valley Oaks

Prologue

Love one another; as I have loved you,
so you are to love one another.
If there is this love among you,
then all will know that you are my disciples.
—John 13:34-35

A tiny woman with primly curled silver hair stood outside the high school gym doors, encircled by a sea of graduation caps and gowns. One by one, boys in royal blue and girls in yellow gold bent to return her hug, to wait for the twinkling blue eyes to register recognition, to receive a personal story. "I remember when you…"

"And this," she said to each one as she smiled at the child standing beside her, "is my great-niece. She wants to be a teacher."

The girl confidently shook their hands, repeating "Congratulations" in a crystal-clear voice. Her close-set blue eyes focused intensely as if she memorized each face; her head tilted as if to better catch every word. Though her blonde braids and chubby cheeks indicated she was only about nine, she was already as tall as the woman.

As the students moved on through the crowd of well-wishers, the girl's eyes widened. "Did you teach *all* of them kindergarten?"

"I did, honey. Do you want to know how I remember them?"

11

The child nodded.

"Because I loved each and every one of them as if they were my own children. In a way, every class is a family. My job is to make sure each member feels that they belong, that they make a difference. Can you be that kind of teacher?"

Again the girl nodded solemnly, her mind almost audibly clicking, storing away the sage advice for future use.

Across the open, central area inside the small-town high school, a young couple faced each other, unconcealed adoration evident in their gaze. She wore the yellow gold cap and gown, her long black hair cascading to her waist. He wore dress slacks, and his football shoulders strained against the white button-down collared shirt. A certain air about him declared that his diploma was already gathering dust.

The girl reached up and brushed a dark brown curl from the young man's forehead. "You want me to open it now? Here?"

He nodded, smiling.

In her palm was a tiny, gold-foil-wrapped gift. Giggling, she swiftly opened it and pulled out a ring box. Her smile rounded into an oval. Lifting the lid, she uttered a small cry.

"It's a promise ring," he explained. "Not an engagement ring."

"But it's a diamond!"

"It's called a chip." He removed the narrow gold band from the box, took her left hand, and slid the ring onto the third finger. "I promise to always be on your side, to always take care of you. No matter what."

⤙⤚

Halfway across the country on the West Coast, an outdoor ceremony had just been completed. A slender young man stood before an older couple. His face, partially shaded by the dark bill of his white cap, was fresh, teetering on the brink of manhood. Yet, somehow, he exuded the sense he was already there.

He wore the Marine dress blues of the Honor Grad as if the uniform had graced his closet for some time, waiting only until the boy's height and breadth would fill the white-belted blue jacket and blue pants with the red stripe along the sides. Something evident in his sharp eyes, square jaw, and rigid posture added years that had scarcely begun to accumulate.

The older man spoke. "Son, you'll make a fine Marine."

"Thank you, sir."

The woman dabbed her eyes with a handkerchief. "I'm very proud of you."

"Thank you, ma'am."

She clutched his white-gloved hand and laughed. "But I would appreciate a little eye contact and a smile!"

He grinned and looked down at her. "Sorry, Mom."

His father asked, "Are you still thinking career?"

"Yes, sir. I don't foresee a reason to ever leave the Corps."

"It's what you've always wanted." He smiled, nodding in approval.

The woman tucked her handkerchief into her purse. "Just don't forget to call me on Christmas."

"*Semper fidelis*, Mom. I'll always be faithful to you, my country, and my fellow Marines."

One

Twenty years later

Britte Olafsson hated goodbyes.

In no hurry to say another one, she inched her white Jeep down Acorn Park Lane. At last she parked, a short distance behind a U-haul trailer. And there she sat, lost in goodbye thoughts.

Naturally, there had been the unavoidable loss of elderly grandparents. Perennially, on the last day of school, she had dreaded the parting with yet another favorite teacher. The ongoing departure of pets—and on the farm that included cows and horses—never ceased to stun her.

The first almost truly unbearable goodbye occurred when she was 13. Her best friend moved across the country. Again, at 16, her next best friend left. Three weeks before graduation, a senior boy, a close friend, died in a car accident.

In college she had tried *not* to make best friends, an impossible challenge at a small Michigan school where she spent four years playing basketball with four other women who knew her better than anyone ever possibly could. Of those four, the nearest now lived 300 miles away. Then there had been Eric—

Britte opened the car door, jumped out, and slammed it shut.

And now there was Isabel Mendoza.

A cold November wind whipped Britte's ponytail against her cheek as she jogged across the front yard. Frozen grass crackled beneath her running shoes. Snow wasn't yet in the forecast, but the steady north wind left no doubt that winter had arrived. Crummy day for moving.

Britte recognized her brother's lanky form backing against Isabel's glass storm door. She pulled the door open for him. "Hi, Brady."

"Hey, sis." He turned, his arms hugging a kitchen table chair, and stepped down to the sidewalk. "Where's your coat?"

"I'm wearing a coat." She saw Isabel's favorite padded rocking chair now approaching, carried by someone hidden behind it. She kept the door open and waited.

Brady tsked, only half jokingly. "How many times do Mom and I have to tell you? A warm-up jacket does not count as a winter coat."

"Yeah, well, it's 30 degrees and you're bundled up like an Eskimo, ready to race a dogsled across the tundra. You're going soft on me!"

Walking toward the truck, he called over his shoulder, "Windchill is five degrees. You'll get sick, Itty-Britty!"

The nickname was a taunt left over from their childhood, his final zinger that typically caused her to smile. At the moment she didn't feel like smiling. She shouted, "Brady, your persnickety side is showing! Has Gina seen your persnickety side yet?"

The door shifted in her hand. She pulled it wider, making room for the rocker's exit. The high school principal came into view, carrying his usual stoic demeanor right along with the chair. "Mr. Kingsley!"

"Afternoon, Miss O. Thought I recognized your coach's voice."

"Who roped you into this?"

Only a slight lift of his brows changed his expression. "Your brother has a way with words."

She laughed. "Tell me about it. I grew up with Mr. Motor Mouth. At least he's put it to good use by writing books for a living."

As he continued down the sidewalk, another kitchen chair appeared in the doorway. Big Cal Huntington had an arm looped through it. He carried a second one behind him. "I can't believe you two call each other 'miss' and 'mister' outside of school."

"Habit. We can't risk some student overhearing us and realizing teachers and principals actually have first names. Our mystique would be destroyed in no time. Hey, congratulations, big guy! Engaged, huh?"

"Yep." The deputy sheriff grinned in a distracted sort of way as he lumbered down the steps. It was the same grin Brady wore these days, the one that must have spread across Isaac Newton's face after the apple whacked him. They, too, had been hit over the head by a new law, the law that governed their hearts and sent them scurrying off to buy engagement rings. She grinned to herself. Watching these guys fall in love amused her to no end.

Brrr! Britte dashed into the house, her nose and fingers numb from the cold.

Isabel's front room was a disaster. Her things were making their way out to the U-haul, while Lia's furnishings were shoved willy-nilly out of the way. The men had previously made quick work of moving Lia out of her apartment above the pharmacy and into the rental house Isabel was vacating.

The sound of female chatter drew her down the hall. She found Isabel and Lia in a bedroom making up the bed.

"Hi, Isabel. Lia!" she cried as she wrapped the pharmacist in a bear hug. "Congratulations! Mom told me the news this morning!"

"Oh, thank you, Britte. I am *so* happy." Lia returned the hug and then held out her left hand. The sparkle of a diamond mirrored the one in her dark, almond-shaped eyes.

"It's beautiful. Cal's out there grinning like he just won a million bucks. Actually, I think he has."

Lia smiled and caught the bed sheet Isabel was tossing her way.

Britte plopped down on the carpet. "Hey, sorry I'm late."

Isabel threw her a smile. "You're not late for lunch, Coach."

"Impeccable timing, if I do say so myself." She gave her friend a thumbs-up. "You know, if you had planned more than a week in advance that you were moving from Valley Oaks to Chicago, I could have rearranged my practice schedule."

"It's the day after Thanksgiving. You shouldn't make those girls practice on a holiday weekend!"

"It was a simple shoot-around and only mandatory for the coach."

Isabel tucked in the sheet. "I hate the thought of missing your game Wednesday."

Their eyes met, acknowledging the unsaid. Isabel would miss every game this season after three years of not missing a single one.

Lia piped in and eased the tension in that calm way of hers, "Next Wednesday? Chloe and I will be there! She loves basketball now. Come to think of it, she loves all sports now." She grinned. "Probably has something to do with Cal enjoying them."

Isabel burst into laughter. "You think?"

Britte sighed to herself. Couples were cropping up everywhere. Cal and Lia. Brady and Gina. Isabel was moving to take a new job and live near Tony Ward, a likely candidate for fiancé in the not-too-distant future. Was there something contagious in the village well-water system? She always drank bottled water.

"Isabel, where's Tony?"

"Picking up pizzas for lunch."

"Sounds good. So what's with Mr. Kingsley? How'd he get involved today?"

Isabel shook a pillow into its case. "Britte, you make him sound like an old man. What is he, 37, 38?"

"Something like that. He's my principal. As in my immediate boss. He has a permanent 'mister' aura about him. Can't seem to get his first name onto my tongue. What is it, anyway?"

Isabel threw the pillow at her. "You're hopeless. Cal never takes a moment off from being a cop. You never take a moment off from being the prim-and-proper schoolmarm, except during basketball season, but now it's even worse. Schoolmarm morphs into fire-breathing coach."

"You have a problem with that?" She threw the pillow back.

Isabel just shook her head in reply and straightened a blanket.

Lia cleared her throat and flipped back her bobbed, jet black hair. "Um, I've seen Cal take quite a number of moments off from being a cop."

Britte and Isabel collapsed into laughter.

Lia's deadpan expression didn't change. "But you're not getting details."

Britte gasped for a breath. "Puh-lease! I don't want any details! All this romance is getting just a little overdone for my single taste."

Lia smiled. "Cal and Brady invited *Mr.* Kingsley. They've been playing basketball together at the Community Center. They thought it appropriate to include him; make the new guy in town feel welcome."

Britte pushed out her lower lip in a sort of facial shrug. "No problem. The more the merrier. Lia, how long before we move you into Cal's house?"

She laughed. "Not long at all."

"Oh, really?"

"Some of my stuff is already there. I've just brought the minimum here." She sat on the bed. "Did you hear about last night?"

"A little. Did Pastor Peter really threaten to tackle Brady?"

"He did. Your brother is quite the talker, isn't he? He doesn't give an inch."

Britte laughed. "You've noticed."

"And of course you both know Cal isn't normally a talker, but the two of them got going with Gina's dad, Reece. They squabbled like little boys over who had the right to reserve the church first for a wedding. So Gina, her mother, and I talked. Maggie has no problem with them renewing vows on Friday night. And," she said, grinning, "Gina and I think a double wedding the next afternoon would be perfect."

"Double wedding!" Britte clapped and whooped. "I like it!"

"It turns out that neither of us have definite ideas about a big, fancy wedding. We're both delighted with small and simple and letting the mothers plan it."

"I'm sure the guys agreed with that."

"Not until this morning! We all met early in Peter's office and figured it out. It'll be the weekend after Christmas. So." Lia raised her hands, palms up. "I know it's fast. I only met Cal a few months ago, but he's everything— No, he's *more* than everything I ever hoped for in a husband. He loves Chloe as if he were her own father."

Isabel's dark eyes shone. "And we all know that's a major tap from God. Cal never kept it a secret that little kids bothered him, to put it mildly."

Lia nodded. "We trust God is directing traffic every which way here. We see no reason to wait."

Britte said, "It'll probably be a tax advantage, getting married before the year is over."

Lia laughed. "That's exactly what Gina said."

"I knew I liked my brother's choice for my sister-in-law. But how can you plan all this in less than six weeks and during the Christmas season?"

"Maggie and my mother are chomping at the bit at such a challenge. Mom knows Chicago shopping, and Maggie has connections through her work in women's apparel."

"And Brady knows flowers," Britte added.

Everyone laughed. His extravagant habit of sending flowers to Gina was well known.

Brady appeared in the doorway. "I heard my name. What are you all laughing about?"

Britte stood, hurried over to him, and flung her arms around his neck. "Woo-hoo! The wedding's set! I'm laughing because I am so, so happy for you!"

He returned her hug and whispered, "Thanks, Itty-Britty. Thanks."

For a moment or two, the fire-breathing coach blinked repeatedly. It just wouldn't do to have salt water dousing the flames.

~

Of course Britte knew his first name. It was Joel. Mr. Joel T. Kingsley.

From her perch now on a kitchen countertop, she balanced a paper plate stacked with pizza slices and watched him across the crowded room. He sat at the table with others, eating and occasionally almost smiling like a regular person. To a certain extent, he even resembled a regular person. Short hair, just this side of a buzz cut. A shade of black, the kind that would turn to iron gray because that color fit his disposition. Bit of an elongated face with furrows already embedded in his forehead and jawline. Nice ears. Yes, he had nice ears...attached lobes, not flappy ones like Cal's.

Unlike a regular person, though, he exuded *military,* appropriately enough considering he was an ex-serviceman from the Marine Corps. He wasn't as tall as Brady nor as broad as Cal, but his ramrod posture and clear, deep voice effortlessly commanded the attention of students and staff alike. She guessed that at one time he must have been accustomed to giving orders. That fit his leadership position, and yet to her way of thinking, the man was just a bit out of sync in his role as high school principal.

He had made sweeping changes at the school, an unsettling action despite some good results. Teachers for the most part adopted a wait-and-see attitude. The community hadn't yet reached a consensus on whether or not it approved. On the other hand, the students thought he was great. Britte estimated their approval rating at 74 percent, unheard of in her experience.

Which all added up to the fact that, after five months in town, Mr. Joel T. Kingsley remained an enigma to her.

Britte glanced around. Isabel sat close beside Tony. Cal sat on the other side of the sink, also atop the counter, sharing his pizza with Lia, whose arms were crossed on his knees. Gina and Brady stood beside Britte. He had his arms around his fiancée in a bear hug, warming her. She had just arrived a few moments ago, wearing only her veterinarian's lab coat over a turtleneck sweater and jeans.

All couples. *Yes, there must be something in the water.*

"Gina," Brady's tone chided, "I'm taking you shopping today. You've got to get a winter coat. This isn't California."

Britte extended her leg and poked his with her toe. "This is his persnickety side, Gina. Do you know about it yet? Are you sure you want to go through with the wedding?"

She laughed and untangled herself from him. "Yes and yes. Britte, I have something to ask you." She leaned near and lowered her voice. "Will you be my maid of honor?"

Caught unaware again, Britte choked up and swallowed a bite of pizza with difficulty. There were way too many emotions playing tag with her today. "Really?"

She nodded. "Except for Brady, you're my closest friend."

Britte set aside her plate, slid from the counter, and hugged her future sister-in-law. "Gina, it would be an honor."

"Thank you!" She returned the hug. "We're keeping things simple. You're my only attendant. Chloe is going to be Lia's. And Isabel will sing."

"And the guys will be each other's best man?"

"Of course. Etiquettely speaking, it may not be proper, but we don't mind." Her entire face glowed. Gina was beautiful, inside and out, a compassionate veterinarian with brilliant green eyes and a Miss America smile.

"Brady." Britte turned toward her brother. "I don't know how you won this woman's heart, but I'm so glad you did."

He draped an arm around each of them. "Me, too."

"Brady." Joel Kingsley stood behind him. "I'm taking off."

"Hey, thanks for your help, Joel." They shook hands. "Thursday night at the Center?"

"Sounds good to me. Gina, it was nice meeting you again." He shook her hand and then glanced at Britte. "See you Monday, Miss O."

"Bright and early."

As he made his way through the kitchen, Britte picked up a slice of pizza, her appetite suddenly restored. Good. She could tell Isabel goodbye without his supervision.

It was as if she didn't want to let her guard down in his presence. There were no warm fuzzies oozing from this principal's office! At the school he was all business, and that attitude produced results. He had made great strides in establishing changes, restoring much-needed order. The kids respected that and found him fair and trustworthy, even approachable. She felt that the 26 percent who didn't approve of him were simply lazy.

Yet, the thing was, she didn't know the color of his eyes. Eye contact with him was fleeting at best. He was always on to the next moment, leaving a trail of accomplished tasks in his wake as well as a distinct impression of...detachment.

One of the teachers had dubbed him "the General." It fit. School was beginning to feel like a military academy. His intensity surpassed even Britte's, and she found that somewhat disconcerting.

Which was why she had no inclination whatsoever to call him Joel.

Two

On his way home from helping Cal and Brady, Joel stopped by Swensen's Market. It was a day earlier than the norm for his weekly grocery shopping. He greeted a few high school students who worked there and a set of parents in the produce aisle, stocked up on supplies, and then drove home.

His newly constructed, two-bedroom condominium was on the south edge of town, just three blocks from the high school's athletic field. It was a great location, affording him the opportunity to walk to work. Open corn and soybean fields surrounded three sides of the small complex.

In the kitchen he started a pot of coffee, put away his purchases, made a salad for dinner, and poured marinade over a T-bone steak. By then the coffee was ready. He carried a large mugful into the spare bedroom, which he had converted into an office. A wide, L-shaped, cherry-wood desk dominated a corner. Manila folders were neatly stacked on a credenza to the left, a computer sat on the right side of the desk. At the bookcase just inside the door, he flipped on the portable CD player. Soft, contemporary jazz floated from small speakers. On another shelf, books were stacked in the order of to-be-read. He was looking forward to beginning Brady's first novel that evening.

Joel set the mug atop a coaster on the desk and sat, rolling up the sleeves of his flannel shirt and scooting the chair on its wheels toward the center of the desk. A sheet of paper lay squarely in the middle of his work space. It displayed a typed, to-do task list. There were reports to write, parents to call, schedules to consider, problems to ponder, lesson plans to peruse. But first...

He propped his elbows on the desk and rested his forehead on his hands.

"Dear God. Thank You for today, for the ability to meet new people and to help. Thank You for this community. Thank You for the friendship of Cal and Brady. Thank You for Britte and other teachers like her, the ones who take their job seriously and don't need my constant supervision. Give them the strength to fulfill their duties. Help me now in this work You've given me to do. In Jesus' name, amen."

He fingered the sheet of paper, musing about the orderly developments of the past few months. Cal, a deputy sheriff, had introduced himself the week Joel arrived in town. They talked on numerous occasions. The cop kept a close eye on the kids. Six weeks ago, he had introduced Joel to his friend Brady at the Community Center. They started regularly playing basketball once a week, sometimes racquetball. It was always a good workout.

Even before he heard Brady's last name, he suspected he was related to Britte Olafsson. He learned they weren't twins, though they could have passed for a set. They were both blond with slender but strong athletic builds. Attractive. Tall. Not that she was 6' 4". The eyes weren't identical either. Hers were set close together. That proximity and their piercing blue grabbed your attention, almost as if they audibly announced, "Hey! I'm talking to *you!* Pay attention." Valuable asset for a teacher. As was her coach's voice, low and clear, at times raspy after practice.

Joel turned his attention to the large-faced clock positioned dead center on the ledge at the back of the desk. Its second hand swept away the moments.

Musing time ceased. He read the first item on his to-do list.

Britte and Isabel exchanged a fierce hug but didn't say goodbye. They stood in the front yard. Britte knew the bone-chilling wind would cut things short.

She turned to Tony. "You'd better take excellent care of her or I will hunt you down."

Tony grabbed her in a hug. "Don't worry. She'll be in good hands." Then he held her shoulders and looked her square in the eye. "You know that, don't you?"

She nodded.

"We're only 90 minutes away. We'll visit often."

"Right. That's what they all say. My biggest dilemma is, who's going to keep me supplied with salsa verde?"

Tony and Isabel laughed, holding hands, noses reddening.

"Okay." She gave them both a brave smile and a thumbs-up. "I'm out of here."

"See you, Britte!"

She ran down the street to her Jeep. Not waiting for it to warm up, she drove past the house and waved at the couple still standing outside the front door.

What she was going to horribly miss was their common ground. Isabel led a Bible study for high school girls. Some of them Britte had coached; all had been in at least one of her math classes. Though the group was unaware of it, the two women bathed them in prayer.

There was going to be a hole in the community.

A few blocks from Isabel's, Britte pulled into her own driveway and pressed the automatic garage opener. The yard looked so bare this time of year, except for the junipers hugging the far corner of the house. Above the roof the backyard's massive sycamore was visible, a few giant leaves still clinging to its branches. In front, the two maples' barren limbs rocked slowly in the wind.

Britte liked her house. It was one level, with three bedrooms, the third being only slightly larger than the bathroom, the ideal size for an antique library table and school-related paraphernalia. There was a wonderful old fireplace in the living room, its brick chimney running up the outside beside the front door, which was recessed in a brick arch. The dining room also faced the front. Its diamond-paned windows reflected the corner streetlamp already burning in the dark late afternoon.

She had bought the house three years ago when the owner, Great-Aunt Mabel Olafsson, passed away. Of course the transaction was a good deal because her dad had inherited it along with three other nephews, none of whom wanted to keep it. As of last month, the house had belonged to a Miss Olafsson for 43 years. It carried a legacy as well as a bit of a stigma. Mabel Olafsson had been a beloved Valley Oaks kindergarten teacher for ages. She had also been a "miss" for eight and a half decades.

Britte drove into the attached garage, closed it up, and hurried into the kitchen. She was a few months shy of three decades. Although it disturbed her mother, Britte wasn't overly concerned at the thought of following in Great-Aunt Mabel's "old maid" footsteps. As a teacher, Britte's life overflowed with activity, challenge, and young people. What else was there?

She flipped on lights and pushed up the thermostat on her way to her bedroom. Shedding her warm-up jacket, she pulled on a thick sweatshirt and then returned to stand in the living room in front of a heat register, looking out at the darkening backyard, waiting for the warmth to reach her bones.

"I know You love me, Lord."

Her parents had taught her everything about Jesus, but it was Great-Aunt Mabel who embodied His boundless, passionate love for students.

Britte shivered and crossed her arms. A feeling of uncertainty hovered. Not a common occurrence. *Time to check the emotional barometer, girl!*

Life was satisfying. Teaching and coaching consumed her in the way that whitewater rafting in the Rockies left her breathless and exhilarated. When she wasn't engaged at school, she was, generally speaking, a loner and she liked that. Tonight she would watch a favorite video, eat popcorn, and snuggle up with Brady's latest five chapters he had asked her to critique.

Snuggle up with a stack of printer paper?

She shivered again.

This feeling must be from telling Isabel goodbye...from hanging out with only couples...well, not counting General Kingsley, but then he didn't count any which way...from the thought of turning 30... Loner was distinctly different from lonesome.

"Jesus, I know You're with me. I know I am the love of Your life. Sit with me tonight?"

The furnace heat rolled up from the register now, surrounding her with a comforting warmth. She replayed the day's events.

Breakfast with Mom and Dad and younger brother Ryan at the farm—it was a tradition to haul Christmas things down from the attic the day after Thanksgiving. Shoot-around with the team—the girls looked good, their attitude was top-notch, their free throws out of sight. Brady and Gina's announcement—Brady loved that woman so much. She would complete him, fill in the empty patches of his life. Helping at Isabel's—knowing her had enriched Britte's life. Perhaps Lia or Gina would fill in at the girls' Bible study. God, of course, wouldn't drop the ball in the teens' lives. And, above all, Jesus beside her every moment of the day—

Britte grinned and laughed softly.

"If I'm all that lonesome, I can always drink a *jug* of tap water."

Three

The hotel room's door handle rattled.

Anne Sutton uncurled herself from the plush armchair and, with her nose still buried in a paperback book, walked across the room. She pulled open the door. "Hey, mister."

"You'd yell at the kids if they did that."

"Did what?" Turning the page, she moseyed back to the chair.

"Opened the door without asking who's there."

"Oh, Alec," she objected with a little smile, eyeing him over the top of her reading glasses. "You're the only one who would be standing out there in the hallway fiddling with the card key."

"Most ridiculous thing ever invented." He tossed it onto the desktop and unfastened his watch. "Why are you still awake?" Not waiting for a reply, he headed toward the bathroom, peeling off his long-sleeved, sage green polo shirt.

Anne returned to her reading, eager to finish the chapter. It was a thrilling courtroom scene. Who was the bad guy? *Oh no!* Cliff-hanging last sentence. She peeked at the next chapter and then smacked the book shut. *Save it!* She set it aside with her glasses and scurried to the bathroom, where her husband stood at the sink, splashing water on his face.

She slipped her arms around his middle. For a 39-year-old, he had a nice waist. She spoke to the back of his head, at the naturally wavy nut brown hair. He needed a haircut. "I'm awake because it's our annual one night in a hotel without the kids. I want to savor the awareness that I do not

29

have to listen for them in the night, that I do not have to hear cartoons at the crack of dawn, that I do not have to juggle carpools tomorrow."

Alec wiped his face with a towel. "You need to get out more, sweetheart."

With a sigh, she straightened and leaned against the door-jamb, watching him brush his teeth. He'd change his tune when he saw what she wore beneath the hotel's complimentary white terry cloth robe. Her new nightgown was red silk. Well, not silk. It was polyester, but just as soft as silk. He liked her in red; he liked the contrast with her black hair. She pulled the scrunchie from her hair, loosened the ponytail, and snuggled against him again, this time shoulder to shoulder.

He edged away.

Their eyes met in the mirror.

"It's late," he mumbled through foaming toothpaste.

"It's only," she glanced over her shoulder at the bedside clock's red digital numbers, "twelve-seventeen?! Twelve—! What have you guys been *doing?* We finished dinner hours ago. I thought the meeting doesn't start until tomorrow."

He lowered his face and rinsed the toothbrush. "It doesn't. I've been talking with Kevin."

"Until midnight?"

He swept past her.

She turned. "Okay, help me out here. What is wrong with this picture? On the one hand, we have Kevin," she held out a hand, palm up, "the podiatrist, whom I love dearly as the husband of my best friend. A guy who seldom strings more than two sentences together in a social setting."

At the closet door, Alec pried off his loafers.

"Talking for two solid hours— Where? In the *lobby?* On the other hand, we have this." She untied her robe and held it open. "A fetching wife in a fetching new, ruby red silk—

extremely silk-like anyway—nightgown. The French would call it a *negligé*."

His back to her, he stood at the closet, attaching his slacks to a clothes hanger.

"Alec!"

He glanced over his shoulder. "Fetching."

"I thought so, too. Okay, Alexander," she teased, "what gives here? Normally you would not have let me read *this* late. Normally you would be kissing me by now. *Passionately*, I might add."

He slowly shut the closet door and rested his forehead against it.

Struck with the realization that nothing about his actions was normal, she swallowed her bantering tone. "What's wrong?"

He blew out a loud breath and turned, leaning against the door, holding out an arm. "Come here, fetching wife of mine." She stepped into his embrace, and he buried his face in her hair. "I'm sorry. I don't know how to tell you."

And then she knew. "It's Kevin."

He straightened, placed his hands around her face, and whispered, "He's leaving Val."

The world stood still for just a heartbeat, and then it spun again, but Anne knew it was off-kilter, knew that from this moment on it would always be so.

"No!" she wailed. "No! They said—"

Alec pressed her head against his chest. "Oh, Annie. I'm sorry. Shh."

"They can't!" She pushed herself from him, crossed the small room, and sank onto the turned-down bed.

"Sweetheart, it's not as if it's a surprise."

"They're seeing a counselor!" Suddenly chilled to the bone, she wrapped the robe tightly around her.

"The counselor agreed that a trial separation could—"

"How can a *Christian* counselor tell them to *separate*?" Her voice rose, and the tears started flowing. "*They're* Christians! This isn't supposed to happen!"

"Annie." He sat beside her, enfolding her in his arms again. "You know it happens to Christians."

"Does Val know?"

"Yes."

The sobs erupted. "Then why didn't she tell me? I should be with her. Why now? Why this weekend? We're in Chicago! On a church council retreat—"

"Shh." He stroked her hair. "Kevin said they... They had a discussion late last night. It was their first calm one. And they reached this decision. He's..."

She felt Alec's intake of breath.

"He's moving out on Sunday. Val didn't want to ruin your weekend. Instead," his tone grew sarcastic, "she let me do it."

"Alec, that's not fair."

He sighed and tightened his arms around her. "No, it's not fair. I don't know what to do with this gut-wrenching emotion. And I hated passing it on to you."

They held each other, absorbing the pain they felt for their friends. Friends who, like them, were 30-something and had three children. Who, like them, lived in Valley Oaks, attended Community Church, car pooled, and volunteered whenever necessary for anything related to the elementary, middle, and high schools. Three kids, three schools.

Finally, Anne whispered, "I can't imagine their hurt. What can they be doing right this very minute? They don't have anyone to hug them." She burst into fresh sobs, envisioning Val and Kevin hugging opposite sides of a king-sized bed.

Alec tightened his hold around her until her tears slowed. She fumbled with a tissue from the robe pocket. "What else did he say? How is she?"

"Well, apparently she's all for this. You know Val. She's strong, stronger in her faith than he is. She'll get through it."

"I thought they were making progress."

"Kevin says no way. It's time they stepped back and got a new perspective. They thought it'd be best to do it before Christmas." He took a breath. "*Kevin* wants it before Christmas. He'll step down from the church council. We've got to tell Peter. I don't know what he's going to do, but since he's the pastor, I guess that's his job. He can figure out what effect it will have on our planning session tomorrow."

"Oh, Alec, the kids!" She plopped her head down on the pillow and pulled her knees up to her chest. They brushed against Alec as she rolled over toward the center of the bed. Her stomach ached. "Theirs and ours! It's like a ripple effect. From their kids to our kids, from them to us, from the council members to their wives to the whole church."

He crawled over her, pulled the covers up over both of them, and laid down facing her. "Annie, don't internalize this."

She looked at her husband's face just inches from hers. His easy smile was missing, making his jaw appear a rigid square. He needed a shave. The crow's feet were pronounced around his cinnamon eyes. "How can I *not* internalize this?"

He encompassed her hands in his. "I don't know. But you can't fix it."

She caught her breath, struck with a new image. "What'll we do at the basketball games? We've always sat together— Oh! What'll we do for Christmas? Our families' traditions—"

"Anne! Just take it one day at a time. Okay? Now, it's late. We've got to get some sleep."

"I can't sleep!"

"Well, I have to. I have to be coherent tomorrow." He kissed her forehead and rolled over. "All you have to do is shop."

She ignored his snide comment. After 17 years of marriage, she knew this was how he grappled with uncomfortable emotions.

He rolled back over. "I didn't mean that like it sounded. I love you, sweetheart." He pulled her to him and kissed her soundly. "Please try to sleep?" He rolled back again facing the windows.

Within moments his breathing eased into sleep mode. Tears still burned in her eyes, and a wave of loneliness washed over her. She reached up to turn off the lamp.

Dear Father, comfort Val tonight... And Kevin. Hold both of them close.

Sleep was the furthest thing from her mind.

~

Early morning sunlight streamed into the hotel room. Alec sat quietly on the edge of the bed and watched his wife sleep. Her thick black hair was mussed, spread out over the pillow, as if she had tossed and turned. The tiny scar was more noticeable when she was motionless like this. It was a subtle fold in the right corner of her upper lip, the result of a dog bite when she was six years old. It wasn't discolored. It simply made the smile of her wide mouth a little...quirky.

Should he wake her or not? She probably hadn't slept much. He mulled over the consequences. They wouldn't be alone again until late that night when they arrived home. He reminded himself that they were each other's best friend. Sleep was secondary to the comfort she would need when she first awoke.

He pushed strands of hair from her face. Her eyes would be dark today. Lack of sleep and this trauma would widen the black that rimmed the smoky gray, leaving only a trace of the lighter color showing. Annie didn't wear her heart on her sleeve, but it was right there in her eyes for anyone who dared to look close enough.

He noticed red silk poking out from under the covers and felt a twinge of disappointment, but he couldn't help smiling. How she could feel romantic was beyond his comprehension! Most of this 24-hour trip was spent with seven other couples. They were there for a mini-retreat, not an intimate getaway. As far as he was concerned, they could have doubled up on the rooms, put the women in a couple, the men in others, saved some money.

After arriving late Friday afternoon and checking into the hotel, the entire group had met for dinner. Today the wives would shop. The men—all members of the church council— would meet with Pastor Peter for an extended time of prayer and Bible study, followed by lunch and a business session. Relating with his wife wasn't on the schedule of events.

Not so with Anne, but that was just her way, grabbing the moment and wringing everything she could from it. In their short time away, she would catch up in detail on the lives of seven women, luxuriate in the hotel's bathtub, read an entire novel, finish the year's Christmas shopping, and wear red silk to please her husband.

He tapped the tip of her turned-up nose. "Hey, sweetheart. You want to wake up?"

"Hmm?" She peered at him and smiled. "Hey, mister."

He gave her a gentle smile, waiting for the memory of last night's news to register.

It didn't take long. A tear slid out before her eyes were fully open. Her lower lip trembled. "Oh, Alec."

"Why don't you call Val? Have her come over for a room service breakfast before you all go shopping. Our treat. You two can emote for a couple of hours before heading out."

"What time is it?"

He glanced at the bedside clock. "It's 6:20. We're meeting for breakfast at 6:30. I'd better go now, try to corner Peter, clue him in on the situation." He kissed her. "I'm sorry I have to leave you like this."

"I know."

"Hug Val for me."

She grabbed his arm. "Alec, you wouldn't leave me, would you?"

"Of course not. Anne, you're internalizing. This is them, not us."

"But why them and not us?"

"Because..." He stared at her a moment. "There's no simple answer."

"But I think we need an answer."

He stood up. "Because you're a fantastic cook and look great in red."

She blinked. There was no gray showing in her dark eyes.

"Hey, sweetheart, it's good enough for me." He smiled and went to the door. "I'm easy."

"That's all you want from me?"

"Annie, I love you. If you love me, that's all I need. I gotta go. See you at four."

Waiting in the hall for the elevator to reach the nineteenth floor, Alec gazed through a window at the Chicago skyline and pondered Anne's last question. *Was* that all he wanted from her?

He'd never thought about it. He had wondered at times, when he wearied of the treadmill, if this was all there was. Wife, kids, mortgage, church, school activities, family vacations, work. Evidently Kevin didn't think so.

For a moment he imagined chucking it all. What would he do? He drew a blank. He couldn't think of serious discontentment on any front. He liked all three of his kids. He liked living in his small hometown. He liked being on the church council. He even liked his job. And his wife? Not only did he love her, he liked her!

The status quo was about as perfect as a guy could ask for.

Four

Best friends since the fifth grade, Anne and Val didn't need words to arrive at the heart of the matter. They simply burst into tears and hugged.

Now they sat in Anne's hotel room, chairs turned to face the large window overlooking the Chicago River. To the far right, sunlight danced on Lake Michigan. They sipped coffee, disinterested in the basket of muffins and croissants on the table between them.

Over the past year, Anne had been privy to deteriorating events in her friend's marriage. She sensed that rather than a rehash of those events, a shoulder was best for the moment. Still, it seemed a sudden decision to separate. She ventured a question. "Val, why didn't I notice anything at dinner last night?"

Scrunched in her armchair, feet propped on the wide windowsill, face half hidden behind her mass of chin-length, dark natural curls, Val shrugged. "I didn't want you to."

"The curse of the healthy glow."

Her friend chuckled, a sound without humor. She was an aerobics instructor and fitness devotee, compactly built and shorter than Anne's 5' 9" by four inches. Her physical features exuded an air of confidence, even now. "Celeste noticed something."

Celeste was their friend and their pastor's wife. "We all know Celeste has a direct hot line to the supernatural. Not even our lifelong friendship can compete with that. What did you tell her?"

"That I'm tired. Which is the truth."

"Why did you two come?"

She blinked and looked toward the window. "Kevin's sense of duty and honor."

Anne choked on coffee and pressed a linen napkin to her mouth.

"I know. Go figure. But that was it. The weekend was already planned, and he didn't want to leave the council hanging. He felt he should explain in person, resign in person, and not just see Peter privately and dump it in his lap."

"Thoughtful."

"Uh-huh."

Anne felt heat bubbling in her chest. Her throat constricted.

"Annie-banannie." Puffy eyelids shrouded Val's blue-green eyes. "Promise you'll keep me from charging an extraordinary amount of money today?"

"Val, we always charge an extraordinary amount on this day. It's tradition! But we've saved for it and do most of our Christmas shopping and get the kids winter coats—"

"No. I'm talking a nasty, abhorrent, shameful amount of money." She bit her lower lip. "I know revenge is God's department. I know we can't afford it, especially now, but there is this voice inside that keeps telling me to punch Kevin where it hurts. And at the moment that voice is screaming to spend money like it grows on trees. So promise me. I'm counting on you."

Coffee churned in Anne's otherwise empty stomach. *Oh, Lord.* "How about if I just help you spend it?"

Val's mouth fell open.

"You know you could use a new dress for Christmas. Let's actually *buy* something at Saks—"

"Anne! I'm serious!"

"And while we're into splurging, let's not forget about eating. You are not passing up desserts today, nor snacks of fudge and ice cream. Nor caffeine breaks. It's only lattés with extra dollops of whipped cream for you."

The corner of Val's mouth lifted.

"Mission accomplished." Anne smiled. "We can always mail things back. And you'll only need one day in aerobics class to work off the extra calories. Okay?"

"Okay."

While Val stepped into the bathroom to wash her face, Anne studied the tabletop. *Lord, we need Your grace for this day. Moment by moment. Please!*

The hotel logo caught her eye. It was stamped in gold calligraphy on the room service receipt. *The Renaissance.*

Renaissance. Now that's ironic. I think we're into a death here, Father. What's with this rebirth business?

She thought of the day that stretched before them. Celeste would catch a nuance, a vibe. They would have to tell her. She needed to know, and she should hear it from them, not late tonight from Peter. Anne imagined Celeste's reaction to the news. How would she pray? She was the pastor's wife and, although close in age to Anne, possessed a faith usually found only in women twice her age. Respect for her had grown by leaps and bounds during her five years at Valley Oaks Community Church.

Celeste would immediately bring Jesus into focus. She would say He died, and there was rebirth in that death for everyone.

Tears sprang to Anne's eyes. *Jesus, how in the world are we to expect a rebirth in this nightmare?*

Anne loved the old farmhouse she and Alec had moved into ten years ago and spent nine renovating. The white two-story sat on Acorn Park Lane at the end of a long front yard at the edge of Valley Oaks. Fourth Avenue ran along the west side, turning at this point into a little-used, graveled country lane. Bordering their property were fields owned and tilled by a farmer who lived elsewhere in the county.

A red barn stood in the backyard and housed the over-flow from the single-car, unattached garage. Three children accumulated a lot of bicycles and sporting equipment. The minivan and riding lawn tractor were parked in it. Their two big dogs, the black lab, Madison, and the golden retriever, Samson, slept and ate in the barn.

Late Sunday afternoon, the day after returning from Chicago, Anne stood in her beautiful kitchen and felt as if its three walls were closing in on her. There was no fourth wall. It had been replaced with a breakfast bar. The effect was a large open space, a combination kitchen and family room. Which meant that at the moment she was witnessing firsthand a noisy confrontation between the three Sutton children.

Anne turned on her heel and walked into a short hallway located just inside the back door. She breezed past doors leading to the back staircase, the basement stairs, a bath-room, and the living room. Without a pause, she rapped her knuckles on another door while opening it and strode into the den tucked away in the rear corner of the house. It was Alec's hideaway.

She shut the door and announced, "It didn't work."

Her husband sat at the desk, eyes glued to the computer monitor, fingers tapping.

She gave him a moment. Then another. "Alec."

"Mm-hmm. Just a sec."

She flumped onto an overstuffed armchair and swung her legs over the side. Alec could get lost in work any time of any day or night. He was a corporate trainer for a big company called Agstar. He taught managers how to manage others. Those others made or sold farm equipment. It sounded boring to her, but he thoroughly enjoyed the teaching aspect and working with a variety of people. And, it paid the bills. If they stuck to their budget, their needs were met and Anne didn't have to work full-time. She helped out part-time at the pharmacy. During the winter, she coached the sophomore girls basketball team and assisted with the varsity. She was a PTA officer, Booster Club officer, and Mandy's room parent.

Alec continued typing. He wore his comfy, Sunday afternoon clothes: old brown cords and an ivory cable-knit sweater.

The guy hadn't changed much through the years. If anything, he had simply grown into the promise of what he had been as a teenager. She had fallen for him during her sophomore year, when he was the senior quarterback hero, homecoming king, and student council president. Energetic and focused, he was still good-looking, a cross between rugged and executive. At 5' 11", he wasn't much taller than she was. He was more broad-shaped than lanky.

It was those crinkly cinnamon eyes that had drawn her in the first time she passed him in the high school hallway over 20 years ago. He turned them toward her now, swiveling in the high-backed desk chair, and asked, "What's up?"

"It didn't work."

"What didn't work?"

"Sending Drew alone to rent a video." Their oldest had been driving for only a few months and had not yet wearied of running errands. "He didn't get what the girls wanted. They're all fussing at each other."

"So what's new?"

She went over to him and slid onto his lap, nestling into the arms he wrapped around her. A faint hint of his familiar, spicy Aramis cologne comforted her. She touched his rough cheek. "Alec, let's go to the Pizza Parlor, have calzones. Just you and me."

"The kids—"

"I'm not up for refereeing tonight."

"You've had a rough weekend. I'll handle it."

"They need to learn to handle it. Drew can take the girls back to Swensen's." The grocery store carried a limited video selection, but it was their only source. The video store hadn't yet re-opened after the owner was arrested a few weeks before.

"I've got to finish up a couple of things here for a meeting first thing tomorrow morning. And, besides, it's our family night. I feel like I haven't seen the kids all week. Thanksgiving was full of relatives, and then we left for Chicago the next day. We are committed to our Sundays together, right?"

Energetic and focused parents meant they had produced three children of the same ilk. Even before nine-year-old Mandy was born, they were all going different directions. They had carved Sundays into the schedule years ago. "Of course we're committed to Sundays. I'm only talking an hour and a half to—"

"Anne, we just told them about Kevin and Val this afternoon. How do you think they're processing that?"

"I don't know how *I'm* processing that!"

"Exactly. We all need to be together. It'll give them security. They're probably fussing because they feel a sense of loss. Bewilderment."

"I *need* to be with *you*."

"You'll be with me here."

"*Alone* with you."

"Hey, we're alone now."

She laid her head in the crook of his neck. "For two whole minutes. Then you'll turn back to the computer, and Amy will walk in and announce in her 13-going-on-35-year-old voice, 'Alec and Anne Sutton, your son is absolutely impossible!' Then I'll go fix soup and sandwiches."

He chuckled. "But at least we had the two minutes. They've got to be worth 60 at the noisy, over-priced Pizza Parlor."

"You just don't get it, Alec."

"Do you?"

"No. All I know is that I feel out of sorts here. I need to get out."

"Go see Val. Kevin should be gone by now."

"Her mother and Celeste are there. Besides, I think I should step back from that situation. It's throwing me for a major loop."

"Annie, Kevin and Val will survive, independent of one another. He was never home anyway. They disconnected a long time ago. This is probably for the best."

"Don't say that."

"Kids are resilient. There will be less stress in their home. Val can spread her wings a little more."

She sat up straight. "You're defending him!"

"No, I'm not. There's no excuse for what he's doing. What I'm saying is the end result could be some change for the good."

Tears stung her eyes. "But it's not *right!* He's causing irreparable damage to all of them! He shouldn't get away with it!"

"Shh." He pulled her nearer again and pressed her face against his shoulder, catching a deep sob. "I know. I know."

How she hated crying! She hated feeling helpless. She hated the ugly words forming in her head, obscene words she wanted to scream at Kevin Massey.

Alec's arms tightened around her. There was a knock on the door. He called out, "We're busy. Go away."

The door opened. Anne heard Amy's voice. "Alec and Anne Sutton, your son is absolutely impossible! I don't know how you raised— Mom! What's wrong?"

Alec answered, "She's upset about Aunt Val. Go on, honey. We'll be right out. Just give us two more minutes."

Anne spoke into his soft sweater, "Tell your brother to drive you and Mandy back to the store so you can all take care of it."

Amy sighed dramatically. "Thank you!"

The door closed with a loud click.

Alec kissed her wet cheek. "Got you four minutes, sweetheart, not just two. Worth 90 at the Pizza Parlor."

She sighed loudly, mimicking Amy's performance. "Thank you!"

"You okay?"

She envisioned the next five hours. Alec would get back to work, she would prepare supper—at least it was a simple one—they would prompt the kids to discuss what they learned about God at church today, how it applied to real life. They would watch a video, after which she would clean up the kitchen, fall exhausted into bed, and start all over again tomorrow... It was simply what a wife and mom did. Just like Val had done for 17 years.

Alec kissed her head and tightened his arms. "Annie?"

She nodded against him. "I'll be okay."

Maybe four minutes were better than none at all.

Five

"Jordan!" Britte called across the high school gymnasium. "Practice is over. Go home already!"

"Ten more free throws, Coach," she hollered back, bouncing a basketball. Its staccato beat resounded off the court's hardwood floor. "Dad said I have to do 50 a day."

Britte stifled a sigh. "Watch the elbows!" She turned back to Anne, sitting beside her on the second row of bleachers, and muttered, "Jordan Hughes' dad will be the death of me yet."

The assistant coach looked up from the clipboard on her lap, eyeing her over horn-rimmed reading glasses. "Fifty free throws a day is not bad advice."

"That isn't the point. The man has been telling me how to do things ever since I joined the coaching staff. In six and a half years Jordan hasn't missed one camp or league. Her dad hasn't missed an opportunity to point out my mistakes." Britte shook her shoulders as if someone had just told her there was an ugly bug crawling up her back. "Sorry. Didn't mean to get off on that subject."

"First-game jitters." Anne pushed her glasses up along her nose. "Or *ego*."

"Probably both. I mean, look at this lineup." She pointed at the clipboard Anne held. "I feel like we're cheating! We've got five seniors who have played together since they were little tykes in rec leagues. Four of them are the fastest and smartest I've ever seen. And two of them are the tallest in the conference."

"Supersectionals this year?"

45

Britte slapped her friend's raised palm. "For sure."

"I see you're pulling Jordan out before the end of the first quarter."

"Liz is more talented. Agreed?"

"Agreed, but Liz is a junior, less experienced."

"She needs playing time, but I wanted to start all seniors this first game. It's their big night. For most of them, it's the beginning of the end of their career."

Anne shook her head. "You do such a great job straddling that fine line."

"What fine line?"

"That one between focusing on the win and focusing on giving *all* the girls a chance to play, junior, senior, experienced, or not."

"Hey, we're in this together, Miss Assistant Coach." She smiled. Five years ago Britte was sophomore and assistant varsity coach. Anne had just joined the staff, taking over Britte's former position coaching the freshman. Though the older woman's basketball skills were rusty, Britte would have been lost without her influence. "You're my anchor. I always count on you to make sure my head's on straight."

Anne gave her a distant smile and set the clipboard on the bleacher. Propping her feet on the bleacher below, she leaned forward and crossed her arms over her knees. Dressed in warm-up pants and a T-shirt, hair tied back in its high, bouncy ponytail, she appeared her usual, relaxed self.

But Britte sensed she wasn't. "Annie, you're not all here today."

She gazed away, a vacant look in her eyes. "Did you hear about Val and Kevin?"

"No. What—"

"Jordan!" Mr. Kingsley's strong voice interrupted their conversation. He strode across the gym toward the lone team member. "You can't stop on a miss!"

"I told Coach I'd leave after 50."

"Throw another one."

The girl walked back to the free-throw line. Her shot missed.

The principal hustled after the rebound, his yellow gold tie fluttering with the quick movement. His dress clothes—black slacks and royal blue shirt of some shiny fabric—added an elegance to his athletic movement. "Try it this way." He passed the ball back to Jordan and went to her side.

Even with his back to her, Britte overheard his advice in that distinct voice of his. She watched him mime a throw and then position the girl's elbows. "Great," she said under her breath, "another expert."

Jordan made the shot, and Mr. Kingsley applauded. "That's it! One more time."

Anne removed her glasses. "Britte," she said in an undertone, "why don't you just admit it? You think he's attractive."

She laughed quietly and murmured, "In your dreams, *Mom*."

"You don't have to like him, but you've got to admit he is magnetic."

Mr. Kingsley strode toward the bleachers, watching Jordan over his shoulder. "Good. Five more." He turned and greeted them. "Afternoon, ladies. I got your note, Anne. Sorry, I wasn't available when you stopped by."

"No problem, Joel. I just, um..." She glanced around the gym.

With a start, Britte realized her normally straightforward friend was at a loss for words. "Anne, should I leave?"

"No, it's what I was going to tell you." She inhaled sharply. "Jason Massey's father moved out Sunday. His parents have officially separated."

Britte groaned, "Oh, no." She reached over and gave Anne's shoulder a squeeze. "I'm sorry."

Mr. Kingsley echoed the sentiment. "I'll notify his teachers. We'll all keep a close eye on him."

"Thanks. He and his mom told his coach last night, so he's aware of the situation."

"Good. Miss O, you have Jason for geometry, right?"

The man's memory was astonishing. "Yes."

"I'll schedule a session for him with the counselor. I can pull in the district's psychologist, too. She's better equipped to offer help in this type of situation."

"Joel," Anne said, "will you talk with him? He's going to connect better with a man, and he respects you. I know the counselor and the psychologist. They do a fine job, but, as my Drew said, guys sugarcoat things they say to their grandmothers. That's what the kids call those women. Grandma."

Britte was glad to hear the usual punch underline Anne's words.

Mr. Kingsley's eyes narrowed as if he was deep in thought. Always the professional, he stood with his feet slightly apart, his arms crossed. His long sleeves were rolled up his forearms, but the shirt collar was still buttoned to the neck behind the firmly knotted tie. He gave a curt nod. "Understandable. I'll meet with him."

"Thank you."

"Thank you for telling me. Anything else I can do for you? I'll pray for the family."

"Now *that*," Anne's voice quivered, "covers everything."

"That's been my experience. Miss O, have we missed anything?"

She mentally conducted a split-second debate. His unexpected attention settled the issue. "On an unrelated matter." She tilted her head toward the court where Jordan was still shooting. "There is the free-throw issue."

He raised his brows, deepening the ever-present furrows lining his forehead.

Britte started. Eye contact! He stood a distance from the bleachers, and she noted only what she already knew. His eyes were not dark, nor were they a pale shade. "I mean, if she gets to the line in tomorrow night's game, she'll need that elbow-tuck reminder. Coming from you, it seems to have worked. How about you sit on the bench with us?"

He laughed. "Oh, I'm sure you girls can take care of yourselves." He walked away, still chuckling.

Britte and Anne sat quietly. He exited through the open gym doors. His footsteps echoed in the hallway and then faded.

Britte broke the silence. "Girls!"

Anne smiled. "You deserved it, Coach. I think he got your not-so-subtle message that you *know* Jordan's problem. That you don't need *his* help."

"Hey, I was complimenting him on his ability to get through to her."

"Uh-huh. Maybe you could lighten up your tone a bit."

"Mollycoddle a Marine?"

Jordan's free throw twanged off the basket's rim.

"Britte—"

"Notice he was wearing the school colors?" Adrenaline pumped straight to her jaw. She was on a roll. "You know why, don't you?"

"Of course I know why. There's a boys game in Orion tonight. I think it's great how he's caught on, wearing royal blue and gold like so many of the fans do."

"Did he wear that shirt or even that tie to our games last week?" Their team schedules were identical. Anne's sophomore game always preceded her varsity's.

Anne paused. "He didn't come to our games."

"Exactly."

"Oh, Britte, they were more like scrimmages. Preseason stuff. Two away games with nonchallenging, nonconference teams. Alec didn't even come to watch me coach, and he always comes. Amy had tests and Mandy was sick; I told him not to bother. Maybe Joel's not even going tonight."

"Want to bet? I suspect he's like most of the male admin-istrators in our school *history,* from 1909 on. Like the entire male coaching staff, Tanner Carlucci excepted." She referred to the freshmen girls coach. "Just like my brothers. They believe there is not a shred of evidence to indicate that God endowed woman with the ability to play basketball."

Anne howled with laughter.

"Brady actually said that to me when I was in high school."

"Well," she wiped her eyes, still giggling, "let's not forget anything your big brother ever teased you about!"

"He was serious! He denies it now, but I suspect it's what he truly believes deep down. You *know* girls sports are low on the totem pole around here."

Anne stood and stretched. "Things are changing. We do have Tanner."

"Tanner was raised correctly and in Rockville, which is not as backward as Valley Oaks. And besides, he's only a part-timer. He's not going to change the attitude here."

"Hey, it's a start. I hesitate to ask, but are you coming to the game tonight?"

"Of course. *I* support *all* of our athletic events, whatever the gender, whatever the location." She looked over Anne's shoulder and called out, "Good work, Jordan! See you tomorrow."

"Bye, Coach!" The girl waved from the gym door.

"Britte, did you hear what he said?"

She met Anne's gaze. "I heard."

"He'll *pray* about it. When was the last time you heard a principal say that?"

"Never."

"Me, neither. He's a good one, Britte. Mark my word. He is a good one."

Yeah, well, I still don't feel much of a connection.

Six

Alec stretched from the driver's seat and took hold of Anne's hand. "I think Jesus would sit next to Kevin."

She glanced over her shoulder. Mandy and Amy sat in the far back seat of the minivan, the reading lights on, doing homework as they sped along the dark highway to their brother's game at another school. Amy's CD music played through the rear speakers. The girls were out of earshot.

She watched her husband for a moment, his face somber in the reflected console light. "I know." Her stomach knotted. "How do you do that?"

"Do what?"

"I want to punch Kevin, not treat him with kindness. At the very least I want to ostracize the rat."

"Jesus ate dinner with rats and healed their diseases. If I don't show Kevin that type of love, who will?"

"Haven't we shown him that all along, and didn't he just throw it back in our faces?"

"That doesn't mean we stop."

"But I don't want to be nice."

"Sweetheart, it's not being nice. It's being God's instrument."

"Well, I don't want to be His instrument with Kevin."

Alec squeezed her hand again. "I don't particularly want to either, but I know it's the right thing to do in this situation tonight."

She leaned over and rested her forehead on his arm. "How'd you get to be so good?"

He laughed. "If you believe that, there's a bridge in Brooklyn I'd like to sell you."

A short time later they entered the noisy gym where bleachers lined both sides. A pep band played. Dance and cheerleader squads ringed the floor, clapping to the music. Varsity teams warmed up at both ends of the court.

Anne spotted Drew. Taller than his dad already, he filled out his shiny blue and gold warm-up suit and from a distance looked like an older college player. His thick black hair and narrow face were Anne's, but his cinnamon eyes were Alec's. She smiled to herself. He was still her little boy, as evidenced that morning by him asking her to make pancakes.

The awkward moment came. Val was already sitting with the Viking fans, in the lower half of the bleachers, on the edge of the bunched group. Kevin was near the top, on the group's other side. Anne's throat constricted, and she felt a flush spread over her face.

Alec touched the small of her back as people wove around them. He spoke to the girls. "Mandy, you stick close to Amy."

Amy, the big sister with plans of her own, wailed, "Dad!"

"Honey, if you leave the gym and go to the concession stand with your friends, bring Mandy to one of us first."

Amy trudged off with a book-toting Mandy trailing behind.

"Anne, meet me at halftime at the concession stand?"

"Okay."

Now Anne trudged off. For nearly 12 years they had sat side by side, watching their son play, delighting together in his successes, encouraging each other through his inevitable mistakes, sharing a deep contentment simply in his *being*. A product of their love.

She walked in front of the bleachers and then climbed to where her friend sat. "Val."

"Hi, Anne. Saved you a seat."

In reality, saving a seat hadn't been necessary. The entire section to her right was vacant. Anne sat. "Thanks."

Val's eyes were red, but she smiled. "Where's Alec?"

Anne tilted her head toward the back. "With Kevin. He says Jesus would sit with him."

"Jesus would say go and sin no more."

"Well, yeah, you're right. I guess Alec feels he's got to be close enough to say that at the right time. How was your day, sweetie?"

"Yesterday was unbearable. I decided to take off the rest of the week from work. Try to get centered or something."

"Sounds like a good idea."

"Celeste took me out to lunch, and then we tore apart my bedroom. I'm going to paint it."

Anne nodded. "I can help on Thursday."

"That'd be great."

Joel Kingsley climbed the bleachers, heading toward them.

Anne said, "Val, I told Joel after practice tonight."

"Good. Thanks."

Joel reached them and sat sideways on the row below, looking back up at them. "Mrs. Massey, I'm so sorry about developments."

Val bit her lip.

"I just want you to know that we'll do all we can to keep a close eye on Jason. Don't worry about a thing at school. Call me anytime if you need something. Have the secretary track me down if I'm not in the office." He handed her a card. "And here's my home number."

"Thank you."

A group of students stopped at the bottom of the bleachers and called up to Joel. He turned around to talk to them.

Anne studied the back of him. His royal blue shirt fit snugly over shoulders that—though nowhere near as broad as Alec's—leaned toward a trimly defined muscularity. He had nice hair. Thick but very short. In the garish gym lights she spotted a few early gray hairs among the black. There was a solid presence about him, thoroughly masculine, thoroughly take-charge. It was probably what scared Britte.

Britte had always tried to fill her big brother's shoes. She was athletically inclined and had thrown herself into competing against Brady's reputation for being the best, especially when it came to basketball. Given that their opportunities differed, she had succeeded as well as any young woman could by combining her love of teaching, her brain for math, and her passion for the game. But somewhere along the way Britte had eliminated suitors, intimidating them beyond what any reasonable young man was willing to face.

Reasonable young man. Well, that left Joel out. He was about eight years older than Britte, and from what Anne had seen, not all that reasonable. Like a polite Marine assault, he had taken charge of Valley Oaks High School and, against the odds of parents and community and history, whipped it into better shape than it had seen in years. She doubted that anything intimidated him.

Which, under the right circumstances, might send Britte spinning. Hmm... Was there something to be done about promoting those circumstances?

The announcer began introducing the teams. All the Viking fans stood as their boys ran out.

Joel turned around. "Take care, ladies." He climbed up the bleachers behind them. He wasn't headed in Kevin's direction, but Anne assumed he eventually would talk to the man, keep all the communication lines open.

From the corner of her eye, she glanced at her friend. Val's tears flowed freely as her Jason ran out just ahead of Drew.

A nauseating hollowness began to spread from the pit of Anne's stomach. She wanted to be brushing shoulders with Alec as they clapped for Drew, their junior starting a varsity game as forward.

Oh, why would she want to play Cupid to Britte and Joel? Why in the world had God even created love between a man and a woman? It was all so incredibly heartbreaking.

～

Britte considered the high school gym her home away from home. She calculated that by now she had spent almost one-half of her waking life in it.

Late Wednesday afternoon she was the lone occupant in this home away from home. The lights were low, the temperature cool. She sat on the top row of the bleachers, center court, on the side designated for home team fans. She stared at the lacquered hardwood floor with its impressive depiction of their mascot encircled in the middle: a Viking, his arms akimbo, wearing a gold helmet and flowing royal blue garments, gazing out over the helm of his boat.

She let her sight drift first toward the right, at the stage with its drawn blue curtains, at the unlit, black scoreboard high up the wall...then toward the left at the two sets of closed doors and another scoreboard. Alongside this one was a narrow announcement board with removable numbers and letters. At the moment it displayed the list of the jersey numbers and names of her girls... 10—Olson... 15—Taylor... 21—Hughes...

Britte forced herself to look straight ahead at the scorekeepers' table and then, to the left, to the bottom row of the bleachers that served as the team bench. In less than two hours she would be there...with her girls.

She doubled over.

A gym door rattled open, echoing loudly across the empty gym.

"Deep breaths, Britte!" It was Ethan Parkhurst's voice. Ethan was younger, just three years out of college, in his third year teaching English at Valley Oaks High.

Deep breaths? It took all of her energy to manage a single shallow one through the nausea.

The bleachers clanked and shook as he ran up them. She felt him plunk down beside her. "Deeper."

"I—" She gulped. "I can't!"

"Yes, you can."

"Can't."

"Can."

She jerked her head up, leaned back against the wall, and squeezed her arms over her midsection. The gym spun. She shut her eyes. "I'm going to throw up."

"No, you're not. You'll be fine."

She peered at him beneath half-closed lids. "I should go home."

He shook his head. His longish dark brown hair was tied back in a short ponytail. His eyes, a striking color of faded blue jeans, were laughing at her. "You're not a quitter."

"Yes, I am. I shouldn't be a coach. I have no business being a coach. Why am I a coach?"

"You care about the girls. Cassie, Sunny, Whitney, Raine, Jordan, Janine...all of them, in a very personal way like no one else does."

She let his words sink in. "Yes. Yes, I do."

He sighed loudly. "You're still pea green. Aren't we finished yet?"

"It's worse this year, Ethan," she whispered, still in awe of the revelation that had struck her that afternoon in the middle of calculus. "It's this winning-team business. Way, way too many expectations."

"Your *only* expectation is threefold, the same as always: teach them something about basketball, about teamwork, about inner strength."

She looked over at him. "You are good."

"That's why you pay me the big bucks."

"One home-cooked dinner?"

"My fee just went up to two."

"Outrageous." The smile she felt inside refused to reach her mouth. She groaned and lowered her head to her lap.

The scenario was familiar. In her first year as head varsity coach, Ethan had been walking down a hall when she emerged from the rest room. He correctly guessed from her white, panic-stricken face that she had just lost her lunch. He suggested she sit in the gym and get her bearings. Since that day, he had sat beside her like this, before home games. About a third of the way through the season, the terror lessened and the need for therapy vanished.

He gave her braid a playful yank. "You look nice. New jacket?"

"Mm-hmm."

"Perfect Valley Oaks Viking blue, as always. What's that called, that fuzzy material?"

"Boiled wool." Her voice was muffled.

"Looks good with the long black skirt and white blouse."

"Thanks."

"Britte."

She turned her head sideways and looked at him.

"I'll be sitting right here, praying you through four quarters."

She sat up. "I'm counting on that, Ethan."

"God has you right where He wants you. He's not going to let you down."

She nodded.

The side door across the gym behind the bleachers burst open. A few girls entered, laughing and dribbling basketballs. The sophomores, Anne's team, were in uniform, coming in to warm up. Soon, varsity players would begin arriving. They would sit in the second row as the younger girls played the first game of the evening. During the third quarter, she and her team would enter the locker room...and it would begin.

Ethan kneaded her shoulder. "Show time, Coach. Go get 'em."

⌒

Joel stood at one end of the bleachers, near the student section. The gym wasn't crowded, but the cheering group of boys raised enough ruckus to approach deafening at times. Across the gym Britte Olafsson crouched on the floor, surrounded by her team, talking pointedly to the inner circle of five during a time-out. It was the fourth quarter, two minutes to go, and the Vikings were up by six against the number-three-ranked Hawks.

If he were to rank coaches, he'd place Britte number one above the clown leading Hawk Valley. While that guy ranted and raved, Britte remained calm and controlled. From what he'd witnessed at her practices, he knew her girls were in top-notch physical condition. She pushed them as hard as any male coach would a group of boys. Now those girls were scarcely breathing hard compared to the huffing and puffing opponents. Mentally, it appeared she could rein in their focus with a word or two with her voice that easily carried across the court.

All right, he was surprised, if not somewhat impressed. They still ran and shot like girls, but it was a competitive happening, a positive for the school. Of course from a strictly financial point of view, forget it. The gym wasn't half full. An entire season like this wouldn't bring in enough revenue to pay for the referees, let alone coaches' salaries, team uniforms, bus transportation, referees, and extra custodial services.

The boys were a different story altogether. They'd hosted a Thanksgiving week tournament, packing out the place every night they played. It was a town event, not a social outing for friends and families.

Naturally the politically *incorrect* reason for that difference was that one team was made up of guys, the other females. The politically correct reason was... Well, off the top of his head he couldn't think of one.

He smiled to himself, remembering Britte's dig at him yesterday. She knew as well as he did how to shoot a free throw and wasn't about to let him get away before she had informed him of that fact.

He'd better keep all of his politically *in*correct reasoning to himself. Come to think of it, he probably shouldn't have laughed at her comment.

Now, as the team walked back out onto the floor, Joel cheered along with the students. The right thing to do was to be the example, and the example was always about *team*-work. Always about *semper fi. Semper fidelis.* Always faithful.

Always.

Seven

Britte, in the school weight room with her back against the bench, raised the bar until her arms were completely extended. On a good day she could bench-press 130 pounds. This was a good day.

It was Friday. As she had driven to school, the early morning sky was star-studded, promising the appearance of a long-absent sun. Two nights ago her team had beat Hawk Valley, perennial nemesis of the Vikings. Wonderful athletic scents filled her nostrils, scents emanating from rubber mats, disinfectant on the machines, and a stack of unclaimed, used—*very used*—sweatshirts and jerseys. Christian rock-type music blasted from the weight room's portable CD player, leading Britte in a private, albeit loud, session of worship as she worked out. To Britte, it was a taste of heaven.

"Miss O! Morning!"

She cried out and the 130 pounds above her head wobbled.

"Got it!" Hands grasped the bar alongside hers, instantly absorbing the load. Mr. Kingsley's face came into focus above her. He stood behind her head. "Let go."

"I can do it," she grunted the words through clenched jaw.

"Fine. I'll spot you. Ready?"

She blinked. Heart pounding erratically, she knew her concentration was gone. "Take it." She let go.

He laid the bar on its rack and then walked over to the CD player to lower the volume. "Guess you didn't hear me open the door."

She pressed a towel to her face, trying to catch her breath.

"Sorry I startled you."

She lowered the towel and saw him standing beside her, hand extended. She placed hers in it, and he pulled her to a sitting position. "I don't get much company in here at 5:30."

"Company. Is that what you would call a spotter?"

The "General" was reminding her that it was against the rules to lift alone. When students weren't around, she did it all the time. "If you give me a detention, I'll give you one."

He smiled briefly. "Touché, Miss O. I don't have a spotter either."

"The kids would have a field day with this one." She exhaled noisily. Her heartbeat was slowing to normal.

"No doubt about that. I can see the headline in the *Viking Views,* 'Coach and Principal Break Rules.'" He went over to a mat and, hands on hips, began stretching. The man evidently knew his way around a workout. His white T-shirt revealed well-toned biceps and shoulders.

"What are you doing here anyway?" she asked.

His quick laugh resembled a shallow cough. "You do speak your mind."

"So I've been told." She remembered Anne's caution to lighten her tone, an echo of her mother's lifelong advice. "I don't mean to be disrespectful." She grinned. "Just outspoken."

"I'd say you've met that goal with flying colors." His warm-up pants rustled as he sat down on the mat and stretched out a leg. "Normally I work out at the Community Center. The school seems a more convenient place."

"The girls will be here at 6:30."

"Yes, Miss O. I'm well aware of that." There was amusement in his tone.

She bet he knew every detail of the schedule for the entire season.

"I'll be out of here by 6:15."

Britte slid from the bench and headed to the door. Music from the CD still played softly, but her little taste of heaven had soured. She would shower before the girls came in and gather papers to grade while she supervised their lifting. "Oh." She turned back. "Mr. Kinglsey. About the varsity girls going to State."

"State?" He was breathing deeply, rhythmically.

She bit back words on the tip of her tongue. This wasn't the time to be outspoken. So what if they'd already had this conversation? He was new here. Routine business was still unfamiliar to him. "The state tournament in February. We always attend as a team. Not to play, of course, but to watch. The school board needs to approve the trip. It's just a formality, but the request has to come from you at this month's meeting."

"Better write me a memo. Put it in my box."

"Sure." She flicked the volume control up and hurried out the door, closing it against words that threatened to fly off her tongue. Words that were most definitely not respectful.

Walking down the hall toward the locker room, she replayed scenes she had witnessed in recent months. The male coaches of the boys teams asked him detailed requests at lunch, at football pep assemblies, in the hallways, in the parking lot, in the midst of other people and conversations. They weren't brushed off with "better write me a memo" replies.

True, the prejudice wasn't what it was when she was in high school 12 years ago, but it was still there. For all his propriety, Mr. Kingsley couldn't hide what he really thought. Girls sports weren't worthy of his full attention. If she weren't careful, she could someday easily call him on it.

Of course if she did, she'd be able to figure out the color of his eyes then because, without a doubt, at the moment of calling him on his attitude, she would be in his face.

~

Joel's smile turned into a grimace as he bench-pressed. Britte Olafsson never would have made it in the Marine Corps with that attitude.

Physically she might be in shape. And, too, she appeared intensely disciplined as far as coaching and teaching went. Although she recognized when she was becoming disrespectful, that wasn't about to stop her from speaking freely.

He let the music drift into his consciousness. Loud and upbeat as it was, it wasn't what usually emanated from the weight room. The words were about Jesus... Hmm. They were...worshipful.

Joel set the bar in its rack and listened for a moment.

The memories came then. They were why his church attendance was sporadic, why his worship remained...measured.

He understood that he was in a right relationship with God because some years ago he had put his trust in His Son, Jesus. That choice had brought him purpose and hope and sanity. His slate was wiped clean.

But he didn't know what to do with the memories. And so, he avoided them.

Now he sat up and shook them off.

Eight

Alec parked his car in the garage and sat. It was only 2:30 in the afternoon, but he was home, three hours ahead of schedule. He had been driving around the countryside since noon.

He should go catch Peter at the church office, talk to him. This was a spiritual matter, wasn't it? *All* of life was a spiritual matter. This didn't feel like a spiritual matter. It felt like an unforeseen beating by an invisible assailant. His head felt as if he'd been wearing a football helmet and someone had grabbed it and jerked him to the ground. His ribs ached as if they'd been kicked while he was down. Red flags should be floating in the air, calling it against someone, penalizing *someone*.

He made his way across the backyard and walked heavily through the porch and the kitchen door. "Anne!" he called out.

Friday afternoon. What was her schedule? His mind wouldn't focus. "Anne!" he shouted loudly. She was never home. There was PTA, room mother stuff, basketball practice, now Val's extra needs, the pharmacy job—

"Alec! What's wrong?" She ran to him and threw her arms around him. "Why are you home?"

They held each other for a long time.

"Alec?" She undid his tie. "What happened? Who died?"

"Nobody died. Let's sit down." They went around the breakfast bar and settled onto the couch. "That promotion I expected?" He blew out a breath. "Didn't get it."

"Oh, honey." She hugged him and kissed his cheek. "What happened?"

He slouched against the back of the couch. "I went in this morning as a corporate trainer, expecting nothing this first day of the month. Maybe in two weeks I expect to be named manager, make the change at the end of the month. Start out January with a little raise, a little different day-to-day challenge. Just a natural progression. It's what happens to men with my seniority, my reviews, my goals, my company, and above all, with my ability to play their game. I come home, still a corporate trainer for the remainder of December. For the remainder of the entire next *year*. Maybe until I turn 65."

"Didn't your boss get promoted to VP?"

"Frank got *his* promotion, all right, his new office, his raise."

"What about his current position? Who gets that?"

"They're bringing someone in from plant management. Someone they want to put out to pasture until he has the good sense to retire. That's just between Frank and me and you, by the way. As if that helps."

"Then this is a demotion for this man? Why would he take a backward move to Rockville?"

Alec shook his head. "Who knows? Who cares? And to top it all off, there will be no bonuses this year."

She rubbed his shoulder. "We kind of expected that though, didn't we?"

"But we expected a raise, too!" His wife snuggled against him, and he put an arm around her. "I'm glad you're home, sweetheart."

"Ordinarily I'd still be at the pharmacy, but it was empty this afternoon. Lia sent me home. God's timing, huh?"

"Must be."

"Alec, you like your job, don't you?"

"I did. Now I'm not so sure. As manager, I expected I'd be traveling less next year. I expected on getting out of the routine. And I expected a raise! That's not even in the picture now. I want to pay off the van and get Drew a car. I want to buy you something extravagant for a change. I want—"

Anne placed a finger on his lips. "You know the money part will work out. It always does. And I don't want something extravagant."

He pulled her close. She fit so naturally against him. "I've been doing the same thing for ten years. There's nowhere else to move into except manager. You can't become vice president until you've been manager. You know how much Kevin makes?"

"Kevin's a podiatrist. We wouldn't want his headaches or his lifestyle. And yes, unfortunately I know what he makes because Val has given me all the dreary details of what two households cost. Speaking of headaches, do you want some ibuprofen, honey?"

"Yes, thanks. But Val works a full-time job. They can't be hurting too much."

She sat up and rubbed his temples. "In our economy, no, they're not hurting much, but it'll probably turn into a big, ugly issue in the divorce."

"Mmm, that feels great."

"Are you calming down?"

"I've been driving around since I left the office at lunchtime."

"Oh, Alec. This isn't against you personally, you know. It's just politics."

He closed his eyes. What did she understand? She was a woman. "I thought I might call Peter."

"Good idea. Why don't you invite him and Celeste over for pizza tonight? I'll be home from practice early."

"Do you have something you can cook? Pizza gets expensive."

"Alec, our money situation hasn't changed, has it?"

"Not yet. It might if I resign."

~

Anne hadn't seen Alec this strung out since he was studying for his master's, working full-time, and attending Lamaze classes with her.

It was a typical chaotic Saturday morning in the Sutton household. At the moment she wasn't sure where the kids were. All she knew was that as she and Alec crossed paths in their bedroom, she made an idle comment about intending to paint the room in the spring, maybe put some paper on one wall. How opposed was he to something floral?

"Anne! We've got to stop spending money." He hadn't shaved. He wore a sweatshirt he had pulled from the laundry hamper. "That pizza last night cost—"

"We don't buy pizza regularly, Alec. It's a treat. And it was a treat for Peter and Celeste. House maintenance is an ongoing thing. These walls haven't been painted in five years. The pittance I make at the pharmacy will buy the paint."

"You said wallpaper."

"That too. One wall won't cost that much."

"Val makes more than a pittance."

"Yes, and between managing the Community Center and teaching aerobics, she practically lives there."

"Your pharmacy job is more like volunteer. And coaching per hour probably nets you two bucks."

"You're not allowed in the den with the checkbook before dawn again. Come on, Alec! Nothing has changed."

"Don't you get tired of our tight budget?" He raked his fingers through his hair. "I'll be 40 years old in a few months, and I'm still counting nickels and dimes."

"So do our parents."

"They're retired. They have to."

She sighed in exasperation. "We don't go without anything we need. Except for the van and the house, we're not in debt. I only shop for necessities, and that's fine with me. I don't like shopping except at Christmastime. I don't need any more money!"

"Don't buy me anything for Christmas this year."

She burst into laughter. "Oh, Alec! I am not joining your pity party."

"You could get a job like most women. Like Val."

Her smile disintegrated. He was serious. She sank onto the bed. "We agreed from the start that I would be a stay-at-home mom. It was as much your desire as it was mine."

"That was 17 years ago. A lot has changed, especially since yesterday. Since two of our kids became teenagers."

"I didn't finish college."

"I realize that. I know you put me through grad school."

They stared at one another.

He sat beside her. "Anne, I'm just thinking out loud, exploring options here."

"Do you know when the last time was I soaked in a bubble bath?"

"What's that got to do—"

"The first of November. That was the last time I had a spare 30 minutes."

"What if you dropped your part-time work and volunteer stuff?"

"And worked full-time? Forget bubble baths. There wouldn't be enough hours in the day to clean, cook, do laundry, and grocery shop."

"The kids need to be given more responsibilities. They can help more with all that. Maybe that's why God let this happen. So we could all pull together and learn from it. Otherwise He's having a good laugh at me."

"Alec, God doesn't work that way."

"I don't know anymore."

She poked a finger in his chest. "You're losing it, mister. Why don't you go soak in a bubble bath?"

~

Late Saturday night, the old yellow school bus rumbled down the road toward Valley Oaks. The interstate surface was relatively smooth compared to the two-lane county highway which they should hit in about ten minutes. In the front seat across from the driver, Anne felt her bones jar and wondered if, as a late thirty-something woman, she had outgrown her capacity for such treks.

But then, she'd begun questioning every jot and tittle of her life since Alec's career went on hold 24 hours ago. She pulled the scrunchie from her ponytail and absentmindedly fingered the strands loose.

As usual after an away game, the bus was nearly empty. Most of the sophomores and freshmen rode home with their parents. Britte required her varsity girls to ride the bus. By junior year, all of them either had a car or a friend with a car parked back in the school lot. They didn't grumble about their coach's rule.

Anne suspected another reason they didn't gripe was because Britte treated them well. Fast-food restaurants were plentiful along the far-flung routes they traveled. It was tradition to stop as a team and eat on the way home.

"Annie." Britte slid onto the padded bench seat beside her. She had been making her rounds—another tradition— talking individually with the 11 members sprawled about the darkened bus. Rehashing successful plays. Instructing. Listening through their headsets to a curious mixture of music. Joking. *Connecting*.

"Annie," she repeated. "I am so sorry about this schedule."

"Don't worry about it. The schedules don't conflict like tonight's except three times during the entire season. Drew can play three times without his mommy watching."

Britte's face was in shadow, turned as it was from the dimly glowing dashboard, but Anne imagined her friend's eyes. A cartoonist could easily make them dominate her face, poke fun at their proximity. It was that nearness, though, and the royal blue color that made them so arresting.

Britte said, "But can Mommy survive missing him play?"

"Yes, I can. One down tonight, two to go, and Alec's videotaping." *If he remembered.*

"Well, Tanner can take over for you the next two times. I don't mind if you don't mind. He's capable, and those games shouldn't be our toughest." She slapped a hand against her own thigh. "If you're sure it's not basketball, then what's up?"

What was up was Britte, pumped as usual after a game. Anne smiled. Did the community know the treasure they had in this young woman, tucked away in her high school role, growing gracefully into the big shoes of her Great-Aunt Mabel? "You are perceptive, my dear."

"Not really. You just didn't complain once to the refs, and you let me run poor Whitney ragged."

"Alec's job is what's up. He didn't get a promotion we assumed would be automatic." She explained the situation.

"I'm sorry."

"Thanks. It's a major bruise to his ego, no matter how much they downplay it and blame the economy or politics."

"Alec is so likable. And he's always struck me as solid in his faith. He's not going to go wacko on us, is he?"

"You mean, pull a Kevin Massey on us?"

"Yeah, that type of thing. He's too young for a midlife crisis. Too centered."

Anne thought of Alec's demeanor that morning. Centered? Solid in his faith? She pulled her winter jacket more tightly about her shoulders.

"Anne?"

"No, he won't pull a—" She paused. Wasn't it time to admit that her peachy view of Christian marriages smacked of fantasyland? "The fact is, I can't say he won't anything. He's shook up, but God is faithful. God will see us through this."

Britte grasped her hand and squeezed it. "I will pray for you."

Anne nodded. *Yes, please pray.*

Nine

Britte clasped her hands atop her head as she stood on a braided rug in the center of what used to be her bedroom. Her mother had long ago removed the posters and painted white over the hideous royal blue Britte had favored as a faithful Viking. The furnishings, which she had furtively spray-painted gold one spring day when she was 12, had also been restored to their original white. Still, the room resonated with memories of a happy childhood.

Gina lounged on the white chenille bedspread, flipping through a bridal magazine. Winter sunlight streamed through windows behind her, glistening in her brown hair. Barb, Britte's mother, knelt on the rug, running a tape measure down her leg.

"Gina," Britte said, "please tell me this dress has a turtleneck. You could have made ice cubes in the church this morning!"

Gina laughed. "Sorry. No turtleneck."

Barb stood and dangled the tape measure around her neck. "You do have the longest legs, honey, just like your dad's." She wrote numbers on a pad. "Take off that sweatshirt. I can't measure accurately around that thing."

Britte complied. "Mom, since you're making the dress, you can *add* a turtleneck! Tell Gina I look absolutely pathetic in low cut, off-the-shoulder, fancy-schmantzy dresses."

"You don't look pathetic in—"

"But I do! Pull out the old prom photos. Gina, you'll notice that my sister's prom photos are displayed in the

72

family room. Both of my brothers' prom photos are displayed. Mine are stuck somewhere in a drawer."

Barb pulled the tape snug around Britte's waist. "Only because every time I hung them, you took them down."

"I look like a giraffe."

"How you do run on, child!"

"Just stating the facts. Gina, please, please! No skin showing! Else you'll have everyone gawking at a frozen giraffe instead of the beautiful bride."

Gina rose from the bed and brought over the magazine. "Here. This is one of my choices."

Velvety crimson red enveloped the model in a warmth that almost radiated off the glossy page. The dress had a scalloped neck that rose high in the center. From gathered shoulders, long sleeves were held in place with a row of tiny red pearlescent buttons.

"Gina, is this your first or last choice?"

"It's my favorite. Simple, no frills, no fancy-schmantzy."

Britte closed her eyes. "Thank you."

Gina laughed. "Oh, Britte, you know I'd rather be in a sweatshirt and jeans myself! This is as frilly as I can get."

Barb, peering over her daughter's shoulder, sighed. "It's gorgeous, isn't it? And no skin showing!" She nudged Britte. "You'll look beautiful."

Britte handed back the magazine. "Well, I know the seamstress can make that dress look at least as beautiful as it is in the picture."

"Thanks, honey."

"Gina, when do we get to see yours? I cannot imagine choosing a wedding gown. Do they make wedding warm-up suits? Not that I have any reason whatsoever to be concerned about such things."

Her mother tapped her shoulder. "Hold still."

Gina sat again on the bed. "I found one in Rockville, but now Mother's back in Los Angeles and having second thoughts about my choice."

Barb said, "Since she's in the business of women's apparel, I imagine she has quite a number of resources."

"Way too many." Gina grinned. "But she has her own dress to choose, and she can be as frilly as she wants on that one. She'll tire of trying to find a simple, uncreative one for me. Barb, who was it we wanted to ask Britte about?"

"Oh, Ethan Parkhurst. Brady wonders if you'd like to invite him to the wedding."

"Sure." The English teacher was often included in family gatherings. Brady sometimes lectured in his classes. "Is there space?"

Barb and Gina chuckled. Her mother said, "Between Brady and Cal, the list is growing. They seem to be getting into the spirit of a celebration. And how about your principal?"

"Mr. Kingsley? Why on earth—"

"Basketball and Bible study. Hold still."

"Well, then, he's *Brady's* friend. He doesn't need to ask me."

"All done." She rolled up the tape measure. "Why don't you stay a bit and help address wedding invitations?"

Groaning, Britte pulled on her sweatshirt. "Oh, man! I thought I only had to do this dress stuff!"

Gina said, "You don't have to—"

"I'm just kidding. Sort of." She really did have other things to do, other things she'd *like* to do.

"We can watch the game."

Britte returned her smile. "Now that makes it more palatable."

Her mother said, "You two are so much alike, it's funny. And your interests don't even resemble your mothers'." She joined Gina on the bed. "You know, I was always jealous of your mom in high school."

"Really?"

"Mom, I didn't know that!"

Britte and Gina laughed at Barb's teen confessions. The afternoon was another good memory to store in the bedroom. Her mom's stories. Gina, her soon-to-be sister-in-law, participating like a family member. Herself, at the beginning of a winning season. And the feared dress, not too fancy-schmantzy after all. The wedding—well, that felt uncomfortable. It was supposed to have been a small, close-knit affair. Ethan fit, but Mr. Kingsley? Next thing she knew, her brother would be inviting the General for Christmas dinner.

⁓

"Close one, Miss O."

Britte looked up from her seat on the bottom row of the bleachers. Mr. Kingsley stood not far away, just inside the open gym doors. "You're telling me," she said.

The game had ended some time ago. She had struggled through her postgame talk with the girls in the locker room... Accepted the undeserving kudos from parents with all the grace she could muster... Noted from a distance Brady's assessment, a subtle rocking motion of his hand rather than a thumbs-up...

"You kept the fans on the edge of their seats."

"We should have beaten that team by more than one point. It shouldn't have been such an uphill battle."

He shrugged.

She reached down and closed the notebook lying between her feet on the hardwood floor. "Something's not clicking yet."

"Are you ready to go?"

She shoved the notebook into her soft black leather attaché bag and saw the film cassette in a side pocket. Cassie's dad taped the games for her. Eager to review the game, she would do that herself, probably yet tonight. Should they watch it together at practice tomorrow? Could the girls put a finger on the missing ingredient? Anne, uncharacteristically preoccupied, had offered no insight—

"Miss O?"

She looked up. "Excuse me?" His black down-filled jacket was unzipped, revealing a dark green V-neck sweater over a white shirt and red tie. Christmas season appropriate, yes, but school colors? Hardly.

"The custodian has gone home."

"Already?"

"It's 10:45. If you're ready, I'll turn out the lights."

"Ten—?" She glanced up at the clock. "Hmm. Imagine that. Amazing how time flies when you're having fun." She began gathering the clipboards and scorebooks strewn about on the bleachers. "I can take care of the lights and make sure the doors are locked."

"That's my responsibility."

Well, it wasn't. All of the teachers were capable of turning off lights and locking doors.

"And you shouldn't leave alone this time of night."

She zipped shut her bag, stood, and did a slow 360-degree turn. Where was her coat? "You must be confusing Valley Oaks with Chicago."

"City is not the point. A gentleman never allows a lady to walk unescorted in a dubious situation, such as a dark, empty parking lot. Are you looking for this?"

She faced him. Her long wool coat was folded across his arm.

He lifted the coat and held it open for her.

"Chivalry is not yet dead, I see."

A brief smile crossed his face. "It's not dead if you're willing to accept it."

"That sounds like a challenge." She walked over and accepted his help with putting on her coat. "Thank you, sir."

"You're welcome. I'll get the lights."

While he doused the gym lights and closed up, she strolled across the dimly lit area referred to as the commons. It was the center of the school building, a large open area where tables were set up at lunch time. Like the hub of a square wheel, it had "spokes" of four hallways branching different directions. The gym bordered one side, the front doors and glassed-in office another. She reached the back doors leading to the staff parking lot and waited.

As she had concluded before, General Kingsley was an enigma. She wouldn't have imagined him possessing gentlemanly notions. But, now that she thought about it, those notions didn't require emotional commitment, only rote obedience to a set of rules. Either that, or he was just plain chauvinistic and disguising it with courtesy.

He strode toward her, zipping up his jacket.

"Sorry if I kept you waiting," she said. "I lost track of time."

"No problem. I was working." He pushed open the door. "You first, if you don't find that too offensive."

She sailed past him. "Not at all. I don't mind accepting your chauvinistic—I mean, chivalrous—overtures."

He chuckled, his breath frosting the night air. "Now that was intentional. I can tell you're not quite sure which it is."

"The jury is still out."

"There you go, speaking your honest mind again."

She smiled to herself as they walked across the small parking lot. "Where's your car?"

"I usually walk. My condo's only a few blocks beyond the football field."

They reached her Jeep. "Do you want a lift?" She opened a back door and dropped her bag on the seat.

"No, thanks."

"By the way, thank you for *not* offering a coaching opinion on tonight's game."

"You didn't ask for one."

"That doesn't stop most men."

"Pity how rapidly chivalry is dying out. See you tomorrow, Miss O." He walked away, toward the side street that paralleled the back field.

Britte couldn't resist. "It certainly is dying out," she called. "You didn't open the car door for me!"

He looked back at her. "Thought I'd quit while I was ahead."

She murmured, "Chicken," and climbed into the car. While the engine warmed up, she shivered. At the least he could have offered to warm up the car while she waited inside. She laughed at the thought.

He was the first principal to walk her to the car. The first anybody to do so purposely like that. Her mother would adore him. Britte hadn't ever met anyone quite like him, stoic and effective and concerned about dark parking lots in Valley Oaks. And he didn't falsely flatter her about the game. Which made him...an honest gentleman or a chauvinistic boor?

A few moments later she drove alongside him and braked. He halted as she rolled down the passenger window. "Mr. Kingsley. I also appreciate you *not* saying, 'Good job, Coach.'"

In the dim of a street light, she thought she saw him grinning. "Just trying to be honest. Following your example, Miss O."

Ten

Alec sat alone in the family room, staring at the TV but not hearing the 11 o'clock news. He still wore dress slacks and a tie. After working late, he'd gone straight to the high school for the fund-raising taco supper followed by Drew's game. At home he had read the mail, written checks, and tried again to rework the budget. It wasn't happening.

Instead of going upstairs, he sat down in the family room, hoping to neutralize his mind with the news in order to be able to sleep. It wasn't happening.

The past two days, morale at work was at an all-time low. Unpopular decisions had been made by upper management. There was nothing to be done except hang in there, give his all as usual, and convince himself that it was okay not to receive an increase in pay. Believing that was not happening.

Anne walked in, sat on the couch, and snuggled against him. He muted the television and put his arm around her. "Hey, mister. How's it going?"

"She sweetly asked the head grouch."

"I really want to know."

"Don't you remember what curiosity did to the cat?"

"Alexander." Anne didn't easily reach exasperation, but her tone suggested she was nearly there. "I keep thinking this despondency will pass."

"That's a 50-cent word."

Her sigh was audible. "What I meant was, this snarling attitude of yours is getting old." She kissed his cheek. "You're not much fun these days."

"The checkbook isn't either. The ends are not coming together. My car needs tires this month. The van needs some work. I really think we should buy that used car so Drew has his own wheels. It's getting too complicated sharing a car and getting him where he needs to be. He can take care of his own schedule and maybe help with the girls. We promised the kids the Grand Canyon tour next summer. That package deal costs less now than it will next year. I was planning on the promotion or at least the bonus to carry us through."

"What you're saying is that you've already spent the money in your mind."

"Not just. Here, take a look." He reached for the printout he'd laid on the coffee table.

"You know I can never make heads or tails out of numbers."

"I need you to understand this, Anne." He heard the aggravation in his voice and eased off. "I'll explain it." He showed her the figures: the increases in real estate taxes and insurance, the black-and-white of fixed expenses nearly equaling the income.

They discussed ways to cut back, but in the end she said, "Should I get a job?"

He took a deep breath. "I think it would make a difference."

Her forehead was wrinkled. She wasn't convinced.

"We'll pray about it." He nuzzled her hair. "It wouldn't have to be anything major. Maybe something temporary, just to get us over this hump." He tried to encourage her with thoughts of change and adventure, of how shaking up the status quo could be a healthy, stretching experience.

"Kevin certainly shook up the status quo."

Alec pulled her close. The issue of their friends' separation often hung between them like a fine mist, dampening their spirits. "That's different."

She buried her head in his shoulder. "I miss sitting beside you at the games."

"I miss you, too."

They sat in silence for a moment.

"Alec, Kevin has a girlfriend."

He sighed wearily. "I suspected as much. You don't just walk out on a good-looking, hardworking, fun-loving wife."

"But if Val's so wonderful, why would he be attracted to someone else in the first place?"

"It happens. Some guys just want out of the day-to-day rat race. They think a different woman will save them from it." He squeezed her. "You're stuck with me, though, sweetheart. I like everything about our life."

"Except the checkbook."

Anne sat on the edge of the chair, across a wide expanse of a desk. A middle-aged, blonde-streaked, short-haired, perky little woman named Jody sat across from her talking animatedly into the telephone.

Anne was in Rockville, at a temporary staffing office.

Alec had said some things that gave her second thoughts about that old stay-at-home commitment. Overtly, he hadn't pushed her to get a job, but the figures he showed her indicated that the family needed more from her than taking care of the house and volunteering right and left.

She glanced around the office. It was small but bright, full of cute knickknacks, photographs, and floral lithographs, as if this were the woman's home. Maybe it was.

Last night she and Alec had talked further. If she worked, he said, they could afford to buy her new, different clothes. It would be good for her to be out in the world, learn what was going on outside of Valley Oaks and the kids' version of reality. Alec's rambling touched a chord. Was something wrong with her wardrobe? Was her conversation too boring, centered as it so often was around their family?

Maybe it was the Val-Kevin issue that influenced her reaction. The fact that Kevin was seeing another woman— cheating on her most precious of friends—had put her on edge.

Before their talks, before her friends split, Anne had been comfortable with herself. Now she wondered if Alec still found her attractive. She didn't ask him, but the seeds of doubt had been planted.

"Anne." Jody turned to her now. "Tell me about yourself. What's your experience?"

"I'm a mom."

Jody smiled, encouraging. "And?"

"I don't type. I don't know computers. I coach basketball and work as a sales clerk at the Valley Oaks Pharmacy. I know the alphabet. I know how to clean, cook, drive, and condense five schedules into one." She smiled back.

"And what did you do before you had children? Did you go to school?"

"I went to junior college for two years. Then I quit to get married and put my husband through grad school."

"Doing?"

"I worked in an office, doing general clerk-related duties. Seventeen years ago. Computers weren't common."

Jody laughed. "What did you study in school?"

Anne's mind's eye returned to memories long buried. "Art. I studied art."

She was sure the woman had no order to place someone who, in another lifetime, interpreted the world with a paintbrush and oils.

Eleven

The locker room door swooshed shut behind Britte, muting the riotous whoops of 11 girls riding high on a solid Saturday afternoon win. She walked down the hallway, grinning and slipping into her black blazer. The answer to Wednesday night's missing ingredient was coming together.

As she glanced ahead to where the hall opened into the commons area, her steps slowed and her grin faded into a half smile. Separate from the crowd lingering near the concession stand, Jordan Hughes' parents waited. The back of her neck tingled. She knew this dad was ready to pounce.

"Lord," she breathed, "help."

"Coach!" Gordon Hughes called from a distance, not leaving things to chance. It was his way of publicly announcing that he had first dibs on Coach that afternoon. "Good game."

She smiled at him and his smiling wife. When she reached them, she didn't stop completely, but edged her way into the commons. She wasn't about to be cornered in the hall where the teams would soon be filing out.

They stuck beside her. "Britte, we need to talk." Mr. Hughes' voice took on a familiar quality, as if they were friends who lunched together. He was a tall man in his 40s, with large facial features, hands, and feet. In the seven years she had known him, he was always neatly groomed, his brown hair brushed back off of a high forehead. Strutting peacock came to mind, especially next to his attractive but demure wife.

Britte halted on the fringe of the milling crowd. Mr. Kingsley stood across the way, talking with students. He wore a blue sweater today, a school color. Of course, he probably wore it for the boys game, which would begin in a couple of hours. "How about an early Monday morning appointment?" she said. "Seven? Six-forty-five? Or Tuesday evening would work."

"No, I don't need an appointment. It won't take long." He stepped nearer, leaving no room for doubt that he had recently eaten a hot dog with onions. "You changed your lineup."

"Yes."

"May I ask why?"

"Yes, you may ask why." Her jaw muscles tightened as she stubbornly waited for him to ask why.

Lights glinted off his wire-rimmed glasses, and his smile flattened into a grim line.

She bit her tongue before suggesting he go ahead and *ask* why. *Choose your battles, Britte. Answer the man's question, even though he hasn't asked it.* "I thought it best for this particular opponent."

"Jordan didn't start."

She blinked in reply.

"Liz caused seven turnovers."

Britte glanced away. The principal caught her eye. He had moved into her diminished line of vision. She looked back up at Mr. Hughes. "I haven't studied the stats yet."

"Well, believe me, it was at least seven."

"And your point is?"

He lowered his head and whispered, "Jordan wouldn't have made those mistakes."

Britte pressed her lips together. Jordan had been directly or indirectly responsible for nine turnovers in the last game, but that wasn't the point either. "This is about playing time." As most coaches did, she explained at the preseason parents' meeting that she would only discuss with the girls themselves the subject of how much time they were given out on the court.

He straightened again. "It certainly is not about playing time."

"I do not discuss playing time with parents."

"It's about coaching."

Britte's entire face felt hot. She glanced away again. Other parents were watching, unease clearly written on some of their faces. "This really isn't the time or the place, Mr. Hughes."

"Britte." He held out his hands, palms up. "I'm just trying to help. No offense, but you're young."

She knew for a fact the man had never played basketball in his life. "That's true, I am young. And I'm doing my best. We won today, and it wasn't a squeaker. Second half, the girls were finding a rhythm. It was an outside game, and Liz is an outside shooter."

"All I'm saying is…" He droned on, emitting onion scents across her face.

Why was she having this conversation? Mr. Kingsley shifted completely into view now, behind Mr. Hughes' shoulder. She certainly didn't want him in on this, too! "Mr. Hughes," she interrupted him. "I appreciate your help. I'll think about it. Now I've got to talk to Coach Carlucci before he gets away."

"I could come to practice—"

"Mr. Hughes." She pasted on her best placating smile. "If you did that, every dad would want to help. You know what they say about too many cooks spoiling the soup. Excuse me." Lightly touching his wife's arm, Britte made a deliberate sidestep around her and walked away.

The crowd had thinned. The girls were trickling through the commons, calling out plans to meet at the Pizza Parlor. They had time to eat before coming back to the boys game, something they often did as a team. Several girls and parents invited her to join them.

"I'll see," she wavered.

Were Jordan's parents going? Last year they seldom attended such group outings. The thought of sitting across a pizza from them disturbed her. She had to go home, sort this out. Talk to somebody.

Where was everyone? Brady hadn't made it today. Ethan had, of course, but he didn't offer much in the way of technical support. She scanned the commons. He was gone by now anyway. She needed Anne, but she had left immediately after the game, something to do with her family schedule. Anne knew how to run interference for her. She would have been right there with her, reminding Mr. Hughes in her kind but straightforward manner that they did not discuss playing time. Where was Tanner Carlucci? No way could he replace Anne, except perhaps on the bench. He had a good grasp of the game. If she could talk to him now—

"Miss O."

She half turned. Mr. Kingsley was at her elbow.

"Good job, Coach." A brief smile touched his lips, and then he was gone.

Stunned, she almost didn't notice two players waving as they walked past her. "Oh, see you later!" she shouted halfway across the open space.

She felt her shoulder muscles relax, her jaw unclench, the heat in her cheeks dissipate. Of course she'd go to the Pizza Parlor. Why would she miss an outing with her girls?

Warm fuzzies from the principal? Hardly. But, she smiled to herself, it was just what she needed. The General would never say "good job" unless he meant it.

"Amy," Anne called to her daughter down the church hallway, "tell Dad I'll be out soon. Britte and I are going to talk back here." Her daughter waved an acknowledgment as Anne ducked into a vacant Sunday school classroom. "What's up, hon?"

Britte sat on a table, swinging her legs and chewing her thumbnail. "Gordon Hughes."

"Oh, no."

"Oh, yes. Thank you for abandoning me yesterday."

The lump that had taken up permanent residence in Anne's stomach rolled, collecting another layer of discomfort. Everyone was hurting these days, and she was beginning to feel responsible for all of their unhappiness.

"Annie, I'm just kidding. I kept thinking, what would Anne say? That helped. I didn't bite his head off."

"You're growing up. I'm proud."

Britte filled her in on the details. "What do you think?"

"I thought the game went very well. You didn't play Jordan or Janine or Tasha and Katie as much as you could have, but that's your prerogative. It's that fine line we talked about. Do you play to win or play everyone equally?"

"I don't want to straddle it. I want to be fair, but I've got to use this talent we've been given. Everyone would be disappointed if we didn't win like we should."

"It's not your style to keep the fans and parents happy."

"Gordon Hughes knows that for sure."

"What I mean is, in the past, you haven't played to win. You've concentrated on giving all the girls game experience."

She didn't reply, but her legs stopped swinging.

"Is there something personal going on? If so, understandable. With a dad like that, after all these years, I'd have a hard time being civil to Jordan."

"Not you."

"Yes, me. You've got your work cut out for you, Coach. Is it personal?"

"I don't think so."

"Well, you probably should ponder it awhile. Pray about it."

"It'd be a crime to let this team go to waste."

"Agreed."

"Thanks, Annie. Don't let me lose track, okay?"

Anne stifled a sigh. Why was it she had to keep everyone on track? "Britte, I applied for a job this week."

Her friend's eyes widened.

"I won't quit coaching. It's just... Things are getting to Alec. He keeps adjusting our budget. He's angry at his boss. He's losing confidence in his ability to provide. He doesn't listen to me." She held up her hands.

"Ahh, the ever-present male ego."

"I know. At any rate I want to do what I can to support him. Which probably isn't much, even though he thinks I can make a difference. The temp office lady practically laughed me out of the place, politely of course. I'm going to be a little stretched over the next few weeks, whether I get a job or not."

"I'm sorry."

Tears glistened in Anne's eyes. "It'll all work out."

Twelve

Although his Sunday evening schedule didn't accommodate a party, Joel considered the faculty Christmas gathering obligatory and therefore he attended. After two trips to the buffet table, he felt rather pleased with his decision. The event was hosted by the home ec—make that the domestic science teacher. Instead of suggesting a potluck, she collected money from everyone and then proceeded to prove her expertise in the field of cooking.

Her family room was wall-to-wall teachers in festive clothing who were laughing noisily and enjoying a rare moment when students weren't the main topic of conversation. He made the rounds, meeting spouses and evading the perky little divorced French teacher who had recently progressed from subtle innuendoes to outright flirting with him.

Christmas was not his favorite time of year. It was an interruption to real life. Growing up, it hadn't been a big deal. Santa came and went with hints of frivolity; more importantly, needs were met in the modest Kingsley home by his hardworking parents. When he was in the Marine Corps, it had been easy to ignore it. Military training and missions did not always accommodate holidays. Now, his parents spent two weeks with his sister in Florida. Once again he begged off making the trip and promised to visit them in the spring.

Becoming a believer hadn't changed his attitude. To him the commercialism of the season destroyed the symbolic recognition of Christ's birth. Regrettably, even he was induced to shop. Most of it was accomplished online. One evening surfing the Internet took care of his siblings, nieces, and nephews, but for his parents he made a rare trip to the mall. Not that he lingered. Just as he did every year, he bought his father a book and his mother a special piece of jewelry. At least the purchase for the faculty gift exchange had been taken care of at the same time. All of this so-called Christmas-related nonsense fell under the heading of an obligatory nuisance.

He made his way now across the room toward Britte Olafsson, whom he hadn't yet greeted. She sat in a corner with Ethan Parkhurst, laughing hilariously. Joel wondered if the two of them were dating. Lynnie Powell, the school secretary who kept him informed of all the community gossip, hadn't mentioned that they were. They appeared, at the least, to be close friends. As far as teaching went, they fit each other. Ethan was well on his way to becoming an excellent teacher. Britte was already there.

Before Joel reached their corner, Ethan strolled off. Joel slid into the armchair the young man had vacated, just the other side of a lamp table from her chair. "Miss O." The nickname hadn't originated with him. He'd overheard students calling her that the first week of school.

"Hi, Mr. Kingsley." She smiled. She looked different tonight. Her blonde hair hung in loose waves just below her shoulders. "What do you think of the party?"

"Best food I've eaten in a long time."

"Theresa's the greatest cook."

"Mind if we talk shop a minute?"

She groaned. "We're supposed to take the night off."

"I bet you don't take much time off."

Those close-set eyes of hers zeroed in on him. "Bet you don't either," she challenged with a smile.

"Does it show that much?"

She laughed. "Um, just a little. You're worse than I am."

"You think so? How about a contest to see who's the worst? We could have a live-at-the-school marathon. I'll scrounge around for some funds so we can hire Theresa to cook for us."

"Now that sounds heavenly. But how would we measure who accomplishes the most?"

"Good question. We can't have quantity without quality."

"Assign a committee!"

"I'll get right on it." He smiled briefly. "In the meantime, I didn't want to lose sight of your little confrontation with Gordon Hughes."

"Maybe we could have another contest. First one to *not* talk shop for five minutes wins."

"Wins what?"

"A day off."

"Not interested."

She wrinkled her nose. "Me neither. All right, tell me about Mr. Hughes."

"Why don't you tell me? Any problems you'd care to discuss?"

She shrugged. "There aren't any problems really. I've known his daughter for years through our camps and leagues. And through all those years he has been giving me coaching advice. Free of charge, mind you. He thinks Jordan is headed for the Big Ten."

Joel winced. "Seriously?"

"Well, a Division II school anyway. Therefore, he wants her to play all the time."

"That's his coaching advice?"

"It's the main theme of it, yes."

"He called me this afternoon. He made an appointment to talk basketball on Wednesday with me."

She pressed her lips together and glanced away, simultaneously crossing her arms and her legs. When the girl wasn't speaking her mind, her body language did it for her. She wore a soft, bulky sweater, long skirt, and boots. He noticed even a hint of makeup. Typically she wore a warm-up suit or khaki slacks and sweater, her hair in a ponytail, her face unadorned.

Those eyes turned again, nailing him to the wall. "Will you back me up?"

"I don't know the situation yet."

"I just told you the situation." Though her voice maintained a reasonable tone, her eyes blasted missiles his direction. "He won't be happy unless his daughter is the star of the team, and, unfortunately, she's not star material in basketball."

Women and sports do not *mix,* he thought, not for the first time. "I'll listen to what Hughes has to say. See if I can't smooth things over."

"It shouldn't be a political thing." She swung her crossed leg back and forth.

"Smoothing things over is in everyone's best interest. The community pays our salaries."

"That doesn't give Gordon Hughes the right to interfere with *my* team. Will you back me up?"

"My job is to do what's best for the students. Therefore, I've got to hear both sides."

"Well, you've heard mine." She said it matter-of-factly, with only a vague hint of sassiness. Sassiness he could handle. Pouting sent him through the roof. Thank goodness she wasn't a pouter.

"I'll get back to you after our meeting."

"I'd appreciate that. Excuse me." In one quick motion she stood and brushed past Ethan, who approached carrying two plates.

Ethan lifted one plate toward her retreating back. "Apple pie à la mode? No, I guess not. Joel? I've got apple pie here and a mystery dessert exhibiting oodles of whipped cream and chocolate. Which do you prefer?"

He shook his head, baffled at what had just taken place. "Women and sports and politics. There must be a connection, but I certainly don't get it. Oh, thanks, Ethan. I'll take the apple pie, if you don't mind. I've had enough surprises for one evening."

"There you go." Ethan handed him the plate and sat in the other chair. "What'd you say to Britte?"

"I told her Gordon Hughes made an appointment to see me this week."

"Eww. Not a good subject, sir."

Joel chuckled. "Next time, do me a favor and warn me. I like to know when I'm about to face a firing squad."

⌒

Britte gulped a cupful of lime sherbet punch. The icy drink cooled her down.

She really had harbored such grand hopes for the man. Despite his "General's" approach to life, he was effective. He was, as Anne said, magnetic. And yes, all right, he was attractive.

It was his discipline that had caught her attention, a characteristic she always admired in others. Intense discipline absolutely oozed from him. It molded his posture, the set of his lined jaw, the muscular arms and shoulders, the trim haircut, the furrowed brow, the energy. But he carried it way too far! His smile was infrequent, distracted. His eye color still remained a mystery. Even now, focused as he was on their conversation, his gaze had continuously scanned the room, his mind almost audibly clicking her situation off his list as it scrolled down to the next item. In the dim lamplight his eyes appeared a hazel, a mixture of colors, nothing definite.

The only thing *definite* to come out of their conversation was that they disagreed on his responsibility. His adamant refusal to unconditionally defend her made her feel as if she'd been pushed from an airplane without a chute. It left her feeling, to put it mildly, vulnerable.

His job was to catch her, to prevent her from falling flat on her face, wasn't it? It was all she had known in almost six and a half years of teaching.

When she first began her career, the same warm teddy bear of a principal she had known as a student was still at the helm. He retired the end of her second year. Since then, two fly-by-night administrators had filled the post, a brief stopover on their way to positions at larger schools. Then along came Joel Kingsley. She suspected he possessed the same intentions. Get his feet wet as head honcho, and then skedaddle off to a higher-paying situation and hunker down for the duration. With an average of only 400 students, the school had not attracted a leader dedicated to joining the community for the long haul. Still, the three former principals had always backed her. Even the one who disliked her had backed her.

The Gordon Hughes issue didn't matter all that much. There would always be disgruntled parents. That was a given with the job. She welcomed the news that Gordon Hughes planned to talk with Mr. Kingsley—and there was no doubt in her mind that it concerned her—because it took some of the direct heat off of her. The principal could defend her right to make teaching and coaching decisions.

And then he should back her on those decisions.

Britte poured another cup of punch and reminded herself it was Christmas. This was the evening to bask in camaraderie, not review the principal's inadequacies. The faculty members were her friends, a handful of whom had taught her when she was a student at Valley Oaks High.

Sipping the drink, she allowed the ambience to wash over her. Twinkling tree lights. Warm, soothing crackles from the fireplace. Soft candlelight. Cozy quarters. Laughing friends. The enchantment of the season, so eloquent in Theresa's home, worked its way again into her mind-set.

The gift exchange was under way, growing, as always, riotous. She joined the two other math teachers sitting on the plush carpet.

"Britte, it's your turn!"

She eyed the plain, brown paper grocery bag set before her on the floor. The handwriting on the name tag gave no clue as to the giver's identity because Theresa wrote all of them. The gifts were given anonymously, a custom which made the giving fun and the receiving a foreboding experience. The only guidelines were that it be appropriate to the recipient and *cheap*. Of course, the gifts were, more often than not, jokes that poked fun at personal idiosyncrasies. It became a guessing game throughout the year trying to figure out who had given what to whom.

Among the gifts Britte had received to date were one repulsive, fluorescent orange sweat suit, obviously second hand; a trophy with a plaque reading, "Most Losses in a Season BUT Best-Dressed Coach in the League"; and a jersey with letters across the back spelling "1—Bratte." She was still pondering that last one.

And now...she peeked in the bag. A gold megaphone! She pulled it out. "This is great! I love it! Ooo." She turned it on and held it to her mouth. "Batteries included!" Her voice boomed across the room. "Thank you, Anonymous!"

There were boos and guffaws. "Take that thing away from Olafsson! She doesn't need it!"

She laughed and reached back into the bag again. Something else was on the bottom... Out came an elegantly wrapped, long, narrow box. She peeled away the royal blue foil, careful not to smash the tiny gold bow. Lifting the box lid, she saw beneath it a black velvet jeweler's box. How bizarre! She glanced around the room. Someone must be enjoying this joke she didn't yet understand. She tilted the lid back, and her breath caught. This didn't look like a joke.

A necklace twinkled back at her. There was a delicate gold chain. Even without the jeweler's name imprinted on the satin cover, she recognized it as a nice gold, as in 24-karat. In its center hung a small, teardrop-shaped, multifaceted stone. A sapphire? It was blue, at any rate...a blue similar to the school color.

"It's beautiful." Whistles and laughter drowned her murmured words. She felt her cheeks flushing. Who would give this to her? Why—?

"Britte's got an admirer!"

"Way to go, Olafsson!"

The rampant teasing continued until someone called out, "Perfect gift! Britte's speechless. That's gotta be a first!"

She grabbed her megaphone and spoke into it. "I am not speechless! If you'd all be quiet for two seconds I could—"

The room fell instantly silent.

"Uh...okay. Thank you again, Anonymous. This is absolutely beautiful. And you're in big trouble for *nearly* making me speechless. Trust me, I *will* find you out."

Amid laughter and applause, Britte tucked her gifts back into the bag, cheeks aflame, totally blanked on who was responsible. The necklace was appropriate from a close friend, like Ethan, but he wouldn't have chosen tonight to give it to her. Who in the world...?

Thirteen

"Miss O! Miss O!" The muffled cries were accompanied by a pounding on the sliding door in Britte's classroom.

Brushing chalk dust from her hands, she hurried over to it and drew back the curtains that were still shut against the cold gray morning. Two junior girls stood outside, their panic-stricken faces pressed against the glass door.

"Miss O! Fight!"

She undid the lock and swished open the sliding door. "What's wrong, Julie? Rachel?"

"Fight! It's Drew Sutton and Benny Coles!"

Drew? Anne and Alec's son?

Britte abandoned the effort to make sense of the girls' explanation and stepped outside between them. "Go get Mr. Kingsley." She saw a group of about 30 students across the school's frost-covered lawn and broke into a run. The first bell hadn't yet rung. This side of the building was visible to the front parking lot where buses unloaded and kids parked. However, no one in the front office would be able to see it.

"All right!" Britte shouted above the clamor, shoving her way between tightly packed bodies. "Get inside." There were groans of disappointment. "Now! Fight's over."

She reached the center of the circle. Well, the fight wasn't over. "Break it up!" she yelled.

Two boys writhed on the ground, totally ignoring her.

"I said break it up!"

In response, Drew Sutton straddled Benny Coles and pulled back his right arm, fist clutched.

Britte grabbed his wrist. "Knock it off, Drew!"

Too late she realized the normally cheerful, compliant boy was out of control. He jerked his arm away, throwing her off balance and allowing Benny to squirm out from under him. Immediately the boys crouched, poised to lunge toward each other again. In the split second before they sprang, Britte shoved Drew down to the frozen grass, rammed her knee into his back, yanked his arm in an iron grip, and twisted it back and up.

"Andrew Sutton, stop it! Benny! Back off!"

The other boy complied, sitting back on his haunches and wiping perspiration from his face. Drew remained tense, straining against her.

"Andrew, calm down now. Just calm down." She heard his heavy breathing.

He was a lot bigger than she was. He had Alec's breadth of shoulders and Anne's long legs, though his height had passed up his mother and Britte long ago.

"Calm down!" she repeated with emphasis. "Everybody else, get out of here! Benny, you stay put."

Some of the crowd moved off. Drew relaxed slightly, but she didn't loosen her hold.

"Drew, this is Britte. Talk to me."

"You're hurting my arm," he grunted.

"Good. Inflicting pain on students is my favorite Monday morning activity. It's tons more fun than preparing for geometry. Are you about done?"

He went limp.

"You can't pull that one on me anymore, bud. Do you promise?"

"Yeah."

"What?"

"Yes, I promise."

Britte sensed the crowd dispersing. She glanced up. "Ah, reinforcements. Your coach and principal are rushing this direction. I'm letting you up, okay?"

"Okay." His resignation was clear.

"Everybody," Mr. Kingsley roared as he ran across the lawn, tie flapping, "get to class! Now!"

Britte stood, straightening her turtleneck sweater and brushing off her slacks, grateful she hadn't put on a skirt this morning. Her right knee was damp from where it had sunk into the frosty grass. Drew and Benny picked up their jackets and backpacks from the ground. Both of them were disheveled, their faces forlorn. Drew's lip was bleeding. Benny's flannel shirt was torn.

As a bell rang, she greeted Mr. Kingsley and Coach Woodson. "Morning, gentlemen. I'll let you take over from here." She turned to leave.

"Wait up, Miss O."

The glowering General summons. Her back to him, she wrinkled her nose and waited.

"Coach Woodson, please escort these boys to my office. I'll be right there." He fell into step beside her, and they walked briskly toward the building.

She noticed now how cold it was and crossed her arms. Their breath iced the air. "I've lost track of time. Was that the final bell?"

"Britte." His voice was a low growl.

In five months, if he had directly addressed her as "Britte," she didn't remember it. That he did so now in such a tone wasn't a good sign.

As always, though, his demeanor was calm. Only the slightest increase in his volume indicated there was a storm brewing. "What in the...*world* did you think you were doing?"

"Breaking up a fight. The same thing you would have done if you'd gotten there first."

"You could have been hurt! What if they'd had weapons?"

"There wasn't time to assess the what-ifs. I just reacted." They neared the building. Her sliding glass door still stood open. *Swell. Now the room will feel ice-cold all morning.* She caught sight of students ducking away.

He stopped outside her door, hands on his hips. "You just didn't think, did you? You could have gotten punched or kicked! You could have been seriously injured!"

Britte quickly slid shut the door so her first-hour class wouldn't overhear their conversation. "You're right. I didn't think, but I sensed what was going on. It was Drew and Benny. They're top-notch kids. Athletes, high honor roll. This behavior was highly uncharacteristic for them. I know Drew. I used to be his sitter. I've known him since he was a baby."

"Babies grow up and hurt people."

Exasperated, she held out her arms. "Mr. Kingsley, I am not hurt!"

"Why is it you always have to prove how macho you are?"

Her jaw dropped. "I don't have to because I'm not in a macho contest! I simply prevented them from further hurting each other. Why is it you're offended that I can do what you can do?"

He looked away, pressing his lips together. His breath curled vapor around his face.

"Of course," she went on, "*you* might have gone after Benny. I did *think* enough to realize I had a better chance with Drew because Benny's a wrestler. I would have had to use a full nelson on him, and I haven't practiced that one in a long while."

His shoulders sagged. The hint of a smile tugged at the corner of his mouth.

"Mr. Kingsley, will you excuse me? I'm freezing out here."

He turned back toward her. "Britte, please don't do that again. I don't want to have to tell your brother that you're in the hospital because I didn't get there fast enough."

Her teeth were chattering by now. "I can't imagine you ever slacking in your duty. I'm sure you'd get there in time." She slid open the door and stepped inside.

He walked away.

"Mr. Kingsley! It's shorter this way."

"What? Oh, right." He turned back and entered her classroom.

The students were sitting quietly at their desks. As Mr. Kingsley walked silently across the front of her room, one of the boys called out, "Who won?"

Mr. Kingsley stopped at the hall door and exchanged a glance with Britte, his brows raised. He cleared his throat. "Well, Shawn, I'd have to say that Miss O won. But then, women always win. They don't always play fair, but they always win."

The girls protested loudly while the boys applauded.

And Mr. Kingsley threw her a very nice smile.

Fourteen

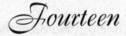

Anne sat in the kitchen. Her favorite Bible lay open on the table before her, but she stared straight ahead, seeing nothing, seeing everything.

There was Drew's cut lip, the purple spreading beneath his left eye, the evasive answers.

There was Sunday's atypical mood, precipitated by Alec's nitpicking everyone and by her teasing him that finally erupted—in front of the children!—in her rather nonsubmissive comment, "Who died and made you president?"

She knew the two incidents were related.

Lord, I'm sorry.

Ever since Alec didn't get the promotion, he had been needling Drew about basketball and grades. She had no idea what Drew and Benny's problem had been yesterday, but she knew beyond a shadow of a doubt that her son's behavior had to do with his parents.

There was Drew's two-day, in-school suspension. He would sit again today in a small back room with an adult monitor and Benny and two pot-smoking, confused boys. He would do class work and practice basketball after school, but he would receive credit for neither. He would fall behind in chemistry and English. He would sit out two of the week's three games. Black and white.

Why can't you make it all black and white, Father?

The phone rang.

"Hello?"

"Anne? This is Jody with Riverside Staffing." Her smile was an audible thing resonating through the line. "I've got a job for you."

∼

Two hours later Anne pushed open the glass door of Manning's Gallery and Art Supply. A tiny wind chime stirred on its handle. Its delicate music tinkled, a jarring contrast to the dull, rhythmic thud of her heartbeat. She took a deep breath. The pungent scent of oils filled her nostrils. Briefly, she shut her eyes. She felt as if she'd come home.

The room was bright and airy and chock-full of art supplies. She turned slowly in a full circle. Oil paints, water color paints, brushes, easels, canvases, pencils, charcoal, paper, sketch pads, frames. In all conceivable shapes, sizes, amounts, and colors.

"May I help you?"

She turned.

An unprepossessing man stood before her. Tall, lean, almost gaunt. His beard more silver than reddish brown, as was the longish hair.

"I was just remembering," she said, "the last time I was in here. My son was a year old." She laughed. "He's 16 now."

He smiled. "My dear woman, where have you been?"

"Are you Mr. Manning?"

"I'm Charlie. My last name's Manning."

She held out her hand. "I'm Anne Sutton."

"Pleasure to meet you, Anne." His hand engulfed hers. "Come into the office."

Unbuttoning her wool coat, she followed him between shelves to a counter along the left side of the store. He was dressed casually in jeans and a green-plaid flannel shirt.

Behind the counter was an open door through which they walked.

"Have a seat." He pointed to a chair the other side of the desk as he sat. The space was a long, narrow, cluttered room with two desks. Charlie nodded toward another open door, opposite the one they had just entered. "The gallery is on that side. You've probably noticed, we have two front doors, leading separately to the gallery and the shop. Of course, if you haven't been here for 15 years, perhaps you haven't noticed." He smiled again, his heavy-lidded eyes almost squinting shut.

"No, I hadn't noticed."

"Ah." His brows went up.

"Kids."

"That explains that. Jody tells me you majored in art."

"Long, *long* time ago."

"But it's in your soul."

She shrugged, wincing in a self-deprecating way.

"I saw it on your face the moment you stepped inside. Did Jody tell you the hours?"

"Days, which works for me because I coach basketball. My evenings are booked solid for the next six weeks."

"Art and basketball? Hmm." His voice was soft, whispery, as if he did not want his words to be an intrusion. "Well, my daytime help just had a baby last night, supposedly prematurely, but he weighed in at seven pounds. The college kids come in at four and work the evening shift. What are your Saturdays like?"

"They differ, week to week."

"How about this Sunday?"

"Sunday?" She couldn't keep the dismay from her voice. Saturday would be hard enough.

"I know. We may as well call it X-mas. We've taken Christ right out of the entire matter. Business is brisk, and

I succumbed for this month. I'm open from one to four. The college kids are going home for the holidays. Since my wife left, that's the only help I've got. I need you nine to four, Monday through Friday. We'll talk about the weekend. Are you interested?"

"But what do I do?"

A slow grin spread across his face. "Just be you, madam. Just be you."

"Meaning?"

"Talk art supplies."

What? No computer? No conflict with basketball? And a premature baby just happening to be born *now?*

It all seemed pretty black and white to her. She smiled. "Okay. When do I start?"

~

"Where did Charlie Manning's wife go?" Alec helped himself to another serving of lasagna.

"I don't know." Anne passed the salad bowl to him. "We didn't get very personal. He wears a wedding band. Maybe she just quit working with him."

"I think," Amy said, putting a hand over her heart, "that she died and he can't bear to say the word."

Mandy burst into laughter. Drew rolled his eyes and shoved a piece of garlic bread into his mouth.

The Suttons were eating a late dinner, atypically all five of them together. Drew's game ended early enough and, given the fact that he was grounded for life, he was present rather than with the guys at the Pizza Parlor.

From the store, Anne had called her mother, who was available to pick up the girls after school. They often walked home, but Mandy would be carrying a large science project.

Anne arrived home just in time to change into warm-ups and make it to practice. The boys games began right after that. They attended, as usual, even though Drew sat on the bench, Anne with Val, Alec with Kevin.

Alec raised his milk glass. "To Mom, for bringing home the bacon."

"Daddy," Mandy said, "this is lasagna!"

He ruffled her hair. "It's an old saying. So, sweetheart, what did you do?"

"I talked art supplies." She grinned. "I felt like I was 18 years old again. It was great! The store kept pretty busy. Charlie was in the gallery most of the time. He sells local artists' paintings and sculptures in there."

"And how much do you make?"

She told him. "Not a lot of bacon, but more than minimum at least. And, I get a big discount on supplies. Mandy, they even have crayons and markers, every color under the sun."

Her little girl's eyes lit up.

By the time they finished dinner, it was after Mandy's bedtime. Anne shooed her upstairs. Amy and Drew tried to follow, but Alec stood in their path.

"Mom needs more help now. You two clear the table."

Amy protested, claiming she had homework. Drew remained wisely quiet and cooperative. They made short work of their chore and immediately dashed upstairs.

"Alec, you put food away, and I'll load the dishwasher. Hey." Hands dripping wet, she sidled up to him and whispered, "Maybe we'll find extra alone time."

"In the kitchen?" He barked a laugh. "Right. Where does this go?" He held up the salad bowl.

"Common sense works well in the kitchen, mister."

"Umm. Leftovers go in a plastic bag. Bag goes in the fridge. I give you the bowl."

"And you get a gold star." She turned back to the sink. He had hugged her when she gave him the news at the game, but they hadn't really talked yet. "So, what do you think? Will it help?"

He came from behind and wrapped his arms around her. "It'll help, sweetheart. I'm proud of you."

"But it's not much. Part-time and temporary."

He nuzzled her hair. "Maybe it's the idea more than the paycheck. I suddenly feel less pressured." He kissed her cheek.

Black and white.

In the end, Anne alone wiped down the counters, swept the floor, and turned off the lights. Alec had gone up to settle down the kids and never returned. As she climbed the staircase, her mind raced. She had to get better organized. At least she had thought to forewarn Lia at the pharmacy. That hadn't been a problem because the pharmacist had taken on a new employee. Anne should make a list of daily and weekly chores, assign them to others, post it on the fridge...write more legible notes on the calendar so everyone knew where everyone else was at any given moment. A new phone list was needed. There were some PTA secretarial duties to be delegated. She'd better get on the phone tomorrow. When tomorrow? There was a game after work.

A shade of gray crept into her thinking, smudging those lines of black and white.

Fifteen

Britte felt Anne touch her elbow and then imperceptibly squeeze it as they stood in the commons facing Mr. Hughes. Same time, same channel, just a different day.

Anne said, "Gordon, we need to give Coach a chance here. She's got to do some experimenting, find the right combinations. We're not even halfway through—"

"The season's only—"

She held out a palm, effectively halting his words. "I know, end of January is it. But we've got the tournament over Christmas break. That'll give us a lot of games."

The man sputtered in Britte's direction. "Didn't Joel speak to you? I met with him this afternoon."

"No. I haven't seen him today."

"Britte, I demand that you start Jordan on Saturday."

Again, Anne's gentle pressure, keeping her still. "I don't think we should interfere." Her voice had taken on that steely edge. "We only make things worse when we tell the coach what to do."

Britte scanned the crowd, blocking out the man's barely concealed tirade. Mr. Kingsley wasn't in sight. *Coward.* He'd been in the stands. Why hadn't he told her about the meeting? Oh, no... She caught sight of Jordan and her mother at a distance, their faces red. *Lord, please don't let me take this out on that girl.* The dad's voice was a dull roar now. *Please don't let him take it out on her either.*

"Gordon," Anne's tone was final now, "no matter her age or her experience, Miss Olafsson is the coach. The girls are undefeated. Not everyone gets equal playing time on winning teams. Excuse us."

"Mr. Hughes," Britte said. "Jordan gives 100 percent. It's not her fault." She let Anne pull her away.

She stuck close to Britte, escorting her out to the parking lot even before the concession stand closed up. "Thanks, Annie."

"You're welcome. That man..." She blew out a breath. "Listen, honey, just for the record, you're not running the show like you did in previous years. And that's fine. That's your prerogative. But parents like Gordon Hughes who counted on a 'low-key, everybody play, have a good time' season are going to be disappointed."

"I don't see it that way, Anne."

"No problem. That's just my two cents. It's impossible to keep all of them happy anyway."

Britte agreed. "Something would be wrong if no one complained."

Anne laughed. "True. Now I've got to go. I'm a working girl, you know! You can't tease me about that anymore."

"I never meant it seriously when I said you didn't *do* anything because you're a stay-at-home mom."

"I know that." She patted Britte's cheek softly. "Lighten up. Try hitting the weight room. It's Christmastime and you're headed to supersectionals." She opened her car door. "At the least. See you."

Britte took her time getting into her own car. Where would she be without Anne? She looked up at the cold black sky, stars twinkling brightly over the small town. *Where would I be without You, Lord? I'm doing my best. Is there a way to please everyone?*

"Miss O." Mr. Kingsley hurried across the parking lot, his coat flapping.

"Well, I wondered where my knight in shining armor was tonight."

He stopped near her car and zipped up his coat. "Off slaying a variety of dragons. Sorry I didn't catch up with you today. Gordon Hughes."

"Ahh, yes. The saga continues."

"He stated his case, concluding that he wants to file a formal complaint if you don't give Jordan more playing time."

"He can't make a formal complaint based on that!"

"I know. Those weren't his exact words, but it's what he meant."

It was an echo of what she had told Mr. Kingsley at the Christmas party.

He went on. "I suggested he make an appointment with you for a time more suitable than after a game in the commons. He needs to talk formally with you before doing anything else."

"Tonight he seemed under the impression that you would tell me to play Jordan more."

Mr. Kingsley laughed.

"That must have been some diplomatic answer you gave him."

"Must have been, if it confused him that much. Britte, I backed you up. I told him you're the coach. My position is to let you coach. I said we can make recommendations, but the final word is yours. Fair enough?"

She grinned. "Fair enough. Thank you, Mr. Kingsley."

"Just doing my political job. See you tomorrow." He headed toward the street.

"So how do you like being a politician?"

"I like it just fine," he said over his shoulder, "especially in Valley Oaks. It's a good town."

Yeah, that's what the other principals said. She opened her car door. "Goodnight."

"Oh, by the way, good job, Coach." He sauntered off.

Britte turned her back to him, grinned, and clenched a fist. "Yesss!"

～

"Last minute, as always."

Britte looked up from her desk and saw Ethan standing in her classroom doorway. She grinned. "This is not last minute."

He waved a notebook. "It's Friday afternoon, 4:25. Next week's lesson plans are due in five minutes."

She grinned. "For your information, I finished that *ages* ago."

"Tsk, tsk," he exaggerated. "You're copying last year's lesson plans again. Not bothering to create new, challenging, and thrilling educational activities for all those young minds thirsting after the knowledge you have—"

"Oh, shush." She didn't take too seriously Mr. Kingsley's requirement that teachers hand in weekly lesson plans for his approval. "I'm writing a memo about next week's school board meeting, reminding him to take care of our trip to State."

"Finished?"

"Hold on a sec."

"We're down to," he glanced at his watch, "three and a half minutes."

She grabbed a yellow highlighter and colored "Mr. Kinglsey," signed her name to the note, and taped it to the top page in her lesson plan book. She shut the book and said, "There. That should be obvious enough for him. Ethan!"

He had disappeared. Britte gathered her attaché bag full of test papers, turned off the lights, and locked her door. Ethan was halfway down the hall. She ran to catch up to him. "Mr. Parkhurst, you carry way too much angst over this silly lesson plan deadline."

"And you're way too flippant." He didn't slow his pace. "There's this little thing called tenure, which you don't have to worry about. I'd better cut off the ponytail this weekend."

"Don't you dare. All the kids think you're cool. You'll get tenure this year. Alec Sutton's on the board. He's in your court, and he doesn't care about your hair. And Mr. Kingsley has given you rave reviews."

"I should offer to coach track. We're still short a track coach you know. And spring is coming."

She laughed. "It's not even Christmas! Not to mention that you detest track!"

They crossed the commons. Voices and the dribbling of basketballs echoed from inside the gym where the boys were practicing. Wrestlers were down in the small gym. With limited space in the school, Britte had become accustomed to ever-changing practice schedules. She had just enough time to run home for a bite to eat before meeting her girls back at the school at 5:30.

She slung her arm across Ethan's shoulders. He was about her height and angular. "If you grew a scraggly beard, you'd look just like a starving artist. Maybe then they'd feel sorry for you."

He stroked his chin. "Now that's a new thought."

Laughing, she preceded him into the office. Mr. Kingsley stood behind the counter, his hands cradling a box chock-full of lesson plan books. Lynnie sat at her desk talking to him. She was the secretary, a short, slender, 40-something mother of two students in the building. Her permed, light brown hair was evidence of a no-nonsense efficiency that kept the school running in an orderly fashion. She turned toward Britte now, her large brown eyes widening slightly behind her glasses, a brow rising subtly. Her message wasn't lost. Britte was pushing it with the General.

"Hey," Britte teased loudly, "it's Friday, gang! What are we waiting for? Let's go home!" She added her book to the stack and tapped it. "There's a note in there for you."

"Mmm." He looked beyond her. "Ethan, by any chance are you a runner? You've got the build for a runner."

She patted her friend's shoulder on the way out. Poor kid. "You all have a nice weekend."

Hurrying across the commons, she wondered if Mr. Kingsley had meant his mailbox when he said to put the memo in his box. The man was a fanatic when it came to order. He had a box or basket or cubbyhole or shelf for everything. Oh, well. He'd get it just the same.

Sixteen

"Mr. Carlucci!" at least half the girls varsity team cried in unison, standing outside the bus. "Come to the dance tonight! Please!"

Britte laughed, shaking her head. "Go home, girls! We've got exactly 97 minutes to get ourselves foo-fooed. And I know you all take longer than I do!"

They eventually drifted off across the parking lot toward their cars. The streetlights were already on. It had been a long ride to their afternoon game and back.

"Tanner, you really can come tonight. That is, on the off chance you've got nothing else going."

The freshman coach stood beside her. Surely the guy had a date. He was single, her age, a pilot for a charter airline, studying to become a high school history teacher, and way, way too good-looking. She had never seen such long, dark eyelashes.

"Actually, it sounds kind of fun."

"Spoken like a true dyed-in-the-wool, soon-to-be high school teacher. Bring a date and get those girls off your back once and for all."

He laughed as they walked to their cars. "You know I'm too busy to date."

"Especially during basketball. Hey, thanks for taking Anne's place on the bus." Because of Anne's new work schedule, she had driven herself to the game.

"My pleasure. We've got a great group this year. You're doing a terrific job with them, Britte."

"Thanks, Tanner. And thanks for giving Gordon Hughes that look."

"What look?"

"You know which one, Mr. Innocent," she teased. "I heard his comments behind my back, and I saw you look up at the bleachers. I doubt you were smiling at him. I hope you gave him the look I've seen you give your freshmen when they're acting particularly flighty."

"Oh, *that* look. No, I was smiling."

She laughed and opened her car door. "You were not. So why don't you come tonight? Chalk up some points for dedication with the administration. Maybe they'll hire you whenever it is you're going to finish college."

"Are chaperones allowed to dance?"

"You bet. Well, at least Ethan and I do."

"Ethan? I figured Joel's more your type."

"Mr. Kingsley? Hardly. Can you picture him doing hip-hop?"

"Hip-hop? I was thinking cheek to cheek."

She hooted.

He strolled toward his car. "Like it or not, Coach, you're definitely more Marine than English lit!"

⁓

Christmas dance. Another obligatory event.

Joel nodded to a group of sophomore girls staring at him and moved along before they started teasing him about not dancing.

This was his third dance of the year. The commons had been turned into a winter wonderland with twinkling lights strung everywhere. The so-called music was deafening, which meant there wasn't much opportunity to converse with the kids or the handful of teachers and parents who were there as chaperones. Cal stood near the front door, arms crossed, gun and nightstick in plain view.

Joel checked the boys' rest room again. At least Suzette the French teacher hadn't shown up. Last dance, he'd spent a lot more time in the boys' rest room, avoiding her. He'd probably rather talk with Gordon Hughes than chaperone another dance. From politician to babysitter... All in a day's work.

The DJ finally took a break and the volume decreased from blast to low thunder. Joel joined Anne and Alec Sutton near the refreshment table.

Britte and Ethan emerged from the group of dancers near the center of the floor. They were laughing, their faces flushed. Those two in particular had a way with the teens that Joel had never attained as a teacher or administrator. Nights like this he doubted he ever would. The English and math teachers even went so far as to dance. Not the slow stuff, only the fast-moving, formless style, joining unself-consciously with the students. They headed his way now, on the edge of the crowd. Were they dating? He had to remember to ask Lynnie. Without sounding overly interested. He was just...curious. On second thought, maybe he wouldn't ask her.

Britte positively glowed, warmed from the exercise, her hair loosened from its ponytail. Unlike the young girls, she wore an ankle-length, high-necked dress suitable for church. He wondered if she were demented or merely winsome. Covertly watching her now, he considered her offbeat characteristics. She was outspoken, unreasonably so at times, which branded her as somewhat controversial. She displayed weight room bravado. She ran practices like a drill sergeant. She hilariously kicked up her heels at high school dances. And—the most bewildering of all—she executed a hammerlock on that strapping Sutton boy! Through it all she somehow

managed to maintain a quality of modesty. Of wholesome-
ness. The woman kept throwing his preconceived notions
back into his face.

She laughed now. "Mr. and Mrs. Sutton! Come out and
dance."

"Drew would have a fit," Anne replied. "This is his space.
We'll stay right here where the kids can't see us. Would you
all like some water or punch?" She passed cups to them.

Joel had noticed the Suttons dancing to the slow music off
in a corner. They were an admirable, respectable couple. He
was grateful for clicking with Alec, a school board member.
They met now and then at the Center for a game of racquetball. Anne was often at the school either coaching or
helping in some voluntary capacity.

Britte turned with a carefree expression directed atypically
toward him. "Mr. Kingsley, the kids want you to dance. Find
a partner. Theresa won't mind. Oh!" She laughed. "What I
mean is, she loves to dance! And you know, you'll make
way-cool points with the students."

"Sorry to disappoint them, but I'm not joining the 'way-
cool' contest."

Britte nudged Anne with her elbow. "Annie, tell him what
you told me the other day when I wanted to get violent with
a certain dad."

"What was that?" she asked.

Britte smiled at him. "Lighten up!"

Lighten up? He was responsible for 250 partying teenagers.
"Any suggestions?"

"A little exercise like dancing might help!"

"I'll hit the weight room tomorrow."

"Chicken."

Britte Olafsson truly did have a distressing attitude. He
considered ordering her to hit the deck with 100 push-ups.
She could probably do them, though he knew it wasn't

appropriate. Still, he wasn't about to let her remark pass. "All right, Miss O. You talked me into it. I'd like to have the next dance with you."

Ethan sprayed a mouthful of water toward the wall and began coughing. Anne buried her face in her husband's shoulder. Britte, for once—well, twice if you counted the Christmas gift exchange—was speechless.

Patting Ethan on the back, Joel grinned at her. "Chicken?"

Her blonde hair was almost white against her reddened face. "No. As a matter of fact, I'd be delighted, Mr. Kingsley."

~

The lights were too dim for Britte to discern the color of his eyes, but the rock-like appearance of his shoulders was for real. Her left hand told her so. She tried to ignore what her right one was telling her, enveloped as it was in his broad left hand. Or what the small of her back sensed about the strength in the subtle pressure of his right hand. This near, he was taller than she thought. More…intimidating.

"Mr. Kingsley, is this appropriate?" she nearly shouted the words to be heard above the staccato beat of drums.

"Certainly, Miss O." His deep voice rose above the music. "The collecting of way-cool points is always appropriate."

"Uh, the music's a little faster than this pace. It might affect your score."

"This is my *only* pace. I think sometimes a harmless display of individualism promotes respect. This pace could very well increase my score. Yours too, for that matter."

She glanced over his shoulder. The teens whirred around them, keeping time with the music, smiling, flashing thumbs-up signs toward them. On the edge of the crowd, Ethan grinned in between coughs. Anne clung to Alec's arm, both of them doubled over in laughter.

"Deal with it, Miss O. Nobody calls me chicken and gets away with it."

She opened her mouth to protest, but he pulled her closer and nimbly steered them out of the way of flailing dancers. Every which way they turned was more of the same. And so he kept her close.

Deal with it? Deal with dancing slowly to a techno beat? What she had to deal with was the beating of her heart that had nothing to do with dancing and everything to do with the General holding her in his arms.

Seventeen

Sunday evening found Britte gripping the Jeep's steering wheel and flooring the gas pedal. Second Avenue's burning streetlamps stretched into elongated streaks. "Lord, please let me get there on time!" She slowed only slightly at the stop sign before peeling out onto Main Street. "Being late for the Christmas cantata is inexcusable. I have students singing in it! They'll think I'm rude. Which I am. I wouldn't let them get away with such behavior. Which they will point out." She let up on the gas and turned into the church parking lot, tires squealing. "At least I finished grading that stack of papers!"

She parked in the first available spot and flew from the car. Her feet hit the pavement at a dead sprint. At the building she yanked open the front door and threw a smile at a greeter as she sailed past him across the foyer and through the open sanctuary door. As if hitting an invisible brick wall, she halted.

The incredible beauty of the church and the season struck her. It was nothing less than *holy*. Her breath caught. She had no right to treat holiness with the flippancy she accorded a trip to the grocery store. *Lord, I am sorry.* She forced herself to stand still and take in the surroundings.

The lights were turned off. Candles glowed in glass chimneys at intervals along the center aisle. Fresh greenery hung everywhere. The floor of the front platform was half covered in red and white poinsettias. The place felt as hushed as a starlit night when fat snowflakes blanketed the field outside her bedroom window at the farm, when all her family slept under one roof.

Thank You, Father.

They were all there in the church, her family under one roof, scattered about the pews. Mom and Dad. Her older sister, Megan, with her husband and their little Tiffie. Her younger brother, Ryan, and his new girlfriend. Big brother Brady and his Gina.

All couples. She muffled a rising sigh.

Britte easily spotted the back of Brady's head towering over most others. There appeared a narrow space to his right. She could squeeze in.

Jesus, I'm sorry for being late. Shall we sit down?

She reached the row and slid beside her brother, grazing her shoulder blade on the high wooden edge at the end of the pew. "Ouch."

"Hey, Britte." Brady shifted slightly.

Gina shifted slightly and leaned around Brady to whisper, "Hi."

Someone else shifted slightly and leaned around Gina. Mr. Kingsley?!

Muted singing diverted their attention. The choir entered from the back of the church, silver robes rustling as they made their way up to the front, singing a cappella.

Squished between her brother and the jabbing curve of wood, now roasting in the long black woolen coat she hadn't the time to hang up in the foyer and now hadn't the space to remove, Britte closed her eyes and shut out the visible world. In time the glory of the season uprooted her discomfort by filling her with a joyful stillness.

Britte tilted the rearview mirror, minimizing the glare of the headlights trailing her out to Brady's place. Naturally, the more she tried to ignore those lights, the more she noticed them.

They belonged to Mr. Kingsley's car.

After the cantata, Brady had said to him, "It's a nuisance to explain how to get there. Why don't you just ride with Britte?"

She could have kicked him. Twice. Once for inviting the man to his house for a party after the service. Once for suggesting the man get in her car. It wasn't that tough to find Brady's place. How big of a problem could a long, winding, dirt road with inexplicable turnouts be to a Marine?

At least he'd had the good sense to reply, "I'll follow her and save us the trouble of coordinating our departures. Miss O?"

Thank you. "Fine."

Brady nodded. "Okay. We'll see you there, then. Britte, the door's open if you beat us. Button up your coat."

She had bit her tongue to keep from sticking it out.

You'd think we'd have outgrown our pecking-order roles by now.

Oh, it wasn't Brady's inveterate words. It was...everything else. The joyful stillness had fled.

She missed Isabel, especially tonight. Not that the choir needed her, but her friend would have sung magnificent, heavenly solos. And Britte could have used her influence now with the girls. Some of the team went to the Bible study that had continued in Isabel's absence, but Britte wasn't personally acquainted with the woman in charge. Isabel would have picked up on nuances about the team, nuances Britte didn't catch in the whirlwind of practices and games.

What were the girls sensing? Was she coaching to the best of her ability? With the girls' best interests in mind?

Anne could have helped. She, too, was familiar with many of the girls outside of school. But Anne was preoccupied with home matters and her new job.

And then there was last night's dance. No, not dance. Rather, there was Mr. Kingsley.

Her eyes strayed to the rearview mirror.

The magnetism Anne kept talking about had finally penetrated the coat of armor Britte so diligently maintained. No one had ever taken her up on a challenge—she couldn't believe she had actually called him "chicken"!—and zapped coherent speech into oblivion. No one had overpowered her with such…such physical presence.

She signaled, turned onto Brady's lane, and chewed her thumbnail.

All right. There. She had admitted it.

～

Anne adored Gina Philips, a second cousin of Alec's. She adored Brady's cozy log cabin house and his golden retriever, Homer, lounging contentedly in a corner. She adored the chattering group still basking in the glow of cantata music that glorified the birth of her Savior. She adored all the yummy Christmas goodies, none of which she had made herself.

But…she was tired. Exceedingly, excruciatingly tired.

"Annie!" Britte cornered her, that focused glaze in her eyes. Something was on her mind. She looked pretty tonight in a light blue sweater dress.

"That's a beautiful necklace, Britte."

"Oh." She touched it. "Thanks."

"Where'd you get it?"

"Um, the faculty Christmas gift exchange."

Joel and Alec joined them.

Anne fingered the necklace. "Pretty nice for a gift exchange. Who got your name?"

Britte huffed. "The whole thing's anonymous. I don't have a clue."

"Did Ethan give this to you?" Anne teased.

"No. It's a special friend sort of gift, but what special friend would give it anonymously in front of the entire group?"

Anne shrugged. "Maybe someone got it in the wrong bag. It's supposed to be for a wife. And now they're too embarrassed to ask for it back."

"No one on our staff would be too embarrassed to ask for it back. I think it's a joke that I just don't get yet."

Joel said, "That's not like you, Miss O. Talking as if the glass is half empty instead of half full."

"Yeah, well, what can I say?"

"You seem to be having that speechless problem quite a bit lately."

Britte flushed.

Anne looked between her friend and Joel and almost laughed out loud. Britte always knew what to say, and she never flushed except when loudly disagreeing with a referee. "Britte, what did you want to ask me?"

"Uh, how's the job going? Is this week's practice schedule all right?"

They'd already discussed that after church that morning. "Fine and yes. But I'm tired. Alec, are you about ready to go?"

"In a minute. I want to introduce Joel to Ed over there. I'll be right back." They continued on their way.

"Okay, Britte, what's up?"

She followed the men with her eyes until they were totally out of earshot. "Was that *tap* water you gave me at the dance last night?"

"Huh?"

She held out her hands, palms up, in a gesture of *well?*

"Yes. We didn't bring in bottled water, silly."

Britte moaned. "I knew it."

"Knew what?"

"There's something in it," she muttered and walked away.

Anne wondered what tap water had to do with anything and why Britte had avoided asking about it in earshot of Joel Kingsley.

Joel and Alec stopped near a group in front of Brady's television. A news program was being aired.

Rather, the war in Afghanistan was being aired.

He turned aside.

Alec said, "Those boys won't be home for Christmas."

"No, they won't." The dull thumping started in the back of his head. "Alec, I'm going to shove off. Thanks for the introductions and the contract information."

"You're welcome. See you at the board meeting tomorrow night."

"Goodnight."

As Joel made his way through goodbyes and out to his car, the dull thumping spread to his chest. The beats echoed one another in an alternate pattern.

The dirt-and-gravel driveway was a dark, narrow serpentine lane through woods, up and down gullies. He drove slowly. At a fork, he curved to the right. A few moments later he realized the road ended on the edge of a clearing. He turned around, retraced his way back to the fork, and took the other choice.

Another fork slowed his progress. By now pinpricks of lights flashed before his eyes, intermittently shrouding the view through the windshield.

At the bottom of a hill, the road dead-ended at the bank of a creek and he stopped. Carefully, he maneuvered the car back and forth until he had it turned around. He made his way out.

A white Jeep sat on the shoulder. Britte stood beside it. If he could follow her rear lights again…

He pulled his car up behind hers and pushed the automatic button to roll down his window as she walked back to him.

"Lost, Mr. Kingsley?"

"This is quite a labyrinth your brother's got back here."

"It's to confuse the bad guys. Are you all right?"

He realized then that he was rubbing his forehead. "No. I get headaches now and then that interfere with night driving. Mind leading me out of the woods, Miss O?"

"Of course not. Want me to drive all the way to your place?"

"If you get me to Fourth Avenue and Main, that would be great."

"I'll go slow."

"Thanks."

She walked away and then came back. "Is there anything else I can do?"

He didn't have much time before the shades would more or less shut and the memories would come. His pills were at home. He struggled against the urge to shout an obscenity at the world. "Britte. Please let's just go."

Well, at least it hadn't been Alec. Although Alec knew Joel's history, Joel still preferred not losing macho points in front of him. It didn't matter that he lost them in front of one rather peculiar girl.

Eighteen

"How'd the game go last night, Britte?" Ethan stood in her classroom doorway early Tuesday morning. "I—missed—" He sneezed.

"Bless you."

"Thanks. I missed the news last night."

"Missed the game, too, I noticed." She took a swig of coffee.

"I'm too ill to figure out whether or not you're teasing."

"Of course I'm teasing." She smiled. "Nobody makes the 90-minute drive to Springdale on a Monday night except parents and the bus driver. Ethan, you look awful. You should go home."

"It's just a cold. I'll be fine once the decongestant kicks in. Zoned out, but at least I'll stop spraying germs. You don't look so hot yourself."

"Late night. I hung out with the MacKenzies in the Rockville emergency room until midnight. Cassie sprained her ankle in the third quarter. We lost in the fourth."

He expressed dismay at both developments. "Your first loss of the season. Is Cassie going to be all right?"

"She's devastated, but she'll take proper care of the injury. We'll have to wing it for a week or so without the tallest, best center in the league." She wrinkled her nose. "Poor kid."

"Poor Coach. This kind of levels the playing field."

"Yeah, yeah. I suppose you missed the board meeting last night, too?"

"Britte, I was asleep by seven! But I am on my way at this very moment to the office. The board minutes are probably copied and in our boxes by now. I will hand deliver your mail to you in penance."

She grinned. "That works. I'm not quite ready for class yet. Thanks. You're forgiven."

He nodded and sneezed his way out the door.

Mid-December was always a tough time of the year. Basketball was in full swing, a daily activity which included two or three games a week, making for cold, late nights. The weather was perfect for one thing only: staying home, curled up with a book in front of a crackling fire. But who had time for that? Add to the schedule a myriad of flu germs circulating at school, playing havoc with everyone's schedule. Not to mention Christmas shopping. To top it all off, there was a wedding! At least she'd had the sense to postpone the shower she was hosting until February.

Britte drained her coffee cup.

And she was drinking way too much coffee.

"Psst."

Finger poised over the phone's keypad, Joel saw Ethan Parkhurst standing in the doorway. He set the phone back on its hook. "Morning, Ethan."

"Heads up."

"Pardon me?"

Ethan glanced over his shoulder and held up a stapled packet of paper. "Board minutes," he whispered. "There will be a firing squad. Oh," he spoke in a normal tone and moved aside, "good morning, Lynnie. I was just on my way out." The guy left.

What in the world?

Lynnie entered his office. "Joel, Matt Anderson's dad is here, and I need you to sign these."

He took a stack of papers from her. "Send him in. Thanks."

Board minutes and firing squad? A memory joggled loose. What was it he had told Ethan? That he'd like to know the next time he'd be facing a *firing squad.* It was in reference to Britte Olafsson and her problem with Gordon Hughes. What did that have to do with last night's board meeting?

A man appeared in his doorway.

"Mr. Anderson? Come on in." He went over to greet him and shut the door.

As he settled in to talk with the father about his son's habitual tardiness, Joel concluded to himself that the job title "principal" was a misnomer. He was a firefighter, constantly stomping out sparks before they flared into major blazes. At the moment it was Mr. Anderson's turn. Evidently Britte's turn was coming, and, as usual, he wouldn't have a moment to himself to figure out why.

⌒

While her first-hour students worked on an assignment, Britte reread her copy of the school board minutes for the— Oh! She had lost count of how many times she had read them. It wasn't there. It simply wasn't there, and she knew for a fact that the board minutes typically included when a member blew his nose. Well, maybe that was an exaggeration, but if the group had discussed her team attending the state tournament, it would have been in the minutes!

All the negatives of the season descended upon her like a torrential downpour. Cassie's injury, last night's loss, Anne's preoccupation, every spare moment spent at the farm trying on a *dress!* Men scheduling *her* basketball games, dictating that the girls travel on a *Monday* night to Timbuktu, needlessly draining their energy reserves for the rest of the week and preventing her from attending the board meeting. And now, one man in particular, squishing their tradition because girls sports did not count enough to warrant attention! In spite of the *memo* she had written to him!

She slapped her desktop and stood. The students sitting nearby jumped in their chairs.

"Class. All of you are 16 or 17 years old and perfectly capable of behaving in a mature manner in my absence. I am going down to the office. If I hear of *one* idiotic move or comment, you will regret it. Understood?"

There were nods around the classroom. No one made a sound.

Caffeine coursed through her nerves, propelling her down the hallway. She didn't care. She was getting to the bottom of this right now.

Her peripheral vision lost in a blur, she entered the office and targeted Lynnie. "Is he in there?" She pointed toward Mr. Kingsley's closed office door as she walked toward it.

"He's on the phone, Britte. Britte!"

She had his door open and was inside shutting it before the secretary could say another word.

Mr. Kingsley looked at her from his seat behind the desk and stood. The phone was pressed to his ear. "Yes. Yes. I'll get back to you. Something's come up. Yes. Goodbye." He hung up. "Miss—"

She held the packet of papers toward him and shook them. "I sure hope there's something missing in this. Is there something missing in this?"

He raised his shoulders in slow motion. "You tell me."

"Oh!" She dropped the papers on his desk and walked around in a tight circle, biting her lip. She faced him again. "Mr. Kingsley! I asked you *twice!* And I wrote you a memo!"

"About?"

She wanted to scream. "About the girls going to State!"

There was a blank look on his face.

"You don't remember."

"Uh, I don't recall reading a memo—"

"And you for certain don't recall *talking* to me."

"I must have misplaced—"

"You are the most neurotically organized man I have ever met. Look at this desk! You can see its top! How could you misplace a memo that *you* requested?"

"Britte, sit down. What do you need me to do?" He sat.

She didn't. She had told him three times what she needed. What was the underlying problem here? What was it she really needed from him? "I need you to pay attention to us! You treat girls activities like some silly phase that'll soon pass from the picture."

"I apologize for being politically incorrect at times—"

"I don't care how politically incorrect you are! Go ahead and wear school colors and go to all the boys games instead of ours."

"I go to—"

"When it's convenient and you have to be here anyway to lock the doors. Oh!" It was a cry of frustration. "You know, that isn't even the real issue. You want to know what the real issue is?" She placed her hands on his immaculate desk, leaned across it, and lowered her voice a notch. "You don't have to do it all. You have a competent staff who can turn off lights and lock up doors. We can write lesson plans without you looking over our shoulder every single week. If you would delegate the details, maybe you wouldn't forget the one *important* thing I asked you to do. And I only asked because it had to come from administration, otherwise I would have done it myself."

"I sincerely apologize. I don't—"

"You're our backup. We're supposed to be on the same team! We're supposed to help each other."

They locked eyes across the desktop, mere inches separating their faces. She remembered how he needed her help finding his way down her brother's road Sunday night. It had been uncharacteristic. Asking for help, delegating…they weren't in his nature. She straightened.

"Britte, do you mind if I complete a sentence?"

She clenched her jaw.

"What can I do to fix what I forgot to take care of last night?"

It felt as if the office walls were tumbling in, suffocating her. She went to the door, opened it, and turned. "I don't know. That's not my job, *General*."

⸻

Well, at least she didn't slam the door.

General? What was that supposed to mean?

Joel walked into the outer office. "Lynnie."

The secretary looked up from her computer.

"What did she mean by that?"

"Which part?"

Of course she would have heard the entire conversation. Britte's end of it anyway, which covered most of the discourse. "The 'General' comment. I pretty much understood and agreed with everything else she had to say."

Lynnie placed a thumb and forefinger around one lens of her eyeglasses and straightened them. "Well, that's what they call you."

"They?"

"Some of the faculty."

"Because?"

"Um, for the obvious, I guess."

"I behave like a general."

"You give orders and you expect perfection and you don't smile a whole lot and you stand like that with your hands on your hips."

"Don't hold anything back now."

She gave him a small smile. "That about covers it."

The bell rang. He exhaled a weary breath and dropped his hands from his hips. "It's only second hour. What did I forget to do for her last night at the board meeting?"

"That I don't know."

"All right. Thank you, Lynnie."

"No problem, boss."

Joel entered the stream of students moving through the commons between classes. He returned greetings, separated a smooching couple, and sent one boy to the office for wearing an offensive T-shirt. At Ethan's room he poked his head inside. "Mr. Parkhurst? May I have a word with you?"

He stepped back out into the hallway and waited, arms crossed, unseeing, pondering recent conversations with Britte.

The bell rang and Ethan joined him. "What's up?" The hall was empty, but Joel kept his voice low. "I appreciated the heads up, but what did I forget last night?"

Recognition registered in the English teacher's eyes. He knew what he was referring to. "She wants to take her team to the girls state tournament. They need permission to miss one and a half days of school. Policy says that you have to grant that and then ask the board to okay the trip. They also need to reserve the district's van."

"And when is the trip?"

"February. If you wait until the January meeting, she doesn't have time to put things in order."

"All right. That helps. Thanks." He turned on his heel to go and then wheeled back around. "Ethan, how did you build a rapport with her?"

He shrugged. "Spent time with her. Wore school colors and went to her games."

"Are you two involved?"

"Involved? As in—?" He burst into laughter, his brows raised as if that were the most absurd question he'd ever been asked. "No. She would drive me crazy."

"Mm-hmm." Joel walked away, murmuring to himself, "Tell me about it."

"Coach!" Anne called to Britte, tilting her head toward the sidelines where she stood. They needed to talk privately.

"Run it again, ladies!" Britte yelled as she left the court. "Liz, call the play!"

Anne stepped around Britte, turning her back to the girls and facing her friend. "Coach, lighten up."

Her eyes narrowed. Not a good sign.

"What's going on, Britte?"

"What do you mean, what's going on? We've lost Cassie. They're practicing like they've never *seen* a basketball before, let alone held one. We've got a game tomorrow night. Bender has a good chance of beating us if we play like this."

"Just back off a bit. You're discouraging them. You usually don't do that."

Britte kicked a foot backwards, ramming the heel against the bleacher. The clang echoed across the gym. "Anne, we have this chat at least once a season."

"This is a bit early for it, don't you think? So how was your day?"

"Thanks for the pep talk, Mom. Sunny," she shouted toward the floor and headed back out onto it, "keep your eye on Katie. Liz, *you* call the shot."

Anne walked along the bleachers to where Cassie sat, her foot elevated and wrapped in a bag of ice. She sat down beside her. The dear girl had come to school today, hobbling on crutches. Her friends took turns carrying around a bucket of ice that she plunged her foot into during classes. She was a trooper and had been a good friend of Drew's since grade school. Anne had known her for years outside of basketball. "Cass, what's with Coach?"

"You haven't heard?" Her eyes widened.

"No. I'm out of the loop." *Especially now.*

"Sunny works in the office first hour. Coach came in and read Mr. Kingsley the riot act."

"What!"

"She could hear her yelling even with the door closed."

"About what?"

"We don't know. Sunny asked Mrs. Powell, but she said it wasn't any of her business. It didn't make sense. Something about wearing school colors and being politically incorrect. And writing lesson plans. When Coach opened the door, she said, 'It's not my job, General.' And she said 'General' in that growly voice she gets when you know she's really mad."

"Oh, good grief."

"I had her fourth hour. She barely said three words. Just gave us a pop quiz and an assignment that she refused to explain. I heard all of her classes were the same. You know what, Mrs. Sutton? I'm kind of glad I don't have to practice today!"

Nineteen

Joel swung his racquet and nailed the small blue ball against the front wall. Kind of like Britte Olafsson had nailed him about six hours ago.

Alec laughed. "Whew! Game point. Want to go another? We've got the court time."

Joel used his T-shirt to wipe sweat from his brow and sat on the floor, catching his breath. "Nah. I told Lynnie I had an emergency meeting with a board member. Guess we better have our meeting before I head back. Thanks again for sparing the time."

"No problem." Still huffing, Alec slid down the wall and sat beside him on the floor. "It feels like we're playing hooky. Feels good, actually."

He grinned. "Know what you mean. Sounds like you're playing hooky all week."

"Not from housework! I told Anne I'd take a few vacation days off before Christmas, help her out in that department."

"How's she like her job?"

"She likes it. Annie's Superwoman. She's amazing. So, what's the emergency?"

"Britte Olafsson. She chewed me out this morning."

Alec laughed. "I'm only surprised that you were the recipient. Anne thinks you intimidate Britte, something no one else has ever come close to doing."

"Really?" Joel chuckled. "At the moment I think I'm here in order to avoid her! Anyway, I deserved the dressing down.

Evidently I forgot she had asked me to get board permission for the girls to go to the state tournament."

"Ouch. You messed with her team. Did she get belligerent?"

"No. In truth, she gave me some things to think about. She said I should delegate more, not be overly concerned about insignificant details." He chose not to mention her title of "General." "I'm not complaining about Britte, Alec. She's the best when it comes to teaching. Gordon Hughes may be complaining soon, however."

"I suppose that would be about Jordan's role on the team." Alec shook his head. "He has to meet formally with Britte first and with the athletic director before the board will listen to him. There haven't been complaints about her in the past, as far as I know. I can't imagine it going anywhere. Hey, I'm sorry I didn't clue you in about the girls' trip. I just didn't think about it. It's odd Anne didn't remind me."

"Can we fix it now?"

"Sure. It's just a formality. We'll call a special meeting. Only take five minutes. Let's shoot for Thursday, seven A.M., superintendent's office. Work for you?"

"That's fine. Thanks. How many members will mark this one against me?"

Alec chuckled. "Oh, three of the seven. You know, Joel, Britte's not the only one you intimidate. Your methods are controversial to some parents, but for most of us board members, your quick, hard-hitting changes have been a godsend."

"I realize alienating some people comes with the job. I just hope you see fit to renew my contract. I like it here in Valley Oaks."

"I'm glad to hear that. Hey, Drew and I finally had a talk. The fight was a girl thing."

"Nine out of ten times…" He shook his head. "Ready?"

They stood, gathered their things, and walked through the door.

"Joel, do you have any Christmas Eve plans?"

"I'm staying in town." He grinned. "That's about it. Catch up on some work. Please don't feel obligated—"

"Anne would have a fit if she knew you were sitting home alone on a holiday. Come on over, about four. The Eatons will be there. You know, the pastor and his family. Val and the kids. You don't want to pass up Anne's cooking."

Food and company? "Thanks. Sounds great. Is there a gift exchange involved?"

Alec laughed as they headed toward the locker room. "No. Just bring yourself. I think it'll be good for Jason and Drew to see you outside the school environment. You can tell them all about life in the Marines."

"Either one of them thinking of joining up?"

"Jason has toyed with the idea. This business in Afghanistan has some of the guys riled up. You were in Desert Storm, right?"

"Right." He didn't offer anything else. Alec knew most of his story.

Alec stopped in the middle of the hall, all trace of his mellow demeanor vanished. "Oh, yeah." The details must have come to him. "Maybe you don't want to talk about it."

Joel slapped his shoulder. "Can't say it's my favorite subject."

～

She hadn't exactly *yelled* at him, had she?

Elbow propped on her dining room table, chin settled into her palm, Britte eyed the cold lump of macaroni and cheese and soggy tossed salad. No sense in pretending. She was not going to eat dinner.

How many times was she going to rerun this morning's office scene in her mind?

It was her voice. It was a perfect coach's voice that carried well. She could effortlessly speak in class. With only slight exertion on the vocal cords, she could make her words understood across the gym. She was born with this voice. She had not yelled at him.

"*It's your tone.*" Oh, great. Now her mother's voice was in on this.

"I didn't use a *tone*, Mom," she spoke aloud to the empty house. "I was angry, and I think I had a right to be angry. It was righteous indignation. He hadn't done his job, and I called him on it. End of story."

Britte carried her dishes to the kitchen and proceeded to clean up.

She had been uncommunicative and a grouch the entire day. No doubt there were rumors racing around the school, probably throughout Valley Oaks by now. Would they know the gist of the argument? Maybe it wasn't even an argument since it was totally one-sided. What they would know was that she had called him "General."

A water glass slipped from her hand and crashed into the sink, breaking apart.

"Nuts!"

She leaned against the countertop and willed herself to stop evading her conscience.

Oh, why had she called him "General"? Up until that point, she was home free. Upset and straightforward were acceptable behavioral patterns, part of life. Calling him that derogatory name was—

A defense. She understood that now.

Facing him across the desk, she had, for the first time, seen the color of his eyes. Hazel with green flecks. And they were not haughty nor condescending nor cold. They were full of— No, not full. They were *overflowing* with care and concern.

She wasn't about to accept that from him. And so she had retreated, put up her defenses, and called him "General."

~~~~~~~

"You're my sergeant!" Britte yelled. "Back me up!"

A part of Joel knew it was a dream, but a heavy blackness wouldn't release him.

The artillery explosions were deafening. The roar of the chopper. The orders screamed from his own throat. Sweat steaming the night goggles. The unbearable cries of the injured.

He felt the sensation of floating. The chopper took off. Britte's shouts faded.

No! Britte wasn't there!

She was gone. He knew she was gone, left to the enemy. They had to go back!

"Go back!"

The sound of his own voice jerked him awake. He sat up, his breath coming in short gasps, his body drenched in sweat. He flicked on the bedside lamp.

The dream was nothing. The worst was yet to come.

"God, don't let them start. Take the memories away." At times, he knew God had answered that prayer.

Why was Britte in the dream this time?

He knew why. He had refused to admit it up to this point. Remembering meant *feeling* again, and the feelings agitated unbearable memories, forcing them to surface. The simple solution to avoiding the memories was to avoid the feelings.

But Britte Olafsson disturbed the feelings, cutting loose emotions long buried. All she had to do was show up.

And between school Monday through Friday, Saturday basketball, and Sunday church, she showed up every single day.

Long accustomed to the discipline of focusing his mind, Joel mentally reviewed chores awaiting him in the morning. In that way he successfully blanked her out.

But the feelings kept churning, and the memories reappeared.

Joel was tired of the incessant struggle. He lay back down and curled into a fetal position.

"God, help me."

He imagined supernatural hands unlocking gates. He saw the deluge of ugliness pouring through, coming into focus. The choice he had made so long ago haunted afresh.

Choice? No, not really a choice. It was a behavior, a mindset drilled into him until it had become second nature. *Semper fi.* To leave a buddy behind was *not* a viable option.

But the *fallout!* The repercussions! Death...court martial...disgrace...oblivion in a bottle...

Until Sam and Jesus.

Forgiveness was a free gift.

Sam prayed that someday Joel would let that fact sink from his head into his heart in order to complete his healing. Was his spiritual mentor's prayer being answered?

For the first time in ten years, Joel Kingsley wept.

Twenty

"Goodbye!" Anne smiled as her customer walked out the door, purchases in hand.

There was a lull in what had been an extremely busy morning, five days before Christmas. Her coworker Natalie, a local college student, was helping the lone remaining customer. Anne took the opportunity to poke her head into the tiny office where her boss sat at the desk.

"Charlie, do you mind if I leave 30 minutes early?"

"Not at all." He smiled his slow smile. Today's flannel shirt was a red plaid. "You've got a game tonight, right?"

"Right. Something has come up, and I need to talk with the head coach beforehand."

Charlie set down his pen and leaned back in the chair. "How's the juggling act going?"

Anne glanced away. The way the man saw things sometimes startled her. She met his clear blue eyes. "You probably wouldn't believe it if I answered fine?"

"Probably not. This has got to be tough for you."

"It is, but I'm learning." She pointed upward, imagining the issues she juggled as if they were indeed merely balls. "Alec and the kids can fend better for themselves than I gave them credit for. The team is in place. I don't need to expend much energy on the girls except when I'm with them. And then there are the cookies. Do we really need a zillion different kinds baked in my kitchen? I don't think so." She could go on...Britte...Val...PTA...parents...in-laws...Christmas... "By the way, what are you doing Christmas Eve? My family would like to meet you. We're having friends over for dinner."

"Thank you for the invitation, dear lady, but I'm going to Chicago. Our son and his family live there. It's the first since Ellen..." His voice faded for a moment. "My wife. She died last spring."

"Oh, Charlie. I'm so sorry."

"Thank you. There won't be a zillion different kinds of cookies in our house this year either."

Her struggle with priorities shriveled in light of his situation. At least all of her family would be together.

Charlie mimed a juggler tossing balls in the air. "And where does your new job fit in?"

"Ah, the job." She smiled. "You know what it's like to visit a place you used to love living in? And suddenly you remember, you *feel* bits and pieces of yourself that made you who you were then? You wonder how you lost them along the way. That's what this job is to me."

He smiled, stroking his beard. "Anne, when was the last time you held a paint brush?"

"Good heavens. I have no—" A memory rushed at her. "Yes, I do. Amy was two months old. Drew was three. I had my little corner in our bedroom where I kept an easel and supplies. One day I was painting. All of a sudden I heard a crash and both kids screaming. Drew had heard Amy wake up from her nap. He lifted her out of the crib, carried her into the kitchen, and tried to put her in the infant seat, which was on top of the counter. The seat flew off onto the floor. Fortunately Amy landed on the counter. I cleared away my things within the hour. Drew held the trash bag."

Charlie studied her for a long moment. "In January our classes start up again. You could join, no charge, and paint once a week."

The bell on the gallery's front door jingled.

Charlie stood, came around the desk, and put a hand on her shoulder. "It's a way to find those lost bits and pieces."

⌒

Wednesday afternoon Anne walked through the deserted high school hallway. The industrial mint green walls had finally been painted an off-white a few years ago. Heavy-duty carpet had replaced the shiny black tile. She could still remember dress-up days when her pumps clicked smartly on that old hard floor.

High up the walls, above the lockers, hung large, framed photo collections of graduating classes. She stopped, as she always did, in front of Alec's class. He was by far the cutest among the 80-some other faces. He looked so young, so full of promise. *Oh, Lord, what's happening to him? Please, take him back to this...this hope. Remind him that in You he can do anything.*

Anne knocked on Britte's open door. She was at her desk. "Hey."

"What are you doing here?"

Anne shut the door. "Wow, I just had this sense of déjà vu. Remember Mr. Robbins?"

"The cadaver? Fortunately he retired before I took Algebra II."

"This was his room. He made me stay after school one day for giggling during his class. He scared the willies out of me." Anne slid into a student desk. "Unlike you, he was totally noncommunicative."

Britte smiled. "Did you get off from work early?"

"There was a break in the action, and I told Mr. Manning the head coach needed to talk to me about being overly communicative."

Britte winced.

Anne shook her head. "You called him '*General*'?"

"Among other things. By the way, I'm sorry for snapping at you at practice yesterday."

"Calling me 'Mom' is not on the same level as calling your boss that horrible nickname."

"I've been trying to apologize to him all day. He was out of the building two of the six times I went to the office. The other times, Lynnie didn't know where he was."

"He's probably avoiding you."

"Probably. Not that I blame him. Annie, he forgot to bring up the girls' trip to State after I asked him to three times. So I called him on it. Then I accused him of not taking the girls' activities seriously, of not attending our games like he does the boys'. He admitted to being politically incorrect."

"He *agreed* with you?"

She nodded. "You know, although I was angry, at least I cleared the air about a few things."

"But '*General*'?"

"All right. I totally blew it with that remark. I will apologize. Okay?"

Anne studied her face for a moment. Britte wasn't herself. True, they did go through times like this during every season. Britte would become strung out and overdone, and Anne would have to remind her that basketball, in spite of what the T-shirts pronounced, really was not life. Something else was going on here, but she couldn't put her finger on it. "Okay. Are you all set for tonight?"

"No. I need to go sit in the gym and gear up. Ethan's home sick today. Want to sit with me?"

"Sure."

"I think we can win."

As they gathered her things, closed up the room, and walked down to the gym, they talked game strategies.

Britte said, "I'm considering pulling up Erin."

Anne stared at her. Erin was her star sophomore player. "Britte, you said you'd never pull up the younger ones. Why this year? You've got more talent than you've ever had."

"Cassie, our *center*, got hurt. What if she doesn't recover?"

"Since when do you start thinking in terms of 'what if'? That's a spirit of fear, and you know better!"

"I just said I'm considering it."

Anne shuddered. That sense of déjà vu settled on her again. Had old Mr. Robbins started out like Britte? Like Alec? Young and passionate, full of potential? Only to cave in to fears along the way?

Like herself? An image came to mind of how she had snapped at the children that morning and practically shoved them out the door so that *she* wouldn't be late to work. She hadn't even hugged Amy.

Lord, why don't You post danger signs?

Maybe He had. Maybe they'd all just been too busy to read them.

Twenty-One

Britte locked the door to the girls' locker room and walked down the dimly lit, vacant hallway. She had stayed later than usual after the game, dissecting plays and lineups.

They'd lost again, but only by three points. The girls had played well. She was certain they felt better about themselves, knowing that Cassie alone did not make the team. They could function without her. It had been a good lesson for all of them.

Some players saw much less playing time, a couple saw none. She wasn't sure how she felt about that, but she knew it was how they would win. There was no explaining that to Mr. Hughes. She had successfully dodged him after the game.

So where was her escort? Anne had pointedly drawn her attention to the fact that Mr. Kingsley stayed for the entire game and that he was wearing his royal blue shirt and yellow gold tie.

How about that? The man had responded. Britte didn't know how she felt about that either. Maybe he was mocking her.

His green-flecked hazel eyes came to mind.

She walked outside now, double checking that the door locked behind her, even though she thought the custodian was still around somewhere in the building. The parking lot was dark. There must be a spotlight out somewhere. No problem. She pointed her key chain toward the car and pressed the unlock button as she hurried through the cold. The car's interior lights flicked on.

All right. He probably wasn't mocking her. She would apologize, even if she had to leave her first-hour class again and track him down when it was most likely to find him—

Something slammed violently between her shoulder blades, viciously shoving her, forcing her body forward until she sprawled flat against the rough asphalt, her knees, palms, and forehead bearing the brunt of the harsh impact. A disembodied voice snarled hateful names.

And then, as instantly as the silence had been ripped apart, it thrust itself against her ears. She lay beside her Jeep, shaking, her heart pounding, her breath in ragged gasps. She braced herself and partially sat up. Pain shot through her right arm.

"Britte!"

Again, unseen hands took hold of her. She struggled against them, flailing her arms and screaming, "No!"

"Britte! It's me."

Mr. Kingsley! Her muscles turned to jelly and her screams subsided into whimpers.

"Can you stand?"

She held onto his arms and let him help her up. "Ow!" Pain exploded everywhere.

"What happened?"

With his steadying hands still on her arms, she leaned against the car. "Somebody pushed me."

"Pushed you!" He scanned the parking lot.

"I'm sure they're gone. Will you hand me my bag, please?" She pointed to the ground. "The keys are somewhere…"

He found the keys, picked up the bag, and opened the driver's door. The interior lights spilled out.

Britte moved to enter the car, but he kept hold of her elbow and held her back, tossing the bag into the car.

"You're not going anywhere. Your face—"

"I'll be fine. I want to go home." She heard the tears in her voice before they sprang to her eyes. "Give me my keys."

"You're shaking and probably in shock." He pulled her toward himself, pocketed the keys, hit the automatic lock and shut the door. "Let's go inside and see how hurt you are."

"I'm all right!"

"You're not all right, and you're going to listen to me this time." He slipped his arm around her waist and began walking.

Britte's knee gave way, and she stumbled. "I'm all right."

"Well, I'm not all right. It's freezing out here, and I'm not wearing a coat. Let's get inside." He draped her left arm up over his shoulders and tightened his grip around her waist, leaving her with no choice but to lean into him as he half-carried her across the parking lot. "Do you think if you keep repeating you're all right, it'll make it true?"

She bit her lip, willing the tears not to fall. Her entire body hurt!

"You're not all right. For one thing, you were insubordinate to your superior yesterday. If there was any decent protocol in place, you'd be on probation by now, Miss Olafsson."

One of the school doors was propped open. They went through it now, and he pulled it shut behind them.

"For another thing," he went on, "you disobeyed orders. I distinctly remember telling you I would escort you outside late at night when the parking lot was empty. Telling you is the same thing as an order. That's another case of insubordination. I don't know what a general is supposed to do around here."

In spite of the pain shooting through her body, Britte felt a tiny smile tug at her mouth. She quickly wiped at her eye, deflecting the tear before it fell.

They went into the main office, down a short hallway, past his and other offices. At the nurse's room he loosened his hold of her and turned on the light. "Let me take your coat."

To her dismay, she couldn't keep her fingers on the buttons.

"Here." With deft fingers, he unbuttoned her coat. "You tell me to delegate, but see what happens when I try to *delegate* the simplest task? I have to do it myself. There." Slipping the coat from her shoulders, he steered her to a high, molded plastic stool. "Sit."

Every muscle ached as she lifted herself onto the seat. "I'm sorry."

"For what?" He took hold of her chin, gently turning her face back and forth, inspecting it.

"For being insubordinate." A tear trickled down her cheek.

He brushed it away with his little finger. His face very near hers, he looked her in the eye. "Hey, if somebody doesn't have the nerve to set the General straight, he could become a real pain in the neck. Where do you hurt?" He held her hands and turned them over. Bloody, bright red scrapes covered both palms.

"But I'm sorry!"

"I'm sure you are." His eyes focused on hers again. "Trust me, Miss O, it's all right. Apology accepted. I'm sorry for letting you down." He waited a beat. "Accept my apology?"

She nodded.

"Okay." He knelt and lifted her right leg. "It looks like you fell on your knees." A hole was torn at the knee of her black slacks.

She noticed his shirt, where she had held onto his shoulders. "There's blood on your shirt." That nice royal blue shirt. He'd worn school colors...just for the girls game.

"It's washable." He went to the cupboard and pulled out antiseptic and bandages.

"I have Band-Aids at home. I can—" Nausea churned in her stomach. "I think I'm going to be sick." Stiffly, she rose from the stool, went into the tiny adjacent bathroom, and shut the door.

Bending over the sink, she turned on the faucet and splashed cold water on her face. It stung her palms and cheeks, but at least the sick feeling subsided. She dampened a paper towel, pressed it to the back of her neck, and straightened. The reflection in the mirror startled her.

A purplish bruise puffed her left cheek. Blood seeped from scrapes along her forehead, nose, and chin. Bits of asphalt clung here and there. Her hair stuck out in every direction. Her eyes looked sunken.

Her right arm felt as if it had been jammed into her back. Pain shot the length of it and into her shoulder blade. Her right knee throbbed. Her wrists felt disconnected. Her hands wouldn't stop shaking. Her head was throbbing. There was blood on the white blouse she wore under the short blue wool jacket.

She removed a paper cup from the dispenser, filled it, and choked down the water. Her breathing was shallow, almost a gasping sound. Another wave of nausea engulfed her. She inhaled several times, forcing air deep into her lungs until it passed.

After gulping another cupful, she opened the door and shuffled back out into the nurse's room. It was vacant. That nighttime quiet of the large building hummed in a way she had never before heard it. Eerily.

"Joel…" There was no reply. She raised her voice, "Joel." Suddenly she heard footfalls thumping and screamed in panic, "Joel!"

He rounded the corner of the doorway, catching hold of the jamb to stop himself. "What?"

Her whole body was shaking again. Tears ran down her face, stinging the cuts. "I... I..."

He folded her into his arms and held her close.

~

He realized it was the first time she had called him "Joel." *Probably a good thing if this is going to be my response.* He stroked her hair and told her everything was all right, that inane phrase she kept repeating. No other words sufficiently conveyed his strong desire to comfort her.

After a time, her body stopped shaking. While her sobs lessened, his rage was shooting off the charts. Who had *dared* do this to her?

There was a pounding on the front door. Britte jumped and looked up at him with terrified eyes.

"It's Cal. I called him. Sit down. I have to open the door." He steered her onto the stool and reluctantly let go of her arms. He rushed out and through the main office. In the commons he could see Cal outside the double set of front, glassed doors, arm poised to bang again. The sight of the big sheriff in his uniform relieved Joel. He let him inside.

"Is she all right?"

"She's bruised and probably in shock." He led them through the office and ushered Cal into the nurse's room.

"Oh, dear God," Cal breathed his reaction to her appearance into a prayer.

"I'm all right. You didn't have to come."

Cal took off his large-brimmed hat and touched her shoulder. "Britte, this is my job and you're not all right. You were attacked."

Her face crumpled at the word "attacked."

Cal turned to Joel. "We should call Doc Thompson."

Britte snapped, "Why don't we have a happy fizzies party? Come on, guys! It's just some scratches. Nothing's broken."

Joel exchanged a smile with Cal and said, "I think she's feeling better." He opened the small refrigerator and pulled out an ice pack. "If we're not calling the doctor, then you'll have to put up with me. Hold this on your left cheek. Here." He positioned her hand. "That's where it's swelling."

Cal unzipped his leather jacket, pulled out a notebook, and sat on the cot, his cop gear creaking and clanking. "Britte, tell me what happened."

While Joel cleansed her cuts, she told the sheriff about being pushed to the ground. "Ouch!"

"Sorry," Joel said. "There's still some asphalt clinging to your forehead." He looked from the wound to her eyes. She had the most intriguing eyes. They drew him in like a magnet. Until tonight, he had resisted meeting them.

"There's blood on your shirt and tie."

He shrugged.

Cal said, "Britte, you weren't just *pushed*. Tell me what happened."

"I already did."

"Tell me exactly what happened this time."

Her face went rigid, revealing nothing, but fear shone in her eyes and made her voice unnaturally high-pitched. She told them how a heavy force had slammed into her. Strong hands not letting go. Shoving, shoving, crashing her into the pavement.

Joel looked at Cal. The cop's expression reflected what he felt: fury.

"Britte," Cal said, "did you see anyone? Hear anything?"

She looked down. "They—he called me a name. That was all."

"So it was a male voice."

She nodded.

"Young? Old?"

She shrugged.

Joel took her right hand and picked up an antiseptic pad. He dabbed at the scrape. "What did he say?"

She told him.

He clenched his jaw.

"Joel," Cal asked, "what time do you think all this happened? When did you find her?"

"I got out there right afterward. I was waiting for her to leave. By the way, I had told her I'd escort her out whenever she stayed late like tonight. That she shouldn't go alone to the parking lot."

"Good idea."

"If she would have listened." He set down the antiseptic and leaned against the counter. "I was at my desk when I heard the door shut and noticed it was just after ten. I went through the office, across the commons and out to the back parking lot. Her interior car lights were on, but I couldn't see her. I went out and found her getting up from the ground. I thought maybe she had tripped." He blew out a breath. "She said she'd been pushed, so I looked around. I think whoever did it was long gone, but there's a broken spotlight. It was too dark to see clearly."

"Britte, who's holding a grudge?"

Again, she shrugged, an almost imperceptible lifting of her shoulders, as if the movement hurt.

"Whatever you say stays in this room. You're not accusing anyone."

"Cal, it depends on what day it is. Did I give someone a wrong grade? Did I snub someone? Did I not listen long enough to someone? Was the test too difficult? Did I not help someone enough to catch up on their work? Was I too hard on someone at practice? Who didn't get to play..." She glanced at Joel. "There's always someone mad at me, Cal."

Cal had caught her look. "Joel, who doesn't she want to tell me about?"

"Drew Sutton."

"No way!" she cried.

Cal asked, "What?"

"She pulled him off Benny Coles. Wrestled him to the ground in front of half the school."

"Britte, of all the stupid—!"

"Hey, don't nag me right now, all right?"

Joel continued, "Then there's Gordon Hughes. He's been on her case for a while, complaining that his daughter doesn't play enough. He spoke with me about filing a formal complaint, bringing it up to the board."

"Britte, what did he say to you? Any threats?"

"No. No threats. Just griping, like I get from at least four parents every year."

"Cal," Joel took the ice pack from her and started cleaning her left hand, "what do you know about the guy?"

"Don't know the man. What do you think?"

"He seems like a regular guy, your average overly distraught, interfering dad."

Britte shuddered.

Cal's eagle eye noticed. "Britte? What do you think?"

"I don't have any proof, Cal. I can't accuse someone—"

"You're not accusing. Just give me something to go on. Your impressions may be enough."

"No, I can't say anything. It goes against my cardinal rule of sharing information. Nine times out of ten, what anyone says in Valley Oaks is repeated and most likely turns into a rumor. I can't express an intuition that has no foundation. That's not information."

"I don't want to scare you, Britte. No, on second thought, I do want to scare you. I want to scare the living daylights out of you. Listen. The back doors are wide enough for a clear view of the commons. The attacker easily could have seen Joel coming and ran off. He may come back because he didn't finish."

She jerked at the words, but immediately raised her chin. "That doesn't change anything." In spite of the brave words, her voice didn't hold its usual confident tone.

"You are the most stubborn— How am I supposed to nail the guy—"

"You don't have to. I don't know how I could ever press charges. I mean, Jesus tells me I have to forgive him."

Joel stared at her. He felt as if he'd been punched in the stomach.

Cal snapped shut his notebook. "That's all well and good for you, but there are two guys—" His cell phone rang. He pulled it out and flipped it open. "According to this incoming number, make that *three* guys ready to tear your assailant's limbs off one by one." He held the phone to his ear. "Yo, Brady. She's okay."

While Cal talked, Joel knelt in front of Britte with another antiseptic pad. "Let me check your knee."

She tugged the torn, loose-bottomed pant leg up. "You called him, too?"

"Left a message on his machine. I was glad I didn't have to tell him you were in the hospital." He began to carefully clean the scrapes above her kneesock. "You know, between this and the scuffle you broke up, that makes twice I was glad for that."

"I know." She reached down and her fingers grazed his temple. "Thank you. Joel."

Twenty-Two

Britte sat in Cal's cruiser. He drove her home while Joel followed them in her Jeep.

Mr. Kingsley.

The General.

Her knight.

Joel.

"Britte," Cal said, "if you have any suspicions, you know the guy might hurt others. It's got nothing to do with your cardinal rule or forgiving him."

She didn't reply. They'd already covered this, and she wasn't going into something as vague as the creepy feelings she felt around Gordon Hughes. Or the even vaguer notion that he abused his wife.

He couldn't really have done this, could he? It was beyond her comprehension that *anyone* was capable of it. If it weren't for her incredibly sore body, she wouldn't believe it even happened.

"All right, I'll do it without your help. But just promise me one thing."

She heard the concern in his voice. Since she'd been in third grade, Cal had treated her like a little sister. Usually in the negative sense, but still...like family. "What?"

"Don't walk alone to your car. Don't be anywhere alone by yourself. Call me if you have to. Just don't take the chance. The guy was obviously waiting for you. You shouldn't even go home alone, especially at night."

158

"No problem with that tonight." Through the windshield she saw Brady standing outside her house, his truck parked on the street. He'd evidently used his key to go inside. All the front lights were on and the garage door was open. Joel was driving her car into it now. And here she came with the deputy sheriff. "Can we turn on your siren?"

He pulled into her driveway. "Promise me you will not get into a similar situation." It wasn't a question.

"Promise."

"Since you think you can forgive the jerk who did this, I take it keeping your word is also a cardinal rule with you." When she didn't comment, his voice rose. "I'm serious!"

"Cal, I said I promise. I mean it. The truth is, I'm scared to death."

He squeezed her shoulder. "And I mean it. Call me anytime for an escort."

"Thanks for worrying."

The car door opened on her side. Brady stuck his head in, looked at her, and sharply inhaled. Wordlessly he helped her out and hugged her. "Thank God you're all right."

She heard the tears in his whisper, and, willing her own not to fall again, teased, "You call this all right?"

Joel and Cal joined them. Great. Now she had three big brothers. No...only two. Joel was in a category by himself.

Joel. It felt good to say it.

Brady announced he was staying the night. Cal agreed it was a good idea.

"Brade," she said, "you don't have to disrupt your life for this. Somebody got mad and pushed me down. I'm sore. I just want to take a hot bath and go to bed. End of story. Go home. You didn't call the folks, did you?"

"No. I figured no reason to wake them up."

Joel cleared his throat. "Britte, if your brother doesn't stay, I'm staying."

They all stared at him. It must have been his "General's" tone that stopped the conversation. She knew he meant it.

He went on. "None of us want you to be alone. You should not be alone tonight. Tomorrow night is negotiable, but not tonight. So who's it going to be?"

What she wanted was to fall into his arms again. For the whole night? That'd be fine with her.

He stepped over and put his arms around her in a brief hug. "You'd better choose Brady. Otherwise, the kids would have a field day. Stay home tomorrow. I'm calling for a sub first thing."

She looked up at him. His face was hidden in the night shadows. "No, don't do that. I'll be there."

He gently touched her bruised cheek and murmured, "Ice it some more."

Cal offered to take Joel home and they left. She walked with her brother into the house, grateful not to be alone.

"Brady, thanks for staying."

"No problem. Anything I can do for you?"

She shook her head. "Just make yourself at home. Keep the bogeyman away." She rambled as she headed toward the hall. "I think the spare bedroom is presentable. There are bagels in the fridge. Why don't we leave a light on—"

Brady laughed. "Stop avoiding it, sis. When did this thing start between you and Joel?"

She paused and looked back at him. "Tonight. Pure adrenaline. It'll pass."

It hadn't passed by morning, but neither had the aches and pains, nor the bruise on her cheek, nor the raw scrapes on her face. But she made it to school, early as usual. She entered the back door and spied Joel across the commons. Not good timing. She was shaking like a leaf after parking in her usual spot out back and replaying last night. Even in the cold sunshine with Brady sitting nearby in his truck, she succumbed to an onslaught of sheer terror.

Joel met her in the center of the area. "Britte, I called a sub."

"Well, call her back. I'm here." She tried to smile, but it hurt.

"Why?"

To see you. To see if his eyes were still warm. They met hers now. They were still warm. She felt intoxicated with the eye contact. "I never miss a day."

"You look like you should be in the hospital." He took the attaché bag from her hand and set it in on the floor. Gently, he grasped her hands in his and turned them over, inspecting the palms. Both were covered with gauze. "What are you going to tell the kids?"

"The truth. There's no reason not to, is there?"

"No. Maybe one of them knows something." He let her hands go and picked up her bag. "I'll walk you to your room." As they turned by the office, he stepped inside and told Lynnie to cancel the substitute. They strolled down the hall. "Are you sure you're up for this?"

"I'm always up for this."

"Britte, you can give yourself a break now and then. That's one reason for lesson plans."

"Uh, my lesson plans aren't ready."

He stopped and stared at her. "You turn your book in every week."

"But I, um," she glanced away, "I just copy into it from last year's, which is pretty similar to the previous year's. In class I kind of wing it. I mean, I have a broad outline. I know where we're going, deadlines for tests, etcetera, etcetera."

She looked back at him. "Things change, day by day. Different kids need different approaches. For example, in calc today, we've got to go over yesterday's lesson again. How I'm going to do that is stored here." She tapped her head. "A sub could follow the book, but the kids would miss a valuable day. Goodness, that sounded repulsively egotistical."

Chuckling, he touched her elbow and urged her along beside him to her room. "A bit. Miss O, you certainly had me fooled about the lesson plans."

"I'm sorry. It was insubordinate." She grinned and then winced. "Ouch. It hurts to smile." She unlocked her door, flipped on the lights, and walked inside.

"Actually, I wasn't totally honest myself about lesson plans."

"How's that?"

"I never read yours."

"You what!"

He shrugged and went to her desk, where he set her bag. "It was quite obvious to me the first week of school that you know what you're doing. You certainly don't need me looking over your shoulder."

"That's awful!"

"I couldn't exactly play favorites."

Their eyes locked again, and she knew it wasn't adrenaline. She was a favorite? He had her fooled, too. "The memo!" She shrugged out of her jacket, draped it across the back of her chair, and slid out a drawer. "I taped it to the page you should have read last week." She pulled out the notebook and opened it on the desk.

He peered over her shoulder. "Yep, still there, right where I would never see it."

"I wouldn't either. I haven't opened this book since I gave it to you. Joel, I really am sorry. I tried to find you yesterday to apologize. My behavior was despicable."

He leaned back against the desk to face her. "You don't have to apologize. I needed—I truly needed to hear those things."

"But I had no right to say them with such anger."

"You had every right. If you said you talked to me twice about the request, I'm sure you did. You obviously wrote the memo." He glanced up at the clock. "In all the commotion last night, I forgot to mention I've got a special meeting with the board in about five minutes. I'd better get over to the superintendent's office and fix what I botched the other night."

"The superintendent's— A board meeting just for my team thing?"

"Hey, your *girls* team thing is important."

She smiled.

"Britte, you have my permission to call me on the carpet anytime I start strutting around like a general again."

"I don't need *permission*. You better make that an *order*, General."

He laughed, a hearty sound, a curious sound because it was...unguarded.

Pure adrenaline it wasn't.

~

Joel rushed down the hallway beside Liz, the student who had come to get him. He could see Britte. She stood outside her classroom, leaning back against the lockers, arms crossed, head bowed. It was only 8:40, halfway through first hour.

He motioned to the panic-stricken student to go on inside the room. Even before the door shut, he was slipping his arms around Britte's shoulders.

"Joel," her voice was a gasp, "I can't do this!"

He pulled her away from the wall, and she sank against him. "You don't have to, Britte."

"But I never run. Not from anything!"

"This isn't running. You've got to take care of yourself first."

"The girls are scared. The boys keep staring, but they don't say anything. Nobody can work. This stupid incident shouldn't interfere! Those kids should be teasing me about it!"

"It's not a teasing matter. Shh," he soothed, his voice muffled against her head. It crossed his mind that he had himself physically separated numerous teen couples in the hallway standing nowhere near this closely. "Lynnie took one look at you and told the sub to stand by. I'll take over until she gets here. I want you to go home right now. And that is an order, young lady. I'll go in and get your things. All right?"

She nodded.

Reluctantly, he willed his arms to let her go.

A few moments later they made their way out to the back parking lot. He sensed her fear, sensed that his arm around her would encourage her, but he kept his distance. He tried to convince himself it was because too many classroom windows faced their way, too many eyes were noting their progression. On another, deeper level he admitted that he didn't touch her because of the simple fact that he wanted to so badly.

She reached over and gripped his elbow. "I'll come back for practice at 3:30."

"No, you won't. Let Anne and Tanner run practice. I will personally call them and tell them the situation. Britte, give this some time. Stay home tomorrow, too. It's the last day before Christmas break and only a half day. You won't miss that much."

"I'm not saying I will, but if I do, please tell the sub to read the paper that's in my upper right-hand drawer. It has assignments for the break."

"You taskmaster, you. Christmas homework?"

"Naturally. Where did I say the paper is?"

"Upper right-hand drawer. I won't forget." He risked a glance at her. "Not this time."

"I know."

He squeezed the fingers that held his elbow. They reached her car, and he opened the door for her. As she settled behind the steering wheel, he leaned inside. "Now that I think about it, even though it's broad daylight, I don't want you going home alone."

"Well, guess what?" Her voice wasn't back to full power yet, and her eyes kept filling. "I don't want to either. I'm going to my mom and dad's."

"Good. I hope your mom will make you some chicken soup."

Her smile didn't quite lift the corners of her mouth. Her eyes immediately teared up again.

"I'll call you later."

"Joel, you don't have to be so attentive—"

"But I do." The words flew out, as if they'd bypassed his mind. And they kept coming. "I don't have a choice in the matter. I can't remember what else it is I'm supposed to be doing."

She closed her eyes and whispered, "Why?"

"I think you know why."

"Adrenaline."

If she hadn't opened those magnetic eyes of hers at that precise moment, he might have been able to agree with her and escape what he hadn't meant to start. "I don't think so."

Twenty-Three

"Britte." With that one syllable, Joel's voice conveyed anxiety, hope, and tenderness.

I never should have drunk that tap water! And to think I drank even more in the nurse's room! Phone to her ear, she snuggled back against the pillows and pulled the down comforter up around her shoulders. It was Friday, and she was at the farm still, in her old bedroom. "Good morning."

Silence hung between them. It was the first time they had ever spoken over the telephone. Britte suddenly thought what an awkward mode of communication it was and wondered why it was she had called him. She wanted to see his eyes. Was Wednesday night and yesterday all a dream? Were his eyes distant, his mind moving on to other tasks at hand?

He cleared his throat. "Given the fact that it's nine o'clock, I take it you're not coming in, Miss O?"

"I should have called sooner, but I just woke up."

"Getting lazy, are we?"

"I don't know what it is. I went to sleep at noon yesterday!"

"It's called recovery. How are you?"

She hesitated. He had called twice last night, her mother said. But this was a school morning. "Joel, you're busy. I was only checking in—"

"I'm not too busy." There were muffled noises indicating that he was walking. A door clicked shut. "Talk."

She smiled at his "General's" tone. It meant he was serious. "Before I opened my eyes, I thought it was a bad

166

dream. Then I opened them and realized I wasn't at home. Then I replayed it all again."

"Any new thoughts?"

"No. I just want it to go away."

"It takes time. You'll have to be patient, a virtue I don't imagine you're very comfortable exercising."

"That's a rather impertinent assumption!"

He chuckled. "One of my specialties. Seriously, I know you well enough to realize that not being able to work is probably more difficult to endure than the injuries. Speaking of which, how are they?"

"Well, I don't hurt as much. The swelling's down, but the purple has spread, so now I have a black eye. I need to come to practice at noon today."

"No, you're not allowed back here yet."

"But Anne and Tanner are both working. They can't do it, and with the tournament next week—"

"We've got it covered."

"Did you move it to later? I promised the team they could have Friday night off."

"We didn't move it."

"You didn't cancel it!"

"You're sounding *much* better, Miss O."

"This is my team we're discussing! I can't entrust them to just anyone."

"How about to me?"

"You! Joel, you don't have the time to coach a practice."

"It's on my calendar. I'm serious. So, what do you say? Trust me to do an okay job?"

"Of course I trust you to do that, but I can't ask you—"

"You didn't. Britte, I want to do this." He paused. "For you. If you'll let me."

Suddenly, conversing by telephone didn't feel all that awkward. It felt downright intimate. "Okay, I'll let you. On one condition. Don't call them girls. They're ladies."

"Got it, Miss O. Anything else?"

"Nothing I can think of at the moment. You know, your 'way-cool' points will skyrocket with this one."

"Whew! Am I glad to hear that! It's one of my top priorities." Again, he paused. "How about my 'way-cool' points with you?"

She thought a moment. "I must say, General, you've almost dug yourself out of the negative side."

The delightful, rare sound of his unguarded laughter sang in her ear.

⁓

Britte climbed into her Jeep, hit the automatic door lock, and sat, parked inside her garage with its door down, its overhead light on. She hadn't come out to warm up the car before it was time to leave. No way was she opening the big door and turning on the engine until the very moment she was ready to back out and drive away.

She hesitated, shivering. Or shaking in terror? "Lord, I'm having a tough time here. I'm afraid of my own shadow."

It was Sunday, late afternoon, Christmas Eve, and she was determined to make her first venture out alone. That morning her frightful face and aching body convinced her to go back to sleep instead of to church, but at least she had spent last night in her house, alone. Yesterday there had not been a practice, and so she stayed all day at the farm. Her parents accompanied her home after dinner. Dad had double-checked all the door and window locks. Somehow she had convinced Brady to let her go it alone. The lumpy mattress in her spare bedroom probably influenced his decision.

Joel hadn't called after his Friday practice. Just as well. It saved her from having to convince him, too. Maybe he hadn't called because he understood she needed to face it alone and the sooner the better. Or maybe he hadn't called because Christmas break had officially started. He was probably leaving town. She didn't know the first thing about his family. At his age, he very likely had *children* somewhere. And an ex...

Her shoulders sagged. She hadn't thought of that.

But had she heard that he was divorced? No...only that he was single. Which didn't explain a whole lot when it came to divorce, separation, widowhood, unmarried fathers...

Of course, before...before the attack, his marital status or family background or Christmas plans hadn't mattered to her one way or the other.

"Oh, Lord!"

Goodness, enough with the despair.

"Jesus, thank You that I wasn't hurt more seriously. Please be with whoever did this. Let them know in some way that You love them. Thank You for knowing everything about me." She closed her eyes. "Thank You for Joel. I don't know what I'm feeling, I just know I'm calling him by his first name so I must feel something! I give it all to You." She was silent for a moment, struggling to truly let the fear go, to let the unnamed feelings go, and to let that familiar, supernatural peace find its way in again.

It didn't happen. She was still shaking.

"But it's a fact. I know You are here with me, taking it one step at a time." She opened her eyes and punched the garage door opener. "Amen."

She drove through the late afternoon dusk. It was a cold, cloudy Christmas Eve. Normally, she would be at her parents, but this year was different. Ryan was at his girlfriend's. Brady was at some relative of Gina's with her parents. Megan was at her in-laws'. And, wonderful as the two days had been letting her mom fuss over her, enough was enough. The Olafssons would all be together tomorrow on Christmas Day. When Anne called last night and invited her to their home for Christmas Eve with the promise that Alec would take her home, Britte gratefully accepted.

She covered the few blocks quickly and parked on the long driveway near the garage. As she unloaded her vegetable casserole from the backseat, a car pulled in behind hers, its lights blinding her eyes. The Suttons' two large dogs tore across the front yard, barking.

Britte's heart rammed against her chest as if it would burst out.

The car door opened and a man climbed out. "Britte." He approached.

"Ahh!" she yelled. The cry escaped in that split second that passed before she recognized him. "Joel! Don't do that! Oh!" Her tone was a squeal, beyond her control. Her heart didn't slow.

"I'm sorry! Holy cow, that was thoughtless. Here, let me take that." He took the dish and held on to her arm.

"Whoa!" she exhaled loudly, and then she laughed. There was a touch of hysteria to it. "I guess I used up all my nerve just getting here."

"I imagine you did."

"You calling me chicken?"

"I wouldn't do that. Maybe a yellow-bellied, lily-livered coward."

She laughed again. "That about sums it up. Samson, Madison," she yelled at the dogs, "be quiet!" It felt good to shout. Her heartbeat was returning to normal.

"Come on, let's get inside." He steered her across the lawn, the quiet dogs at their heels. "I didn't know you were coming."

"I didn't know *you* were coming."

Britte was torn between chewing out Anne for this setup and being glad that she had accepted her invitation.

They climbed the front porch steps, and Joel rang the doorbell.

Anne opened the door. "Joel!"

Alec peered over his wife's shoulder. "Britte!"

Joel turned to her and smiled. "Apparently they didn't know either."

~

"Alec, how *could* you?" Anne went quickly along the upstairs hallway ahead of him and into their bedroom.

Carrying their guests' coats, Alec bit back a flippant retort asking her the same question. Anne was not on top of her game today. She swiveled on him now, hands on hips, mouth pursed, eyes glaring. He knew the signals. She desperately needed a hug. He laid the coats on the bed. "I didn't think you'd mind if I invited Joel. I'm sorry I forgot to mention it." They hadn't exactly seen much of each other during the week.

"I don't mind, but Britte will! And after what she's just been through— Good heavens! She'll think I'm playing Cupid!"

He laughed. "You're joking! Just tell her the truth. You didn't know he was coming."

"That doesn't change the fact that they're both here now! She'll be so uncomfortable. Did you know she called him the

'General' to his face? Did you know she *reprimanded* him the other day?"

Alec couldn't help but grin. Joel's rendition hadn't included the "General" remark. "That's our Britte. She's been outspoken since she was a kid. Remember that she used to tell us how to raise Drew? What was she, 15?"

Anne only frowned at him.

"You're so cute when you're mad."

"Don't change the subject." Very un-Anne-like, her voice went up a notch. "What are you going to do about this?"

In reply, he dropped his right hand to the ground, bent his knees slightly, and grimaced at her.

"I'm serious!"

With a growl, he lunged and softly tackled her, grabbing her round the waist and lifting her off her feet and onto the bed.

"Let me up!" She pushed at his shoulder.

"Not until you smile. It's Christmas Eve, woman!"

"It's your fault."

"I apologize. I'll take care of it. I won't let Joel near Britte." He kissed her cheek, his lips brushing her face as he murmured, "You've been taking such good care of us, sweetheart." He kissed the tiny scar at the corner of her mouth. "Throw in a full-time job, and you don't miss a beat. What can I do for you?" He kissed her until at last she slid her arms around his neck. And then he kissed her until he wished they didn't have company downstairs.

He came up for air and saw that her eyes were smoky gray. Their lovemaking had chased the blackness away. "I love you, Annie. Tell me what to do. I want you to enjoy the holidays."

She looked him in the eye. "Clean the kitchen tonight. Totally. Without my help."

Uh-oh. That was a tough one. He detested cleaning the kitchen. There were so many details!

"I'm just tired, Alec. Beyond tired. And you haven't exactly been Mr. Mom this week."

He winced. It was true. He had been at home instead of the office, but still Anne had found it necessary to stay up most nights until long past midnight, preparing for the holiday. She had worked at the store yesterday, Saturday. That schedule had kept her up until 3:00 A.M. in order to have time to go to church and be ready for tonight's guests. "I know. I'm food-prep and gift-wrap challenged. But I know how to clean up."

"Until every dish and bit of food is put away and the countertops are washed? No sticky spots on the floor?" A single tear slid down her cheek. "If that doesn't happen, mister, tomorrow will be unbearable."

He hugged her tightly. "Oh, sweetheart, why didn't you tell me?"

"I didn't know it until you asked what you could do."

He wiped away the tears clinging to her eyelashes. "Hey," he teased, "did you know Peter and Celeste and all three of their kids are coming tonight, too?"

It brought a smile to her face. "Did you know Val and all three of her kids are coming?"

He smiled back, hoping they were using disposable tableware for *everything*.

⌒

Before going back downstairs to her guests, Anne stopped in the bathroom to wash her face.

"Dear Father, I'm sorry. I'd rather just curl up with Alec than be with friends tonight."

She checked her reflection and noticed her ponytail was askew. She gave herself a halfhearted smile, thinking how she missed her husband. She pulled out the band and brushed her dark hair. How long had she worn it this way? It was shoulder length in their wedding pictures. Maybe it'd be fun to chop it off. At the least, it'd be practical. Shampooing and drying time would be cut in half. She could use that time to snuggle with Alec...or kiss Amy goodbye...or listen when Drew surprised her with conversation...or do some room mother thing for Mandy...or wait for Britte after a game so she wouldn't be alone in the parking lot...or read a book...

She'd better shave her head and go bald.

"Anyway, Lord, help!"

Hurrying down the staircase she spotted Britte and Joel in the living room and halted. They stood near the fresh Christmas tree, beside the piano, holding cups of eggnog, singing and laughing through Mandy's halting rendition of "The Twelve Days of Christmas," encouraging the little girl to keep going. And...their shoulders were touching.

Anne burst into laughter.

God's clear answer for help took her by surprise.

Twenty-Four

Britte accepted a bowl from Anne. They were in her large kitchen, unloading copious dishes from the oven and refrigerator. Celeste and Val were in the dining room, arranging items on the buffet table. The men were out in the living room; the nine children were scattered about the house.

"You look pitiful, honey." Anne gave her a gentle smile. "But you probably didn't need to hear that."

"Again."

"Hey, *I* hadn't said it yet." On the telephone Thursday, Anne had tearfully said everything else, from blaming herself for not being there to threatening to sue whoever was responsible. "I can't believe you went to school on Thursday."

Britte cocked her head.

"Well, yes, I can. Why would a little assault disrupt your schedule?" Anne shut the refrigerator and, after a glance over Britte's shoulder, conspicuously raised her brows.

Britte set the bowl down on the counter. It was their first chance to talk alone, and she knew what the raised brows asked. *What's going on between you and Joel?* Britte held out her hands, palms up. "You got me!"

Anne giggled. "Give me details."

"There aren't any! It's just something that—that's *there*."

"Well, this certainly makes the evening intriguing! Alec didn't tell me he had invited him. You know I would have told you."

"I know." Britte smiled.

Anne hugged her. "I told you he's a good one."

"Annie, don't go making long-range plans, okay?"

"I'll try not to." Her jaw dropped. "Whoops. I fussed at Alec, and he promised to monopolize Joel all night. You may have to rescue the guy because Alec will not catch on." Her eyes strayed toward the family room.

Britte looked over her shoulder. Joel was entering from the dining room, Alec on his heels, spreading his arms in a helpless gesture, throwing an apologetic look her direction.

Anne murmured, "Then again, our principal is perfectly capable of standing on his own two feet."

~

Late that evening, while the children wound down in the family room, the adults gathered in the Suttons' living room in front of a crackling fire. Britte sat on the carpet, her legs curled underneath her long skirt. Her back to the fireplace, she leaned sideways against a wing chair, comfortably close to Joel, who sat in it.

She looked around the cozy seating arrangement. Alec sat in another wing chair on the other side of the fireplace; Anne was on the floor near him. Celeste and Peter sat on the love seat facing the fireplace. A square coffee table was in the center. Only a dim lamp, the Christmas tree lights, and the fire lit the room.

Val had gone home. The evening had been packed with laughter, music, food, and games, but it had clearly been a struggle for the suddenly single mother. Britte felt that her own ordeal was hardly worth mentioning in comparison, but the others were eager to hear what had happened since the Wednesday night attack.

Joel touched Britte's shoulder now and spoke to the others. "Cal came to the office on Thursday. Lynnie gave him a complete list of team members, parents, addresses, and phone numbers."

Peter rumbled. He was their pastor, a barrel-chested, redheaded 45-year-old who sometimes spoke eloquently without saying a word.

His wife Celeste, so small and fine-featured beside him, asked in her lilting voice, "What is it, Peter?"

"This is going to upset a lot of people," he replied. "They will feel they're being unfairly singled out."

Britte's heart sank. "I'm not even going to press charges."

Alec said, "But Cal has to do his job, Britte. Did he talk to everyone already?"

Cal had stopped by Britte's house yesterday. She had already told the story to Joel. "Most everyone. A couple of families left town for the holidays."

"Any suspects?"

"No." She didn't look back at Joel. He knew Gordon Hughes had been unavailable. "It's probably just a student who was mad about something. I mean, it's no secret that I make kids mad now and then."

Peter looked from Joel to Alec. "Are the high school students talking about it yet?"

Joel replied, "No. Hopefully, it's only a matter of time before they start."

Alec propped an ankle across his other leg. "I talked with Drew. I think he was being straight when he said he hadn't heard anything. And for the record, Britte, he's not mad." He grinned. "Anymore."

She smiled. "I know. He's like a little brother to me, and his friends know that."

Anne said, "The feeling's mutual. If he finds out who's responsible, there'll be another fight."

Joel put a hand on top of her head. "Which you are not going to break up."

"Yes, General." She caught Alec's confused expression and bit her lip to keep from laughing.

Anne didn't let it go. "Britte!" Amazing how the woman could chastise with one syllable.

Joel chuckled. "It's a promotion, Anne. I keep telling her I only made it to staff sergeant."

Peter asked, "What's Cal doing next?"

Yawning, Britte set her cup of decaf mocha on the coffee table. "He'll probably hang out at the girls games now, too, rather than just the boys. At least I've gained a fan. If you'll all excuse me, I need to go home. Cal will be proud of me because I'm going to ask for an escort. Any offers?"

Joel's voice rose above Peter's and Alec's, and she gladly accepted.

⁓

"I feel like such a wimp." Britte walked around Joel and locked the kitchen door they had just entered from the attached garage. "Here you are, standing in my kitchen, and I'm locking up. I can't even come home alone, and I've left a light on in every room in the house. There is something wrong with this picture."

No, Joel thought, *everything is right with it.* He had caught himself more than once in the past few days nearly thanking God for Britte's dilemma. That didn't seem an appropriate response and yet, without the impetus of the assault, would they have grown so close so quickly? "Under the circumstances, you're simply being cautious, as you should be."

She held out a hand. It was visibly shaking. "That's not caution; it's being a chicken."

"Yellow-bellied, lily-livered coward."

"Exactly." Her entire bruised face scrunched into a frown.

"Britte, you believe in Jesus, right? That He's with you all the time?" It had been evident tonight in conversations with the Suttons and Eatons that her faith was an integral part of her life.

She nodded.

"He's supposed to be in charge, not you."

"I don't want to be in charge."

"Then stop worrying about the need to be escorted home. That's just the way it is for now. You'll get through it and be your sassy self again in no time."

She crossed her arms, evidently balking at his reprimand. "Shall I look around?"

"Please."

He smiled. "That wasn't too hard, was it?"

"You're pushing it, Mr. Kingsley. When I get sassy again, you'd better watch out."

He raised his shoulders to his ears and exaggerated a shudder.

She gave him a half smile and shrugged out of her coat. Her long blonde hair hung in loose waves. It was brushed off of her forehead, and he saw the creases there smooth out at last. Her squinched eyes opened enough for the blue to shine.

The whole effect sent him spinning. Literally. He circled the kitchen, unzipping his jacket but not removing it. "Everything looks in order here, Miss O. Nice place, by the way."

"Thanks. The dining room is through here."

He followed her into the next room. An oak table and buffet shone under an old-fashioned crystal chandelier.

"This was my great-aunt's house. My dad and uncles inherited it, so I was able to buy it from them. I talked them into selling me everything in this room, too. I remember sitting at the table with Aunt Mabel when I was a kid. She was a kindergarten teacher, and I helped her cut and paste things. I loved being here."

"Is that when you decided to become a teacher?"

"That was it." She grinned.

He followed her into the living room. A mathematician's orderly hand was evident everywhere. Nothing was out of place. There was even a neatly decorated Christmas tree in front of the window. "You have a tree!"

"Of course. Don't you?"

"Uh, no. Seems somewhat pointless to go through the motions for myself."

"So you don't have children?"

The question broke new ground for them. He glanced at her sideways and circled the room. "No. Do you?"

"You would have known by now if *I* did. Do you have a wife?"

"No. Do you have a husband?"

"No. Do you have an ex of some sort?"

He halted his circling and studied two abstract paintings on a wall. "Probably of some sort, but not as in wife. How about you?"

"Uh, fiancé. There was one— Do you have— Never mind."

"Do I have a current of some sort?" He turned and looked at her. "No. Do you?"

"Basketball."

Smiling, he gave her a moment. "Any more questions?"

"That about covers it."

"I agree." So...they were both available. Whatever that meant. "Do you want me to check the bedrooms?"

"No! I mean—" She shook her head and gazed at the ceiling.

"Speechless again?"

"This is getting way too awkward. Why don't you go down to the basement while I finish up here?"

"If I'm not back in five minutes, call Cal."

She strode past him toward a short hallway.

Chuckling, he returned to the kitchen and went down the basement stairs. Maybe it was a sugar rush from all the wonderful food he had eaten tonight. Maybe it was a high from the evening's honest-to-goodness fellowship, something he hadn't encountered since he first became a Christian. Maybe it was just those blue eyes connecting with him. Whatever, he hadn't felt like this— Wrong. He hadn't *felt,* period, in a long, long time.

He explored the basement, an unfinished, concrete-walled L-shape beneath the house. Neat-as-a-pin laundry room and storage shelves. He checked the small windows up near the ceiling. *Lord, keep her safe and help us find who's responsible for the attack.*

A few minutes later he met Britte in the living room. She stood in front of the tree. "This is so ridiculous. I can't do this every time I come home after dark!"

"Then we should help Cal find the guy. Even if you don't press charges, at least that way we can monitor things. How can you not go after whoever is causing this havoc in your life?"

"Because Jesus loves me and forgives me. If I can't do the same to my enemy, then Jesus hasn't made one iota of a difference. But...maybe I should press charges to get him off the streets."

The power of her words knocked the wind from him. "Still, that's incredible faith to even want to forgive him."

"Well, this is an easy situation to understand. Forgive your enemies. It's the subtle, day-to-day kinds of things I don't often catch the first time around. Would you like some coffee or something?"

In days gone by, he would have asked for the something. But this was a new day, and he wasn't quite sure of how to go about that request. The rules of engagement hadn't been explained. "No, thanks." He zipped up his jacket. "It's late. You should probably get some rest."

At the front door she rushed the words, "Are you sitting home alone tomorrow?"

"That's the plan."

"Would you, um, like to, um— Oh! Probably not!"

"Will you be there?"

She nodded.

"Probably yes, then."

She bit her lower lip.

He shrugged, smiled, and opened the door. "I'll call for directions."

Twenty-Five

Anne stood on the landing of their staircase and rubbed sleep from her eyes. She was *never* the last one to wake up. How in heaven's name had she managed to do so on Christmas morning? She could hear Alec and the kids in the living room. The girls were reading gift tags and distributing the presents into separate piles. Their family traditions had started without her!

Despite her dismay, she was still groggy. Instead of continuing down the open staircase toward the living room, she turned and went down the enclosed back way to the kitchen. She needed coffee.

She remembered last night. When she went to bed, the kitchen was in a typical postcelebration shape: a mess. At the bottom of the steps, hand on the door that opened into it, she paused and reminded herself to lower her expectations about entering a spotless kitchen. Alec was not a detail person when it came to housework. The room was not going to look the same as it would if she had cleaned it.

She mustered up a Pollyanna take on the day. *Okay.* It was all right if the kitchen did not meet her standards. The point was Alec had asked what he could do, she had told him, he had offered, and then, last night, she had taken him up on the offer by going straight upstairs after closing the door on the Eatons. She hadn't looked in the kitchen, and she hadn't even heard Alec come to bed. He had tried, and that was what counted. Today everyone was on their own for breakfast. She only needed to prepare two dishes to take to

183

her parents' house later. That would require a little counter space, a cutting board, a knife, a clean bowl, and access to the refrigerator.

She opened the door, peeked around the corner, and studied the kitchen. There was not one inch of uncluttered countertop. Closing her eyes, she leaned against the door-jamb and whispered a prayer, "Lord, if it's as bad as it looks, please give me the grace to show him mercy." *Lower, Anne,* she admonished herself, *lower those expectations a little more. Alec does not see things the way you see things.*

Tightening her robe belt, she entered the room. Her slippers didn't stick to the floor. The good china was stacked. Clean, but stacked there rather than on the dining table or put away in the hutch. A few cookie platters were out...uncovered. Two casserole dishes sat atop the stove, their crusted stains soaking in water.

Her breath returned, and she noticed the coffeemaker. Fresh coffee was dripping into the pot. Alec must have heard her moving about upstairs and started it. She wiped a tear threatening to slide down her cheek and sniffed.

"Merry Christmas, sweetheart!" Alec's voice came from behind her.

She hurriedly sniffed again.

He put his arms around her waist and nuzzled the back of her head. "It's not too bad, is it?"

"Is that coffee for me?"

"Yes. So, what do you think?"

"It's...fine."

"I know it's not perfect. Amy and Mandy are going to put the dishes away later, and Drew promised to scrub those pans."

"Okay." She knew that "later" could mean three days from now. Minimum.

"Go join the kids. I'll bring your coffee."

She turned. His cinnamon eyes resembled a little boy's, anticipating and eager to please. That was the point, not the kitchen. She kissed his cheek. "Thank you. Merry Christmas."

There was a roaring fire in the fireplace and a Christmas carol CD playing. Alec's coffee wasn't half bad. The children were not only civil with one another, they were kind and teasing. They all enjoyed the surprises she had wrapped for them and appreciated the necessities...a dictionary, socks, jeans...

Still, the tenor of the Sutton family Christmas morning was off. Anne suspected it was her exhaustion, her sleeping late, her not giving herself the time to get settled into that sense of her hand in Jesus' before she started the day. *If Mama ain't happy, ain't nobody happy.* Glancing around the snugly scene, she chided herself. They appeared happy enough. Maybe it was her imagination.

"Mom," Mandy cried, "open the big one first! It's from all of us."

Anne carefully tore off the shiny red paper from a large box and lifted the lid. Beneath the tissue paper lay a silky red robe. Holding it up, she ooh-ed and ahh-ed until she saw the back of it. No one would have heard her oohs and ahhs at that point. They were all laughing hysterically.

"Get it, Mom?"

Imprinted on the back of the robe was a royal blue triangle with a large, red "S". She got it. *Superwoman.*

After a moment she gave up her attempts at smiling. "Cute, guys."

Alec came over and kissed her forehead. "You can do it all, sweetheart. You are Superwoman."

And what had she been for the past 17 years?

"Here." He handed her a small gift that hadn't been under the tree.

It fit in her palm. The paper was gold foil. She knew it was jewelry, knew it was the special gift he had mentioned wanting to buy for her. Except for the plain gold band and a promise ring with a tiny diamond chip, he hadn't given her jewelry. They had teased that maybe for their twenty-fifth wedding anniversary they could afford her engagement ring. Jewelry wasn't in the budget. Through the years she had admired Val's collection, and somewhere along the way she had dealt with her envy. Jewelry had become a nonissue. And now this...

Was this part of the anticipated bonus Alec had already spent?

He sat at her feet, clearly eager for her to open the gift. She reminded herself that she always kept Alec's gifts unless the size had to be exchanged. He gave her thoughtful gifts, filled with his love. Now, she picked at the wrapping paper and uncovered a black velvet jeweler's box. She eyed him.

He smiled and winked.

Inside the box was a pair of diamond stud earrings. While not ostentatious, neither were they minuscule. They were, quite simply, beautiful. "Alec!"

The girls squealed. Drew patted his dad on the back. "Way to go, Dad."

Anne wondered if it was the entire bonus.

~

Britte chewed her thumbnail and glanced around the farm's big kitchen table. The remains of a Christmas breakfast feast littered the tabletop. She, Gina, and Brady had joined her parents and Ryan for breakfast. Megan, along with her husband and two-year-old, would be coming later, as well as Ryan's girlfriend...as well as Joel Kingsley.

Her mother reached over and pulled Britte's thumb away from her mouth. "Want some more coffee, honey?"

"I can get it."

Barb stood. "I will."

"I'm not an invalid."

"You could have been."

Britte stifled a sigh. Her mom and dad were not helping matters. Their concern for her welfare brimmed in their eyes and coated their words. And they wouldn't stop waiting on her! She stood and clanked a spoon against her juice glass. "Listen up, everybody. I have an announcement to make."

Everyone quieted.

"I look a hundred times worse than I feel. Five days have passed. I'm getting over it." That was easy to say. The sun was shining, and she was spending the night here. "I need you all to get over it, too."

Her dad cleared his throat. Though less talkative, Neil was an older version of Brady in looks: tall, lanky, with more gray than blond hair, and perpetually tanned from living outdoors year round. "Honey, you've got this 'deer caught in headlights' look, you keep chewing your thumbnail, and you haven't made one smart-alecky remark all morning."

"But I'm fine!" She plopped back down onto the chair.

Ryan, a shorter version of their dad and brother, grinned. "Dad, she invited company for today. If you'll note, our little Christmas enclave this year includes our immediate family with Grandma and Grandpa Swanson, Megan's *husband*, Brady's *fiancée*, and my *girlfriend* of *six* months, for whom I had to get a special dispensation in order to invite. Where exactly does *Joel Kingsley* fit into this picture?"

Brady hooted and raised a hand toward his brother for a high five. "Brilliant."

"He's just a friend," Britte raised her voice to be heard above their laughter, "who doesn't have any family nearby!"

Gina put a protective arm around her shoulders, but the male raucous continued, and her mother smiled that funny smile she hadn't had an opportunity to direct Britte's way in years.

Oh, what in the world had she been thinking last night?

Twenty-Six

Britte scooped snow with her mitten-covered hands and formed a snowball. Her right arm still ached, but she managed to hurl the ball ten feet and splat it against Joel's shoulder. A barrage of snowballs sailed toward her, and she screamed, ducking behind her team's fort wall.

It was an intensely beautiful Christmas night. The snow had started falling early in the afternoon, huge, fat flakes that quickly transformed the barren fields into a fantasy winter wonderland. Inches upon inches accumulated as the storm blew in. The wind lessened by nightfall, but the flakes continued to fall, weightless puffs of elegance adding brilliance to the already sparkling white carpet. Reflected in the overcast sky, the snow lit the night in a soft glow and cushioned the countryside in silence.

Britte and Joel were outdoors with Megan and her husband, Ryan and his girlfriend, Brady and Gina. Earlier they had all rummaged through the basement mudroom for thick socks, boots, jackets, mittens, and stocking caps. As far back as Britte could remember, the supply had been there. The odds and ends had accumulated over the years, furnishing visitors with warm clothes for winter play and even ice skates for when the pond froze.

Once outside, they'd discovered ideal conditions for snow-packing. Though Megan kept trying to build a snowman, everyone else rolled massive balls and stacked them into three-foot-high walls. Two forts immediately arose on the

189

front yard. Teams were created, the Olafssons against the Others.

Now sitting in the snow behind a wall, Britte lifted her chin and stuck out her tongue to catch the flakes. *Thank You, Father!* It had been such a perfect day. Her dad and brothers had behaved themselves. There was plenty of food and activity and topics of conversation. Joel had been welcomed and evidently enjoyed himself because he was still there. She had heard his laughter often. They teased each other in front of others about their intensity toward work.

Megan slid down beside her. "Britte, it's too quiet over there. We think we should attack."

"Please don't use that word."

"I'm sorry!"

Britte laughed. "I'm kidding. You're pregnant, Meg. You should go back and work on your snowman."

"I am not an invalid!" Her sister was the only one of the four of them who resembled their mother, and not just in looks. Eighteen months older than Britte and 18 months younger than Brady, she was short and had naturally wavy, light brown hair with matching eyes. Her motherly attitude had been an integral part of her personality since they were children.

Brady and Ryan joined them on the ground. "They're out of ammo," Ryan announced. "We've got plenty. We're going over. Are you with us, Britte?"

Before she could answer, a loud cry arose from the other fort. "Charge!"

Brady and Ryan flew to their feet. Britte, still stiff from her ordeal, rose more slowly alongside Megan. A free-for-all was in progress, snowballs flinging every which way. Britte spotted the bright red ski jacket and yellow stocking cap charging straight for her. *Uh-oh.* She turned and trudged clumsily away through the deep snow.

She made it to a split-rail fence now half-buried in snow. Her body protested, but she boosted herself atop the cross-beam and swung her legs to the other side just as Joel caught up. He grasped her sleeve and lunged over the fence, pulling her with him. Both wildly laughing, they tumbled into the soft snow, the fence rail clanking loudly.

"Ow!" Britte's cry was half-serious. "That hurt!"

"Are you all right?"

"Better than you're going to be if you broke my dad's fence."

"I'll deal with that Olafsson later." Joel raised himself on his elbow and looked down at her, his other hand holding aloft a snowball.

"Don't you dare!"

"Do you surrender?"

"Never!" She whacked his arm and the snowball fell away. "Olafssons rule!" she yelled.

Before she could scramble out of reach, he had both of her wrists in his left hand and was scooping snow onto her face with his right. "Surrender!"

"All right!" she sputtered. "I surrender!"

He released her arms and laid back in the snow, laughing again. "*Others* rule!"

She sat up, tore off a mitten and brushed the ice-cold snow from her face. "Okay, okay. You don't have to gloat. I can't believe you did that. I'll probably get pneumonia!"

"You're a sore loser, Princess."

"What's that supposed to mean?"

"I know you don't let your girls get away with that whining attitude."

"No, not that. I meant the 'Princess' tag."

Joel got to his feet, held his hands out for her, and pulled her up. Letting go of her hands, he took off a glove. "There's still snow in your hair." Finger-combing the damp strands of hair that hung below her stocking cap, he slid his gloved hand around the back of her head. "I take it you grew up here on the farm? That this has always been your home?"

She nodded, distracted by his closeness.

He touched her face now, deflecting the snowflakes falling on it, his hand warm against the cold dampness. "The way I see it, you've got this magnanimous family. I show up with a tin of homemade candy and a poinsettia plant, both of which my mother sent me. You all welcome me like one of the family and even give me a gift."

She smiled. "Ryan's old yellow tie to replace the one of yours I ruined hardly counts."

"But it does count. And then you've got all this open space and enough winter clothes and boots to outfit a platoon. It's like a fairy-tale castle. All it needs is a princess." His hand stilled, cradling her cheek. "A beautiful, benevolent, joyful young woman."

She blinked at the snowflakes floating onto her eyelashes, but she saw him lower his face.

"Someone just like you." And then he kissed her.

~

It was after midnight, but still Joel lingered. He felt somewhat like a teenager. Except for their few moments outside in the snow, he and Britte hadn't been alone all day...and he wanted to be alone with her.

Now at last everyone had gone either home or upstairs to bed. Brady and Gina had finally driven off ten minutes ago, promising to call if the roads were impassable for anything less than a 4x4. The snow had tapered off, but there was some wind, some drifting, and the county road plows had already quit for the night. They'd be out before sunup, though. He said that seemed an archaic practice. The Olafssons explained to him it was just the way things were done in Jacob County. One either drove a 4x4 or stayed put.

"Joel." Britte turned to him now. They sat side by side on the carpet in front of the fireplace, their backs against a couch. "If you won't spend the night here, then drive my Jeep home. I'm staying put, and your car won't make it through the drifts out on the county road."

"If you say so. Is that my exit cue?"

She smiled. "Only if you want it to be."

He slouched down, laid his head against the couch, picked up her hand, and held it between his. It was her eyes that scrambled his thoughts. He chose to stare at the fire instead. "I'd like to just sit here awhile and hold your hand. Will that upset your dad?"

She scrunched down, settling her arm against his. "Not if you fix the fence."

He chuckled, and then they fell silent. The large fire snapped and crackled, throwing heat across the raised brick hearth and enveloping them. Joel held up a foot to catch it and dry his sock and pant cuff still damp from the snow that had lodged in his boot. Lights twinkled from the Christmas tree. "Well, Princess, what do you think?"

"Umm."

He lowered his foot and glanced sideways at her. "You're not going shy on me, are you?"

"Oh!" It was a loud, exhaled syllable. "Oh." That one sounded more like a whimper. "I am. You tell me first. After all, you're the oldest."

"Don't remind me. I feel like I'm robbing the cradle."

"How old are you?"

"Nine years older than you."

"How do you know—?"

"Personnel file. You're 29."

"I see. What else did you learn from that thing?"

"College. GPA. Honors and extracurricular activities. Reviews. Johannah." Her middle name. "That's gotta be a family name."

She laughed. "My great-grandmother's."

"And then there was the negative stuff."

"Holmes." He was one of her former principals.

"He didn't like your attitude much, did he?"

"He didn't like *me* period, though he stood by me a few times. Actually, he helped me become a better teacher. He was the perfect example of what I did not want to become."

"You're ruthless, Miss O." He squeezed her hand. "Oh, sorry. Does that hurt?" He inspected her palm. The scrape wasn't as raw.

"It's fine."

He curled his fingers more gently round her hand and gazed into the fire for a few moments. "I hate that this happened to you, but the silver lining is I'm holding your hand. I don't know if I would have been otherwise. Not yet, anyway. I mean, the incident allowed you to be vulnerable." He looked at her profile in the firelight. "You're not a very vulnerable female. You're even a tad bit intimidating. Are you aware of that?"

"I know," she said quietly.

"I don't know what would have gotten your attention."

She turned her face toward him now. "Were you *trying* to get it?"

"Not consciously." He dropped her hand and reached over to touch the sapphire necklace at her throat.

Her breath caught and she sat up, surprise in her raised brows. "It's from you."

"Took you long enough." He grinned and straightened, turning sideways to face her. "I don't like shopping. I guess this is what I mean by not consciously trying to get your attention. I had drawn your name, and I knew I was to buy something appropriate. The megaphone caught my eye on the Internet. That was appropriate."

She giggled. "And the necklace? You obviously didn't catch the 'cheap' part of the guidelines."

"Uh, no. I was at the mall, buying my mother a Christmas gift. It's a tradition to give her a special piece of jewelry. I saw the necklace there, and I thought, hmm. That looks like the school color Miss O always wears. I'll throw that in with the megaphone."

She laughed out loud. "You're right. That's not conscious. So when did it become conscious?"

He hesitated, wondering if he should stop this unchecked flow of revelations. Then he remembered the kiss in the snow. "Well, it tried to get into my conscious mind at the dance. I mean, when I held you, it was practically kicking down the door. But I successfully ignored it...until that morning when you chewed me out."

"Oh, no," she groaned.

"You were wearing the necklace that day."

"I was?"

"Yes. And as you were leaning across my desk it kind of dangled and the light caught it. I realized it matched your eyes. I also finally admitted I could get lost in those eyes, if I wanted to."

She blinked.

"Last night, after I left your house, I admitted I want to get lost in them." He smiled. "Your turn."

She stared at him for a long moment. "Oh, Joel," she whispered. "I want you to get lost in them!"

It felt as though something inside of him burst. *Is this what joy feels like?*

"Nah, on second thought," a tiny smile tugged at her mouth, "you're way too old for me."

He sighed and shook his head in disbelief, even as he reached for her and encircled her waist with his hands. "I liked you better when you were speechless and shy."

She grinned, sliding her arms around his neck. "I'm not finished."

"Excuse me."

"You may be too old, but there's this big brass band playing somewhere inside of me."

"What's it playing?"

"Something like, 'Whoa, Nellie! Hold on to your hat!'"

He burst into laughter and drew her close. She laughed with him, her head against his shoulder. As their chuckles died away, a wave of emotion washed through him. "Britte, I've never been here before."

"Me neither."

"Do you know what I'm talking about?"

"Well, I don't think you're talking about this house."

"Got any words for what it is?"

She shook her head.

"Me neither."

He kissed her then for the second time that night, and when he did, he knew that the "it" was something beyond words. As if he'd landed on Mars, he didn't have a clue what to expect in such strange territory. "Brady hasn't called. The roads must be passable—"

"Joel," she murmured, her lips brushing against his ear, "you talk too much."

"I should go home."

"Mmm, late hours are kind of tough on old folks."

On second thought, maybe it wasn't time to go home just yet.

Twenty-Seven

Alec wasn't sure what it was his wife wanted, but he was sure she wanted something. The black rim of her irises obliterated any gray.

It was the day after Christmas. He sat on a stool at the kitchen counter, drinking coffee, while Anne spread peanut butter on bagels for the two of them. She was dressed in a sweater, skirt, and boots, ready for work. He had cleared last night's snow from their long driveway with the blade on the lawn tractor. The car was warming up. He needed the van today.

"Annie, isn't this weird? Me staying home, you leaving for work." His company always shut down the week between Christmas and New Year's.

"Mm-hmm." She pushed aside some dishes on the counter and set down a paper plate with his bagel on it.

"Thanks. Your whole face sparkles with those earrings." She gave him half a smile and bit into her bagel.

"I knew you'd look beautiful in them."

"But the money—"

"I told you, I'd saved most of what they cost. I wanted to treat you extravagantly for a change."

"Well, you did that."

"What's wrong, sweetheart?"

She took another bite, chewed, and swallowed before replying. "Do you see anything out of place in the kitchen?"

He glanced around. It appeared to be more cluttered than usual, but they had been gone most of yesterday at his in-laws'. Not to mention that it was the holiday week. Things were hectic!

Anne pointed to the stack of china and the soaking casserole pans.

He grimaced. "We'll get to it today."

"Before or after skiing? Before or after Drew's practice?"

"You know, we could go skiing tonight instead, so you could join us. Drew and Jason could drive out after their practice." It was a family tradition to ski the day after Christmas with the Masseys if there was snow. Today he was taking all six kids by himself. Anne and Val were working; Kevin was out of town with his new friend.

"Alec." She bit her lip.

"Annie, what is it?"

"The thing is, what's bothering me is the fact that this kitchen situation *isn't* bothering me."

"Huh?"

"I just don't care."

"That's good. Spic-and-span is insignificant."

"It's *not* good, Alec. I just said that I don't care. I don't care what any room in this house looks like. I'm not Superwoman and I don't want to be. I was Superwoman from the day I took this job until yesterday. Superwoman only has a life span of two weeks. Where's my coat?"

He saw it on the family room couch and retrieved it for her. As he slipped it onto her arms, he said, "Are you saying you don't like the robe?"

"I don't like the robe." She buttoned the coat and pulled gloves from the pockets.

"You're just tired. Things won't look so bad after the holidays."

"I'm not all that tired today, and things don't look bad at all. They just look *different*." She gave him a quick kiss and strode across to the back door. "I'll be late tonight. There's some end-of-the-year inventory stuff I need to help with. And I think I'll run over to the mall and get my hair cut." She held up her ponytail and smiled. "Show off my new earrings better. Bye."

Alec stared as the door closed behind her. The heavy scent of her new perfume, a gift from her mother, lingered.

Who was that woman?

Twenty-Eight

The squeak and thud of rubber-soled shoes hitting the hardwood floor resounded through the gym. The girls were running sprints back and forth on the court, their breathing an audible huffing and puffing. It was Tuesday, the day after Christmas. Although there were no classes, sports continued unabated. The gym remained open nearly 365 days a year.

Britte yelled encouragement, but she was pushing them hard. They were out of shape. Maybe she shouldn't have given them three days off.

At last she blew her whistle. Some of the girls collapsed on the floor, moaning. Sunny Taylor, one of her seniors, shouted, "Mr. Kingsley! You should fire this coach!"

Britte turned and saw Joel seated at the far end of the bleachers, halfway up, and called over her shoulder. "Take a lap, Sunny."

"Co-oach!" It was a whine.

"Two. Your mouth still has way too much flapping energy."

The girl obediently took off. Britte climbed the bleachers to Joel, wondering how long he had been sitting there watching.

He smiled as she approached. "You know, if you ever decide to leave coaching, you have a promising future as a Marine drill sergeant."

"I'll take that as a compliment, thank you." She grinned and sat down a short distance from him. "They are dragging today. Too much Christmas, I think."

"Or more likely," he murmured, "too much hanging out with their boyfriends until all hours."

Yet again at a loss for words in his presence, she turned to watch the girls gather their things and begin to trickle out the door. Some called out goodbyes. She simply gave them a thumbs-up. Sunny cut a corner; Britte chose to ignore it. The guy had such a bizarre knack…

Joel interrupted her thoughts. "I was going to apologize for not getting in here sooner to give you a hand. From the looks of things, you didn't need it."

She glanced at him. He wore khakis and a forest green V-necked sweater. It would bring out the green in his eyes, but she didn't look for it. What was wrong with her? The tips of her ears felt warm, and her throat was closing up. She had thought about him through the short night, first thing in the morning, and all day until practice at one this afternoon when at last the matter at hand took precedence over that other, whatever *that* was. *Adrenaline…a crush…a moment in the snow…Christmas magic…*

He reached across the distance between them and squeezed her shoulder. "Miss O, you look like a deer caught in headlights."

She'd heard that one before!

"If it helps any," he said, "my deer's wearing a mask."

She turned toward him at last. He was smiling his rare smile; the one that diminished the ever-present military aura, the one that tricked her body into believing it was on a roller coaster, on the whooshing down side of the steepest climb. "I was trying to chalk it up to Christmas magic."

"Me, too."

The roller coaster careened around a curve.

"Coach!" Sunny stood at the bottom of the bleachers, panting, the whine gone from her tone. "Is practice at the same time tomorrow?"

Britte found her voice. "Taylor, if you don't know the answer to that, you'd better take one more lap. See you tomorrow!"

The girl lifted her hand in a discouraged wave and trudged off.

Britte called out, "Hey, Captain! Good workout."

Sunny threw her a smile and left the gym.

"Britte, you are great with the girls."

"I don't know." She settled back against the bleacher and looked at him. Good, safer subject. "I miss Anne, not so much for the physical part of running a practice, but her sense of balance. She's my anchor. I'm still feeling a little unbalanced."

"How'd the girls handle your bruises?"

She smiled. "I think they made allowances, until they realized I'm still—as my friend Isabel calls me—the fire-breathing coach."

"*Apropos* title. Will Anne be around at all this week?"

"No, not with her new job. Practices and the tournament are scheduled for during the day. Tanner's available for the tournament games on Thursday and Friday, though. That'll help."

"Cal called today. He wanted to make sure he had your correct game schedule. He plans to be there."

"In Twin Prairie? It's two days of a drawn-out round-robin. And his wedding is less than a week away!"

"Well, he said he'll be there."

"I hope he's not going to interview parents!"

"He mentioned he only wanted to sit in the stands and keep his ears open. He'll take Chloe with him and make it appear a natural outing."

Chloe had been attending most of the games with Lia. It would appear natural. "I hadn't thought of the guy, the...assailant, sitting in the stands, watching me. But of course he would be, wouldn't he? If he's…one of the dads or students."

"But you won't be alone for a moment. Tanner will be there, and Cal. Of course I plan on coming."

"Joel, you'll have a building full of people here." Valley Oaks was hosting a holiday boys tournament at the same time.

"I can slip away for a while. The ladies are just as important, you know."

"'Ladies,'" she repeated. "You're getting pretty good at that, General."

"Thank you. I'm trying. I wouldn't want a certain math teacher reading me the riot act again."

"Oh, I think you cured her of that tendency." *Nuts.* They were back on it again. She looked out at the empty gym.

"Britte, I've been thinking. I'd like to have dinner with you."

She felt a delicious tingling sensation. But… She turned toward him. The furrowed brow told her he was thinking along the same lines she had been. "But…it's Valley Oaks."

"So my thoughts are valid?"

She nodded. "Someone would see us at a restaurant, even in Rockville. If I cooked and you came to my house, someone would know. The gossip would start. I don't know if we want to get that going."

"Not just yet, anyway."

Not yet?

"Britte, we don't really know each other very well. Once you get to know me, you may not even want to have dinner."

"And vice versa."

"Then all that good gossip would have been wasted."

She smiled. "People would be sorely disappointed."

"We'd lose our way-cool points."

"And we definitely don't want to jeopardize those!"

He chuckled, and then he grew somber. "So, we're in agreement? We'll..." He held up a palm.

"Go slow," she finished his sentence, thinking that if he kept looking at her in that way, they wouldn't need to be seen at a restaurant in order for the gossip to begin. Because at the moment, Joel Kingsley resembled a deer caught in headlights.

～

That evening Joel sat in his condominium at the large, L-shaped cherry desk and stared at the phone. He tapped the eraser end of a pencil on a pad of paper. On the top sheet was a scribbled phone number.

The girl had reduced him to *hesitancy*. Wavering. Vacillation. He felt as if he needed to go back to boot camp and learn all over again. Magnetic blue eyes did not override the brain.

Should he call her? That wasn't against the guidelines they had informally agreed upon, was it? Valley Oaks couldn't witness a phone call. Unless she had guests. He could call under the pretense that he was concerned. Was she in for the night? Was she safe? And then, if she was alone, they could talk.

On the other hand, he should probably disengage now, until a more suitable time. She was preoccupied with basketball. He was preoccupied with making necessary changes at the school, of making them palatable to the board and parents. Emotions such as those which Britte threatened to ignite always complicated things unnecessarily. They interfered with clear thinking. Life required clear thinking. His walk with Christ required clear thinking. He had never met a female who understood that. If any such woman existed, she would resemble Britte.

The phone rang.

"Hello?"

"Joel."

"Mom?" They had talked yesterday. He detected a new anxiety in her tone. "What's up?"

"It's Nicky. Aunt Julie and Uncle Nick never heard from him yesterday."

His heart jumped into a double beat. "That's normal. I didn't call you every Christmas."

"Six out of eight times you did! They haven't even had a note from him in three weeks."

He's in the middle of a war! Joel wanted to scream the words.

"Please, Joel. Call your aunt. It'll help."

"All right. I will. Is the sun still shining down there in Florida?"

They each talked about their day for a few minutes before disconnecting.

By then, the dull thumping in the back of his head had started.

Dear God. Give me the words. With shaking fingers, he punched in his aunt and uncle's number. They weren't much older than he was. He had practically grown up with his Uncle Nick, his father's youngest brother. The families were all close.

His aunt answered the phone.

"Julie."

"Joel?"

"Mom told me you haven't heard from Nicky."

Through tears she talked about her 24-year-old son.

"Listen, I know you know this, but it's normal. All right? It's normal. Keep that in mind. God is with him, and He loves him even more than you and Nick…"

By the time he hung up the phone, he saw pinpricks of light flashing from a great distance. Maybe it wasn't going to be bad. Maybe he could skip the pills.

Without thinking anymore about it, he picked the phone up again and pressed the numbers he read from the pad.

"Hello?"

"Hi, Miss O."

"Joel. Hi." Her tone was soft, personal. She must be alone.

"Are you all right?"

"Snug as a bug in a rug. I'm not going out, if that's what you're wondering. I came home before dark and have stayed put. Besides that weirdo out there, it's too cold and snowy."

"Good. I'm glad to hear that."

"What are you doing?"

"Calling you." The dull thumping moved to his chest. "I'm meeting Brady and Cal at the Center to play some basketball."

She laughed. "I can't believe those guys have time to play basketball and come to my games. They have a wedding in four days! You'd think they'd have to do something to get ready for it. Even I have to go for another dress fitting."

Her voice was a tangible thing, weaving through the pulsating vibrations in his chest, neutralizing them. "You're in the wedding?"

"That was an easy one. You could probably guess that I wouldn't bother with a dress fitting unless someone was making me. It's supposedly a small affair, but are you invited?"

"I am. I plan on attending." *Since you'll be there.* He closed his eyes. The flashing lights were brighter.

"But the boys tournament will still be going on."

"I know. I'm working right now on a plan to delegate responsibilities so I don't have to be there for the entire thing."

"Woo-hoo!"

"Yes. Such progress from one little confrontation with the math teacher."

"Little? That was a major battle."

"Hardly." His voice was low, gravelly.

For a moment, silence filled the line. "Joel, maybe this is just your telephone voice, but you don't sound like yourself."

"I, um…" He rubbed his forehead.

"Well, I'm glad you called. It's a way to get to know each other without the public watching. Or listening. At least we don't have party lines anymore. Not that I remember those. Maybe *you* remember those. So, you want to talk about it?"

In spite of himself, he barked a laugh. She had a knack for catching him off guard. "I just talked with my aunt. Her son, my cousin, is in Afghanistan. They haven't heard from him in over three weeks. The thing is, Britte, he's in the middle of a war. He's with the Special Forces. He's deep into it. He'll be out of touch for a long time."

"Oh, Joel. I'll pray for him. What's his name?"

"Nicky Kingsley. Thanks. I'll let you go now. Sorry. I didn't mean to unload—"

"Hey, Joel," she chided gently, "that's how we get to know each other. That's the whole point of a friendship."

"Friendship?"

"What would you call it?"

"A guy-girl thing."

She sighed dramatically. "There you go with the 'girl' word again."

"All right. Man-woman."

"Much better. Don't you think friendship is part of the man-woman thing?"

"Guys aren't friends with girls. I mean, women."

She whistled in disbelief. "Why not?"

"You're too emotional. There's no point of tangency."

Her laughter grew loud. "Mr. Kingsley, your chivalry is beginning to look an awful lot like chauvinism!"

He waited for her hilarious laughter to slow. "I think I mentioned you may not want to have dinner with me once you came to know me."

"You're not getting off that easily. We're having dinner together Saturday night at the reception. Got it?"

"Yes, ma'am. See you tomorrow, Britte."

"All right. Bye, Joel."

He hung up the phone and maneuvered his way to the bathroom. His knee hit the corner of the desk, his shoulder smacked the doorjamb. He reached inside the medicine cabinet and dislodged several things before putting his hand around the prescription bottle. He fumbled with the lid, thinking that, at the moment, all that mattered were magnetic blue eyes.

Twenty-Nine

Anne walked through the screened-in porch and unlocked the back door of the house, wondering why no lights were on. It was after nine o'clock. She thought her family would have been home from skiing by now.

She flipped on the overhead kitchen light and hung her coat on the wall rack. No reason to hang it in the hall closet. She'd be putting it back on first thing in the morning.

She walked to the center of the kitchen and looked around. It appeared pretty much as it had this morning, except now there were cereal bowls soaking in the sink.

"Lord, am I supposed to clean this up? Or should I let it go? Let them do it, as they promised? It's beginning to look unhealthy. Pretty soon there'll be mold—"

Laundry!

Anne went to the back hallway and peered into the laundry room.

For a moment, while praying, she had sensed she could dig into a deep reservoir of energy. She knew it was sometimes supernatural how she had the energy and the desire to keep up on the daily tasks. But that peek into the laundry room quenched it. In a split second, she felt as if she had slipped her coat back on and it weighed a hundred pounds.

She turned up the thermostat, grabbed the wall calendar, and made her way upstairs. Superwoman was a myth that Anne refused to buy into. She could *not* do it all, not all at once, and she would not try. For the time being, until she taught all three kids how to do their own laundry, they

209

would have to go without a favorite shirt or two. Alec would run out of socks by Friday. Perhaps she could manage to keep up with the linens without buying new sets of everything. The kitchen would be a perpetual disaster area with five people constantly doing their own thing. Somewhere along the way, somebody was going to miss an appointment, a practice, a lesson, or be late for a game.

That was life. Different from what they were accustomed to, but not earth-shattering, was it? Not life-threatening. She let out a deep, audible sigh. There. The hundred-pound weight was gone.

In the bathroom she stared at her reflection and ran her fingers through the short layers of black hair. She had had it chopped off, not trimmed, not cut. Chopped. Alec and the kids would be surprised. She hoped they would like it as much as she did. It was simply different, like the rest of her life.

The diamond earrings sparkled. They were more noticeable with this haircut. She would always wear them because Alec had given them to her. On the whole, she was more... dramatic looking. She smiled.

A short time later, she heard them come in. She was already sitting in bed wearing her fuzzy robe, writing on the oversized calendar in clear printing with colored pens.

"Mom!" Mandy raced in first. She stopped just inside the door. "What'd you do to your hair?"

Amy followed. "Wow! You look so cool!" She came over to the bed and gave her a hug. "Can you just blow-dry it?"

"Don't even have to do that. I can just put—what do you call it?—mousse on it and let it go."

"Your hair was so long. Did you give it away like Lia did, for wigs for ladies with cancer?"

"I did."

Mandy approached, a look of dismay on her face.

"Punkin, it's me." She hugged her nine-year-old baby.

"You look so different."

"Whoa, Mom!" Drew shouted from the door. "What happened to you?"

"What do you mean, what happened to me? I've joined the new century."

"Which century is that?" He laughed. "Just kidding. It's not that bad."

"Well, thanks."

Alec appeared. "What's all the commo— Anne!" He walked across the room, tilting his head and examining her hair. "It's different."

"Do you like it?"

He nodded. "It'll take a little getting used to, but, yeah, I like it."

She could tell. "You hate it."

"N-no."

Amy said, "Dad, she gave her hair away. And this will be so easy to take care of."

Anne noticed Mandy still staring at her. She kissed her cheek. "You'll get used to it, too."

Alec pulled the girls aside and sat on the edge of the bed. "Last one downstairs is a rotten egg!"

Amy squealed, "I get Drew on my team!"

Mandy raced off behind her, yelling, "I get Dad!"

"'Night, girls!" Anne called. "It must be a Ping-Pong tournament."

Alec smiled. "The only time Amy and Drew choose to be on the same side. You beat us home."

"Not by much. How was skiing?"

"Great. The snow was perfect. Val ended up going with us."

"She did?"

"She took the afternoon off and met us out there. The boys drove her car back for practice. The rest of us stayed awhile longer, and then we stopped for pizza."

"You've been at the Pizza Parlor?"

"No, we went into Rockville. You know Val can't stand the Pizza Parlor. She seems to be doing a lot better than she was on Christmas Eve. I think having the holidays over probably helps."

"Why didn't you stop and see me?"

"What?"

"I was at the shop. Why didn't you come in?"

He shrugged and got up from the bed. "Didn't think about it." He disappeared into their bathroom.

Anne felt a knot in her stomach. Was she jealous? Of Val? No... She was confident in Alec's love for her. Of Val's love for her. It was good that Val had played hooky today and enjoyed being with her kids. It was good she and her kids had some of Alec's male input.

But all that time they had spent together... All that time stolen from her...

Suddenly cold, she shoved the calendar to the floor and scooted down under the covers, not even bothering to remove her robe.

∼⌣∼

Alec opened his eyes and stared at the clock. Seven-thirty? He patted the other side of the bed. No Anne. She was probably already gone to work. He hadn't heard a thing. Of course, he'd stayed up extra late, playing Ping-Pong with the kids in the basement.

He went into the bathroom. The jeweler's box caught his eye. He opened it. The diamond earrings were stuck in the little cushion. Strange. She had put them on Christmas morning and not taken them off. She'd said she wouldn't take them off for a long time, if ever.

Why wasn't she wearing them two days later?

Thirty

From her seat in a pew at the back of the chapel, Britte swallowed, collecting herself after a mad dash across the county. She had slipped inside just minutes ahead of the Friday evening ceremony. Gina's parents, Maggie and Reece Philips, were about to renew their vows.

The chapel was the original building of the first Valley Oaks church, built in 1890. It was located in a rural area, not far from Brady's acreage. Although the town never expanded in that direction, the chapel was maintained as a historical site. Tourists stopped by to read about the early Swedish settlers. Occasionally special services were held in it. Once, when Britte was a teenager, the king and queen of Sweden had even visited there.

The old wooden pew was hard, the floor was creaky, and the stained glass windows were drafty. But the Christmas poinsettias, candles, pine garlands, and the organist's classical music erased all of that. It was a beautiful setting, perfect for a small wedding.

Britte smiled to herself. Normally during the winter season, life in Valley Oaks truly was basketball, especially so the week between Christmas and New Year's when both varsity teams participated in tournaments. *Not true this year,* she thought. It was the year of the Wedding with a capital "W".

First thing that morning, instead of mapping game strategy, she was at the other church, rehearsing for Brady and Cal's wedding; then she was in Rockville eating brunch

213

with the wedding party and families. Prompted by numerous comments, she had slipped into the ladies' room and studied her face in the mirror. The bruise on her cheek was down, but it was now a yellowish color. The scrapes were more pink than red. She'd better hit the pharmacy tomorrow and clear Lia's shelf of cosmetics.

After the meal, she drove to Twin Prairie for her girls game. Tanner was in charge of bus rides, allowing her to make it to the chapel in time for the wedding. Now she looked around. Alec and Vic Sutton, cousins of Maggie, were serving as ushers rather than attending the boys tournament. Although the Valley Oaks team wasn't playing that evening, Vic, an assistant coach, and Alec, a player's dad, would normally be in the stands, taking notes on opponents. And Brady—who only missed a boys game if he was out of town—was sitting up front beside his fiancée.

Maggie and Reece had been gracious to invite her entire family. How bizarre that the Olafssons would all be sitting there to witness the momentous event that involved the woman her father had married as a teenager! How bizarre that her brother was marrying that woman's daughter! And...how great was God, the healer of all wounds.

Cal appeared now at the end of the pew. He slid in, exchanging smiles with her. Lia and Chloe were already seated up front. Britte didn't know why Cal was so late. He had been at her last game without Chloe, but surely he would have left before she exited the locker room. Like her, he had been dressed for the wedding. The sight of Cal in the stands wearing a tie had caught her attention, partly because it was so uncharacteristic of him, partly because she was looking in that direction. Behind the team bench. Away from the court.

She shouldn't have been, of course. They had lost again. They had lost three of the five games, and she blamed herself.

She couldn't shake the thought that the same eyes that watched her walk out to the parking lot the night of the attack were watching her throughout the game. She wanted to meet them, to reason with them, to apologize for any hurt she had unintentionally caused, to offer forgiveness. But those eyes remained faceless. Like thornbushes in a ravine, the thought grew wild in her imagination that every pair of eyes watching judged harshly her every word, her every gesture.

Cal nudged her and whispered, "Move over."

She looked sideways. Alec was ushering in a dark-haired woman— Anne?! Britte mouthed a "wow," gave her a thumbs-up sign, and slid along the pew. She'd had her hair cut short, and she looked like a totally different person. She was amazingly attractive, more so or in a different way. Anne's personality was one of those that was just always "there" in a solid sense of the word. She was down-to-earth, practical, straightforward, no-nonsense. Now she appeared the same, but somehow to another degree, another level. It was almost...unsettling.

Kind of like the attack...like Maggie and Reece's wedding...like Cal attending all of her games...like her non-coaching...like falling for Joel Kingsley.

Talk about a bizarre winter!

Anne bit her lip. Maybe the tears wouldn't fall. As if on cue, Alec, sitting beside her in the pew, reached over and covered her hand with his.

At the front of the chapel, Maggie looked absolutely elegant. Her blonde hair, always just so, was curled to perfection. Tiny pearls were scattered throughout it. Her dress was ivory and long; a delicate, crocheted layer covered it. Reece looked almost as elegant in his black tuxedo.

They were speaking their vows, a rendition of the classic ones they had probably spoken almost 31 years ago. They promised again to love, honor, and cherish. A maturity in their tones, however, underscored the phrases. It revealed a depth of profundity, attained only through years of grasping at those abstract terms, of looking back and recognizing that they were no longer abstract. They had crystallized somehow, somewhere along the way.

Hindsight would also reveal...mistakes...when they as a couple had worked against the process.

Anne wondered if she would ever reach that vantage point of hindsight. Seventeen years was not much over just half of Maggie and Reece's time. She wished she could talk with Maggie, but after tomorrow's double wedding, she and Reece would be leaving for their honeymoon.

Maggie's Aunt Lottie was Alec's grandmother. In other words, they were related and therefore had met often through the years. Last month, at Thanksgiving, they had been together. Maggie had shared briefly with her about falling in love again with Reece. It had come after years of growing apart.

At the family Thanksgiving dinner, Anne hadn't a clue what the woman was talking about. Tonight she understood what that meant...that growing apart.

Now, as Maggie and Reece kissed, what Anne could not comprehend was how to bridge the chasm widening itself between her and the man holding her hand.

∽

Shortly after the ceremony, Britte parked her Jeep in the garage. She climbed out, punched the wall-mounted, automatic garage opener, and hurried out under the closing door. Cal had invited her to ride with them to Maggie and Reece's buffet supper in Rockville. His car was parked in her driveway.

As Britte approached it, Lia got out. "You sit up front, Britte."

"Don't be silly. I'll sit with Chloe in the back."

Lia touched her arm and whispered, "Cal needs to talk with you, and he'd rather Chloe didn't hear."

She got in the front seat and turned. "Hi, Chloe. What have you been up to over Christmas break? Oh, wait. Let me guess. You've been doing the same thing I've been doing. Trying on the bridesmaid's dress."

Chloe giggled. "A *million* times."

"I tried mine on a gazillion times. How are the kitties?"

The nine-year-old reached up and patted Cal's shoulder. "Soot and Nutmeg are fine. They like their new house. I made a bed for them in my room at Cal's."

As they sped along the highway, passing headlights lit up Cal's face. He twisted his nose in distaste. Children he was beginning to handle with a smile. Cats were another matter.

Britte laughed. Cal had come a long way, indeed, to fall in love not only with the pharmacist, but with her niece as well. His family was expanding even to cats and parents. His mother, who seldom traveled north in the winter, was in town for the wedding. Lia's parents, who would care for Chloe during the honeymoon, were staying at Lia's.

They made small talk about tomorrow's events and their plans to spend Saturday night in Rockville before flying to Hawaii. Brady and Gina were taking a Caribbean cruise.

As Lia drew Chloe's attention elsewhere, Cal turned toward Britte. "We got him."

She started. "You *what?*"

"It was Jordan's brother, Trevor."

"Trevor! But he's just a freshman!"

"And he's a big kid, with a big mouth and an ax to grind."

Britte felt confused. A child? "How did you find out?"

"I watched him during your games. He was angrier than his dad about his sister not playing. Red-faced, shouting derogatory statements about your..." His voiced faded.

"Coaching. Cal, I hear a lot of it. I know parents disagree with me right and left, and it comes out during games. I didn't know kids would be concerned about it. Obviously, Trevor gets it from his dad."

"Right. His opinion *and* his temper. I pulled Gordon Hughes aside at halftime this afternoon and told him I wanted to talk with his son."

"Oh, Cal. During the game?"

"Sorry. Had a wedding tonight and another one tomorrow. No time to waste." He flashed a grin at her. "The Twin Prairie principal let me use a classroom. Trevor Hughes said he was in bed that Wednesday night after your game. Britte, the kid was lying. His dad hesitated for a split second—he couldn't prove he saw the kid in bed at that time—and then he started blustering, defending him."

"So you don't know for a *fact* that Trevor is responsible?"

"My gut tells me. Almost the same thing as fact."

Britte wasn't sure she agreed with that summary, but she didn't argue. "Now what?"

"I filed a report after the game. Trevor knows I'm on to him. He won't make a wrong move for a long time. If he's tardy or jaywalks or looks cross-eyed at a teacher, I'll be on his case."

What had she just been thinking about Cal handling kids with a smile? Maybe it was only Chloe. "Cal, we're not talking about an older, belligerent teenager. He's a child."

"Who assaulted you. Britte, he's a belligerent teenager in the making. If somebody doesn't crack down on him now, he's headed for disaster. The point is, I don't think you need to worry about him coming after you again. I told him if anything happened to you, I'd nab him so fast it'd make his head spin."

"Oh, Cal. What did Mr. Hughes say to that?"

"He didn't hear me say it."

Thirty-One

Saturday afternoon Joel sat in a back pew, along the side aisle, and wondered what he was doing at a wedding for two couples he had only recently met, people who were not connected in any way, shape, or form to a single one of his high school students or to the school board. He was all for building community relations, but attending a wedding went far beyond that obligation.

Of course he knew why he was there. Not that it made sense, but he knew why. Britte Olafsson. The girl who was never far from his thoughts, whether he was awake or asleep. The girl who shot his orderly routine, his *mind*-set, all to pieces simply by showing up. The girl who had an uncanny knack for breathing life into feelings that were best left *unfelt*.

The headaches had returned. The sleepless nights. The memories. Would Nicky's disappearance in Afghanistan alone have triggered those reactions? He didn't think so. Nicky was military. Joel was military. Feelings were disassociated. He would have prayed for his cousin—as he did now—but it would have been routinely, not emotionally, not spontaneously, not with his own baggage, the baggage he had given to Christ years ago.

Kissing Britte was spontaneous. Kissing Britte broke the dam that had always separated real life from the uncontrollable. Real life was disciplined. Black and white. Two plus two equaled four. Anything outside of that was unnecessary and detrimental. It led to unnecessary complications.

Jesus was real life. Jesus came to earth and did what had to be done. He explained the way, and then He went to the cross. Disciplined. Following orders. Black and white. Two plus two equaled four. And He wasn't married.

Up front now, the pianist, flutist, and violinist paused in their playing, shuffled sheet music, and began a new piece. Pastor Peter walked out of a side door, followed by Cal and Brady, formal in their tuxedos. As the music changed tempo, people stood and turned toward the back of the church. Joel followed suit.

He glanced at the dark-haired little girl starting down the aisle, at Lia on the arm of her father. His gaze was drawn beyond them, to the foyer, to blonde hair glistening in a streak of winter sunlight pouring through a front window.

Now she stood in the doorway, waiting for Lia to reach her destination. While other eyes followed the first bride, Joel could not take his from Britte. Her hair was up, a few loose wisps grazing pearl earrings. From this distance, the bruise on her cheek was only a slight shadow, only conspicuous because he looked for it. She wore a soft-looking red dress and a pearl necklace as well as the sapphire on the gold chain he had given her.

Britte wasn't a classic beauty. She wasn't the current version of cute. In a word, she was striking. Her Nordic height and blonde hair and blue eyes attracted attention. But those were merely physical attributes. Joel knew it was her personality that had prompted him to take a second, longer look. Her character, her dedication, and her focus intrigued him to the point of…to the point of Christmas night.

Now, as she glided down the aisle, she looked every inch a princess. She turned her face his direction, looked directly at him, and smiled.

And why was it a princess would be interested in a murderer?

Biting the inside of her cheek, Britte managed to kept the tears from falling as she stood at the front of the sanctuary alongside Gina. The young woman who would become her sister-in-law in a matter of moments was gorgeous. She wore a simple white satin gown. Her natural beauty didn't require enhancement. Her chocolate brown hair was turned under, tucked behind her ears, adorned with a circle of pearls from which flowed a short, lacy veil that only partially hid the gazillion tiny, satin-covered buttons down the back of the dress.

Between Gina and Lia stood Brady and Cal, both magnificent in black tuxedos with white cummerbunds and white bow ties, their broad shoulders dominating the space. Next, Cal's beautiful bride wore a luscious gown more frilly than Gina's, which suited Lia. Pearl-studded lace covered the satin. A thick, pearly headband secured her jet-black hair off of her face; a pouf of a veil floated out behind it.

Last but not least stood little Chloe, a miniature portrait of Lia, her blunt-cut, thick black hair vivid against her red dress and ivory skin. At the moment she looked uncertain, probably concerned about when to take her aunt's bouquet, when to hand it back, when to turn.

Britte caught her eye and winked. The girl rewarded her with a smile.

There was a movement near the piano. Isabel was standing now to sing. Unable to get away from her new job in Chicago, she hadn't arrived until sometime last night with Tony. She had stayed at Lia's, he at Cal's.

Britte swallowed. The moment was too much. Brady...her brother and childhood friend. While their sister played with dolls, Britte tagged after him, getting under his feet when he shot baskets. Today he was marrying his perfect match. Then there was Cal, in many ways another brother to her, grown into a man and marrying a lovely woman. Gina and Lia...two cherished new friends marrying the old sports buddies. And Joel...the mystery, sitting out there, the object of her anticipation. Would they go through the buffet line and sit together at the reception? Would they dance again? And now Isabel, the dear friend she missed so...adding the final, glowing touch with her incomparable voice.

Britte resumed biting the inside of her cheek.

~

In the sun-drenched church foyer, at the end of the receiving line, Britte stood next to Brady. The couples were greeting friends and family before the photo session, which promised to be long given the fact that there were two wedding parties involved.

During a lull in the activity, Brady said to her and Gina, "Do you know how you can tell if the wedding is in the Midwest?"

Britte groaned. "Gina, didn't you make him promise no Midwest jokes today?"

She giggled and shook her head. Evidently the woman was in love. Who else would so graciously endure his sappy humor?

Brady grinned. "When it's a *double* wedding and *still* you know every single person in the crowd."

The newlyweds laughed while Britte shook her head. Her brother did not know every single person in the crowd. Not even close. He didn't know Lia's friends from Chicago.

Gina didn't have any out-of-town friends, which saddened Britte. Naturally, Valley Oaks was a little far for Californians, but in recent months Gina told how her entire life revolved around her veterinary work at a wildlife preserve. When that job went haywire, her friends, who were all work-related, grew distant. On the other hand, she had more Valley Oaks relatives than they did. Between them and the Olafssons, she had easily been drawn into a loving circle.

Joel approached, his height making him visible over a group of Gina's cousins now passing. Britte tried to ignore the first notes of that brass band warming up somewhere in the vicinity of her heart.

At last he reached her. He grasped her outstretched hand in both of his, and then, in the manner of old friends, he leaned toward her until his cheek touched hers. "Hey, Princess," he whispered in her ear.

Speechless. Again!

He looked her in the eye, still holding her hand between both of his. There was warmth in his gaze, but he didn't smile. He squeezed her hand. "I have to go see my aunt and uncle. In Chicago."

"Oh, Joel. Your cousin?"

"No word yet. They need moral support. I'm sorry. I'll miss the reception."

"Of course." *It couldn't wait a few more hours?* No. She refused to whine. She was 29 years old. She would not whine. She would not ask for more than he was willing to give. "Thank you for coming to the wedding. I know Brady appreciated it."

He let go of her hand. "I'll see you Tuesday."

"Bright and early, Mr. Kingsley."

Alec steered little Mandy around the dance floor to the instrumental version of a vaguely familiar, slow tune. "Mind if we change partners, honey?"

His little dark-haired replica of Anne smiled up at him. "Oh, Daddy, you're not asking me to dance with my *brother!*"

"Hey, he's all dressed up and behaving like a human being tonight. And I want to dance with Mommy."

Mandy giggled. "All right."

He swung her between other couples and neared Anne dancing with their son. "Drew. Your sister wants to dance with you."

He smiled, kissed his mother's cheek, and held his arms out for Mandy.

Laughing, Alec caught Anne in his.

"Hey, mister."

"Hey yourself, sweetheart. What's gotten into Drew? He even danced with Grandma Lottie without my prompting."

She smiled. "He's showing off. Have you noticed that pretty girl over there? The blonde in the sparkly dress?" She tilted her head.

Alec turned that direction. "Ahh, that explains that. Who is she?"

"A distant Olafsson. Her family lives over in the Quad-Cities."

He smiled at her. "Having a good time?"

"Great time. We haven't had a family outing like this since I can't remember when. Our kids don't have one personal friend here. We should regularly check out receptions at this hotel and invite ourselves in. It's such a treat to see all three kids interacting with others."

"Even strange girls in sparkly dresses?" He winked.

"Even that. Not counting the wrestling match with Britte, he's growing up, isn't he?"

"He certainly is. I like our kids, Annie."

"I do, too. I was thinking we could let them take care of each other while we go out for dinner tomorrow night."

"New Year's Eve?" Every place would be crowded and noisy, impossible to get a reservation. "We said we'd chaperone the youth group's all-night party."

"That doesn't start until 8:30. We could meet Drew and Amy there after they take Mandy over to Chloe's."

"Sounds complicated. And then we'd have to stay up all night after a big dinner. You look sensational tonight, by the way."

She leaned into him, placing her chin against his shoulder. "Thanks."

"What is this song?"

For a moment she was quiet. "Something or other 'Melody.' Something about God speed your love to me."

"That's it!" He hummed a few bars, and then he sang the one line he knew, "Are you still mine?"

"If you take me out tomorrow night."

He chuckled softly in her ear. He'd always loved her sense of humor.

⌒

Late Saturday night after the reception, Britte and Isabel sat on the carpet amidst pillows in front of the fireplace in Britte's living room. The gas log emitted more glow than heat, but it added a cozy ambience along with the Christmas tree's twinkle lights. They wore flannel pajamas and munched from a large bowl of popcorn.

"Oh, Britte." Isabel's caramel eyes and auburn hair shone in the soft light. "It was so great seeing everyone. I miss living here. Sort of." She winked.

"Sort of. I take it Tony has something to do with the 'sort of' remark?"

"Whatever gave you that idea?" She laughed. "It's so kind of your parents to let him stay at the farm."

"It's so kind of him not to mind. With Lia's parents and Chloe staying at your old house and Cal's mom at his place, there wasn't much of a choice. There's enough space for you out there, too, you know, but I'm glad you're here instead."

"Of course you are." Isabel raised an arm, bending it at the elbow and placing a fist against her forehead. "I'm well known for my bodyguard prowess."

Britte laughed. "Thank goodness Cal took care of that need before he left town."

"Good old Cal, the cop. I never would have imagined him romantic enough to plan a honeymoon in Hawaii."

"I was impressed. It was as good as Brady's surprise Caribbean cruise."

"Do you think they did their planning together?"

"You know they did, Isabel. Those two talk about everything. So which honeymoon would you prefer?"

"Mmm, I'd probably choose Mexico." Isabel smiled. "Tony would like that."

"Is it serious, then?"

"It's...progressing. Beautifully progressing, step-by-step. He's growing in his faith. We see each other about three times a week. He's attentive, but not pushy. In a way, we picked up where we left off in college, but in another way everything between us is brand new."

Britte's throat felt dry. "I'm happy for you. And envious."

Isabel reached over and patted her arm. "But we know how to be single, right, Britte?"

"Right. Jesus is with me, and no human could replace Him or love me like He does. He keeps me from being unbearably lonesome. I think I'm feeling the envy because of all the wedding stuff and— Oh, I don't want to go there."

"Joel Kingsley." It was a statement.

Britte stared at her.

"It showed."

"It did not."

"It did."

"It couldn't have. He wasn't even at the reception."

"Things were sizzling in the receiving line."

"No way."

Isabel smiled apologetically. "'Fraid so. And I know it's not my imagination, else you wouldn't be blushing right now. So, 'fess up. What have I missed in five short weeks?"

"Adrenaline and Christmas magic."

"Huh?"

"Isabel, I think it's *my* imagination. I mean, I thought something clicked between us. I finally admitted that I was— had been—attracted to him." She relayed the details of the confrontation in Joel's office, of being together Christmas Eve and Christmas Day. "It was probably just because we spent so much time together. We were both alone. I needed a knight in shining armor. He was available. He kissed me Christmas night, outside in one of those wondrous snow-falls. We kissed a few times." She stretched out on her back, on the floor, and groaned loudly. "And now he's out of town. Legitimate excuse, but the timing isn't."

"Fire-breathing coach wants her man *right* now."

"Isabel!"

"Well, my goodness, Britte. It sounds as if things just started developing about a *week* ago. Give it some time."

"I saw it in his face. Things aren't going anywhere. There's something else going on in his life."

"Tell me about him."

Britte sat up. "He's whipped the school back into shape. The community at large still isn't sure about him. He steps on toes, but he gets results. I don't think there's marijuana exchanging hands in the rest room anymore."

Isabel wrinkled her nose. "I keep hoping Valley Oaks is innocent. Wasn't Joel in the military?"

"Marines, for eight years. He's lived all over the world. He doesn't talk much about it." They exchanged a look. "He's old enough for Desert Storm."

"Bingo."

"What do you mean?"

"My oldest brother was there, with the army. He doesn't sleep well. And he doesn't talk much about it."

Britte felt suddenly tired, as if the plug had just been pulled on her reservoir of energy. "Well, it doesn't matter. He's like the other principals. He won't be around long."

"But it does matter. You care about him, don't you?"

She fingered the necklace chain and smiled softly. "I admire him. I wish he would stay. And...at some point in every conversation with him, I'm at a loss for words."

Isabel howled with laughter. "That never happens!"

"Exactly."

"Then don't give up so easily. If he's lived all over the world, he's probably got some great ideas for a honeymoon destination!"

Thirty-Two

Anne eyed Alec over the large menu. He was fidgeting like a six-year-old. But then, that was Alec's way whenever his meticulously planned agenda was disrupted. He thought she'd been teasing about New Year's Eve dinner out, just the two of them, before chaperoning the church youth lock-in at the Community Center. Now, admitting that his discomfort might not go away, she wondered if she should have pushed for the date. After all the energy poured into prepping the kids—laundry, packing, timetable—and calling a long list of restaurants, she wasn't so sure she wanted to be there either.

But something had driven her to force the issue of spending time alone together. Some innate sense said that healthy marriages required maintenance. Theirs was past due for an overhaul.

"Pasta will put me to sleep," Alec grumped.

"So have the antipasto salad." She winked at him. The Italian Village in Rockville was the only place that could squeeze them in before ten o'clock. Well, not counting the Rib House in Valley Oaks. The choice had come down to cozy booths or an open room of tables peopled with acquaintances.

"Their ravioli is pretty good. Maybe I can grab some court time with one of the other dads and run it off." After placing their orders, he pulled out his pocket calendar.

"Alec, this is supposed to be a date. As in *romance*."

"But we only have an hour, and then we have to spend the night with a bunch of teenagers."

"So? Isn't a little romance better than none?"

He smiled, his cinnamon eyes crinkling. "How about a little practical catch-up talk about our life? Isn't that romantic?"

She glanced around the dining room, fighting the sense that she was sinking in mire.

"Once I go back to the office on Tuesday and we're both working full-time—"

"I'm part-time. The holidays are over. No more Saturdays for me, and I can be home soon after the girls get there."

"Then there's basketball."

"Only four more weeks. Well, not counting assisting Britte at regionals."

"You'll go beyond that tournament, don't you think?"

"Probably." She did not want to talk about Britte and basketball tonight.

The waiter slid salads before them.

"Anne, your financial contribution is really helping."

"It must be. I didn't hear you complaining about the prices here."

He reached over and squeezed her hand. "I'm sorry I get so overdone about money."

"I'm glad I can help, but the house is a pit."

"I don't even notice it."

"So you're saying that when I kept things neat and orderly, it didn't matter?"

He squinted, a sheepish look crossing his face. "No. I just didn't want to lay a guilt trip on you. Truthfully? The house is a pit, and the schedules are driving me bananas. I don't know how you did it all."

"Thank you."

"Annie, I always appreciated what you did, even though I didn't always tell you."

"I know, but it's good to hear it now and then. Well, the tough stuff hasn't even started yet. There are some school holidays coming up. Martin Luther King Jr. Day, teachers institute, Lincoln's birthday, Casimir Pulaski Day, etcetera. I don't like the thought of leaving the kids alone."

He eyed the calendar laying open on the table beside his salad plate. "The first one looks like Monday, the fifteenth. I'll take that day off. I'm sure the office can get along without me, considering my duties haven't changed for January. Or February, for that matter."

She heard the disappointment in his voice. "Alec, are you going to be all right with work?"

"You mean, will I be obnoxious and vocal about this grudge I have?"

She smiled. "That's putting it succinctly."

"I'll be civil. No, I want to be more than civil, more than just grin and bear it. I have to believe that God has a reason for this."

"We know He does. Maybe it's me working."

"But that's temporary. Won't the lady with the baby be back after six weeks?"

"Eight. But you know how new mommies are. I think she's able to stay home, like I was. She may choose that." She smiled. "She brought the baby in on Friday. She loves being at home, I could tell."

"Just like you did, huh? Once we get over this financial hump, we shouldn't need your paycheck. Things will even out again. I'll get that car for Drew next week. He'll be getting a job after the season; he can help out with gas and insurance."

"Alec, I like working."

"Maybe Lia could have you come in more often at the pharmacy."

Anne shook her head. "Her new assistant runs circles around what Dot used to do. And Chelsea Chandler is there every day. What I'm saying is, I *like* working at the art store."

"But you liked being at home."

"I did, but now I've smelled the paints again. Alec, you pushed me into this—"

"I pushed you? You went and applied for a job. It was a mutual decision."

"Well, so to speak, mister. According to you, our future was pretty bleak. I thought we could get by, but I trusted your judgment over mine because I don't pay too close attention to our finances. We both know you're smarter than I am in that area. The point is, honey, I'm glad it happened." She smiled. "I want to paint again. Why are you looking at me like that?"

He shook his head slightly. "I keep looking for Annie, but this stranger keeps popping up."

"And? Do you like her?"

"I don't know her."

"Do you like my hair?"

"I, uh, I'm getting used to it."

"Mandy is so much like you."

"How's that?"

"If it's not written in her little calendar, it's not supposed to happen." She reached over and covered his hand with hers. "Alec, write this down. Your wife is sprouting wings."

Alec drove them home from Rockville while Anne snoozed. She had eaten a plateful of fettuccine Alfredo as well as tiramisu. At least that side of her was familiar, grabbing the moment and squeezing everything she could from it. If the two of them were having dinner at a restaurant on New Year's Eve, then by golly it was a special one and should be treated as such, no matter what the next moment was scheduled to bring, according to the calendar.

Her calendar remarks annoyed him. It was her polite way of telling him to deal with it. He didn't like to be told to deal with it. He'd rather negotiate.

Take her working, for example. Shouldn't they decide together whether or not, say next month, it'd be best if she cut back her work hours? Evidently she wasn't planning on quitting the art store. He didn't know how long he could put up with unmatched socks, a coffee pot hidden behind stacks of dirty dishes, routinely running out of bread and milk and laundered shorts. And all this while he and the kids were on vacation!

He'd seen other wives sprout wings. They were the divorced women in his office, the ones with fancy haircuts who couldn't care less if hubby's socks were folded together according to style and color.

This wasn't what God intended for them, was it?

Thirty-Three

Joel pulled his car alongside a snowbank-covered curb on Second Avenue, braked, and turned off the headlights. Britte's house was just across the street. Her curtains were drawn against the night, but lamplight shown through from her living room window.

He reminded himself of a lovesick teenager sitting there outside a girl's home with the engine running, undecided about his next move. It was after eight o'clock, Monday night. On his way home from Chicago, he had entered Valley Oaks and turned right instead of left, which put him at Britte's instead of his condo.

It had been a rough two days with his aunt and uncle... and Sam. Sam more so than his family.

Sam was 62, but his sparse gray hair and hunched back gave him the appearance of at least 70 years. He was a husband, a father and grandfather, an ex-Marine, a Vietnam vet. In his spare time he hung out at the VA Hospital. His "Volunteer" name tag gave him the necessary official capacity. Twenty minutes after meeting the guy, the white slash of a scar down his right cheek faded from view, as did his deformed shoulders. In their imperfect place Jesus appeared, dispensing grace and mercy, wisdom and forgiveness.

Yesterday Joel had complained to him about the recurring headaches and sleeplessness.

"What's her name?" he had asked.

"I told you about Nicky."

235

"It's more, Joel. I know you. You're always protecting that heart of yours."

"Britte. Britte Olafsson."

The old man had smiled.

"And it's Jesus who has my heart. That's what you taught me."

"Aw, son, that doesn't mean you disengage your emotions. I've told you that time and time again."

"Engaging means headaches, and so on and so forth."

"What's your point?"

"I can't function that way. I can't do the work He's given me to do."

Sam had studied his face for long moments, his expression unreadable. "This Britte may be the only way you'll get rid of the headaches and so on and so forth." He reached over and patted Joel's cheek. "I can't tell you how. When it's time, you'll know. Come on. Let's go do my rounds."

When it's time, I'll know what?

Joel watched her house as if it would give him an answer, but he reminded himself that he knew better.

"Lord, I feel something for this girl. This woman. I don't know what to do with it. I know, though, what I can't do with it. I can't function at 100 percent. That aside, she's a hometown girl. I don't know how long I'll be here. There's no future in a relationship, not that we can even pursue one in the first place. It'd be another community black mark against me if I took her to dinner. And so I guess I'm asking that You'd help me...distance myself. And get back to work."

He should get out and knock on her door and nip it in the bud right now, tonight. But they would be in her house and he would look into those blue eyes and maybe he would change his mind. If he went through with it, there was a chance she would be upset and explode like some emotional land mine. He would lose the night. He couldn't afford to lose another one.

No, tomorrow was better. At school. She'd be less likely to get distraught in public. He wouldn't be tempted to hold her, to kiss her.

There. It was settled. He turned on his headlights and pushed the gearshift into drive.

Christmas break had been abnormally short due to some school-year schedule changes. On Tuesday, the first day back, Britte wasn't sure she was ready. She walked across the commons, attaché bag in hand, unzipping her jacket and pretending her two bites of cereal weren't rumbling in her stomach. It was early, but not her usual early. Other teachers were in the building. Through the glass walls of the office, she could see Lynnie...and Joel.

Britte had struggled this morning. Correction. The struggle began yesterday as she put away Christmas things and prepared to return to routine life. About 2 A.M. the realization struck her that she was afraid. That's all there was to it. Fear was not her style, and it certainly wasn't her Lord's style.

At least she had fallen asleep after that. Recognizing the problem, admitting it, and praying about it was half the battle. The other half, of course, was walking into the school.

Joel spotted her now. He raised a hand in greeting, all the while conversing with Lynnie.

Okay. Back to routine in *that* department...the Joel-mystery department. Maybe Christmas didn't happen.

She walked with a purposeful step down the hallway toward her classroom. Ethan suddenly appeared at the intersection with the other hall. For a split moment, her breath stopped, and then it rushed back into her lungs.

"Hey, Britte. Welcome back."

She swallowed. "Thanks. How was Colorado?"

He fell into step beside her. "Great. Super skiing. How was the wedding?"

"Great. Beautiful. Tearful. Fun." She unlocked her classroom door and hesitated. The last time she was inside, she couldn't string three words together.

Ethan reached around her and pulled open the door. "Welcome back," he repeated.

She went inside and turned on the lights.

"You doing okay?"

She chuckled weakly. "Yes and no. Cal thinks Jordan's little brother was responsible. He's a freshman."

"You're kidding."

She shook her head and dropped her things onto her desk.

"Your face looks fine. Changing subjects, how'd the tournament go?"

"Not so good. Two-three." She picked up a sheet of paper and began reading notes that the substitute teacher had written for her.

"Hey, Britte."

She looked up. "What?"

"Things will get better. Okay?"

"Sure." She didn't bother to tell him the rest of the story.

There was a knock on the open door. She turned and saw Joel standing there.

"Morning, Britte. Ethan. Just checking in. You all right, Miss O?"

"I'll be a lot better once people stop asking me that."

The men exchanged a look, and Ethan said, "Sounds like she's back to normal."

"That it does. See you later." He ducked back out into the hall.

Had that man really kissed her eight days ago? Maybe there wasn't any rest of the story to tell.

⌒

He owed her an explanation. Of some sort.

Joel walked across the commons, Britte's coaching voice nearly at full volume even through the closed gym doors. He discreetly opened one wide enough to slip inside and sat on the nearest bleacher.

Her back to him, she gathered the panting girls around her, like a hen with her chicks. They all sat on the floor, Britte along with them. He couldn't decipher what she was saying in low tones. The back of her red T-shirt was dark, damp with perspiration. She must have scrimmaged with the team. Earlier he had noticed Anne leave with her sophomores, evidently cutting her practice short in order to get to the evening's boys game on time in another town.

Britte dismissed the girls now, turned, and spotted him. She didn't hurry over.

The girls trailed out past him, calling greetings. When the door closed on the last one, he joined Britte halfway down the stretch of bleachers where she was changing her shoes, one athletic pair for another.

"Rough practice?"

She glanced up. "You know it. First day of the new year is rough on all of us. I'm surprised the boys have a game tonight." She stood and pulled on her jacket.

"Glitch in the scheduling system. How did your day go?"

"It went." She blinked and her expression softened in a subtle way. "Sorry. Fire-breathing coach converts to civil teacher. The day went well. It's good to be back. How was your weekend? Any word on your cousin?"

"No, which is good news. If he'd been hurt or captured, we would have heard, but try telling that to his mother."

"I can't imagine. Did you put your mother through that?"

"All the Kingsley women have been put through that. Joining the Marines is genetic. My dad served, my younger brother served. My uncle, Nicky's dad, was in 'Nam. My grandfather was in World War II. Another cousin in Bosnia."

"And you? Besides living all over the world?"

His eight-year stint had taken him to U.S. embassies in Latin America and Europe. And... "The Persian Gulf."

"During Desert Storm?"

He nodded.

"I'm sorry."

He forced himself to meet those eyes now brimming with compassion. "It's life. Are you going to the game?"

"Of course. You? Of course you are. You're wearing your royal blue shirt and 'new' yellow tie."

"Gotta keep stacking up those way-cool points with the kids."

"Oh, you're set there, Mr. Kingsley."

Unfortunately, the student population didn't vote on renewing contracts. "Walk you to your car?"

A brief smile played at her lips. "Thanks."

They left the gym and headed across the commons. "Britte, if you were a guy, I'd just casually suggest we ride together to the game."

"Likewise if you were a woman."

They were treading softly, trying to avoid tripping the land mine. He followed her through the doors to the parking lot. "Too many eyes are watching right now. I don't think it's going to work."

She pointed her key chain at the car and popped the locks. "Oh, I agree. Too many eyes, too many what-ifs. Unnecessary complications."

He opened the car door for her.

She threw in her attaché and slid behind the wheel. "Thank you, Mr. Knight."

"You're welcome. Princess."

She gave him a thumbs-up as he shut the door.

Oblivious to the cold, he watched her drive away. Good. No explosion. They'd reached an agreement on their nonrelationship without tripping any land mines.

Thirty-Four

Britte and Anne hurried across the cold, vacant parking lot Saturday night.

Apparently vacant, Britte mentally corrected the perception. Even with the restored spotlight brightening the far corners, it might not be totally vacant.

"Britte, you're coaching like the guys." Anne's voice was low.

"Thanks! I take that as a compliment."

Anne stopped and eyed her over the hood of the Jeep. "It wasn't meant to be one."

Opening the car door, she motioned for her friend to climb inside, too. Britte started the engine. "Why not? The male coaches get kudos for playing to win. We're going to super-sectionals this year. This is how we do it. We don't play Jordan and Haley and Tasha. Michaela, Janine, and Katie help *part-time*."

"Britte!" Anne exploded. "That is not your style! You're alienating all of them!"

"Who? The parents? I know that, but they're not the team. The girls want to win. They're scrimmaging harder than ever because they're seeing the results of teamwork." Which Anne didn't know about because of her work schedule, but Britte didn't say so. "We just won our third game this week. Who's complaining? Besides Gordon and Trevor Hughes?"

Her friend was silent for a moment, her expression lost in the shadows. "I'm complaining."

"Annie," she implored.

"Listen, Britte. The guys pretend they're professional ball players. Drew plays because he's talented, but a lot of those not playing, especially the seniors, are having their self-confidence undercut. Meanwhile, the hotshots—and Drew's included—think they're headed for the Bulls. The U of I at the least. It's ridiculous."

"Of course it's ridiculous. It's the guys."

Anne didn't laugh at their inside joke. "The girls don't care about playing professional ball or Big Ten. What happened to your threefold philosophy?"

"It hasn't changed. They're learning about basketball, teamwork, and inner strength."

"More inner strength than you can imagine sitting on that bench. You never sat on the bench in high school or college."

Britte ignored the charge and flipped the heater fan to high. "What should I do with this gift of a team I've been handed? Just let it slide into oblivion?"

"You're a good coach because you care about the girls as individuals." Her tone softened. "I'm just asking you not to lose sight of that. All right?"

The conversation didn't resemble any they'd ever had through the years. Not that they'd ever had a season like this one. "All right."

Anne reached over and touched her arm. "Nothing personal. You know I love you like a little sister. What's up with Joel?"

Miffed at Anne's accusation, it took her a moment to jump subjects. "Joel? Oh, adrenaline and Christmas magic. And they're both past tense."

"What happened?"

She shrugged. "We have separate lives. Valley Oaks is between them. Who knows? Cupid's on vacation."

"Oh, Britte. I'm sorry."

"Nothing to be sorry about. It just didn't...pan out."

"But you still care about him."

"Why would you say that?"

"Because you still wear that necklace. Because Christmas didn't just happen out of the blue. Emotions led up to it. Situations led up to it. All that doesn't go away at the drop of a hat. You're not running away, are you?"

Britte fingered the chain at her throat. "There's nothing to run from."

Alec sat on the bed folding laundry, matching socks, waiting for Anne to come home after the Saturday night girls game. The boys had played out of town that afternoon. He and Anne had driven separately to watch Drew play, giving Anne plenty of time to return to Valley Oaks to coach her own team. Complex, but routine for the Suttons.

It was now after 10:00. Drew had permission to stay out until 11:00. Mandy was giggling in her room with Chloe, who was spending the night. Amy was at a slumber party.

Yesterday morning the pastor had resumed the men's Friday morning Bible study. Alec had caught Peter for a few moments afterward and given him a nutshell version of the New Year's Eve conversation with Anne and his take on it.

"Alec," Peter had said, "you're really not saying that socks are all that important."

"Okay. What is it I'm saying?"

"I mean, that would be pretty superficial. The point is, you miss the essence of you and your wife. You're losing track of each other. This didn't just happen since she started working. Changes come, buddy, and you need to know what's going on in Anne's heart. Where have you been?"

Peter wasn't much older than Alec, but he carried an air of authority underscored by his deep voice and wild red hair. "You've been concerned with Alec Sutton getting and then not getting a promotion. You've been concerned with kids, racquetball, committees, and the school board."

"Just give it to me straight, big guy."

Peter laughed and lightly slapped his shoulder. "Date night. Get one on the calendar."

The new routine of life with Anne working had begun this week, and it had produced more stress than anticipated. Tuesday, a neighbor's phone call to Alec at the office alerted him to the fact that the dogs hadn't been tied up. It took an hour to resolve that issue. Wednesday, he and Drew picked up the car he purchased from a coworker; Drew had promptly put it in the ditch on his first foray into the countryside. No harm done, if he didn't count time, energy, and panic. And those were just the tip of the iceberg.

Now he could hear Anne down the hall, talking to the girls. He put away his socks.

"Alec! You folded the clothes." She closed the door behind her.

"Least I could do. You washed them."

She brushed a kiss on his cheek as she passed on her way to their bathroom. "Ah, one of the perks of the career woman."

He considered offering to fold clothes even if she didn't work. Make that didn't work outside the home. Tucking other laundry into drawers, he called out, "How was your game?"

"We won, 54 to 48! I really like this sophomore group. Have I said that before?" She laughed. "Varsity won, too."

He puffed pillows, climbed into bed, and leaned back against them. "How's Britte doing?"

"Don't get me started. She's coaching like Vic and the others."

His brother Vic coached the freshmen boys. "What's wrong with that?"

She peered through the open doorway, a toothbrush in her mouth, her eyes wide in disbelief.

He grinned. "Just kidding."

She turned away.

He knew her opinion, that the men were too serious about high school athletics. That she and Britte balanced things more appropriately and had more fun in the process. He tended to agree with her, although he was tremendously enjoying Drew's experience.

A few moments later Anne climbed into bed beside him and snuggled under his arm. "I am so tired. Alec. The calendar is in bed with us."

"I know. I brought it from the kitchen. I was thinking we ought to schedule a weekly date night."

"Oh? What brought this on?"

"I miss us."

She went still beside him. "Since when?"

"Since...our new schedule."

"You mean since you went back to work and I'm not here to take care of your socks."

"Annie, it started before that, and I'm just now recognizing the fact."

She remained quiet for a long moment. "I've been missing us for some time."

"Why didn't you tell me?"

"I think I've been trying. Remember Thanksgiving weekend?" Her voice was a monotone. "I wanted us to go to the Pizza Parlor, but you didn't want to. You didn't want to go out New Year's Eve. Those weren't the only times. I've suggested

Chicago without the church council; I've suggested other outings for the two of us."

"I'm sorry. Men are slower at catching on to this sort of thing."

"Men tend to be more controlling. This requires spontaneity, Alec. I mean, look at that calendar. Six out of seven nights we have something going."

"There's that seventh night." The school board had made it a policy that no school extracurricular activities should take place on Thursday nights.

"If it's not my monthly book club that night, we catch up on whatever. We'll especially be doing that now. And look at next Thursday." She pointed at the calendar. "It's your office Christmas party. The one without spouses."

"I have to go, otherwise I don't look like a team player. Annie, we can fit us in *somewhere*."

"You schedule it. Let me know where and when. I'll try to be there. Goodnight." She slid down under the covers and turned her back to him.

"You haven't worn your red silk nightie for a while."

She rolled over and looked up at him. "I didn't think you'd noticed."

Truthfully? He hadn't, not until tonight.

She saw it on his face. "You hadn't. I did wear it that night I got my hair cut. But you had dinner with Val and didn't stop in to see me at the shop."

And then he played Ping-Pong with the kids, and the next morning she hadn't worn her diamond earrings.

"That's when I realized I was missing us." She yawned and rolled back over. "I love you, Alec, but I am not Superwoman. 'Night."

He stared at her back, bombarded with emotions, no coherent words coming to mind.

What had he done? How could he have missed the signals? Annie was his best friend. Their marriage was a joint venture. They were each other's backup, each other's sounding board, each other's right hand. He had never belittled her staying home. They had both agreed on that and what it would mean to their lifestyle. He lost sight of God's provision, angry at not being promoted. She was right. He had pushed her. His anxiety had pushed her. She applied for a job to please him, to help him out.

And it had backfired in his face.

Already now her breathing was in sleep mode. Shouldn't she be angry at him? Shouldn't she be upset? Shouldn't the gray be blotted from her eyes? Shouldn't she be fussing at him?

Well, *he* was angry. Angry that she had stuck with a course of action that pulled her away from him and the children.

No, not angry. Scared was the word.

⁓

Anne awoke with a start. The red dial on the clock said 1:20.

What was it?

The conversation with Britte. The conversation with Alec. *Have a conversation with Me.*

It was more a mental nudge than a thought.

Dream remnants came back then. In it, she had been scurrying around the house, from the basement to the attic, unplugging electrical cords from every single socket.

Talking with Britte earlier tonight, she had sensed her friend was shutting down, pulling away from the girls, from Joel. Anne hadn't been able to put it into words, but now she realized that Britte wasn't living from that deeper level, from her heart.

And how about Anne, herself? Unplugging. Shutting down. Telling Alec in essence that yes, she missed their oneness, but she had dealt with it and moved on. It was their life at this point in time.

"Oh, Lord, it's how Britte and I cope. If we had to feel the pain, we'd crawl off into a corner and just shrivel up."

For a time she lay there, dry-eyed, wondering how Val was doing.

Thirty-Five

"Miss Olafsson, the wheels seem to be falling off."

Britte tapped a pencil on top of her desk pad and stared at Janine Larson's father. He sat across from her in a student desk pulled over for the occasion. The occasion being a parent-coach conference early Monday morning. "Can you be more specific, Mr. Larson? The way I see it, we won three games last week."

"You've got a solid bench, but for the majority of the time you only played your starters." He held up a hand. He was a tall, soft-spoken accountant with thick brown hair and horn-rimmed glasses. "I'm not talking about playing time for Janine."

"I know you're not."

"The wheels fell off during the Christmas tournament. They will again if you keep pushing those same five to perform without consistent help from the bench."

She listened to him talk strategy, things she knew, things she considered, some things she even was doing. His daughter was one of her seniors, a girl who admitted to Britte that she was *not* serious about the game and only played to support her friends.

Britte noticed Mr. Larson was avoiding eye contact. Strange.

"What's your response then, Miss Olafsson?"

"My response?" She thought she'd been responding throughout the dialogue. "I'm doing my best. I'll continue to do my best."

Thirty minutes after the man left, Joel entered. "Morning, Britte."

"Good morning, Joel." She remained seated behind her desk, wishing she could nonchalantly stand and lean against it. Evidently their mutual agreement to disengage—from adrenaline and Christmas magic?—hadn't yet reached her leg muscles. Vocal cords were a bit slow, too, but her heart knew better and would supply the determination to not look back at what might have been.

Joel sat in the student desk Mr. Larson had vacated, but he didn't speak. His shoulders hunched.

She gave him a thumbs-up. "Nice royal blue sweater for tonight's game."

"Rah rah for the girls." He smiled, but it was in a distracted way, not reaching his eyes. "I mean ladies."

"What's up?" The first bell would ring in a few minutes.

"Mr. Larson. He's filing an official complaint against you to the school board."

She dropped her pencil on the desk, leaned back in the chair, and folded her arms. "It certainly has been quite a season. Did he say why, exactly?"

"Didn't he talk to you?"

"Yes."

"Supposedly he told you."

Her face felt flushed. With great effort, she searched her muddled thoughts for the gist of the man's conversation. "Basically, I suppose he said I'm an incompetent coach." She laughed mirthlessly. "That would be a reason enough to complain. I honestly didn't take him seriously because his examples were weak."

"I agree."

"About which? That I'm incompetent or his examples?"

"Britte." His voice soothed. "He doesn't have a leg to stand on."

"Why now? Why not leave it until it's time to renew my contract?"

"They—"

"*They?* They who?"

"Larson, Hughes, and Fleming. They want your attention. They want you to ask for help coaching at tournament time."

Britte squeezed her arms more tightly across her midsection, fighting the urge to pick something up from the desk and throw it. "This will disrupt everything. The girls will find out."

"The whole town will find out. I'm sorry, Britte. I did what I could to stall him, but I think he's going through with it." The first bell rang and Joel stood. "I'd better go." He moved toward the door. "We'll talk later."

"Joel!"

He stopped near the door and looked back.

The sound of lockers banging open and shut resounded from the hallway, but she had to know. "Are you backing me on this?"

It took him only a split second to recross the room. He leaned across her desk, his hands on the blotter. "Listen, I know I backed off. I backed off on...us. That was—"

"Miss O!" a voice shouted from the doorway.

Joel snapped his head around and pointed. "Out! And shut the door, Shawn." It was his best General's voice. "*No* one is to come in here until I leave."

"Yes, sir." The boy did as he was told.

"Britte." Joel paused, his eyes never straying now from hers, his lips pressed together as if he fought for control. "That...that backing off was personal, born out of a need I cannot begin to explain to you." His voice had softened, but it was still the determined General's. "This is different. You're on my team, and I don't hang team members out to dry. I will not let you down. Understood?"

"What am I supposed to do?" Frustration pushed her own voice up an octave. Frustration? Try anger. Try fear.

"Britte."

No, try jumping out of an airplane without a parachute because that was exactly what this felt like.

"Britte! Look at me."

Still frozen in position gripping her arms, she blinked. Hadn't she been looking at him?

"You're zoning out on me. Hey, all you have to do is take care of your team. Do what you know how to do. We're rooting for you. All right?"

He was too close. She saw where he had nicked himself shaving this morning. She saw the green flecks in his hazel eyes and smelled the faint scent of his spicy cologne. He was confusing things, but she realized he wasn't leaving until she responded coherently. Reining in her scattered thoughts, she nodded. "All right."

"Good." His gaze lingered for a moment on her, and then he was crossing the room. "I'll let the troops in. Call if you need anything." And he was gone.

She bit her lip and blinked back angry tears. He had said they were rooting for her. Who was rooting for her? Not the team parents. Not Anne. Not Joel, not really. She wanted him to hold her. He hadn't even touched her arm in the way any encouraging friend would.

"Heavenly Father," she whispered, "what do You want from me?"

Thirty-Six

Late Thursday afternoon, Alec stepped into Manning's Gallery and Art Supply shop. The door gently swished shut behind him, an overhead bell tinkling in its wake. Muted voices came through an open door behind a counter, but no one was in sight.

He looked around. It was like stepping into some futuristic setting. He couldn't relate to a thing he saw, and the scents nearly gagged him. This was Anne's world.

She emerged now from what looked like an office door, laughter subsiding in her voice. "May I help—Alec! What are you doing here?"

"Hi." He walked over to the counter, spreading his arms, palms up. "Date night."

Her eyebrows scrunched together. "It's your office Christmas party night."

"I know. The one with no spouses or friends. I'm skipping it. I have more important things to do." He smiled. "You said to let you know where and when. This is it, sweetheart."

A man appeared behind Anne, who still stood in front of the office doorway. "Is this Alec?"

Anne moved aside. "Uh, yes. Alec, this is Charlie, my boss."

Alec shook his hand. The man was younger than Anne had described him, despite the gray in his reddish brown beard, despite the fact that he was reed thin and a widower.

"Charlie! Nice to meet you. I was wondering if I might steal your employee away a little early."

The man's face softened into an easy smile. "No problem with me. Anne, show him around. I'll be in the gallery. Nice meeting you, Alec." He ducked back into the office. Literally ducked. The guy was tall.

Confusion still covered Anne's face, which had turned rosy. "Alec, I have work—"

"I'll wait."

"I wasn't planning on this."

"You look great."

She looked exasperated. "I'm not talking about my clothes. You weren't going to be in all evening. I was going to bring home a sketchbook."

He waited for her to continue.

The hands of a normally cool, calm, collected Anne flapped wildly. "And sketch!"

She hadn't sketched in how many years? He sensed it wasn't the question to ask at this point. "Let's be spontaneous. How about dinner first?"

Charlie reappeared. "Excuse me. Anne, may I show you something in here? It concerns tomorrow when I'll be gone. Just take a moment."

"Of course." Anne followed him.

And Alec twiddled his thumbs, wondering if he had time to step outside for a breath of arctic air...wondering if he should just keep on going and forget about the date stuff. Was it really worth it? Peter claimed it was, but then he hadn't gone into a Plan B: What to do if the wife balks.

"Alec." She came up behind him. "Do you want to see the gallery? I know this supply store side doesn't interest you."

"Lead the way."

"We'll go through the office here."

He followed. It was a tight squeeze of an office. Charlie smiled from behind his desk as they passed through.

The gallery was light and airy. Anne showed him a variety of paintings by local artists, telling him about the ones she had met. Clearly she felt at home. "That's most of it." She faced him. "Shall we go?"

"Do you want to go?" He forced himself to meet her eyes. There was a glimmer of smoke gray within the black perimeter.

"I'd love to go."

"Really?" He grinned. "I thought we'd start with a movie. Unwind, forget about the kids. At dinner maybe we could talk about the movie instead of the kids." He didn't want to talk of real life. He was tired of real life, schedules, a disordered home, and resentment at work.

"The kids! What have you done with the kids?"

"Grammy's in charge of getting the girls home and fed. Drew and Amy can take over from there."

"You asked my mother?" Surprise and a hint of admiration crept into her voice. "A movie? On a Thursday night?"

He nodded. "I like your hair."

She blinked. "You got used to it."

"No. I just finally saw it in the proper environment. The one where you've sprouted wings."

Annie smiled. "Thank you." Her eyes sparkled. Only the gray was showing.

⌒

Sitting on the team bench during halftime of Saturday night's varsity game, Anne concluded that the turning point occurred that morning. A thoughtless word by Alec effectively unraveled the fragile bond that had begun to develop

between them Thursday night. She shook her head in disbelief. There she sat—in the midst of thumping basketballs and
rock music and high-strung girls with a one-point lead and
chattering fans—pondering her and Alec's relationship.

Beside her, Britte was quiet. Out on the floor, the girls and
their opponents were shooting. Inside of her, built-up emotions pounded in her chest, threatening at that very moment
to cut off her air supply if she didn't somehow release them.

Yes, she admitted it, *emotions.* Those abstract things she
recognized only at the shop because that was the only place
in her life where they made any sense. Take the phone conversation that morning, the one of Alec's she overheard.

The two of them had been in the kitchen discussing the
day's schedule when the phone rang. He answered it. The
conversation was work related, and so she cleaned up breakfast dishes while he talked. While he laughed. While he said
"sweetheart." *Into the phone.*

He had first begun calling Anne that when they were newlyweds. She cherished the special name he had chosen for
her. It was hers alone. For keeps.

Until today.

It wasn't that she suspected Alec had a girlfriend. For
goodness' sake, she was standing right next to him when he
said it into the phone. No, it was that the name was no big
deal. It was just Alec talking in that casual, friendly way of
his.

And she wanted to throw the pancake griddle at him.
Which made no sense whatsoever. Such emotions weren't
right. They weren't safe. Therefore, she ignored them.
Instead of discussing them with Alec, her ex-best friend, she
bottled them up. While she was at it, she might as well admit
that adding fuel to the combustible mix was her Superwoman struggle. Although she had been denying it, guilt that

she couldn't properly take care of everything weighed more heavily day by day.

Thursday's surprise date had been nice, fun, a temporary reconnection, a respite. She might have missed it if Charlie hadn't pulled her into the office and pointed out that when a husband offers, it's a shame if the wife turns a cold shoulder. However, now, two days later, the date was ancient history. There was a growing chasm between her and Alec, and she didn't know what to do about it. Actually, even if she did know what to do about it, she wouldn't have the time to do it. The new lifestyle they had chosen was in the way, gobbling up precious moments like a rabid cuckoo clock.

The buzzer blared harshly, startling her back into the present. Britte was standing already, surrounded by the girls layering their hands together in the center of the huddle and shouting, "Go team!"

Five girls ran out onto the court as the others settled onto the bench. Tanner sat at the far end, his freshmen girls behind him. The other team was Hawk Valley, nemesis, contender for second place in the conference. It should have been no contest, but then Anne had thought that more than once this season. Something was off-kilter, and that something's name was Britte.

Tonight her friend coached hesitantly, relying on her five starters to pull it off without much direction from her. Anne had spent the first half interceding more than she thought proper. It was Britte's team, and taking over for her wasn't being her assistant, nor was it being her friend.

Those pounding emotions went into triple time as Cassie smacked the tip-off into Liz's hands and Britte didn't budge. She resembled sculpted stone. Anne flew to her feet, unable to keep the lid on her emotions a moment longer. She shouted encouragement and direction.

So what that three dads had filed a complaint that week? So what that Britte had been physically attacked? So what that Joel had inexplicably tangled up her friend's heart? All of that was real life! None of those things excused Britte's behavior at the last few games. In Anne's opinion, the woman needed to grow up. As a matter of fact, maybe she needed a little shove in that direction right now before she totally lost her team.

Anne focused on one of the referees. His calls against them had been borderline all night. As he blew his whistle now, Anne's vocal cords tingled in anticipation. As he signalled his reason, she loudly sang out, "Aww, crummy call, Ref!"

It was better than throwing a pancake griddle.

"Annie!" Britte yelled from the bench.

Practical Anne Sutton, wife, mother of three, faithful follower of Jesus, PTA officer, and respected community presence was nose-to-nose with a referee.

The man in the black-and-white striped shirt stepped back, turned stiffly toward the official scorekeeper, flung his hands together into the shape of a "T" and pointed toward Anne.

Britte jumped up. "Annie, you just got a technical!"

"Sorry. I know it's not enough."

"Not enough!"

Anne grinned at her in a strange way. "Got you off the bench. Are you in the game yet?"

Britte stared at her.

"No?" She turned and, as a girl from the other team headed to the free-throw line, Anne shouted to the ref, "You owe us *three* of those!"

It was an instant replay. He made his "T" signal again, along with a few words. He was kicking Anne out of the game. The crowd was going ballistic, most loudly in favor of Anne.

"Annie!"

"Listen, hon, this is *your* team. This is *your* game." Her words were rushed, her eyes boring into Britte's. The referee was approaching, the game halted until the troublemaker left the gym. "Coach it your way. Sub a little more. You know how to do it. They need you, Britte. Help them win. And in case you haven't noticed, this ref is hurting us." She glanced over her shoulder and held up a hand. "Okay." She raised her voice. "I'm going."

Amidst booing, Anne walked graciously toward the exit. Passing Tanner, she called out, "Let her do it! Don't help."

As Anne disappeared through the open gym doors, a burst of anger ignited in Britte. How dare she! Anne was her last holdout. Joel was gone even if he was standing across the court. Brady was gone. Albeit on a honeymoon, still he was gone. The parents of her players were physically present, but gone nonetheless. Tanner was gone. Ordered not to help, he leaned back now, elbows propped on the bleacher behind him, legs crossed, a smug little smile on his face.

Gone. All of them.

"Coach!" Liz yelled from the court. Her arms were raised, blocking a possible pass to the girl she guarded.

Correction. Not everyone was gone. The girls were here. *Her* girls were here.

Britte flipped her a thumbs-up sign. "Let's go, ladies!"

⌒

Across the court, midway up the bleachers, Alec sat frozen in horror. His wife had just been evicted from the game. Not his son, the hotshot player. Not his brother, the mouthy coach. But his *wife* from a *girls* game. He knew Anne could be outspoken, but this was...this was...ludicrous! What was she thinking?

He hustled down the bleachers, rattling them and bumping people. "Excuse me. Excuse me." *My wife has lost her mind.* Why, oh why, had Drew's game been an afternoon one rather than evening, allowing Alec to return in time to Valley Oaks to witness this?

He found her in the nearly deserted commons, just outside one set of gym doors...laughing. "Anne!"

"Quick, Alec! Hide me. If that ref sees me, he might make me leave the building!"

"Anne! What are you doing?"

She giggled. "Trying to see the game. Scoot over. Woo!" she shouted and raised a fist. "Yesss! Cassie scored! Turn around, Alec. You missed it."

"What's going on?"

"The game!"

"Why did you do that?"

"Oh, Alec." She glanced at him, but quickly diverted her gaze above his shoulder toward the gym. "Britte needed a little kick in the pants. She's been wallowing in fear long enough. I figured if I made her mad, she'd snap out of it. Go, Liz! Oops, I better not yell and draw attention to myself, huh?"

"You did that on purpose? You got kicked out on *purpose?*"

"Of course. And it feels pretty good!" She met his eyes now. "Did I embarrass you?"

In high school he had been the jock, the one with the popular friends. She had been the artist, the one with the friends who wore strange clothing and didn't join in normal activities. She quietly ran cross-country, but didn't play basketball until after he had graduated. At first he had been embarrassed to admit he was attracted to her. After finding the nerve to ask her out, he was embarrassed to be seen with her. Eventually he figured out that the reason he was nuts about her was because she was who she was. He'd only been 18. He had an excuse.

Now he was 39, and he had begun to lose track of who she was. He had no excuse.

Alec smiled and made a show of brushing her shoulders. "No. I'm just having a hard time getting used to those wings."

Thirty-Seven

Joel poured coffee beans into the proper slot, set the timer for 5 A.M., and wondered what Britte would think of the General and his most prized possession, a coffeemaker that not only ground the beans but brewed them when he dictated?

Then he wondered why he wondered about Britte. He shoved aside that dead-end thought for the umpteenth time and flipped off the kitchen light. His mind went to the night's game, definitely more solid ground than that other line of thinking. Although it was now after midnight, he still chuckled over the spectacle in the gym. Anne Sutton had been thrown out of the game, and Britte had come alive and actively coached the girls to a solid win. It gave the team a good shot at tying for second place in the conference. Not bad for a rather inconsistent season.

The phone rang. His heart kicked in as if a starting pistol had fired. *Nicky? Dear Lord.*

He ran back into the kitchen and grabbed the cordless from its cradle. "Hello."

"Joel, it's Cal. Do you know where Britte is?"

"No. What's wrong?"

"I'm in the ER at the Rockville Hospital. Gordon Hughes beat up his wife."

Joel sank onto a chair. "How bad is she?"

"I hope bad enough to file charges. She was barely conscious when Jordan called 911, but she'll be okay."

The incident probably wasn't the first for the family. What was it he had said about Hughes? That he was a typical parent? So much for his ability to read character. "Cal, how'd we miss this?"

"It's the norm. Families cover it up. She's probably gone to different doctors, different urgent care facilities. Listen, Joel, Britte's not answering her phone, and Hughes hasn't been found yet."

The implications hit him like a blow to the stomach, and he couldn't breathe.

"Jordan said he was drunk. An aunt just picked her up here. Trevor wasn't home when it happened. He's at a friend's. I called that family, so he's accounted for. Point is, I'm 20 minutes away, and Hughes threatened to finish what his son started."

"I'm out the door."

Like an Indy 500 race car driver, Joel tore across the sleeping town. Ignoring stop signs, he flung bursts of prayer toward an overcast sky and felt that they bounced right back at him. He started making deals with God, not caring that he sounded like a confused child.

"Father! Keep her safe! Oh, God, give me another chance. Keep her safe, and I'll stop running away. I promise!"

Britte's house came into view. The lights shone through the front windows. She was home!

No, not necessarily. The outside lights were on, too. She had developed the habit of leaving all the lights on when she wasn't home. He knew that from those times he had walked her inside.

He screeched to a halt, parked on the street, and jumped out. The snow had been scooped from the sidewalk leading to her front door. Did she shovel her own snow? Shouldn't someone help her do that?

He rang the doorbell and pounded on the storm door. He tried to open it, but it was locked. He pounded again and jammed his thumb into the doorbell.

She wasn't home. The lights wouldn't be on.

Unless Hughes got her when she pulled into the garage.

Joel ran to the attached garage. There was a small window, covered like front windows with opaque curtains. He couldn't see inside.

He plunged into the snow, going from window to window, hammering his fist against each one, working his way around the house. No neighbors turned on a light or came outside. No one heard him. No one would have heard her either. He had to get inside. She had to be home. Why wouldn't she be home by now? Could she sleep with all the lights on, through all his pounding? He'd get the tire iron out of the car, break a bedroom window and climb in, and— Find her?

Back on the driveway, his heart thumping erratically in his ears, his breath frosting the air, he cried out, "Oh, God! Please, don't let anything happen to her!"

Britte tooted the horn as she drove from Anne's house. "Oops," she spoke aloud to herself, "guess I shouldn't honk in the middle of the night on Acorn Park Lane!" She laughed. It felt so good that she laughed again, heartily.

After the game she and Anne decided they needed some serious coaches' bonding time away from everyone they knew. Before the gym had emptied, they were in the Jeep, on the road to Rockville.

Britte smiled, imagining what she and Anne looked like at the 24-hour restaurant, sprawled for hours in a booth, eating copious amounts of food, laughing and crying. They had apologized for losing sight of their teamwork as coleaders in the basketball program. Annie confessed to losing sight of that very same thing at home with Alec and the kids. Britte confessed that she had lost it in regard to the girls.

They concluded that they'd lost their way and didn't have routes plotted for the way back...that they'd been lousy ambassadors for Christ lately, not displaying much love and compassion...that it was past time they started praying for each other along those lines.

Now, as Britte drove through the midnight town, she began to pray. "Jesus, I've taken my eyes off of You. I'm sorry. I wanted to win so badly! The whole kit and caboodle. State champs. Well, at the least, be a Sweet Sixteen contender for the championship. You gave me this passion, right? This team? Oh, Lord, I get it. It was a test. What can Britte do with extravagant gifts? How about make such a mess of them I've got parents filing complaints? And while we're on the subject of complaints, what was that business with Joel all about? You get my attention with this guy and then—"

The words caught in her throat as the Jeep's headlights fell on a car in front of her house. Someone was bending over its opened trunk. She slowed and the man stood, turning toward her. When the lights picked out his familiar black jacket, relief flooded through her. Dread quickly followed on its heels. It was 12:30...the middle of the night.

At the driveway she braked and put down the window. "Joel! What are you doing here?"

His face was in shadows, but she saw that he shook his head and pointed toward the garage. "Go on inside."

She tapped the garage door opener, pulled the car inside, and quickly hopped out. He was still in the street, leaning back against his closed trunk. She hurried to him. "Joel?"

His face was down, propped against a hand. Slowly he lowered his arm and held it out toward her. "Britte," he whispered, "come here. Please."

"What's wrong?"

"I thought you were dead."

She stepped to him. "Joel!"

He drew her near, his arms encircling her. His cheek against hers was damp and cold.

"You're freezing." What was wrong with him?

"Yeah, well, I'm melting on the inside." His voice was hoarse, his mouth against her ear. "And that, Princess, is a miracle."

Even through their heavy coats, she thought she could feel the hardness of his muscles as he tightened his hold around her. Something was terribly wrong, but she leaned against him, hoping to give him time to collect himself. A shudder tore through him. "Joel! Let's go in the house!"

He nodded.

They walked in through the garage, his arm heavy around her shoulders. She pushed the button to close the big door and unlocked the kitchen door.

"I'll go in first," he said.

"There's no need to..." Her voice trailed off at the look on his face, at his narrowed eyes and sternly set jaw. What had he said? That he thought she was dead? "Tell me what's going on!"

He brushed past her. "Gordon Hughes beat up his wife. She's in the hospital. He said he would finish what his son started."

Britte followed slowly and made her way to a chair at the table. Oh, why hadn't she said something? Couldn't this have been prevented? It was exactly what she suspected, what she feared. *God, I'm sorry. I've let You down again. I knew—*

"How is she? What about Jordan? And Trevor?"

"They're all okay."

The phone rang at Joel's elbow on the kitchen counter. He answered it. "Hello...Yes, it's me, Anne...She's fine...I'm staying with her. Don't worry...All right. Thanks. Bye."

"Anne?"

"Yes. Cal called Alec right after he talked with me. She was checking to make sure I was with you."

She nodded. "You said Jordan and Trevor are all right?"

"They're with friends and relatives. There's nothing to be done."

"But there *was* something to be done! I knew he did this. I knew it! If I'd told Cal—"

"You had proof?"

"No, but—"

"Then you couldn't have helped. Cal couldn't have done a thing. It happened in private." They stared at each other. "Cal called from Rockville. He couldn't reach you. Gordon Hughes is on the loose. I came over. I thought you were..." His voice faded. "In here. Hurt. Or worse. When you pulled up, I was getting the tire iron to break a window..."

The enormity of the situation suddenly struck her, and she burst into tears. Poor Jordan had lived with the horror, probably for *years,* and Britte had had the audacity to let the girl get on her nerves?

Joel slid the other chair next to hers and sat on it. He wrapped her in his arms and soothing words began to flow from him. "Britte, it's over. Shh. It's all over. Holy Father, thank You for keeping Britte safe. Have mercy on the Hughes family. We pray for Your healing touch on the broken bodies, the broken spirits..."

Thirty-Eight

As they sat in her kitchen and Joel prayed, Britte felt a quiet settle about her like the hush of a gentle snowfall. She rested in it as easily as she rested in his strong arms. The world was a place of fear and ugliness. Much as she wanted to deny it, the sheer physical presence of Joel offered a respite. His faith, a shelter of immense proportions.

He whispered an "amen," but he didn't release her. The front of his down jacket became damp with her tears. He smoothed back her hair, still murmuring words of comfort.

At last her tears slowed, and she straightened just enough to look up at him. "I'm sorry."

"For what?" He gently brushed his thumb across her cheeks.

"Crying all the time. I haven't really cried for years." She sniffed. "You hang around and I'm blubbering twice in one month. I am not a weepy female."

"Maybe you should cry more often." He smiled at her crookedly. "Those are the times I seem to wind up holding you. Would you like some coffee?"

"Don't change subjects. Why is it *that's* when you wind up holding me? When I'm at my most vulnerable?"

"Are you kidding? You don't even let your girls get close to your normally all-sufficient self."

That stung. She pushed herself out of his arms. "I'm fine now. Why don't you go home?"

"Because I haven't answered your question yet. But I need some coffee first. Have you got any?" He stood, shrugged off his jacket, stepped over to a cupboard, and opened it.

Of all the nerve! Walking out of the kitchen, she offered in a caustic tone, "Make yourself at home, Mr. Kingsley."

"I love it when you call me that!" he called after her. "Hey, don't you have any whole coffee beans? This stuff is already ground."

She ignored him and walked through the house into her bedroom, pausing only long enough at the thermostat to turn up the heat. It was as freezing inside as it was out.

Especially so since he'd stopped holding her.

Changing into fluffy, powder blue sweats, she felt a fresh aching wave of pain for the Hughes family. What could she do to help? Find a role for Jordan on the court? Make sure basketball was a positive experience during the upcoming tournament time? Appoint Trevor to help the girls keep stats? Keep him close, forget what he had done to her?

In the living room, only soft light from one lamp shone. She pulled the afghan from the back of the armchair and wrapped herself in it, settling cross-legged onto the seat and undoing her braid. Sleep was out of the question at this point between Gordon Hughes on the loose and Joel Kingsley in her kitchen. And what a cutting thing for him to say! She was close to her girls.

He entered the room now, carrying two steaming mugs. He looked different in worn blue jeans, a navy blue sweatshirt, and stocking feet. "Black, right?"

"Right." When had he noticed that? "Thanks."

He handed a mug to her and settled into the recliner directly across from her chair. "Britte, I didn't mean to hurt your feelings, but that's the way I see things."

"Mmm, this coffee is good. Really good."

"Thanks." He smiled. "Now who's changing subjects?"

"You can go home. I'm safe and sound."

"I'm not going anywhere until that guy's locked up."

"I am close to my girls."

He eyed her over his mug and took a sip. "I think you're holding back. I've been watching your game tapes from previous seasons."

"Why would you do that?"

"Just trying to pinpoint the missing ingredient. But that's another matter. I want to answer your question."

"I can't get too close to them. I'm their coach and teacher, not their buddy."

"Don't you want to hear it?"

Hear his answer to her question about why he hugged her only when she was displaying vulnerability? "No. Not really. It's not necessary."

Even in the dim light, she could see his eyes boring into hers. "Chicken."

"I think I'm tired of playing games."

He set his mug on the end table and pulled up the footrest of the recliner. "I am too, Britte. I promised God tonight I'd stop if He brought you home safely. It was one of those in-the-trench, bullets-flying-overhead prayers, but still…I promised."

"And why would you pray a prayer like that?"

"Because I thought you were dead, and I finally admitted that if I couldn't see you at school Monday morning, I may as well just lie down in the snow right now and quit breathing."

She stared at him, speechless.

"When you were crying, I couldn't help but hold you. When you weren't crying, I convinced myself it was for the best if I didn't hug you."

"Why would that be for the best?" she whispered.

"For my sake." His voice faded. He pushed against the chair arms until the back reclined. "I'm getting a headache."

Britte set down her mug and untangled herself from the afghan. "Do you want some ibuprofen?" She went to him and knelt on the carpet.

"That stuff won't touch it. It's…it's a migraine." He closed his eyes.

"Joel." She touched his hand. "Do you have something to take for it?"

"Not here. Do you have an ice pack?"

"Does a coach have an ice pack? I'll be right back."

"Not going anywhere," he mumbled. "Got to protect you from that idiot."

Britte rushed about the house, gathering an ice pack and her balm. Back in the living room, she covered Joel with an afghan. She lifted his head and placed the ice pack behind his neck. "Is that good?

"Mmm. Why is it you only take care of me when I'm vulnerable?"

"Why don't you just be quiet? I have this super-duper balm with menthol and camphor." Standing behind him, she opened the container and scooped balm onto her fingertips. Gently she began to rub it into his temples. Its sharp scent permeated the room, making her own eyes water. "How's that?"

"Great."

She applied some to his forehead.

That forehead with its furrows already etched in place. She studied his straight, narrow nose. His square jaw, stern in appearance even now, dark with middle-of-the-night stubble.

What had he meant? To lie down in the snow and quit breathing if he couldn't see her? Was it a declaration of love? Followed by a migraine? He got migraines?

Joel Kingsley was still an enigma.

Joel sank into the pain while Britte's fingers softened its sharp edges.

Thank You, God. Thank You, God.

She was safe.

Was that what loving was? Opening the floodgates, loosing pent-up emotions until they roared, imploding in his head? Sam had told him he would know when it was time. Well, it was time. He didn't ever want to let her out of his sight again.

From a distance he heard a knocking. Was he asleep?

"Britte! Don't answer that!"

"Shh." Her hand pressed his shoulder. "I'll just see who it is." A moment later, "It's Cal."

The opening of the door. A blast of cold air. Murmured voices.

"Joel, they've got him." Her voice was a whisper near him.

Thank You, God. Thank You, God.

"Joel." It was Cal. "Want me to take you home, bud?"

"No way. The kid's not locked up, is he?" He tried to smile. "There are some pills. In my car."

"Joel!" Britte scolded softly. "Why didn't you tell me?"

"Is the car locked?" Cal asked.

He didn't have the strength to reply. They could figure it out.

"I'll check his coat pockets."

Good girl.

Was it moments or hours later? Britte touched his hand. He recognized her long fingers, her feminine skin. "Joel, how many?"

"One."

She touched his lips. "Open." A capsule slipped inside. "Here's water." A glass met his mouth.

He swallowed.

"Joel, why didn't you tell me earlier that these were in the car?" She was close, stroking his cheek.

"I didn't want you outside by yourself. And I had to stay awake." He tried again to smile. "So to speak."

"Oh, Joel, you silly knight in shining armor."

"Told you that you might not want to have dinner once you got to know me."

"Forget dinner. It's almost time for breakfast. Do you want to lie down on the couch?"

"No. This chair is good."

"Then I'll take the couch."

He should protest. Tell her to go to bed.

Her hand stopped on his jaw, and he felt her breath on his face. Something softly brushed the corner of his mouth. "Goodnight," she whispered.

On second thought, he wanted her on the couch, as near as possible.

Thirty-Nine

Joel opened his eyes to the grainy light of early morning. In spite of the confines of the recliner and his stiff body, he didn't move. Just a few feet away, in his direct line of vision, lay Britte. She was on the couch, fast asleep, huddled under a huge quilt, her wavy blonde hair spread over a pillow.

He felt like a kid on summer break. Anticipation crackled in the air. No school, his mom cooking bacon and eggs, his dad coming home early to take him to a Cubs game.

No. It was beyond even that. It was every moment he'd ever experienced of pure...Contentment? Bliss? Delight? Joy? All rolled into one.

Remarkable.

Maybe he'd stay in the chair awhile. Try to imagine what he was going to feel when she opened those amazing eyes.

Or when he kissed her again.

Yes. He would most definitely be kissing her again.

~

Britte awoke to the sound of Joel in the kitchen. Sunlight was streaming in through the draperies. She glanced at the clock on the mantel and took stock of the situation. It was after nine. Her head protested at the thought of scurrying about to make it to church on time. Her conscience prickled at the thought that a man was in her kitchen making—she smelled it now—coffee. And that his car had been parked in front of her house since around midnight.

It shouldn't prickle. It wasn't as if anything immoral was going on. Even if she had kissed him goodnight. Even if they had slept in the same room.

What would her mother say?

Britte kicked off the quilt and shuffled through the dining room and into the kitchen. At the sight of Joel Kingsley peering inside her refrigerator, she knew the root of the prickle.

She *liked* the whole scenario!

Nuts. She never should have tasted that tap water.

"Morning," she mumbled.

He turned and smiled. "Morning." There were dark half-moons beneath his eyes.

"How are you?" she asked.

"Better, thanks. Mind if I cook breakfast?"

"Go for it." *Oh my gosh. He cooks.*

"Do you like eggs?" He was kneeling in front of the fridge. "Sautéed veggies? Cheese?"

"I have all that?"

"I think I can rescue enough for us." He held up a hair-sprouting carrot and a chunk of unrecognizable fuzz. "Biology experiments?"

"Basketball season." She went to the coffeepot and bumped into him. "Sorry."

He took her by the shoulders and pointed her toward the table. "Go sit down. I'll wait on you. I thought you were a morning person."

"Not after a night like last night. Isn't the coffee ready yet?"

"Just a couple more minutes. Mind if I turn on the radio?"

"You can stop asking if I mind."

He looked over his shoulder at her and grinned.

The only thing I mind is that this situation is unnerving me. "Joel, I, um, don't know, uh—" She cleared her throat. "The point is, I've never had male company in my kitchen for *breakfast.*"

He turned and leaned against the counter, studying her face now. "Somehow I knew that. Look, I don't want to make you uncomfortable. I just thought since I was already here, maybe we could spend a little coherent time together. You know, last night when I was pounding on all of your windows, not one neighbor noticed. But if you prefer, I'll leave now."

She shook her head. "I just wanted you to know."

He smiled.

"Okay." She stood. "I'm going to wash my face."

In the bathroom she surveyed her own eye baggage. Her sweats were rumpled, her hair a tangled mess. Not a pretty sight. She brushed her hair, twisted it up, and stuck a banana clip on it.

Back in the kitchen and seated at the table, she sipped coffee and watched him work. He seemed completely at home opening drawers and cupboards, effortlessly finding pans and utensils, humming to the hymns playing on the radio, turning on the stove. The scents grew more fragrant by the moment. Butter, garlic, vegetables, herbs, spices. Her stomach was growling by the time he sat down across the table from her.

"Wow!" she exclaimed after her first bite. "This is fantastic."

"Thanks."

"Thank *you.*" *Maybe you should come by more often and cook and...and whatever.* "Do you always cook like this?"

"Like what?"

"Like just whip up whatever and have it taste so yummy?"

"You don't have to flatter me. I already gave you a good review."

She heard that brass band in the distance, as if it were warming up in the deep recesses of her chest. "I was trying to ignore the fact that my overnight guest is also my boss."

"Forget I said that. It's in the spices. And I enjoy cooking."

"I detest cooking."

"You know what they say about opposites attracting." He smiled.

The smile did it. That slow, rare smile that lit up his eyes even this morning in their haggard state. Britte felt a stab of loneliness. "Are we attracted?"

"I thought we had established that at Christmas. I know. I have a strange way of showing it."

"Extremely strange way. We go from Christmas to barely speaking to last night."

"I'm sorry. I didn't mean to play games or lead you on. The simple explanation is that I haven't felt for a long time."

"Haven't felt what?"

He blinked and fiddled with his fork. "Anything."

She thought of his stoic, general's demeanor. Of his no-nonsense attitude with the students. His ruthless pursuit of enforcing new policies. His rare smile.

"Things...happened when I was in the service. I basically just shut down years ago. It was how I survived. And then you came along." He connected with her eyes again. "Somehow you sneaked in through the back door when I wasn't looking. I was going along, minding my own business. The next thing I know, I'm in the jeweler's, buying a necklace for the math teacher."

"Joel, you can't tell me you haven't been attracted to women."

"That's a totally different thing, unrelated to emotions."

"That can't be a totally different— What?"

He was smiling again. "You're such a princess, up in your ivory tower, protected from the world out there where physical attraction happens and it's totally detached from the heart. It's one of the most appealing things about you."

"I am *not* a princess! I'm just a girl from Podunk, as Gina would put it. Quite happy to stay put in my own little world."

"Well, whatever. All I know is that suddenly I'm mushy inside."

"That doesn't sound very general-like."

"I know. My image is going down the tubes."

"I think you'll ratchet up way-cool points with the ladies."

He reached across the table and took her hand. "There's only one lady I care about. May I court you, Miss O? As publicly as the community can handle?"

The brass band was blaring now, drowning out the warning that he was a likely candidate for breaking her heart. "I don't think I have a choice, Mr. Kingsley."

Forty

In the crowded church foyer after the service, Anne made a beeline for Lia, who had recently returned from her ten-day honeymoon. "Welcome home!" They exchanged a quick embrace.

"Thank you." The young woman's dark eyes sparkled; her entire face glowed.

"How was Hawaii?"

"Absolutely gorgeous. Oh, the blue sky and flowers in the middle of January! It was heavenly."

Anne grinned. "I'm sorry I haven't had a chance to stop by the store since you got back. I did check in on that substitute pharmacist."

"Did he do all right?"

"He seemed fine. Not nearly as pretty as you, though. I think married life agrees with you!"

"Anne, when does this go away? I mean, it must go away. All I can think about is Cal. I'm so grateful for Leslie." She referred to her new pharmacist technician. "She's caught five mistakes I've made on prescriptions in the two and a half days I've been back!"

Though Anne felt her smile fade, she forced a perkiness she didn't feel into her tone. "That's the honeymoon phase. It'll pass, but things get better…in a different way." At least she had believed that for a long time. "You couldn't live on the mountaintop forever."

"You're right. I can hardly breathe up here, let alone dispense drugs! Is Britte all right? Cal filled me in this morning."

In spite of the horrible circumstances, Anne couldn't help but smile. "I called her before church. Joel Kingsley fixed her breakfast."

Lia's eyebrows shot up.

"This was after he spent the night in her recliner, making sure she was safe."

"Certain tongues are going to wag."

"Wait until they hear that they have a dinner date tonight."

Lia giggled. "It's times like these I wish Dot still worked in the store so I knew what was going on. Speaking of which, how's your new job?"

"It's great." *The rest of my life is falling apart, but the job is great.*

"I'm glad to hear that, though I miss you at the store." She squeezed her hand. "I'd better go. I know Cal's hungry. See you later."

"Bye."

I miss me, too.

"Hey, Annie-banannie." Val was at her elbow.

"Hi, stranger." She hugged the friend she seldom had time to even catch on the phone these days. They quickly caught up on tidbits concerning the kids. "Val, you look well. You okay?"

She nodded, her curls bouncing. "Most days. I only cry three times a week now and only at night."

Anne smiled softly. "Progress."

"You bet. Anyway, I'm taking the girls into Rockville this afternoon. It's our only time to shoe shop. I know Sunday's your family day, so you probably don't want to come?"

"No. Thanks, though. Actually Sunday has turned into a major catch-up day. The washer and dryer go nonstop."

"Maybe you won't miss Alec then." Val winced. "I was talking about a plumbing problem, and he said it's no big deal, he could show Jason how to take care of it. I'm sure it's not what Jason had in mind for a Sunday afternoon, but his other choice is to hang out with us girls. So is it all right if Alec does surrogate father?"

"Of course it's all right." They chatted for a bit longer, until the lump forming in Anne's throat cut off her voice.

～～

"Where's Mom?" Alec folded the Sunday newspaper and put down the footrest of the recliner.

His three children were scattered about the family room, their attention focused on the TV. Only Drew replied, and it was with a shrug. The video they watched was G-rated, which was probably why he had heard the question.

"Drew."

"Huh?"

"Thanks for participating."

Drew turned toward him with an exaggerated look of astonishment on his face. "Why, Dad, whatever do you mean? I love watching animated characters sing and dance and restructure historical fact."

Alec laughed and walked past him, ruffling his son's hair.

He found Anne upstairs in their room, sitting in bed with a book.

"Annie, are you sick?" He walked over and sat on the edge, facing her. Her short hair still grabbed him unawares at first glance, causing him to take a split second to orient himself to the fact that this person was indeed his wife. He hoped she didn't notice.

"I'm not sick, just exhausted."

"That's not like you."

She glared at him.

Wrong thing to say. She hadn't been herself all day, though. He felt as if an invisible wall hung between them, allowing them only to get so close. "Do you want to talk about it?"

"Not really." She removed her reading glasses. Her eyes were dark.

"I think we should. I miss you."

"You have a funny way of showing it."

He wrinkled his brow, puzzled.

"Oh, think about it, Alec. Friday night, Drew's game. You sat with Kevin, as usual. Saturday our paths didn't even cross except when I got kicked out of the girls game. You played racquetball while I played chauffeur. Today, the kids sat between us in church. You spent the afternoon with Jason, which I know was really important, a priority. But meanwhile I caught up on housework and helped Amy with a math project that I truly did not understand."

"The kids are off tomorrow. I'm home. We could have done all that then. Remember, you don't have to be Superwoman!"

"You're missing the point."

His temper was doing a slow burn. "Enlighten me."

"Not that much has changed. We've lived like this for years. I'm just beginning to recognize it. You didn't miss me before because I didn't acknowledge that we're really not first in each other's lives. You made it very clear yesterday on the phone when you said 'sweetheart' to whomever was on the other end. Now that I see where I stand with you, I'm tired of pretending. I have better things to do. Like read this book." She put her glasses back on and propped the book on her knees.

He said "sweetheart" on the phone? His temper gave way to a solid knot of dread pressing against his ribs. "Come on.

We have to talk about what's bothering you. We've never gone to bed mad at each other."

"I'm not mad, Alec. I'm just being realistic. And probably unemotional because I am so tired. I'm sorry. I didn't want to talk about it tonight. Are you mad?"

Disgruntled. Confused. Scared to death. "Upset."

"I am too." She stared back at him. "But we can't fix it tonight."

"We'll talk...Thursday."

"There's a new art class starting Thursday night. Charlie said I can join it, no cost. I—I think it's something I need to do. For now."

Who was this woman with the short black hair? Didn't her eyes used to be gray?

Forty-One

Sunday night Joel took Britte into Rockville, to a Chinese restaurant because it was her favorite. He wanted to spoil the girl who diligently chipped away at the brick wall surrounding his heart just by showing up. When she smiled at him or touched his arm, large chunks fell away. Their crashing threatened to trigger another migraine, but so far he was handling things fine. One step at a time.

They lingered over the meal, slowly opening up, making discoveries about each other.

"His name was Eric." Those singular eyes of hers focused elsewhere as she talked of her old boyfriend.

"What happened?"

"He was from Detroit, where his family ran some business related to the auto industry. He had no intentions other than going back and joining them after graduation. I had no intentions of doing anything but teaching in the Rockville area, preferably in Valley Oaks." She shrugged. "Somewhere along the way we had missed that about each other."

"But you were engaged?"

Again she shrugged, attempting to make light of what must have been a painful situation. "It was a beautiful diamond. Really too large for my tastes. I think the family business was a prosperous one. How about you?"

"Engaged once, mostly long distance. I'd been in the Marines for a while when I thought I wanted to get married. When I got out, she...changed her mind." Should he tell her now? On their first official date? Casually mention over the

mu shoo pork and wonton that he had killed a fellow
Marine? That Marti had dumped him like yesterday's newspaper? "Mind if we save that story for another time?"

She reached over and traced a finger along his cheek. "Is
it the 'things' you referred to this morning?"

He nodded.

"Are you getting a headache?"

"No. I'm good."

"Do you have those often?"

"When I'm stressed, which is why I do my utmost to avoid
stress, keep my life cut and dry, stick to a master activity list
every day."

"That's why you're neurotically organized." She smiled.

He chuckled, remembering her accusation when she had
stormed into his office. "And why I disassociate myself from
feeling too much." The compassion on her face sent his heart
into a double-time beat. "It's why I pulled away."

"Then why are we here, Joel? On a date? Why would you
even consider this…this wooing?"

"Because…the tension of not pursuing this was becoming
unbearable."

After dinner Joel followed Britte into her house to say
goodnight. Though she wished the evening wouldn't end,
they both admitted they were too spent to stay awake much
longer.

She unbuttoned her long coat. "Joel, dinner was great.
Thank you so much."

"You're welcome." He looked at her, his exhaustion
showing plainly on his solemn face. "Uh, I'm not sure about
the rules of engagement here."

She laughed. "That sounds like a military term. What on earth are you talking about?"

His eyes were at half-mast. "What I mean is, in this Christian wooing business, is kissing acceptable on a first date?"

She laughed more loudly. "You haven't dated since you've been a Christian?"

"No, that's not it. I just haven't dated a Christian, not a true-blue, dyed-in-the-wool one like you."

"And exactly how long have you been a Christian?"

"Seven years."

Overcome now with giggles, she leaned against the door. "No wonder you get migraines, Mr. Kingsley. I think you're desperate for female companionship!"

"Now you sound like Sam, my spiritual mentor."

"Maybe you should call and ask him about the rules of engagement." She crossed her arms, trying to hold in the snickering.

"Hey, I'm being vulnerable here. The least you could do is stop laughing at me."

"Joel, we've already kissed!"

"That was different. That was unofficial."

"You are an enigma, but then I've been saying that for a long time. Now that I think about it, we should forego the kiss. Since you're in this desperate mode, I think maybe you'd kiss *anybody* walking by in a skirt. We really should hold off until you're sure."

He stared at her for a full minute. "You're getting sassy and I'm bushed. I'll see you tomorrow. We'll go over those game tapes." He squeezed her shoulder and opened the door. "Goodnight."

Still chuckling, she told him goodnight, shut the door behind him, and abruptly stopped laughing. A wave of disappointment washed over her. How had she managed to chase him away? She really was too mouthy at the most inappropriate times.

She yanked off her long black boots, hung up her coat in the closet, checked the answering machine in the kitchen, turned off the lights, and started down the hallway. Well, so what if she was mouthy? That was just the way she was. Her mother hadn't managed to change her in 29 years. She certainly wasn't going to roll over and play nicey-nice because a man who 99 percent of the time behaved like a *general* couldn't handle it!

The doorbell rang and her heart leapt into her throat. She took a deep breath. Gordon Hughes would not ring the doorbell. And besides, Cal had him locked up.

She went back into the living room and flipped on a light. At the door, she peeked through the curtain covering the narrow window alongside it. Joel stood on the stoop.

She opened the door. Without a word, he stepped inside and shut it. His eyes never left hers, the glint in them a tangible force that prevented her from speaking.

He cupped her face in his hands, and then he kissed her...rather...deliberately.

He raised his head slightly and announced in his low General's grumble, "We're going to have to work on that sassy attitude of yours, Miss O."

He walked out the door, once again leaving her speechless.

Forty-Two

Anne nestled against Alec, in his arms. They stood in the kitchen. He had already been outside to start the car so it would be warm for her.

"Thanks for the bagel and coffee," she said. He had made an effort to treat her sweetly that morning.

"You're welcome. Annie, I didn't mean to say sweetheart. I didn't even know I did it."

She felt herself stiffen. "You sound like Drew. 'I didn't mean to punch him. I didn't even hear Britte tell us to stop.'"

He kissed the top of her head and drew back, dropping his arms. "Okay, okay. I'll work on taking responsibility for my actions."

She pulled on her gloves. "Alec, I don't want to be your mother. I only told you because it hurt my feelings." *Not to mention that it clarified where I stand with you.* But she wasn't going there. It was time to leave for work.

"It's all right. I deserved that one."

"Who was she anyway?"

"Tracy."

"Ahh, the cute, bubbly, young one."

"Well, you wouldn't want me calling just anyone 'sweetheart,' would you?"

"Nope." She put her hand on the doorknob.

"I didn't mean anything by it."

"Alec, I know that." She looked over her shoulder at him. "Which translates that it doesn't mean anything when you call me that. So," she shrugged, "let's stop pretending and move on."

He swallowed. "I'm sorry."

She went to him and kissed his cheek. "Bye."

"Bye. Be careful. I'll put the rest of those Christmas boxes in the attic today."

Right. She'd heard that one before.

Alec trudged up the narrow staircase with the last of the boxes packed with ornaments. He walked across the attic to the designated Christmas corner, sneezing on the dust swirled into motion with his footsteps.

The attic was unfinished business, with exposed rafters beneath the slanted roofline and only half the floor area covered with boards. The walls were insulation packed between the studs. However, there were two nice dormer windows overlooking the front yard. The space would make a great playroom. Of course, the kids were almost grown out of playrooms. Amy thought it'd be perfect for sleepovers, though. All it needed was a floor, ceiling, walls, bathroom, and, she added, why not a kitchenette?

That knot of dread had grown overnight and was now twisting, demanding attention. He shuffled over to another corner and sat on a trunk.

How was it the kids had outgrown a playroom before he had had time to build it? If he started today, Mandy might enjoy it for a few months, before she got caught up next year in middle school and stopped playing dress-up or imaginary classroom or with dolls. Maybe if he created it, though, she wouldn't stop playing those games. She could keep pretending.

Alec propped an elbow on his knee and put his hand against his face in time to catch the sob. What did Annie mean, she was tired of pretending? Their life was good together. They were busy, productive people. They were friends. Friends that confided, friends that spent time together— Yes, they spent time together!

Another thought nagged. *Oh, Lord.*

He closed his eyes and let it develop.

Their time together...their *alone* time together was...limited. Limited? One Thursday night date in how many years? Make that infrequent. No, truth be told, their alone time was nonexistent. Is that what she meant, that she wasn't first in his life? That he wasn't in hers? That she wanted to quit pretending that they were and get on with other things? What other things?

She had sprouted wings because she had been pushed from the nest, her Valley Oaks nest. And yes, he had encouraged it. He had panicked, imagining their growing needs and feeling like a failure as a provider when the promotion didn't happen. He had taken his eyes off of God, the One who had always met their needs.

I'm sorry, Lord! Make it right again. Make us right again. Annie's my everything. How do I show her that?

He let the tears fall now. How could he have done this to her? She was always there for him, supporting who he was with her quirky smile and beautiful gray eyes and her great capacity for not complaining.

And he'd let her down. Broken that promise that they would do it the old, traditional way. He would financially support them and— The vows! There were vows. They had literally written down that promise in their vows, not the public ceremony vows, but— What had they promised? They'd kept a copy, hadn't they? They would have kept a copy. Where—?

The trunk he was sitting on. Annie called it their memory treasure chest. It was an old hand-me-down, her version of a cedar hope chest she could never afford. He opened the lid and the scent of cedar floated out. She must have placed cedar blocks inside to keep their treasures from smelling like hand-me-down stuffiness.

Two hours later Alec sat on the floor beside the trunk, memories strewn about him. Memories in the form of dried flowers; high school football programs; ticket stubs; packets of letters; a shoebox of photos; a handkerchief; a scarf; his letter sweater wrapped in tissue paper and plastic; a sketchbook of her drawings, mostly of their college campus and a nearby state park; a large manila envelope.

He held each memento, racking his brain for its significance. They should do this together. Between them they would remember everything. The two of them together... They needed each other.

He reached into the envelope and pulled out a handful of loose papers. There were favorite quotes, poems, scraps of paper with notes to each other...and, in a folder, in plastic covers...the vows.

Anne's were written, of course, on pale pink stationery, now faded, in calligraphy. His were printed in block letters— his cursive was unreadable—on copier paper with a black ballpoint.

Alec wiped at his eyes. He felt like a kid who, while digging a tunnel to China, had unearthed a box of priceless gold coins.

They had written these for each other. During the wedding ceremony at the church, they had recited the traditional vows, promising to love, honor, and cherish, whatever those vague terms meant. That night in the hotel's honeymoon suite, they had exchanged their personal ones, hoping to make the abstract specific.

His young wife had promised to kiss him every morning with a smile...make the coffee...run the household...pay for his grad school...change 95 percent of the diapers they hoped to need...bake his favorite cookies and always have some in the freezer...always be pleasant to his mother...clean the gunk out of the sink strainers...and pray for him every single day...

Alec smiled. Last time he checked the freezer, they were down to a dozen chocolate chip cookies, still his favorite after 17 years. Was she praying for him?

He hesitated before turning to his. What had he forgotten?

The biggie jumped out at him, as he feared it would. "I promise to—right after grad school—totally support us financially. We will always make ends meet on my check alone so that you can be a stay-at-home mom until all six kids are out of high school."

It wasn't the way he had grown up. His favorite, most comfortable memories as a little boy were of staying at his Grandma Lottie's. His earliest memories were of spending summer days with her and Grandpa Peter. Their house felt more like home than his own. Even with a younger brother and sister, he was often lonely. And so, he had wanted six kids for him and Annie to love to pieces day in and day out.

They had lost the fourth baby, five months in the womb. There were no more after that.

"I promise you will always be my one and only *sweetheart.*"

The tears flowed now. *Dear God, what happened? I didn't mean for it to happen.*

After a time, Alec felt a cleansing effect. He had come to the end of himself and realized there was no other place to hide. God was carrying him now.

His eyes fell on the loose papers. In those early, exhilarating, romantic days Anne often copied poems and quotations that

moved her. He picked one up. It was a poem by Edgar A.
Guest.

"Send Her a Valentine"

Send her a valentine to say
You love her in the same old way.
Just drop the long familiar ways
And live again the old-time days
When love was new and youth was bright
And all was laughter and delight,
And treat her as you would if she
Were still the girl that used to be.

Pretend that all the years have passed
Without one cold and wintry blast;
That you are coming still to woo
Your sweetheart as you used to do;
Forget that you have walked along
The paths of life where right and wrong
And joy and grief in battle are,
And play the heart without a scar.

Be what you were when youth was fine
And send to her a valentine;
Forget the burdens and the woe
That have been given you to know
And to the wife, so fond and true,
The pledges of the past renew.
'Twill cure her life of every ill
To find that you're her sweetheart still.

"Daddy! Daddy! Where are you?"

"Up here, Mandy." Alec wiped his flannel sleeve across his face and took a deep breath.

His daughter's light footstep tapped on the wooden stairs. "Here you are! Mr. Kingsley is on the phone." She handed him the cordless.

"Thanks, punkin." He held out his other arm, inviting her to sit on his lap. She settled in. "Joel. Morning."

"Hi, Alec. Hope I'm not disrupting anything."

"Not at all. What's up?"

Joel cleared his throat. "I need some advice from a school board member, preferably one of my allies."

"At your service."

"Thanks." He took an audibly deep breath. "Is there any rule against a principal dating a teacher?"

Alec chuckled. "I don't think so. I hear female teachers can even be married now. And if you were to smoke and have a few at the neighborhood bar, only a handful of folks would frown."

"I suppose that's my real question. How many would frown if I courted Britte? No smoking and drinking involved."

Alec laughed now, as heartily as he had been crying earlier. "Congratulations!"

"Uh, thanks, but you didn't answer my question."

He glanced at the poem on the floor near his knee and hugged Mandy. "Three unfortunate, miserly wretches come to mind, but then their faces are always pinched and only one of them has a vote on the board. Joel, it doesn't matter what Valley Oaks thinks. If you're falling for Britte Olafsson, don't let *anything* get in your way. I've been married for 17 years, and nothing, absolutely *nothing,* compares to that relationship. Don't let life get in the way. That *is* life, real life."

"You're sure about that?" he asked, his tone facetious.

Alec smiled at his own adamancy. "You caught me at a strange moment. By the way, do you have any ideas on how to be romantic? I'm a little out of practice in that department."

It was Joel's turn to laugh. "Tell me about it."

"Come on, help me out. What are you doing with Britte today since there's no school?"

"She's coming over and we're talking coaching."

"Now that certainly sounds romantic."

"It's who she is, you know. And I'm cooking dinner for her."

"Ahh, now we're getting somewhere."

"I want to take her to Chicago to see the Bulls play because I think she'd like that."

"I bet she would."

"Valentine's Day is coming."

"When?"

"Man, you are out of practice. It's always the same, February 14. That'll be here in about a month. So I want to buy something special for her. Britte's not the roses-and-candy type, but I'll figure something out."

"Anne's not the roses-and-candy type either."

"Well, you've known her for a long time. Shouldn't be too hard. Thanks, Alec. I really appreciate your encouragement."

"What if I had told you instead to forget dating her?"

Joel was quiet for a moment. "I'd have put a message on the Community Center sign. 'Kingsley Woos Olafsson.' Maybe put an ad in the kids' *Viking Views*."

Alec laughed. "I think that's why we hired you. Great attitude. Have a good one!"

"You, too. See you."

Alec pushed the off button. True, he had known Anne for a long time...so why didn't it feel as though he *knew* her?

"Daddy, does Mr. Kingsley love Britte?"

"Sounds like it."

She grinned up at him, her face a miniature of her mother's. "Britte needs a husband."

"And why is that?"

"All my favorite teachers are 'Mrs.'"

He smiled. "Hey, do you think Mommy would like me to cook dinner for her?"

"Yeah. Then she could paint."

"Paint?"

"She wants to paint. She said if she didn't cook, maybe she'd have time to paint." Mandy pointed to the scattered piles. "What is all this stuff?"

"Uh, memories. Want to see what your mom and dad looked like when we were Drew's age?" He reached for the shoebox and began to share his and Anne's love story. The youngest proof of its reality listened intently, her gray eyes rapt with delight.

Forty-Three

Britte studied Joel's condominium complex as they pulled into his driveway a few blocks behind the high school football field. Nice place. New construction. Minimally landscaped with small evergreen bushes. Not many units. Uniform beige siding with forest green trim. Unhindered views of snow-covered fields. "Joel, I could have driven myself over."

"But I would have followed you home anyway." He tapped the garage door opener and glanced over at her. "Cal called. Hughes is out on bail."

"Here we go again." She wrinkled her nose.

He drove into the attached garage and cut the engine. "He said you need to get a restraining order. If Hughes gets within a hundred feet of you, he gets arrested."

"Guess that means no more games for him." She felt again a heavy sadness for his family.

Joel touched her shoulder. "On a cheerier note, I called Alec Sutton earlier and asked him what he thought as a board member. About, you know, us."

She laughed. "You didn't! He probably wonders if you've lost your mind going out with me, of all women. He knew me when I was a spoiled child and smart-mouthed adolescent."

"Has anything changed?"

"That remark is going to cost you."

"How about a home-cooked dinner?"

"Sounds great." They climbed from the car, and he opened the door leading into the condo. "So what was Alec's response?"

"He thought I'd lost my mind."

She stepped through the door he held open. "There is a glint in your eye, Mr. Kingsley." It was, in fact, a gleam of delight that erased years from his face. She had never seen him so unguarded. "I don't know if I believe you."

He smiled and shut the door. He really had an awfully nice smile.

"You should do that more often."

"What's that?"

"Smile. Christmas is over, you know."

He chuckled, understanding her reference to the dictum that teachers shouldn't smile before Christmas. "The timing is different for principals and generals. We have to wait until Easter to crack a smile. May I take your coat?"

With his help, she shrugged out of it. "Nice kitchen." Talk about gleaming. The walls and countertops were white, as were the apparently new appliances. There was a sliding glass door overlooking a deck and a field. A square, light-colored wooden table completed the décor. She slipped off her athletic shoes. "Spotless, too, of course."

"Of course. It's not too tough to clean, living alone."

"You saw my kitchen."

"But you're in the middle of basketball season. Come on. I'll give you the grand tour."

She followed him through the wide doorway that led into a large hall. One end of it was open to the living room. Around its other sides were the front door and a smaller hall.

Joel went to a closet and hung their coats. He gestured. "This is it. Bedrooms down there, one of which is my office away from the office. Living room here." They walked into the sparsely furnished, contemporary room.

"It's all so bright and new."

"Bachelor pad. No Aunt Mabel ever lived here. Did I pass inspection?"

She gave him a puzzled look.

"Based on my home, do you think we should continue getting to know each other?"

"You're passing with flying colors, General. How about vice versa?"

"Flying colors, ma'am. Your house conjures up cozy grandma memories. And no, I'm not comparing you to my grandmother."

She smiled. "Good. So what did Alec really say?"

"We're not breaking any rules."

"I wouldn't want to break any rules. What are we going to do about the gossip?"

"Ignore it. How about some coffee?"

"Love some. Mind if I watch you make it? After drinking yours, mine didn't taste quite right this morning."

"I'll teach you." In the kitchen, he talked her through grinding beans and measuring water. "How did practice go?" Though it was a school holiday, both of them had gone in to work, greeting each other from a distance.

"Fine. Jordan wasn't there. I talked with the girls about the situation. Naturally, they'd already heard about it. They'll support her. Hopefully they can talk her into coming back to school tomorrow. I suggested we bring Trevor on board as a manager. They liked the idea."

"You are something else, Britte. I want to suspend him indefinitely."

She smiled. "You know that wouldn't help him."

"It'd help me. Cal told me the kids are staying with relatives for the time being. Their mother's gone to a shelter."

"I wish we could fix it for them."

He touched her shoulder lightly and reached behind her into a cupboard. "Maybe lock up Gordon and throw away the key?"

"Mm-hmm. Something like that."

Leaning against the counters, they chatted like old friends as the coffee dripped into the carafe. Its strong scent eventually engulfed the kitchen, and Joel filled two mugs. He wore blue jeans today with an olive green fleece shirt that highlighted the green flecks in his eyes. When he handed a cup to her, his fingers brushed against hers. She kept her eyes lowered, concerned they would betray her thoughts, which jolted as if electrified. Why was it that for nearly six months she hadn't noticed how attractive the guy was?

In the living room she sat on the couch, leaving the recliner for him. He chose, instead, the floor, his back against the couch.

"Ready?" he asked.

"I guess." She eyed the stack of videos, clearly labeled as girls basketball games, dated last year. "If you think this will help."

"I think it will." He pointed the remote at the television and VCR.

Instantly she came into view, huddled with her girls on the court. The scoreboard indicated zero to zero. It was at the beginning of a game.

Joel lowered the volume and began narrating in a quiet tone. He fast-forwarded through much of the game, focusing instead on Britte's interaction with the girls. He praised, pointed out inconsistencies, made suggestions, compared her style with what he had seen of it this season.

"Okay?" He stopped the tape and looked back at her.

She nodded.

"I think I've figured out a pattern. Mind if I show you more?"

"Please." She set her mug on the end table. "I respect your opinion."

"All right, then." He turned around again and aimed the remote.

Britte watched the start of another game. She truly didn't mind being critiqued by someone who knew what he was talking about and didn't have a daughter on the team. What she found disturbing was the idea of Joel diligently studying her on tape. It was an unparalleled act of outright caring. The impact of it interfered with her effort to concentrate on basketball.

Well, that and the movement of his shoulder against her leg every time he lifted the remote.

She pulled her legs up on the couch and tucked them beneath herself, stifling a sigh.

Over two hours later, Joel flicked off the television with the remote and swiveled on the floor to face Britte. He rested his arms on the couch. "Does that make sense?"

Those eyes of hers that mesmerized him were clouded. Avoiding eye contact with him, she nodded.

Had he misread her? He thought she was strong enough to handle the criticism. "I didn't mean to—"

"Oh, Joel, how could I get so far off track? It's as if I totally forgot the definition of teamwork. And what's happened to my focus? The girls are first and foremost. I know that!"

He moved up to the couch, put his arms around her, and kissed the top of her head. "Hey, we all do it. You don't have to be perfect."

"I blew it." Her voice was muffled against his shoulder. "I've alienated them."

"Only for the moment. It's been a tough season every which way. And I wasn't much help. You were right insisting that I back you up." He remembered the faculty Christmas party when she had asked for his support against Hughes. "Britte, I'm sorry for being political. Just like you, I lost sight of my team." He looked down at her. "You're my team first. We are in this together, on the same side. And I promise I will always be faithful. Nobody messes with my faculty."

She stared back at him. "Do you know how much that means to me? I feel like a two-ton weight just fell away."

Respond to those in need. It was ingrained in him to comfort Britte the moment he saw her hurting, and so he had jumped again to her side. But maybe it wasn't such a good idea, sitting closely, holding her, losing himself in that royal blue gaze...in the thought of that wonderful mouth, so close—

"*Semper fi*, right?" she asked. "Always faithful."

"How'd you know that?"

She grinned. "Do you remember working out with the boys basketball team one afternoon? You rolled up your T-shirt sleeves."

He groaned.

"Drew told his mom about the tattoo, and she told me, and then Alec told us it's a Marine phrase." She laughed. "Guess you can't say much against tattoos to the kids. They all know about your eagle and your *semper fi* banner. Youch! Didn't that hurt?"

"To a Marine?" he scoffed. "No way."

She smiled again. Such a great smile. "Anyway, thank you. For all of this. Those tapes helped. I can't believe you put so much time into watching..." Her voice faded.

"My pleasure." He tilted her chin up and hesitated. She fit too well in his arms, in his home, in his thoughts. Best not to even start. "Mmm. This is not a good idea."

"Rules of engagement?" she murmured.

"I'm making them up as we go along." His eyes lingered on hers. "We'd never get to dinner, Princess." Reluctantly he let go of her chin and stood. "And I promised to cook for you."

"Can I help?"

"Uh, no." He gave her a crooked smile and headed toward the kitchen. "Why don't you stay put and relax?" *While I go out here and cool down...*

Forty-Four

Alec pirouetted Mandy around the kitchen as they both sang loudly and off-key. His younger daughter's favorite music—a children's chorus singing Christian lyrics to a hip-hop beat—blared from the stereo. At the counter, Amy shredded goat cheese, singing at the top of her voice. It was late afternoon, and they were preparing tacos for dinner. Drew was at basketball practice.

What a day! Alec laughed, leapt in the air, and clicked his heels. The girls squealed and giggled at his antics.

Sifting through the memories earlier in the attic was like jump-starting a dead corner of his mind, the corner responsible for creating romantic ideas. Once that was charged, the energy flowed. He finished long-standing plumbing and carpentry projects around the house. He planned Anne's favorite dinner complete with chocolate cake. He wrote three notes that said "I love you" and posted them on the vanity, in her sock drawer, and on her pillow. He made a list of possible gifts he could buy her for Valentine's Day. He thought of things he could do for her.

He checked the calendar and noticed with dismay that he was scheduled to be out of town on business February 14! Why had he scheduled that? Because the date hadn't meant a thing. His mind raced. Could he reschedule? He *had* to reschedule.

Think about it. Pray about it.

The phone rang. Amy answered while Alec turned down the music.

"Dad, it's Mom."

He took the cordless phone. "Hi, sweet—" Pausing, he consciously dropped the automatic tone. "*Sweetheart.* Annie. Love of my life. Bearer of my children."

"What did you break?"

"Nothing. Actually, I fixed a few things."

"Great. Alec." There was an edge to her voice. "It's sleeting here. The forecast says it's going to get worse. What's it doing there?"

"I haven't noticed." He stepped over to the sink and peered through the window above it. It was too dark to see anything. "Can you leave now?"

"Cars are sliding across the parking lot." Her voice trembled slightly. "It looks like a sheet of ice. It was fine 20 minutes ago when the last customer left."

They both knew how drastically winter weather could change within a few moments time. Those caught unawares... The silence hung heavy between them. Images played in his head, and he knew they'd been in Anne's before she picked up the phone to call. "I'll come get you."

"No! Please, Alec," she nearly whimpered. "Don't come. Don't put me through that."

"Okay, okay. I won't." He wouldn't. She had put him through that, traveling when she should have stayed put during an ice storm...

"I'll wait it out."

Drew walked through the door.

"Hold on, Anne. Drew's home." He noticed his son's odd expression, but thought it best not to ask what was wrong with Anne listening. "What are the roads like?"

Drew shrugged out of his jacket. "Bad." He chewed a corner of his lip and turned to hang up his coat.

Alec darted over to him and laid a heavy hand on his shoulder. Drew came back around. Alec looked up at his tall son. Alarmed at the little boy visage he saw there, he pressed the phone against his chest and mouthed, "What happened?"

"The car's fine." His overgrown hands fluttered. "I sailed past a stop sign, but nothing happened! I wasn't going fast, honest!"

Alec patted his cheek, relieved. "Now you know how to drive on ice." He put the phone to his ear.

"Alec!"

"I'm here."

"This is a toll call!"

"Oh, yeah. Drew says the roads are bad here, too. Stay put."

"Charlie said I can go home with him. He doesn't live far and it's flat between here and there. I'll call you in a bit. Bye."

"Bye. I love—" He heard the disconnection click.

So much for wowing his wife with romantic surprises. With disgust he punched the off button. Romantic surprises? That was the least of his concerns! Charlie Manning was right where he should be, comforting Annie through one of her worst nightmares.

⌒

In the midst of yet another public service announcement to stay off the highways, Anne snapped the radio's power dial and walked out into the shop. She crossed her arms in an effort to stop her hands from trembling. "Charlie, what are you doing?"

Her boss stood in front of the display of brushes, poking through them, lifting out one, then another. Had he heard her? Today's flannel shirt was blues and grays that highlighted his eyes and hair. In his left hand he held a shopping bag. Now he deposited a handful of brushes into it as he stepped over to the paints.

Anne went to the window and shivered. Truthfully, she didn't even want to ride down the street with Charlie. The city streets would not resemble the two-lane state highway or the parking lot. Still, to go out at all on a night like—

"Anne."

She turned to face him.

"You seem troubled."

Once again his perceptiveness sliced through her jumbled emotions. She didn't know where to begin.

"Perhaps staying at my house isn't such a good idea. Your husband might get the wrong impression."

Anne chuckled at the absurd idea. "I told you that you remind me of my brother." Tall, gaunt, artistic, a shade on the odd side. "The illustrator who lives in Oregon."

"And you remind me of my daughter, but Alec has no way of knowing that since I've never mentioned it to you. So I put myself in his shoes. If my wife were in this predicament, I'd risk life and limb to get to her."

"Alec won't do that."

"I gathered that from your conversation. Sorry, I over-heard that part. At any rate, he's a red-blooded male who will not be comfortable with you at another man's house. Therefore, I've taken the liberty of calling the motel next door on my cell while you were on the other phone. They have a room. My treat. It's what I would do for my daughter. And, I'd give this to her." He handed her the shopping bag. "We'll grab a canvas, too."

Anne stared at him, speechless.

"Go and paint, dear lady."

"Oh, Charlie!" Tears sprang to her eyes. "This isn't nec-essary."

"I think it is. Why don't you get your coat?"

A few moments later they stood again at the front door, coats on, lights off. Charlie held a canvas and an easel under one arm.

Anne peeked in the shopping bag she carried; there were oils, brushes, a palette, a sketch book. "Charlie, I can walk to the motel." The parking lot of the mini-mall in which the art store was located abutted the motel's lot. A ten foot snow bank separated them.

"You'd have to walk out to the street and around. I'll drive you." He moved to open the door. "It's not exactly out of my way."

"I prefer to walk." Her voice sounded like a stranger's.

"Anne, what is it?"

"I...I don't want to..." She waited for the shudder to pass. "It's the ice. I was in an accident seven years ago. The weather was like this." Over the years she grew used to snow driving again. Ice storms were rare. If conditions predicted one, she simply didn't drive.

She went on. "Alec was home with the kids. I was in Rockville, finishing up Christmas shopping at the mall until late evening. I ignored the radio warnings and drove right into the storm. The car slid off of the highway." She paused. "I was five months pregnant." Another pause. "He would have been our fourth." She wiped a tear from her eye.

Charlie crooked his elbow and held it toward her. "Come on," he said in his soft voice. "I'll walk you over to the motel."

Forty-Five

"Joel, this is wonderful." Britte closed her eyes and inhaled the scents wafting from the forkful of fettuccine Alfredo she held up. "Mmm. Cheese and garlic. Salmon with some kind of honey-mustard sauce. French bread. Salad. Where did you learn to cook like this?"

"That fiancée I mentioned? She was studying to become a chef." He shrugged. "I kind of got hooked on the process when I helped Marti practice."

"Is she a chef now?"

"I have no idea." Soft jazz music filled the quiet space. He eyed her over a bite of salmon. Did he detect a waver of disbelief? "Really. It was a long time ago. Remember? I'm much older than you. Lots of water under the bridge. It's like that Bible verse about old things passing away and everything becoming new."

She smiled. "I keep forgetting how *old* you are."

And he kept forgetting how young she was, how naïve. "Joel, what's your family like?"

"Typical middle-class, hardworking. Churchgoing, but not Christ-centered like yours. I'm guessing you were a little girl when you met Jesus?"

"Nine."

"Then you're ages ahead of me in that department. I was 30 years old."

"How did it happen?"

Now the junk would come out. He saw the compassion in her eyes and knew she was indeed eons older in a spiritual

310

sense. Could they ever truly meet on a level playing field? "Britte, it's not a fairy-tale story like yours."

"I did not grow up in a castle!" Her tone was indignant. "My parents made mistakes. And I haven't been perfect!"

He couldn't help but laugh. "That's a relative term. What's the worst thing you've ever done? Cut class? Gotten a speeding ticket?"

"You know that's not the point. There are no degrees of badness. In God's eyes, if we're angry with a brother we're as guilty as if we've committed murder. But if we have faith in Christ, He sees us as perfect. And one time I had two speeding tickets within a year."

"No!"

"Yes!"

"I'm shocked."

"I thought you would be." She reached over and squeezed his hand. "You don't have to tell me about the worst thing you've ever done."

He met her blue gaze. "You are one of a kind, Britte Olafsson. For years I've been successfully avoiding feeling too much. Jesus has given me work to do. And like a general, I can disengage the grayness of feelings and deal in the black and white. One, two, three, get it done. Now, every time I look at you, emotions just sort of...explode. Part of me wants to run away so I don't have to deal with them. I don't really know *how* to deal with them."

A momentary pain registered in her eyes. "Jesus dealt with them. He laughed. He cried."

"Yeah, but He was perfect."

"Maybe we could do it together."

He took her hand still covering his, brought it to his lips, and kissed the palm. Already he had said so much more than he intended, revealed the tip of that unfathomable iceberg of emotions. *Lord, give me the strength to deal with them when the meltdown comes.*

~

Britte sat on the couch. This time Joel had chosen the recliner, a large one that suited his long frame. The footrest was down. He crossed his legs, ankle to knee, and sipped coffee. They had switched to decaf. The music still played softly. Blinds were shut against the cold night. She could hear the wind howling.

Since kissing her hand, Joel had kept his distance, even while they cleaned the kitchen together. She sensed he was ill at ease after opening up to her. Had he ever discussed emotions before? She doubted it. From what little he had revealed of his family, she deduced that he came from a tradition of stoic, military males. Of course, she had almost guessed that from her own observations. No wonder he had migraines.

He was telling her about becoming a teacher. "That's genetic, too, from my mother's side. She taught for 30 years before retiring. She'd still be teaching if Dad hadn't retired as a mechanic and wanted them to spend more time together. She still volunteers. In the Marines, I liked every aspect of teaching, of bringing order to the chaos of untrained minds. After the service, I went to college. Then I taught high school history for four years. Once I saw how chaotic secondary school environments could be, I went to work on my master's in administration."

"Let me guess. You became a principal to bring order to the bigger picture."

He grinned. "Do you know how ridiculous a general looks in a puny classroom?"

She laughed. "Well, you have done a tremendous job of bringing order to Valley Oaks High. You've got my vote."

"Your vote doesn't count."

A vague sense of disquiet threaded itself through her chest. "Joel, they'll renew your contract after all the good you've accomplished. It's so obvious what you've done." They *had* to renew it.

"Some people don't like knowing we've got big-city-type problems at the school." He shrugged. "If we don't highlight them by attempting to remedy them, then they don't exist. You look like you're going to pop."

"I might." Her face felt warm with anger.

He smiled. "Don't worry about it, Miss O. Want some more coffee?"

"No, thanks." They looked at one another for a moment, and then she prompted, "And so after the Marines you became a Christian?"

"Not immediately. Britte." He set his cup on the end table and looked at her again. "I was dishonorably discharged."

"What does that mean?"

"Forfeiture of veteran's benefits. I had a good lawyer; he got the confinement sentence reduced to six months."

"*Confinement?* As in jail?"

"I was court-martialed for disobeying orders. It's a dishonor that doesn't go away. The school board knows all about it and decided to hire me in spite of it." He gave her a wry smile. "Other than that, my record was spotless. So to speak. Another relative term."

"*Did* you disobey orders?"

"Oh, definitely. I was leading a four-man recon team in Kuwait. There were other teams out. Iraqis had been spotted. It was our job to figure out exactly where they were. My team split up. When all was said and done..." His voiced trailed off. She suspected his thoughts skimmed details, reliving, eliminating what he didn't want to tell her. "One of my guys was wounded. His partner couldn't get him through alone. I was ordered to pull out." He gave her a tight smile. "We don't leave anyone behind. My partner and I were in a good position to get the other two out. I informed my CO of my decision, told him not to send the chopper. It was getting near dawn. The timing was wrong. The chopper came. A Marine on board was killed picking us up." His face went blank.

"Joel?"

He blinked.

"I'm sorry."

He nodded.

"If he hadn't died, would they have given you a medal for saving the other two?"

His chuckle was a dry rumble. "You sound like my dad. Bottom line, I disobeyed orders. Automatic discharge with dishonor."

In spite of the circumstances, she wanted to add, but knew that he would not hide behind excuses. Britte set the empty mug she had been clutching on the end table, sickened at the thought of what he had lived through. "Does that make you feel betrayed?"

"Now you sound like Sam, asking questions about my feelings." His stare and set jaw challenged her.

"I think," she offered softly, "this is how we deal with your emotions together."

"You really want to tackle that?"

"Yes. It's called friendship, Joel. I can't have a relationship without being friends. I can't do the man-woman thing without a friendship. Do you want to tackle *that?*"

He propped his elbow on the chair arm and stuck his chin in his hand, quietly studying her for a moment. "You mean get rid of my politically incorrect biases?"

She raised her brows. "If that's what it takes."

"You drive a hard bargain, lady. Kingsley Marines don't laugh much, and they sure don't cry."

"All things are possible through Christ."

He rubbed his chin, the struggle evident on his face. At last he said, "No, I don't feel betrayed. Not anymore. The Corps was my life from the time I could walk. I'd do it all over again. But the aftermath was...ugly. Marti bailed out. I was over the edge, aimless for about a year. Sam's a 'Nam vet. He found me outside the VA hospital, drunk, feeling betrayed. He volunteers at the hospital, but he couldn't get me inside for treatment. He took me home, later kept tabs on me, got me through the rough spots, got me into college in Chicago. All the time talking about Jesus. *He* didn't really sink in for a few years. Not until I saw, truly saw, all that order He brought into this chaotic world. Britte, don't cry."

She wiped at her eyes.

"It all turned out for the best, Princess. It all turned out for the best."

Joel watched her trying to compose herself. He gripped the arms of the chair, refusing to comfort her...refusing to give in to the anguish rumbling through his chest like an armored tank. She could cry for the both of them.

"Joel, how can you keep all of that inside of you?"

He couldn't, not without repercussions. There was a telltale thumping in the back of his head.

"Joel." Her voice was a little shaky. "Are you getting a headache?"

"No," he lied.

She was beside him, pushing his hands from his head, pressing her fingertips against his temples. And then she was kissing his forehead, his cheeks, her tears falling on his face. Her face blurred before him, and then he knew.

The iceberg was melting.

Forty-Six

Alec did his best to bolster the kids' festive mood around the dinner table, but each tasteless bite he took intensified the ache in his stomach. His efforts lagged.

The girls took it in stride that Mom wasn't driving on the ice; she'd come home when the storm quit. No big deal. Mom always took care of herself. They saw no reason not to go ahead and eat on the good china in the dining room and use linen napkins. Mom wouldn't mind. She liked special occasions.

Drew laughed with his little sisters. Recovered from his near brush with the need of a tow truck for the second time in one season, he probably was elated as well at the fact that his mother was safe, wherever she was. He would remember the accident; he had been nine at the time.

Elation didn't describe anything near the emotions tearing through Alec. He was disappointed, angry, relieved, upset, frustrated, defeated, seething. The overriding one? He was really ticked off at Anne, the weather, Charlie Manning, and probably God. He wanted to break something.

To divert his attention, he interrupted the discussion about what the kids planned to do if school were canceled tomorrow. "Hey, gang, won't Mom feel bad," he hoped she would feel extremely bad, "that we had her favorite without her?"

Drew held a taco in front of his mouth. "Favorite? Tacos aren't her favorite." He took a bite.

"Sure they are."

317

He shook his head and mumbled around his mouthful, "They're mine and Mandy's."

Alec glanced at the girls. They shrugged. "So, Andrew, what is her favorite?"

"Salmon."

"We never have salmon."

"Because you three don't like it. Whenever there's salmon on a menu, that's what she orders. And when you're out of town, that's what she fixes for herself. It's not bad, actually."

Alec stared at his son as the boy stuffed another huge bite into his mouth. *Salmon?*

Mandy reached over and patted Alec's arm while glaring at her brother. "Yeah, well, smarty-pants, we baked her favorite dessert. Chocolate cake."

Drew's laughter turned into a minor choking episode.

Alec gave up all pretense of eating and waited. What else didn't he know about Anne?

Drew gulped water. "Amy, what's Mom got stocked in the freezer downstairs? Those cartons we're not supposed to touch?"

"Ice cream. Praline."

He gave her a thumbs-up sign. "Mandy, what does Grammy bake for Mom's birthday *every* year?"

"Pecan pie!" She met her brother's high five across the table.

Alec frowned. "I knew that."

"She doesn't like chocolate, Dad."

Alec knew that too. He'd just...forgotten.

I wonder if Charlie Manning knows?

⌒

Anne spun around the motel room and giggled. Sleet pelted against the window, but her children were safe at home with their father. She was warm and cozy. And there, under a ceiling light, stood an easel with a blank canvas.

On the way through the parking lot, she had stopped at her car and retrieved warm-up pants, sweat shirt, socks, and athletic shoes. After telling Charlie goodbye and checking into the room, she had immediately filled the bathtub and slipped out of her sweater and slacks. She soaked in the steamy water until the tensions melted away. The thought struck her that the working woman did indeed have time for a bath. Her only regret was she didn't carry bubble bath in her gym bag. Next time she'd be prepared.

At that she had smiled, and then she began to imagine what she would paint.

She went to the phone. Alec would be anxious by now and wondering if they had made it to Charlie's house. On second thought, she should use the cell and not add charges to the room bill. She dug it out of her purse and pressed her home number. The phone at the other end rang and rang. She counted 15 rings and started over again. When the same thing happened, she realized that the phone lines were probably down.

Not uncommon, which was why they had two cell phones. She punched in the number of Alec's and reached his voice mail.

"Hey, mister. I can't get through to the house phone. I suppose it's the storm. I'm at the Stratford Inn next to the store, in room 212. Charlie insists on paying for it. He said he wouldn't want *his* wife staying with another man. And guess what?" She giggled. "I've got an easel and canvas and paints! Right here in the room! I'm going to *paint*. If I can't be home with you all, this is my second choice. Just me and the paints. Call me. I'll keep the cell phone turned on. I love you."

Anne stared at the blank canvas. "Oh, Father, thank You."

~

"Daaad!" Amy whined, stretching the one syllable down the hallway and into the den.

Alec had been staring at the computer screen, pretending to work, pretending his stomach wasn't churning, pretending the image of Anne cooking with that tall artist in that tall artist's kitchen wasn't rerunning in his mind's eye.

He swiveled his head around. "What, Amy?" His tone was sharp.

His daughter didn't seem to notice. "The phone's not working!" she wailed.

Alec yanked the desk phone from its cradle. There was no dial tone. He rubbed his forehead. "It happens, honey. The ice storm—"

"It's not fair!"

No, it's not! he wanted to scream. *Your mother can't get through! She's hanging out with another man. I don't even know if she tried to call!*

"Dad. Can I use your cell phone just this one time? We won't talk long, I promise!"

Cell phone! Where was the cell phone? "Drew!" Alec shouted and rushed out the door and into the family room where his son sat on the couch. "Drew, what'd you do with the cell?"

A sheepish look crossed his face and he jumped up. "It's still in the car. I'll get it."

"*I'll* get it!" Better to expend his energy going out to the barn rather than throttling the kid.

"I'm sorry, Dad. I know I'm not supposed to—"

Alec shut the kitchen door on his words, walked across the porch, and out the door. He stepped gingerly down the steps, although he had already sprinkled rock salt on them.

The sleet stung his face and felt as if it would penetrate his sweatshirt.

That other night came back to him with a fury. The sheriff had called. *There's been an accident... Your wife will be all right, but she's in shock, bruised. The ambulance is transporting her to the hospital, just to be sure.* Someone witnessed her car leaving the highway and notified the sheriff's office. She wasn't exposed long to the cold. Still, it had taken awhile to extricate her from the crumpled car that had rolled, coming to rest on its side...

Alec entered the barn and flipped on the lights. The two dogs bounded from their warm straw beds, tails wagging. He patted them cursorily and went to Drew's car. After several moments spent checking on top of the seats, below the seats, the floor, the glove box, and the door pockets, he mentally reviewed what being grounded would mean to Drew a second time around in one season.

As he backed out of the car, the small silver phone caught his eye. It was in the backseat. The backseat?!

He retrieved it and turned it on. Nothing happened. Dead battery.

Alec ran his hand across his face. "Okay, Lord. I quit. *You* know where she is. *You* know what she's doing. *You* take care of her. Please. Keep her," he took a deep breath, "keep her from driving home in this."

Forty-Seven

A distant chirrup startled Britte awake. It sounded again. Her foggy brain registered that it was a cell phone. Not hers. Abruptly, Joel was on his feet, and she was toppling onto the couch cushion where he had been sitting close beside her, his arm around her.

He loped to the kitchen. She sat up and noticed from the VCR's digital clock that it was 10:35. Considering Joel's chest probably wasn't going to be her pillow for the rest of the night, she should go home.

He returned to the living room now, cell phone to his ear. She watched him as he talked. His face was becoming increasingly familiar. A short while ago she had kissed his furrowed brow and stern jawline, his stubbled cheek damp with tears shed by them both. When she sat on the arm of the recliner, he had buried his head against her neck, his shoulders heaving.

After a time he had looked at her as if to say something, but instead stood, gathered her into his arms and wordlessly guided them to the couch. He kissed her then…passionately kissed her as she'd never been kissed before.

He raised his face a mere fraction of an inch. "Britte." His voice was a low rumble, his eyes at half-mast. "What's a princess like you doing hanging out with an old, broken-down Marine?"

She touched his chin. Her throat was dry; her heart hammered 100 miles an hour. "I have no clue."

He chuckled softly and lowered his head again.

After a time he sighed deeply, his arms still around her. "Mmm, those rules of engagement keep revising themselves. Not a good idea. I should take you home." He hugged her tightly. "But can I just hold you for a while?"

Nodding, she snuggled against him, trying to catch her breath, almost frightened at the depth of her response to this man. She *should* go home. Instead, they both fell asleep.

He closed up the phone now and smiled at her. "Hi."

"Hi."

He slumped back onto the couch, his shoulder against hers, reached for her hand, and yawned. "That was Bruce Waverly." The school district's superintendent. "Evidently we're in the midst of an ice storm and the phone system is down. That's why he called on the cell. Some of the districts are already canceling tomorrow's classes, but he's decided to wait. Forecast says it'll warm up through the night." He yawned again.

"Ice storm? I'd better go home."

"Mm-hmm." He turned toward her. "Hey, Britte. I just found a better cure than a pill for migraines. Kissing you! Maybe we could patent it."

They laughed like two silly teenagers. Britte knew he was spoiling his General's image, but she wasn't about to point that out.

"Joel! Ice storm!" She stood, pulling on his arm. "Let's go."

In a slaphappy mood, they managed to put on shoes and coats. Outside in the garage, she stood by the large automatic door as it rattled open. "Uh-oh."

He came up behind her. "What?"

"Look at this." The streetlight shone on the blacktop road, his driveway, bare branches, and evergreens. A thick layer of ice coated everything in sight. Like falling needles, frozen raindrops pelted the snow-covered lawn with a steady rat-a-tat-tat.

"It's beautiful."

Surprised at his comment, she peered over her shoulder at him. "It is, but I can't believe we didn't hear it from inside."

"No mystery to me why we didn't hear it." He tugged at her sleeve. "Come on. I shall get you safely home, O Damsel in Distress. Piece of cake."

"Joel, have you ever driven in this stuff? Out in the country?"

"I'm sure I have. Chicago is in the Midwest, isn't it?"

"Your armor is looking a bit smudgy, O Knight. Promise to go slow?"

They climbed into his car. He inched it in reverse down the driveway. All the while she narrated a litany of harrowing incidents that resulted from driving in this type of storm.

"See, Britte? So far, so good. Got your seat belt on? No more stories. Please!"

Half a block from his condo, they crept toward a stop sign. Joel braked and the antilock brakes went into action, but to no avail. The car didn't respond. It just continued moving, as if in slow-motion, through the intersection.

The center of the blacktop road rose slightly higher than its sides. The car, its steering nonresponsive, followed the gentle line of the slope toward the left, sliding slowly until at last coming to rest in a shallow ditch.

"Whoops," Joel announced.

Britte sighed dramatically. "Well, Knight, your armor is completely corroded now."

"Never fear, Princess. I shall *carry* you home." He cut the engine and pushed his door open a few inches. "But we'll have to get out your door. Mine appears to be blocked."

She opened hers and climbed out, her athletic shoes crunching through the snow. He followed her. "Joel, you don't need to walk me home. Then you'll have to walk all the way back. I can go by myself—"

"Are you kidding? I wouldn't let you do that even if Hughes were still locked up. Don't you have a hat or a hood?" He was tying on his own hood, and then he held out his gloved hand. "Give me your hand. Why aren't you wearing gloves?"

"Because I was just going to ride in your car for eight blocks." They climbed up to the road. "I can walk home. Nobody's going to be out on a night like this."

"You think we're the only numskulls out? I'll go— Whoa!" His left foot hit the iced pavement and, like the car, kept on going.

Britte, still on the snow, steadied him. Inwardly she moaned. Things were not looking good.

He managed to reel in his left foot. "Careful. We'll cross here and then just stay in the snow as much as possible. But first we'll go back inside and get you some gloves and a hat."

He was beginning to sound persnickety like Brady, which annoyed her. "Mr. Kingsley, I already have a mother and a father." Hands locked, they walked by millimeters. "And a big brother and a big sister."

Britte's foot slipped. Joel lost his balance. They rocked back and forth, exclaiming "Ohhhh" in unison with increasing volume. And then they fell.

"Ouch!" she cried. Her hip and elbow took the brunt of the fall. She gave up resisting it and lay back on the street.

Sprawled beside her, Joel asked, "Are you okay?"

"Sure. Falling flat on the pavement is a favorite pastime of mine. Are you okay?"

"Yeah. Assuming we can make it across the street to my place, will you spend the night with me?"

"No! Of course not! Don't be ridiculous!"

"Tough. I was only asking to be polite because I don't think you have a choice." His chuckle was low. Infectious.

She joined in. The whole scene was so absurd. Soon they were howling contentedly while ice accumulated on their coats and in her hair.

Again with the phone! The ring shrilled near Britte's head, rousing her from a deep sleep. She reached toward the noise, her arm floundering, her vision hampered by sleep and the fuzzy light of the predawn hour.

"H'lo?"

"Uh, may I speak to Joel?"

Joel? The mere sound of his name even in dream zone ignited sparks somewhere deep in her being, diffusing heat, liquifying her bones. But he wasn't with her now. "Mmm," she replied sleepily, "not here."

"I'm terribly sorry." The voice was familiar.

"Mmm," she said again and fumbled to replace the phone. She clunked it against the nightstand. The cradle wasn't in its usual spot.

It wasn't in its usual spot because there was no nightstand. She wasn't at home!

And she had just talked to the school superintendent on the phone. She shot straight up and yelled, "Joel! Joel!"

"What?" A large shadow came barreling around the hall corner into the living room.

"Waverly just called."

"Huh?"

"Bruce Waverly! I told him you weren't here. I think that's what I said anyway."

"What!" He sounded awake now.

The phone rang again, and he stepped over to answer it.

In the hazy light she could tell he wore long pajama pants without a shirt. She peered at his left upper arm, searching for the tattoo the kids talked about. It was too dark to see anything. Curious that she would be drawn to a military guy. Not that she'd ever known one before. At least the tattoo didn't have some other woman's name on it. Now that would really be bizarre.

"Thank you, sir. Goodbye." He hung up the phone. "Temperature's up. School's a go. Coffee." He headed toward the kitchen. "Call a tow truck…"

"Joel."

He turned.

"Did Waverly say anything? About a woman answering your phone?"

"Huh? Oh. No."

"He probably thought he had a wrong number. Of course, when word gets out that I spent the night here, you'll probably have to tell him the truth." She noticed Joel shuffling away and called out to him, "I thought you were a morning person?"

"It's not morning yet. I was still awake at 3 A.M."

Britte snuggled back down on the couch, under the covers. It didn't feel like morning to her either. What time was it? The VCR clock was flashing, signaling a power failure.

Last night, after laughing like hyenas in the deserted street, they had inched their way back to the condo, wet and freezing. His laundry room adjoined a bathroom. She took a hot shower while her warm-up suit tossed in the dryer. They drank hot chocolate, gently fussing over sleeping arrangements. She opted for the couch, refusing to take his room. He finally seemed to catch on that for her, that would be too…intimate. He had smiled in an odd way, and she knew he thought her old-fashioned and naïve. Well, he was right. She had tossed and turned on the couch. The last thing she remembered was peering at her watch sometime after two.

Innocent as the situation was inside the walls of his home, outside them somebody was going to believe they had this time indeed broken a rule. And they would pay for it.

Forty-Eight

Alec dozed fitfully, lying atop the bedspread fully clothed. Every few minutes he checked the cell phone on the nightstand. Plugged into an outlet, it was recharging, taking forever and a day... And then the power went off.

What was Anne doing? Was she sleeping on a couch? In a guest room? Could she hear *him* snoring?

It wasn't that he didn't trust her. Of course he trusted her. Implicitly. He even trusted Manning. He seemed a decent sort; he paid his employees well. A believer, Anne said.

Kevin was a believer.

Kevin. Kevin and his much younger girlfriend. Women were attracted to older men. Even men with beards and graying hair? But Annie wouldn't feel that.

Would she?

At last, emotionally spent, he slept. A tiny ding woke him. Voice mail message alert! He reached for the phone. Beside it, the clock's red digital dial flashed 12:23, which didn't mean anything except that the power had clicked back on 23 minutes ago. He turned on the lamp. The tiny digits on the cell phone read 2:40.

He fumbled with the correct sequence on the number pad. At last succeeding, he found six new messages.

Alec rubbed sleep from his eyes. He listened to three messages from the office, cutting them off immediately after hearing the first utterance. The next *two* messages were a girl's voice, talking to *Drew*. The kid was grounded. Heart throbbing in his throat, he waited for the last message.

"Hey, mister." His bones felt like rubber. It was Annie. "I can't get through…"

He replayed the message three times, his grin broadening with each repeated sentence. She was at a motel. She loved him.

Should he call her? No, she needed to rest. But…he'd be there when she woke up.

⌒

"Who is it?" Anne peered through the peephole of the motel room door but saw only a white paper bag.

"Breakfast-in-bed delivery man."

"Alec!" She hurriedly undid the locks and opened the door. "Alec!"

Grinning, he held his arms wide, a bag in each hand. "Coffee and bagels. Cream cheese with pecans."

She laughed and tugged on his coat lapel, guiding him inside the room. Bagels and cream cheese? *That* coffee shop was nowhere on the route between home and the motel. He had gone out of his way. "You've been busy."

"I got an early start. Nice room." He set the bags on the desk and removed his coat while she took out the styrofoam containers. "Thanks." He accepted a cup from her; then he set it back down. "But first things first." He took the other cup from her hand and set it aside.

"What?"

He smiled, wrapped his arms around her shoulders, and looked into her eyes. "Annie, you are so beautiful."

She slipped her arms around his waist. With those cinnamon eyes so focused on her, she thought she was still dreaming. When he kissed her, she hoped she'd never wake up.

"Good morning, sweetheart."

"Morning, mister."

He kissed her again, and she began to lose interest in drinking hot coffee.

"Did I wake you?"

"Mm-hmm." She nodded, her forehead against his. It wasn't even six o'clock.

"I couldn't sleep," he murmured. "I wanted to make sure you were all right. Did you sleep well?"

"Mm-hmm, but not until late. I think it was after one. Are the kids okay?"

"I woke up Drew and put him in charge of the morning." He kissed her eyelids. "He's working off some jail time. He promised to get the girls to school."

She smiled. "Really?"

"Yep. You don't have to go anywhere. I brought clothes for you."

"*Really?*"

He grinned. "Really. And shampoo and that hair mousse stuff and some lotion I think you put on your face. Oh, and some bubble bath."

She laughed. "What's gotten into you?"

His face sobered, and he kissed the tip of her nose. "I don't want to lose you. I don't want Charlie Manning to know you better than I do. I don't want to lose track of us. Annie, I did break something. I broke our vows. I am so sorry, sweetheart."

Her chest felt as if her heart skidded to a halt. Suspended, life crumbled within her. She withdrew from his embrace and sat on the bed.

Alec knelt before her. "I'm sorry. I never should have made you go to work full-time. It's dividing our family."

"What are you talking about?"

"The vows. You know. I promised we would always live on my income. That you could be a full-time mom and keep painting. You gave up school for me. I never wanted you to quit your art altogether."

"The vows!" Her breath flung itself back into her body, jolting her senses. "The ones we wrote! Oh, Alec! I thought—" She covered her mouth with her hands.

"What is it? What did you think?"

"I thought you did what Kevin did!"

"What Kevin—? Oh, no, Annie." He sat beside her and held her tightly. "Never. I could never do that to you. No, I'm talking about what we wrote. I'm sorry. I let you down."

They sat quietly holding each other. Anne silently thanked God. If he had—but she didn't have to think what if. The working situation, the financial situation...that could be remedied. "Alec, something good is coming from it. Look." She pointed across the room toward the easel.

"You painted!" He went over to it and studied it. "Annie, it's beautiful."

"You think so?"

"It's our house." His voice caught.

It was their house in springtime. Lilacs bloomed at the corner of the front porch, multicolored tulips and yellow daffodils surrounded its base, the peonies along the drive were full of buds, the flowering pear blossomed, and bright green leaves emerged from the maple's branches. The upstairs windows reflected the morning sun's rays.

She went and stood beside him, slipping a hand into the crook of his elbow. "Well, technically it's rough. It was so hard to begin, but I did it. And it feels— Oh, Alec, it feels like I've come home."

He kissed the top of her head. "Then you should keep painting."

"I agree. If I keep working, I can keep myself in supplies."

He stiffened.

"You know the woman who took time off to have the baby?"

He nodded.

"She's not coming back. Charlie needs me full-time. If I want."

"Do you want?"

She touched his cheek. "I don't know. Do you want?"

"I don't want to tell you what to do or coerce you into something because of my anxieties."

She smiled. "We know God brought us this far. He won't let us down. Can we leave it for now?"

"Okay." Though his tone was strong, his facial expression remained tentative. He wanted the issue settled now.

Well, she wasn't ready. "Are you wearing jeans to work or are you going home?"

He shook his head. "Neither. I brought my work clothes, too."

"Really?"

He gave her a half smile. "Really."

"Then I do know what I want."

"What?"

"Bagels, bubbles, and you." She slid her arms around his waist. "And not necessarily in that order."

Forty-Nine

Joel opened his office door and peered out into the main area. "Lynnie, get Britte down here, please."

The woman gave him a look. *The dismissal bell just rang and a slew of anxious adolescents have descended in need of who knows what and the phone is ringing and Britte's more than likely as swamped as I am and on her way to the gym.*

He gave her a look in return. *I know all that! Just do it.* He ducked back inside his quiet space wishing he had adolescents to deal with rather than Bruce Waverly. "Bruce, would you like some coffee?"

"No, thank you." The man stood facing the window, his hands clasped behind his back. The superintendent of schools was a long time Valley Oaks fixture and the consummate politician. Joel respected the man's ability to smooth ruffled feathers and keep the district sailing along under budget.

"I forgot. You're a tea drinker."

Bruce turned. He was shorter than Joel and compact. His dark brown wavy hair should have been gray by now. As always, he was dapperly dressed in a dark suit. "Tea would be great."

"Be right back."

In the nearby kitchenette, he stuck a mug of water into the microwave. While it heated, he found a small bottle of orange juice in the refrigerator and downed it in three gulps. There was a storm raging in his head. In spite of the ibuprofen he'd been swallowing all afternoon, he knew he had a fever. Lynnie had come after him with a thermometer, but he insisted it didn't matter. He wasn't going home.

He carried the hot mug into the outer office. Britte approached from the other direction.

In spite of feeling as though he'd been run over by a semi, he smiled and for a split second forgot he wasn't one of the teenagers. The sight of the woman turned his insides to mush. If students weren't milling three feet behind her... Maybe they could have dinner...

She smiled back. "I'm kind of busy."

He mouthed "Waverly" and put his hand on the doorknob.

"Oh."

He whispered, "Are you sick?" Her eyes looked as red and glassy as his felt.

She shook her head and sneezed into a tissue.

Joel pushed open his door and followed her inside. "Here you go, Bruce. I brought you a few choices." He set the mug along with a box of assorted tea bags on his desk and stepped around to his chair. He needed to sit.

"Thanks. Hello, Britte." He busied himself with his tea.

"Hi, Bruce. How are you?"

"Just fine. I know you're both busy. Please have a seat." He settled into one of the chairs facing Joel's desk. They followed suit. "I wanted to tell you the latest on that complaint filed by Hughes and Larson. Obviously Hughes is out of the picture. The man has major problems. It turns out that Larson works for an accounting firm whose biggest client is a wholesale company of which Hughes is a partner. Alec Sutton dug up that bit of information yesterday. I imagine there was a little coercion going on from Hughes to Larson. Their allegations won't be taken seriously by any board member. So just keep on coaching to your heart's content and don't worry about that stuff."

Britte's eyebrows went up. "Whew! I don't know whether to laugh or cry. I wish Jordan and Janine had better role models for fathers, but it's a relief to know I can keep coaching."

"Yes, you're home free on that matter, so go ahead and laugh. You've put up with a lot of bunk. But speaking of role models..." He sipped his tea.

Joel felt his pulse quicken and kept his eyes on the superintendent. If he glanced at Britte, they would look guilty. Of course...they were guilty...in a sense.

Bruce cleared his throat and set his mug on the desk. "My neighbor walks her dog early in the morning, oftentimes on your street, Britte. She has three elementary age children and has ambitions, I believe, to win a seat on the board and run the district single-handedly. Nice enough woman, but she is a bit of a," he paused, tapping his fingertips together, "busybody. Sunday she told me that she saw your car, Joel, parked at Britte's house. By then I had heard about the Gordon Hughes business and told her it was probably related to that. Today she called to report that she had just seen you drop Britte off at her house about 6:30. I told her you were both athletic nuts and had probably already been to the Community Center gym. After I hung up, I remembered dialing what I thought was your number at 6 A.M. A woman answered."

"At the risk of sounding like a teenager, sir, it's not what it looks like."

Bruce held up a hand. "I don't want details. I don't want excuses." His voice hardened. "Your private lives are your own. However, I will not tolerate inappropriate *appearances*. If my neighbor gets wind of anything like this happening again—and she will be watching closely, I guarantee—I will not cover for you. We don't need this kind of gossip, especially about you, Joel. It's contract time. Not to mention that you're both a little controversial as it is. Although, quite frankly, she's not after *your* hide, Britte."

Joel knew Britte was about to pop and said quickly, "I promise nothing that looks inappropriate will happen again, sir."

"Glad to hear it. I don't want to lose you, Joel. You're doing a good job here, but we need to keep the constituents happy." He stood. "Well, I'll let you two get back to work. Thanks for your time."

Joel shook his hand. "Thank you, Bruce."

"Britte. Good luck at regionals. By the way, you both look as if you should see a doctor. Goodbye." He left, leaving the door conspicuously wide open behind him.

Britte's face was crimson now. Joel went for diffusing and said in a low voice, "Guess that means no more overnights."

She didn't smile. "How could you sit there and not explain?" At least she spoke through clenched teeth. People in the outer office wouldn't overhear their conversation.

"He didn't want explanations." Joel leaned across his desk. "Britte, he's the ultimate politician. He has to keep the community as happy as possible. If we interfere with that happiness, he can make waves concerning our future. Big waves."

"It's not fair!"

He couldn't help but smile. She was so idealistic. "That's not the point. We're in the public eye. I have to court you in the public eye, not in each other's houses."

"Politics shouldn't enter in at all."

"But everything he said was true. I didn't choose the best course of action. Saturday night I should have had Cal get some off-duty cop to watch your house. I should have let him take me home. Last night I should have tried harder to get you home." They could have walked it, if he hadn't been so...so *giddy*. Giddy! Marine Staff Sergeant Joel Kingsley, giddy!

"But nothing happened!"

"It's the appearance, Britte."

A sudden change came over her face. Her eyes widened as if she were struck by a new thought. Her clenched jaw slackened, but she didn't tell him what was going on inside that mind of hers.

"What?" he asked.

She shook her head. "I'm late for practice." With that and a sneeze, she was out the door.

He sat back in his chair. Well, whatever, she'd get over it. Bruce Waverly's ultimatum changed nothing between them. As Joel had told her, he would just have to do his courting in public. They were both committed to being role models to the students. It would be a challenge to show the kids an appropriate example of courtship and marriage.

Marriage?

That was a brand-new thought, but... Maybe he was ready for brand-new thoughts. He knew for certain that his heart beat differently these days. He also knew that Jesus had given him a brand-new life. Now, for the first time, he *felt* with joyful anticipation what that meant. There was no way he was going back to living in the emotionless void.

❦

Britte rushed through the vacant halls to her classroom, gathered her attaché bag, coat, a box of tissues, and then raced to the gym. Her throat ached and her eyes burned, but what hurt even worse was her heart.

Ten to one Joel Kingsley would be out of here by the end of June.

Why hadn't she caught on sooner? She had been duped by their compatibility, his ability to capture her attention unlike anyone ever had, and, yes, even their shared penchant for being controversial figures. And now she felt her heart cracking, deep fissures splitting it open, ripping the breath from her.

Lord, why did You let this happen?

Britte walked into the gym, surprised to see Anne and Tanner there with the girls who were already doing warm-up drills. She dumped her things on a bleacher as Anne walked over to her.

"Britte." There was immediate concern in her voice. She touched Britte's forehead. "Go home, girl. You've got a fever."

"What are you doing here?"

"I got off work early. Tanner and I figured you could use some extra help with only two games left this week and the tournament next week."

"Who's that up there?" She nodded toward a lone figure sitting high in the bleachers, his face bent over a book.

"He's a cousin of Jordan and Trevor's, a college student. He's taking them back home to their aunt's in Rockville after practice. Their mom is still at the shelter."

Another wave of anguish flowed through her. "What a horrific situation that is!"

"Hon, we're doing what we can to help. The girls are so protective. And your idea to have Trevor be manager seems to be making all the difference in his attitude. What's wrong with your breathing?"

She stared at her friend for a moment, wanting to blame someone. Why not a school board member's wife? "Oh, Anne, can't Alec keep Joel here?"

"What are you talking about?"

"You know he won't be rehired. Bruce Waverly just said as much in the office."

Anne picked up Britte's coat and handed it to her. "Let's go. I'll walk you to the door."

"I can't leave—"

"Well, you're not staying. You're sick and talking nonsense. The girls don't need your germs, literally and figuratively."

"It's not nonsense," she fussed, but she slipped into her coat and followed Anne out of the gym and across the commons. An overwhelming sense struck her: She wanted to cling to her mother. Annie was the next best option.

Anne stopped, her hand on the door leading to the parking lot, and turned. "Britte, tell me what's wrong."

"Joel's going to leave." Chilled now, she shivered. "And I can't catch my breath."

"You're sick and overreacting."

"He was dishonorably discharged from the Marines! When people hear that—"

"You know people have heard that. What difference does it make? We know what he's made of. He's proven himself here."

"Annie, we spent last night together, too, not just Saturday night."

Anne stared at her, slack-jawed.

Britte gave her a quick synopsis of events leading up to the superintendent's ultimatum. "Basically, he threatened him."

"Oh, Britte!" She burst into laughter and hugged her. "It was just a warning. Don't worry about it. You can both handle a little gossip. And besides, anyone who knows you knows you're a Miss Goody Two-shoes. Now go home and go to bed. Get better. The girls will need you in tip-top shape tomorrow night."

"Thanks, Mom." She shivered again and doubted she'd ever truly feel in tip-top shape again.

Fifty

Early Wednesday morning Britte sat at her desk, staring at nothing in particular. Like airy cobwebs in the corners of her mind, pieces of last night's dream clung.

There had been a field in it. Dried bits of stalk blew about. It must have been after the harvest, late fall. Eric was holding her hand as they ran toward a horizon that never drew near. He squeezed tightly until the engagement ring cut into her flesh. She cried out, but he didn't let go. The pain increased until she could scarcely breathe. And then he was gone, leaving her stumbling forward at breakneck speed.

Then somehow, as only happened in dreams, she was on the roof of the sunroom at the farm house. Brady was on the ground, calling to her. And Joel...there was a glimpse of Joel behind her, begging her not to do it. She went to the edge—

"Britte."

She jumped, startled out of the reverie.

Joel was standing directly across the desk. "Sorry. I thought you heard me come in." He smiled. "Where were you?"

If only he wouldn't smile... "In some crazy dream. It reminded me of the time I followed Brady out to the roof of the sunroom. It's flat, so that was no big deal in itself. But he shimmied down the drain pipe and called me 'chicken' when I wouldn't do it. So, of course, I did it." The moment of falling rushed back to her, and she caught her breath.

"You fell."

341

She nodded. "Not far. I only broke some ribs instead of every bone. I couldn't breathe for..." That was it. She couldn't breathe without excruciating pain. Like now.

"For weeks, probably. I know how that feels." He slid into a nearby student desk. "Britte, I've been thinking—"

"I have, too."

For a long moment they looked at each other. Then he said, "I'd like to take you to dinner tomorrow night." His tone was cautious. "Locally. Waverly didn't forbid—"

"I think he did. I think he didn't want people talking about us any which way. If we're seen together, it will give credence to whatever gossip that woman spreads. I think we should just cool it."

The "General's" countenance returned in a flash, making Joel's expression unreadable. "It's not like you to run from a threat." He spoke softly. "I have a childish desire to call you chicken, Miss O."

Each breath was sheer torture. "Well, I guess maybe I am chicken when it comes to jeopardizing your job."

"*My* job. That means it's *my* decision whether or not to jeopardize it." He shut his eyes briefly. "This isn't the time to talk about us."

"There isn't anymore to talk about. I've made up my mind."

"A little quickly, I'd say. Two nights ago you seemed awfully interested in a relationship."

"That was before your job security came into play. I said my mind is made up!"

"And it's closed to my opinion?"

She clenched her jaw at the glimpse of pain that crossed his face. "It won't change anything."

He stood abruptly. "I suspect there's something else going on here. I can take a hint." He turned and walked out.

So, that was that. *Goodbye.* It had been inevitable. Now worked as well as later. Actually it worked better than later. There were less heartstrings tangled up at the moment.

⌒

Joel fumed all the way down the hall, across the commons, through the all but vacant main office, and into his room where he slammed the door shut. He tore it back open and barked, "Lynnie, I'm unavailable." He pushed it closed again. The loud clicking of its latch resounded in his head, silencing the roaring there of indefinable emotions.

That was rude.

He opened the door. "Lynnie."

She looked up from her computer monitor.

"I'm sorry."

"No problem, boss." She picked up a pencil. "Just give me your next of kin's phone number so I don't have to dig it out of the file when you have your stroke."

He glanced around the room. Two students stood at the counter with another office worker. A teacher stood at the bank of faculty mailboxes. They were all quietly looking at him. "I'm fine."

"You look like a red balloon stretched to its limit and ready to pop."

Kind of how he felt. "If I'm not out in ten minutes, call the paramedics." He went back into his office and shut the door in a civilized manner.

He walked over to the window and stared through it, unseeing.

"Okay, Lord. You've got my attention. What is it you want from me? I'm head over heels for this woman, and she just said the feeling's not mutual. Loud and clear. Cool it.

Not let's take a step back, but just cool it. Zap it. Nip it in the bud. Pulverize it.'"

How could she say that? How could she turn off her emotions as if they were controlled by a spigot? She was fooling herself if she thought she felt nothing toward him. The romantic attraction between them was palpable. She wasn't the type to go around kissing someone she cared nothing about. Besides that, they were friends, something he would not have imagined possible with a woman. She cried over him. Good grief, he had cried in front of her! He admired her and respected her opinion and enjoyed just hanging out with her. If she didn't care for him, she wouldn't be concerned about his job. So what if he lost it in the process of courting her? He could easily get a job somewhere else—

Somewhere else.

His shoulders slumped. What had she told him about splitting up with her fiancé? The guy was going to work in his family business somewhere else, not in Valley Oaks. And she was *not* leaving Valley Oaks.

But that was years ago. Surely she wouldn't be opposed to leaving now if it came to that?

Fragments of scenes rushed at him. Britte and her family. Christmas. Brady's wedding. Her going to her parents' house after being attacked. Her living in her great-aunt's house, carrying on a tradition. A former high school player, coaching in the same gym where she grew up. The memories she must have in the building, in the town!

Of course she would be opposed to leaving.

Lord, if it's from You, then what we have between us is stronger than anything else. Everything else like where we live and work is nothing more than street noise and will be taken care of, right? I ask that You will take care of it because, Father...I love her.

Yes, he loved her. He smiled to himself. It felt pretty good to admit that.

You're not getting off that easily, Miss O.

⌒

Britte stood in her darkened living room near the warm register. The furnace churned heat waves upward as she stared through the window. She could make out the bare sycamore branches spreading across the star-studded sky.

Jesus, sit with me tonight?

Earlier, before the evening's game, the girls had prayed for her. For *her*. Their custom was to bow heads and one of the girls would say a brief prayer, asking that they'd play their best and be good sports. Tonight three girls prayed. Hands had touched her shoulders as the girls asked for God to grant Coach health and wisdom. They had told God how much they appreciated her.

Unprecedented.

They had played well. She had coached well. They had won. She had discerned a role for Jordan where she could help and do little damage. Trevor had made the first eye contact with her since she had brought him on board. Joel had cheered from across the court, wearing school colors, and kept his distance. After the game, Anne walked with her through the parking lot.

Britte knew she would be all right. Perhaps by tomorrow even the pain would diminish, the pain that stabbed with each breath she took.

Fifty-One

Britte stood outside her classroom door between third and fourth period classes, watching two girls approach. Julie and Rachel giggled all the way down the hall. It was amazing how much chitchat could fly during the four minutes of passing from one room to another.

"Miss O," Rachel called out, "we just saw Mr. Kingsley and he says 'hi.'"

Britte clenched her jaw, hoping to stop the flush from spreading.

It wasn't the first time a student had delivered a greeting from the principal. The first time occurred a week ago, the day after the Bruce Waverly ultimatum. Britte had thought the student's so-called "relayed message" must be a joke. Until it happened again with a different student. And then again. All in the same day.

The notes added credence. They began arriving the next day. At least once a day since then she had found a handwritten note in her office mailbox, on her desk, or taped to the locker room door for all to see. Saturday the note arrived in her Valley Oaks post office box. Sunday it was stuck under the wiper on her car in the church parking lot. "Have a great day, Miss O." "Good luck in tonight's game, Miss O." "Thinking of you, Miss O." "You look especially striking today, Miss O."

All of them were signed "the General."

Now the two girls stopped before her. Julie whispered, "We think he has a crush on you!"

Rachel added, "He *never* used to smile."

They sauntered into the room, their giggles lingering in the empty hallway. The bell rang, but Britte stood still, trying to shake off conflicting emotions. He might be smiling, but she certainly wasn't. The man was not playing fair!

"Psst!"

She turned and saw Joel peering around the corner.

"You're late for class!" he called out in a stage whisper, a smile softening his square jaw.

"Oh!" She swiveled on her heel and strode through the doorway.

It wasn't the first time for *that* either.

And then there were the other incidents. Last Thursday he had interrupted her sixth-hour lecture just to say hello. Friday he entered the gym in the middle of practice. Dribbling a basketball, he wound his way between the girls on the court and made a layup. He then grabbed the ball, focused in on her, grinned, and slowly, deliberately *winked*. By the time she came to her senses, half the team was rolling on the floor and laughing hysterically, Anne loudest of all.

Evidently Mr. Kingsley was not going away.

~

The following day it was Cal Huntington who interrupted her class. He arrived first hour wearing his sheriff's uniform, gun and all. In spite of his fuzzy brown hair that begged to be ruffled and the protective appearance of his wide shoulders filling out the leather jacket, he did not exude what Lia called his "teddy bear" demeanor. Britte involuntarily shuddered, hoping he wasn't after one of her kids.

"Can we talk?" He pointed over his shoulder toward the hall.

She followed him out and shut the door.

"Sorry to interrupt, Britte, but I wanted you to know. I picked up Gordon Hughes about two this morning. He was in your front yard, just standing there cursing up a storm."

She leaned against the lockers.

"That put him within 100 feet of you. He broke the restraining order. The judge won't let him go this time. Are you okay?"

Her breakfast cereal was doing a gymnastics routine in her stomach. "I didn't really think he'd do anything."

"He was intoxicated. He even passed out before I got him to the station. I don't think he could have managed to break in. Sober, I don't think he'd ever have the nerve to try."

"Still."

"Still," Cal agreed. "But it's over now."

"Can you keep it out of the newspaper?"

"Yeah, I'm trying. His kids don't need this kind of publicity. How's Trevor doing?"

"He's doing well. He's a big help, actually, and starting to talk to me directly. The girls all treat him like a favorite little brother." She blinked away tears.

"Good. You've shown us how you've forgiven him, but keep your eyes open, okay? If he were to get angry, blame you for his dad…" He shrugged again.

"Okay. Thanks for coming by, Cal."

"You're welcome. Now you don't need Joel to spend the night with you." He grinned. "Unless you want him to, Miss Goody Two-shoes." With that he was striding down the hall, laughing rather loudly.

At a particular juncture near the end of the season, Britte usually lost all sense of connection with anything unrelated to her team and basketball. However, that wasn't happening. And the funny thing of it was, the girls were winning. They won the regional tournament, hands down. Their first sectional tournament game would begin in three hours.

"Ethan." Britte was sitting in his classroom Thursday afternoon when she should have been down in the commons waiting with the girls for the bus and feeding them enthusiasm. "I don't get it. It's tournament time and the fire-breathing coach is taking a nap."

"Ah." Her friend's feet were up on his desk; he leaned back in the chair, hands locked behind his head. "Your heart is otherwise engaged."

She blinked. "It is not."

"Would you recognize it if it were?"

"It's basketball season. My heart can't be anywhere else."

"But Joel Kingsley has never been present during the season."

"And he probably won't ever be again."

"Meaning your heart shouldn't be occupied with him? You are much too practical, Miss O. Hearts don't work that way. Why don't I give you some good literature to read that'll teach you something about the ways of the heart? Get your mind off two plus two."

"I know enough about the ways of the heart. I know that I don't want to mess with a broken one again." Although her relationship with Eric had happened a long time ago, the pain had left an indelible mark.

"You're counting on something that may not even happen."

"Hey, two plus two equals four. I'm staying and he's going."

Ethan shook his head. "Way too practical and way too stubborn. What did he give you today?"

"A few notes." She paused. "And a flower. A red rose."

The English teacher smiled. "Only one?"

She nodded.

"You realize only one means 'I love you'?"

She glanced away. No, she didn't know that. Would an ex-Marine know that? "Says who?"

"Someone unconcerned with two plus two. What did the card say?"

"Good luck at sectionals." She bit her lip. "Princess."

Ethan's smile stretched into a broad grin. "I'd say the guy is hooked."

The guy who was supposedly hooked on her didn't even show up for her game that night.

Like I could care less.

The bus sped through the night. While Britte huddled against a window and chewed a thumbnail, her assistant coach whooped it up with the girls in the back. The sophomores, finished with their own season, were permitted to ride along to attend the varsity tournament games. It was a crowded, noisy place.

Anne plopped beside her now on the bench seat and roughly nudged her with an elbow. "Hey, Coach. Smile. You won!"

Truthfully, it hadn't been that tough of a game.

Anne leaned around her until their faces were inches apart in the dark. "What's wrong?"

"Nothing!"

"Britte, this isn't you. Come on, let it out. This is a crucial week, and I have to know what's going on with you. Else how can I be your surrogate mom and assistant coach?"

"I don't know." Her voice, those strong vocal cords that so effortlessly carried words across a basketball court, was *whining*. "Joel wasn't there."

"He's in Chicago. Didn't you know? A family emergency. He left school right after lunch."

"How do you know that?"

"I asked Alec at halftime why he wasn't around, and he heard it in the stands."

Why hadn't he told her? That was obvious! She hadn't exactly talked with him in over a week. Why would he leave in the middle of the week? Nicky! "Did any of our guys in Afghanistan get hurt today?"

"I haven't listened to the news since I started working." She put an arm around her shoulders. "So you admit that his absence bothered you."

"It always did."

"But that was because you thought he was unfairly favoring the boys. Now it bothers you because, face it, Miss O, you're falling in love with the man!"

⸺

Early Friday morning Britte went into the school office. Anne's words from last night's bus ride home were still ringing in her head, which *flustered* her. Britte Olafsson did *not fluster*. A fact which, of course, flustered her all the more.

"Lynnie."

The secretary looked up from her desk. "Morning, Britte. Congratulations!"

"Thanks. Is Joel still gone?"

She nodded. "He plans to be back tomorrow, in time for the sectional championship game."

"Is it his cousin?"

"Yes. He came home."

"Is he all right?"

"He's all right. It was an unexpected, short leave." Lynnie smiled. "I imagine the florist will be stopping by again today. You know, because Joel can't be here himself to leave notes."

Intense heat flared inside of her, reaching even the tips of her ears. *Does everyone know?* She opened her mouth, expecting a reply to automatically roll off her tongue, but none came. She clamped her mouth shut, waggled her fingers at Lynnie, and walked out.

∼

"Miss O."

Britte peered around the huge floral bouquet that occupied half of her desk. The thing simply had to go. "Yes, Trisha?" she asked the student who addressed her.

"You don't want Mr. Kingsley to get fired, do you?"

After Lynnie's florist warning, she had been somewhat prepared for the arrival of the flowers. She wasn't prepared for the girl's question. Her cheeks felt on fire. Again. The dismissal bell would be ringing in a few minutes. No one in the class was working. Her algebra assignment was light. The class had been shortened due to a pep assembly in honor of the team going to tomorrow night's sectional title game. Because the boys weren't playing tournament yet, the girls were receiving all the attention. It would have been a blast if not coupled with all that *other* attention.

"Trisha, what do you mean?"

"My mom heard that the school board may not rehire him because some people don't like his *style*. We like his style. We want him to stay."

"Do you think Jo—Mr. Kingsley wants to stay?"

Distinctly feminine laughter rippled through the classroom. *Uh-oh.*

Kelli said, "Well, he's smiling like he's happy to be here! He never used to smile."

Yes, he is smiling. His stoicism is totally gone. And it's not even the end of January, nowhere near Easter....

"And..." The girl's voice faded, but she looked directly at the bouquet.

Britte set the vase on the floor.

Danny asked, "Are the rumors true?"

That he's wooing me? She swallowed. For goodness' sake, that couldn't be what he referred to. She wanted to stand and get a clear view of all their faces, but she sensed her legs were incapable of doing their job at the moment. "It's true. Unless they renew his contract, he won't be back."

Voices rose. There were rumbled opinions about shutting down the board.

She held up a hand. "The board represents the community. You're the community. Your parents are the community. What can you do to be heard?"

Answers bombarded her. "Get a petition going! Attend next month's meeting. Write letters to the editor. Get our parents to speak up. Boycott classes! Go on a hunger strike."

"So what's stopping you?" she challenged. "A word of caution. They'll only get upset about boycotts and hunger strikes. You want to be heard, not suspended."

One of the girls opened a notebook. "Will you sign a petition?"

Would she do cartwheels if it would help? Would she camp out on Bruce Waverly's doorstep? Would she carry a placard and march? Would she get on her soapbox at a board meeting? "Yes. I'll sign a petition." *And much, much more.*

Fifty-Two

The weeks passed, two blurry weeks of basketball and Joel.

Approximately 350 teams whittled themselves down to 64 that competed in the Class A Sectional Tournament. Britte's team won, aligning them with only 15 other teams who would compete at the supersectionals. In the entire short history of Valley Oaks girls basketball, a team had never even been a contender.

The entire community was euphoric. Signs went up everywhere around the town and in the school. A fire engine escorted the bus out of Valley Oaks for each game, its siren blaring. Pep assemblies were scheduled almost daily either to congratulate them after a win or to inspire them before the next game. The band played, the cheerleaders led cheers. Joel and the male coaches donned the boys team warm-up outfits and performed a sidesplitting cheerleader routine.

And then the girls won the tournament, making them one of the elite eight that would play at State next week.

In the midst of it all, Joel continued to shower her with notes, surprise hellos, and gifts. One day a student office worker delivered a gift-wrapped package. At least that occurred during her free period. In privacy she tore off the paper and found a coffee bean grinder, a bag of coffee beans, and Joel's recipe for a great pot of coffee.

She was in a dangerously vulnerable state of emotions and nearly caved in on Sunday after church. Snow had fallen during the service; she found her car in the parking lot completely cleaned off. Of course he had done it. She wanted to sit down and cry...with him holding her.

Fortunately, Brady and Gina had parked next to her. She begged them for a lunch invitation. "I'll buy it at Swensen's Market!"

Instead, they made soup and sandwiches together and sat on the floor near their fireplace in the cozy log cabin house. Her brother and his new wife glowed, but it wasn't from the fire. They looked the same in the parking lot, in the kitchen, outdoors, indoors, wherever.

"Okay," Britte announced, "I need to know something. How did you two do it? How did you *give up* your dreams?"

They stared at her. Brady said, "Sis, what's wrong?"

Her voice had cracked. She'd heard it. Between her emotional state and screaming at games and pep assemblies, it was pushed to the limit. As was her heart. "How am I supposed to love Joel Kingsley when he's leaving Valley Oaks and my dream job—my whole *life*—is *in* Valley Oaks?"

In a flash they were beside her, hugging her. Eventually their words of comfort, their experience, and their advice all came down to one word: pray.

And then Brady asked her the question she had been avoiding. "Would your life still be in Valley Oaks if Joel Kingsley weren't here?"

Joel sat in the deafening noise of Illinois State's crowded Redbird Arena, wedged between Alec Sutton and Bruce Waverly. Below on the floor, Britte stood watching her girls warm up. She looked every inch the professional in her black slacks and jacket and royal blue blouse. Her long hair was in a thick braid. He couldn't tell from here whether or not she wore the sapphire earrings he had left in her mailbox earlier in the week. They matched the necklace.

He felt his own pulse race and was glad it was Britte down there and not him. What a nerve-racking couple of weeks it had been for the girls team! And now they were at the state tournament. They had won their first game, guaranteeing them a spot in the top four. He never would have imagined getting so caught up with such a version of basketball. But then, he never had imagined a Britte Olafsson capturing his attention.

Bruce leaned forward and addressed Alec. "Did you tell him about the petitions?"

"No. I figured that was your place."

Bruce nodded. "Joel, there are some petitions going around. People want your contract renewed."

He was surprised. "Really? Does the board pay attention to petitions?"

The superintendent shrugged. "Almost 300 names from the high school are on one alone. Students and faculty. I've never seen anything like it."

Alec said, "If we get anywhere near that percentage from the community, we've got to pay attention."

It doesn't matter. While they talked around him, Joel thought about calling Sam. His friend would understand. Joel's faith had been like an iceberg. Now having melted, it poured freely, a tidal wave carrying him across self-imposed boundaries that had encased his heart. He'd rather watch Britte than talk shop.

She was waving. At him? He sat up straighter and she pointed as if directing him downstairs. He excused himself. Only two and a half minutes remained before the game started.

She met him in the outer passageway.

"Britte! What are you doing?!" He noticed the earrings shining behind wisps of hair. "You'll miss—"

"This can't wait. Oh!" Her hand flew to her mouth. "I'm at the state tournament!"

He grinned. "Yes, you certainly are. Need a hug?"

She nodded, and then she vigorously shook her head no, withdrawing her hand. "Joel, as wonderful as all this is, it just occurred to me standing there courtside that compared to you...it doesn't amount to a hill of beans. Please don't stop wooing me?" Her breath caught as if her own words surprised herself. "There. I said it." She turned on her heel and ran back inside.

The Princess didn't even have to ask. He smiled. "But thank You, Lord, that she did."

⌒

Joel cheered her through that game and one more. When the dust settled, the Valley Oaks girls had taken third place. He couldn't get near Britte, but she caught his eye and returned his smile with a brilliant one of her own.

Contract or no contract, he would win that woman's heart. If he couldn't see her smile every day, he'd just as soon not get up in the morning.

Fifty-Three

"Annie, leave the dishes."

She stared at her husband in disbelief. "It's Sunday night. I've been gone for days. You're leaving town in two days. If I don't catch up now—"

"It's Valentine's Day."

She laughed at his ridiculous statement. "It is not."

"It is in the Sutton household."

Ever since his early morning visit to the Stratford, he'd been surprising her in countless small ways. A note here, an extra hug there, a clean kitchen. A *really* clean kitchen. What was he up to now? Alec never remembered Valentine's Day until after the fact. Then he'd usually promise to do a chore.

"Come, Mrs. Sutton." He held out his hand. "Now, please."

Intrigued, she dried her hands and placed one in his.

He led her upstairs and down the hall to the attic stairs. They climbed those. At the top he opened the door and drew her in. "Happy Valentine's Day."

Anne looked around and gasped. "Alec!"

Not only was the large room spic-and-span clean, it was organized. Not only was it organized, it was finished! There were walls and a ceiling, and the floor was partially carpeted with one corner tiled. In that corner by a window stood an easel with a blank canvas on it. Track lighting hung above. A counter with cabinets beneath it ran along one wall.

"Oh, Alec!" She giggled and flung her arms around his neck. "Thank you!"

He kissed the tip of her nose. "I just wanted to see you smile that way again."

"What way?"

"Like you're doing now. Like you did when you showed me your painting at the hotel. Like you used to when you had an easel in the bedroom."

She kissed him. "I love you, mister."

"And I love you. Go on. Check out your new place."

He showed her around, explaining what he and the kids had done, how most of the material was secondhand, what he still wanted to do.

"It's so great, Alec! Now all I need is to find some time to play in it." She grinned. "Actually, I already took care of that. It's my gift to you."

"What?"

"I figured out a new schedule with Charlie. I'll work just Tuesdays and Thursdays. Happy Valentine's Day!"

He burst into laughter and hugged her. "That's absolutely perfect. But, are you sure?"

It was a compromise that gave her a peace she hadn't felt since before Thanksgiving. "I'm sure. It gives me time that I need here, enough time there to qualify for free art classes and supplies at wholesale, and I can help out a little bit financially."

He kissed her. "Hey, I've got another one for you. Open up that drawer there on the left."

"Another one?" She went to the set of white cabinets. "Alec, what's gotten into you? Oh my goodness! What is this? An airline ticket?"

He came up behind her and wrapped his arms around her waist. "I had enough frequent flyer miles to get your ticket. You'll have to lounge at the pool or art museums during my two days of meetings, but then we'll stay two extra days. Your mom will take care of the girls. Drew can stay at Peter and Celeste's. Vic's got the dogs. It's all arranged. Come to San Diego with me and be my Valentine."

She turned around in his arms. "The day after *tomorrow?*"

He nodded.

"Oh, Alec." Her eyes welled. "I feel like I'm 17 again and we've just begun dating."

"That's the idea. Sweetheart." And then he kissed her.

⌒

Monday morning Britte floated down the hallway. Floating was such exhausting exercise. She had slept through the radio alarm. Students were already in the building, at their lockers, clanging them open and shut, loudly chattering, some calling out congratulations to her.

Her girls had taken third in State, which was inconceivable. Third! The thing of it was, that alone did not account for her floating. No, it was more the knowledge that she loved Joel Kingsley, and, as of late last night, she knew what she was going to do about it.

If he would have her.

In front of her locked classroom door there was a silvery mylar bouquet of helium-filled balloons. Blue and gold ribbons were tied to a tiny sandbag that anchored them to the floor. She opened the attached card. "Way to go, Princess!"

She smiled. He would have her.

But not until summer break. She was adamantly committed to that timing.

A few minutes later, during the intercom announcements, she yawned and took attendance, thinking about sending someone down to the office to fetch a cup of coffee for her. The previous principal had frowned on such things, but the current principal... She smiled to herself. It was probably safe to assume that the current principal was wrapped around her little finger.

Britte floated to the front of her classroom, trying unsuccessfully to wipe the smile from her face.

The intercom hummed again. "May I have everyone's attention, please?" It was Joel's voice now. "I have one announcement to add. Miss O." A clear chuckle resounded through the system. "This can't wait."

This can't wait. She heard the echo of her own words and stopped smiling.

"I want the entire school to know that I am wild about Miss Olafsson."

Her jaw dropped open. He'd gone too far.

"Absolutely, incredibly, insanely wild about her."

Laughter erupted in the room. She heard it coming from another class across the hall.

Joel continued, "I'd like to demonstrate exactly how wild I am about her. You're all invited to the commons in two minutes."

Britte flew from her room and down the hallway. She had to tell him to be quiet. She was his! He had her wrapped around *his* little finger! He didn't have to publicly declare or demonstrate anything. He could at least *try* to keep his job. Oh, she should have given in weeks ago!

"Joel!" she hissed as her feet hit the tiled commons floor and she saw him emerging from the office. "What are you doing?!" They met in the center of the area.

"Miss O, you're early. Mr. Waverly hasn't arrived yet."

"Mr. Waverly?"

"I had to invite him. I don't want him hearing stories from other parties. He should judge for himself what constitutes inappropriate appearances."

She sensed more than saw the commons filling up with people. Was Waverly there? She glanced around. *Oh, my gosh!* He was! Things were getting out of hand! She leaned toward Joel and whispered, "Let's talk about this in your office."

Joel flashed a smile toward Bruce. "No way. That might appear inappropriate. Let's talk here in the open." He went down on one knee and grasped her left hand between his. "Miss O."

The crowd stopped its shuffling. The murmurs halted as if some cosmic finger had twirled a volume control.

"Miss O." Joel raised his General's voice. Nobody was going to miss what he had to say. "I'd like your permission to court you."

"Oh!" Flustered, she waved her free hand about.

The encircling crowd, relatively quiet compared to the rushing noise in her head, drew in its collective breath, waiting for her answer.

"All right!" she cried. "Yes, you have my permission!"

For a split second the spectators stood stock still. Then they roared, a pandemonium of shouts, laughter, whistles, and applause.

"Really?" he asked, his voice scarcely audible above the din. His face was somber, his eyes searching hers.

The crowd faded from her peripheral vision, its noise drowned in the sudden quiet of her heart. Joel Kingsley was her knight, on his knee, behaving foolishly because he wanted the world to know he loved her. Where was his smile? She bent at her waist until her face was inches from his. "Yes, really. Joel, I'm not signing a contract unless they give one to you."

He stared at her for a long moment. Then a smile tugged at the corners of his mouth and he stood, looking down at her, clasping her hands between his to his chest. "You can't blackmail the Board of Education."

"It's not blackmail. I was considering moving anyway."

"Yeah, right."

"Well." She lifted her shoulders. "The thing is, I don't want to be here if you're not here."

He smiled the wonderful smile that transformed his stoic face into that of a caring man. "You don't have to move. If I don't get a contract, I've got a job lined up down at the hardware store."

She smiled. "Really?"

"Really. I love you, Miss O."

"And I love you, Mr. Kingsley."

Eyes not leaving hers, he raised his voice. "Ladies and gentlemen! What you are about to witness is inappropriate behavior for students in the halls." Lowering his face, he murmured, "But I'm the General."

And then he kissed her ever so gently, ever so appropriately for public wooing.

*Other Books by
Sally John*

THE OTHER WAY HOME SERIES
A Journey by Chance
After All These Years
Just to See You Smile
The Winding Road Home

IN A HEARTBEAT SERIES
In a Heartbeat
Flash Point
Moment of Truth

THE BEACH HOUSE SERIES
The Beach House
Castles in the Sand
Beach Dreams
(by Trish Perry)

Harvest House Publishers
Fiction for Every Taste and Interest

Gilbert Morris

JACQUES & CLEO, CAT DETECTIVES
Cat's Pajamas
What the Cat Dragged In
When the Cat's Away

Mindy Starns Clark

SMART CHICK MYSTERY SERIES
The Trouble with Tulip
Blind Dates Can Be Murder
Elementary, My Dear Watkins

MILLION DOLLAR MYSTERIES
A Penny for Your Thoughts
Don't Take Any Wooden Nickels
A Dime a Dozen
The Buck Stops Here
A Quarter for a Kiss

Debra White Smith

THE AUSTEN SERIES
First Impressions
Reason and Romance
Central Park
Amanda
Northpointe Chalet
Possibilities

THE DEBUTANTES
Heather
Lorna

Susan Page Davis

Frasier Island
Finding Marie

Susan Meissner

A Window to the World
Remedy for Regret
In All Deep Places
Seahorse in the Thames

RACHAEL FLYNN MYSTERY SERIES
Widows and Orphans
Sticks and Stones
Days and Hours

Sally John

THE OTHER WAY HOME SERIES
A Journey by Chance
After All These Years
Just to See You Smile
The Winding Road Home

IN A HEARTBEAT SERIES
In a Heartbeat
Flash Point
Moment of Truth

THE BEACH HOUSE SERIES
The Beach House
Castles in the Sand
Beach Dreams

Brandt Dodson

COLTON PARKER MYSTERY SERIES
Original Sin
Seventy Times Seven
Root of All Evil
The Lost Sheep

Siri Mitchell

Moon Over Tokyo

George Polivka

TROPHY CHASE TRILOGY
Legend of the Firefish
The Hand That Bears the Sword
Battle of the Vast Dominion

Craig Parshall

Trial by Ordeal

THE THISTLE AND THE CROSS SERIES
Crown of Fire
Captives and Kings
Sons of Glory

CHAMBERS OF JUSTICE SERIES
The Resurrection File
Custody of the State
The Accused
Missing Witness
The Last Judgment

Roxanne Henke

The Secret of Us

COMING HOME TO BREWSTER SERIES
After Anne
Finding Ruth
Becoming Olivia
Always Jan
With Love, Libby

B.J. Hoff

Song of Erin

MOUNTAIN SONG LEGACY
A Distant Music
The Wind Harp
The Song Weaver